V FOR VENGEANCE

V for Vengeance is the fourth of seven volumes
incorporating all the principal events which
occurred between September, 1939, and May,
1945, covering the activities of Gregory Sallust,
one of the most famous Secret Agents ever
created in fiction about the Second World
War.

It is a story set against the background of
Vichy France and the occupied territories in
1940, with Gregory as determined as ever to
overthrow the iron rule of the Third Reich.

BY DENNIS WHEATLEY

NOVELS

The Launching of Roger Brook
The Shadow of Tyburn Tree
The Rising Storm
The Man Who Killed the King
The Dark Secret of Josephine
The Rape of Venice
The Sultan's Daughter
The Wanton Princess
Evil in a Mask
The Ravishing of Lady
  Mary Ware

The Scarlet Impostor
Faked Passports
The Black Baroness
V for Vengeance
Come Into My Parlour
Traitors' Gate
They Used Dark Forces

The Prisoner in the Mask
The Second Seal
Vendetta in Spain
Three Inquisitive People
The Forbidden Territory
The Devil Rides Out
The Golden Spaniard
Strange Conflict
Codeword—Golden Fleece
Dangerous Inheritance
Gateway to Hell

The Quest of Julian Day
The Sword of Fate
Bill for the Use of a Body

Black August
Contraband
The Island Where Time Stands
  Still
The White Witch of the South
  Seas

To the Devil—a Daughter
The Satanist

The Eunuch of Stamboul
The Secret War
The Fabulous Valley
Sixty Days to Live
Such Power is Dangerous
Uncharted Seas
The Man Who Missed the War
The Haunting of Toby Jugg
Star of Ill-Omen
They Found Atlantis
The Ka of Gifford Hillary
Curtain of Fear
Mayhem in Greece
Unholy Crusade
The Strange Story of Linda Lee
The Irish Witch

SHORT STORIES

Mediterranean Nights

Gunmen, Gallants and Ghosts

HISTORICAL

A Private Life of Charles II (*Illustrated by Frank C. Papé*)
Red Eagle (*The Story of the Russian Revolution*)

AUTOBIOGRAPHICAL

Stranger than Fiction (*War Papers for the Joint Planning Staff*)
Saturdays with Bricks

SATANISM

The Devil and all his Works (*Illustrated in colour*)

Dennis Wheatley

V FOR VENGEANCE

ARROW BOOKS

ARROW BOOKS LTD
3 Fitzroy Square, London W1

An imprint of the Hutchinson Publishing Group

London Melbourne Sydney Auckland
Wellington Johannesburg Cape Town
and agencies throughout the world

First published by Hutchinson & Co. (Publishers) Ltd 1942
Arrow edition 1960
This edition (seventh impression) 1975

Made and printed in Great Britain
by The Anchor Press Ltd
Tiptree, Essex

ISBN 0 09 908470 8

for my friend

ROLAND LE BRETON

As a small memento of the many pleasant hours we have spent together, and in the hope that we may yet crack some good bottles of wine in France again.

Author's Note

The sequence of the seven books which recount the war adventures of Gregory Sallust is as follows: *The Scarlet Impostor*, *Faked Passports*, *The Black Baroness*, *V for Vengeance*, *Come Into My Parlour*, *Traitors' Gate* and *They Used Dark Forces*. Each volume is a complete story in itself, but the series covers Gregory's activities from September, 1939, to May, 1945, against an unbroken background incorporating all the principal events of the Second World War.

Gregory Sallust also appears in three other books: *Black August*, a story set in an undated future; *Contraband*, an international smuggling story of 1937; and *The Island Where Time Stands Still*, an adventure set in the South Seas and Communist China during the year 1954.

Contents

1

The Killers Come to Paris

Madeleine Lavallière stood with drooping shoulders outside the main doorway of the Hôpital St. Pierre. She had just said good-bye to the lean, dark-haired Englishman who was going down the steps. As he half-turned to speak to the driver of his taxi she thought again how ill he looked.

Sister Madeleine was a professional nurse, and she had been called four nights before to Gregory Sallust's hotel, where she had found him still suffering acutely from the effects of a deadly poison. He was still not fit to travel; yet there seemed to be a flame in the man which drove him relentlessly to pursue the secret war job upon which she had gathered that he was engaged. It was that alone, she knew, which had determined him to attempt to reach Bordeaux, instead of taking the easier road, like other English people who had been hurrying out of Paris to St. Malo, or Cherbourg and so home.

The stream of refugees had stopped now, and the sunny streets were practically deserted. It was three o'clock on the afternoon of June the 14th, 1940, and at that very moment the Germans were beginning their formal occupation of Paris with a triumphal entry through the Arc de Triomphe and down the Champs-Elysées.

Gregory stepped into the taxi, and Madeleine half-raised her hand to wave him good-bye; but he did not look back, and as she lowered it again she smiled a little bitterly. She had learnt from his ravings, while delirious, that he was in love with some woman called Erika, and it had piqued Madeleine that he had hardly been conscious of herself. It wasn't that she had actually fallen in love with him, because

11

she was in love with her own dear Georges, but she was an attractive girl—in fact, so attractive that her good looks rarely failed to arouse the interest of her male patients, and sometimes even proved an embarrassment to her—so it had hurt her vanity just a little that the Englishman had not even appeared to notice her deep blue eyes, dark, silky curls, and full, beautifully curved mouth. In some faint way he resembled Georges, and although she loved Georges very dearly and was entirely faithful to him it was now so many months since she had seen him that she would not have minded a mild flirtation with her late patient, had he shown the least willingness.

She even confessed to herself that for her own peace of mind it was as well that she had not accepted Gregory's offer of a lift in his taxi to Bordeaux. A surge of distress suddenly shook her, and the tears came into her blue eyes as she thought again of the Germans, who at that moment were entering fallen Paris. In these last days events had followed one another so swiftly that it was as yet hardly possible to realize the terrible succession of defeats which had been inflicted upon the Allied Armies and that beautiful Paris now lay at the mercy of her brutal enemies. Madeleine would have fled before them, as half the population of Northern France had already done, had she not known that her invalid mother could not possibly survive such a journey. For her there had been no alternative but to refuse Gregory's offer and remain.

As she began to walk down the steps in front of the hospital she thought again of the shocking tragedy, entirely unconnected with the war, which had brought her there. That morning a lively middle-aged man had arrived to see Gregory at the St. Regis. He had proved to be a Bolshevik General named Stefan Kuporovitch, who, a few months before, had decided to shake the dust of Soviet Russia off his feet and return to Paris, with which he had fallen in love a quarter of a century earlier when he had visited it as a young Czarist officer before the Revolution. The hazards of war and many adventures since had prevented his reaching Paris until that very morning, and he had been as eager as a boy, although the Germans were already at the very gates of the city, to sit again at one of the marble-topped tables outside a café in the Rue Royale and drink his *apéritif* with a pretty girl.

Gregory had suggested that he should take Madeleine, and she had gone with the Russian to Weber's, where by his gaiety and a succession of champagne cocktails he had for an hour succeeded in taking her mind completely off the awful doom which was so rapidly approaching her beloved city. Then, just as they had been about to return to the St. Regis, Kuporovitch had stepped off the pavement. A passing car had knocked him down, and his skull had been fractured in two places. They had taken him to the St. Pierre; she had fetched Gregory, and they had just heard the doctor's report. It was thought unlikely that Kuporovitch would regain consciousness, and virtually certain that he would be dead before the morning. Before leaving, Gregory had forced several *mille* notes into her hand with the request that she would arrange for his poor friend to receive a decent burial.

Early that day she had not even known of the Russian's existence, but he had proved a gay and friendly person, and the horror of being a witness at close quarters to a fatal accident had shaken her profoundly; so that this personal tragedy added to her intense depression as she walked homewards through the silent, sunny, shuttered streets of stricken Paris.

Madeleine lived with her mother in an apartment on the top floor of a large block in the fashionable Rue St. Honoré. It was not that they were at all well-off, as Madame Lavallière had only the small pension of the widow of a minor official in the Ministry of the Interior and Madeleine such money as she could earn by her professional nursing; but Paris differs greatly from London in that in the French capital rentals are not always necessarily high in the smartest districts. Such matters are mainly governed by the floor upon which one lives, and in the great old-fashioned blocks that form the bulk of central Paris the first floors are often offices or luxury apartments inhabited by the very rich, while the top floors of the same buildings are frequently let at very modest rentals.

The lift went up only to the fourth floor, and Madeleine wearily climbed the remaining three flights of steep stone stairs. As she let herself into the flat her mother called to her from the bedroom. Madame Lavallière had been afflicted with a stroke some fifteen months before and now being partially paralysed was permanently confined to her bed. When Madeleine had regular work and was out nursing, Madame Bonard, the wife of the *concierge*, looked after Madame Lavallière's simple needs, but she came in only in the mornings to clean the flat and cook a midday meal, then in the evenings to get supper, as the invalid had an apparatus by her bedside with which she could make coffee for her breakfast and the afternoon. On hearing the door open at such an hour she knew, therefore, that it must be her daughter who had come in to see her.

Going into the bedroom Madeleine threw her hat upon a chair and shook back her dark curls. She even managed to raise a smile for the wasted figure with the grey wispy hair, who lay propped up in the large old-fashioned bed.

'My job is finished,' she said. 'My patient has just left for Bordeaux, so I shall be able to be at home with you now during these bad days until things become a little more settled.'

'That is good, *ma petite*,' the invalid nodded. The miserable life to which she was condemned was apt to make her querulous, and she often nagged at Madeleine for going out to work, although this was unjust, as without Madeleine's contribution to the little family budget they would have been hard put to it to carry on; but she was genuinely fond of her daughter and now obviously relieved to think that she had come home for a spell.

She then asked for news, and Madeleine gave her what little there was. No one in Paris knew what was happening outside it. The more optimistic still believed that the French Army was intact and that at any time General Weygand might yet launch a counter-offensive which would roll the enemy back, but optimists were rare in Paris in those days, and a terrible defeatism seemed to have closed like an icy hand upon the hearts of most of its remaining inhabitants.

'So the Germans are here,' the old woman gave a heavy sigh. 'I have heard nothing since this morning, but I was already becoming anxious about you. Thank God that you

14

have come home! You must stay here, Madeleine—in the apartment, I mean—and not go out again. The streets will no longer be safe with these beasts in them, and for a pretty girl like you—promise me that you will not go out!'

Madeleine had already thought of that several times earlier that day with a frightful sinking feeling in the pit of her stomach. All that she had ever read of the fate of the inhabitants in conquered cities, tales of the occupation in 1870 and of the brutalities of the Germans in Belgium and Northern France during the invasion of 1914 lent colour to her fears. Those great strong brutal Germans would, she felt certain, loot the cafés and the wine-shops, and once they had become drunk be capable of any mischief. Woe betide the unfortunate French girl who fell into their hands! Mentally she shuddered to think of the horrible fate which almost certainly would overtake many of them that night, but she strove to make light of it.

'I won't go out tonight at all events,' she promised; 'and perhaps not for a day or two. But we must go on living, and with the many wounded there will be much nursing to do. Even the Germans will respect a nurse's uniform, I feel certain, so you have no need to worry, *maman*. I shall be able to take care of myself.'

Madeleine made the coffee and took some *brioches* from a bag, which had been left ready on the invalid's bedside table. While they ate these they talked, but only perfunctorily, since both were busy with their thoughts and fears as to what the future held in store for them. When they had done Madeleine took the things into the small kitchen and washed up.

She had just finished when there came a sharp ring; it was the door-bell of the apartment. Turning, she crossed the living-room to open it, but in the small hallway she suddenly paused to wonder who it could possibly be.

Madame Bonard did not normally come up to prepare supper when Madeleine was absent until half past seven, and it was not yet five o'clock. Besides, Madame Bonard had a key; yet who could it be, since it was one of Madame Lavallière's complaints that people so rarely came to see her? Perhaps one of the few old friends who occasionally called to relieve the tedium of her bedridden life had thought of her in this sad hour and come to sit with her for a little. Yet, in such a case, knowing that the invalid could not leave her bed, Madame Bonard would have come up to let them in.

The bell shrilled again. Madeleine stilled the beating of her heart, reasoning with herself that it was much too soon for the Germans to have instituted any house-to-house visits yet, and stepping forward opened the door. A cry of gladness and surprise broke from her lips.

'Georges!' and next moment she was clasped tight in her fiancé's arms.

He kissed her hungrily for a moment, crushing her to him, then turned and, drawing her into the room, closed the door softly behind him. She noticed then that his face was tired and strained. He had no hat, and his clothes were thick with the dust of recent travel.

'What a surprise you gave me!' she exclaimed. 'But you are lucky to have found me here. I've only just got back from a job, and you know *maman* can't leave her bed. Why didn't you get Madame Bonard to come up and let you in?'

He shook his head. 'I haven't seen Madame Bonard. No one must know I'm here, *chérie*. I went upstairs in the next block, then over the roof and in through the skylight window on the landing.'

Her elation left her as quickly as it had come.

'Georges!' she whispered. 'What is it? Are you in trouble? Is someone following you?'

'Not yet, I hope,' he smiled. 'But they soon may be.'

And as she stared at him she thought again how his loose masculine figure, dark smooth hair and quick grin gave him a definite resemblance to the Englishman that she had been nursing back to convalescence.

Although the day was warm he was wearing a light mackintosh, and pulling it off he asked her for a drink. Hurrying to a cupboard she produced a bottle of Denis Mounie Cognac and two glasses. As she set them down on a corner of the table her mother's voice came, high-pitched and a little anxious, from the bedroom.

'What is it, Madeleine? Who is it with you out there?'

Madeleine did not wish to alarm her, but for a moment could not think what to reply. Georges was holding his finger

16

to his lips, so it was clear that he too did not wish her mother to know about his visit. Opening the door a little farther she said:

'It is a friend of mine—one of the doctors from the St. Pierre. He was anxious about me now that the Germans are in the city.' Then she firmly pulled the door shut.

Georges had poured out two stiff goes of cognac. She sat down beside him, and they lifted their glasses, staring over them at each other in an unspoken toast. The strong spirit made Madeleine's heart beat faster, but its mellow warmth seemed to give her new strength and momentarily to still her apprehension.

'Tell me,' she whispered, 'who is it that is after you? Why are you on the run?'

Having gulped the brandy he drew a deep breath, set down his glass and took her small hands firmly in his.

'Listen, Madeleine,' he said in a low voice. 'It's a long story —no time to go into details now. You know what is happening—what has happened—to our poor France. Some day perhaps we shall know whom to blame. At present we can only guess that many of our Generals have proved hopelessly incompetent and that many of our politicians have betrayed their trust. No one knows anything for certain, only that France has sustained an overwhelming defeat and now lies at the mercy of the enemy.'

'But the Army,' she breathed; 'it is still intact. Paris was only surrendered to save it from devastation. You cannot mean that the war is over and that we have already suffered final defeat?'

'I'm afraid so. The Army will not fight. It did not do so yesterday or the day before, so why should it fight tomorrow? I don't understand it—no one does—but some extraordinary paralysis seems to have gripped all our soldiers. They just marched back and back, giving ground the moment the Germans appeared before them. They were so bemused that they did not even trouble to blow up the roads, which might have halted the advance of the Germans' tanks. Nine-tenths of our men have not yet fired a single shot, but they are already a hopeless rabble whose only thought is further retreat. In a few days at most it will be over. We must face it, dear heart; for the time being France is finished.'

'But, Georges, this is too terrible! I—I simply can't believe it!'

'Nor I. Yet my own eyes and ears tell me that it is the awful truth, and I have been caught up in the *débâcle*. In such a catastrophe one man's life does not count for much, and if it were not for you, with France enslaved I think I'd almost sooner be dead.' He gave a rueful grin. 'In any case, I will be if the Germans get me.'

Her eyes grew wide with terror. 'But, Georges, what have you done? You are not even a soldier, but a Civil Servant. What have you done that the Germans should want to kill you?'

He was smiling now, right into her eyes, and he held her twitching hands firmly.

'I have deceived you, *chérie*, I confess it; but I know that you'll forgive me when I tell you that it was my duty to do so. I've always led you to believe that I was a clerk in the Ministry of the Interior. You'll remember it was at a dance for the employees of the Ministry that your father introduced us, only a few weeks before he died. When the war came you weren't very proud of me, were you? In one way you were glad that I had a safe job which gave me exemption and kept me out of danger, but there were times when you felt that a man of thirty ought to have been in uniform, and you would have liked your fiancé to be a soldier. Eh?'

'Oh, perhaps; but what does that matter now?' Madeleine knew that he had guessed her feelings rightly. It was that almost unconscious feeling that he should not have skulked behind his Civil Service job while France was in peril which in recent months had made her feelings towards him a little less warm than they had been before the war, and caused her to contemplate, just at odd moments, entering into a flirtation with some other attractive man. But she knew now that she could never have thought of anyone but Georges seriously. Gripping his hands again, she murmured:

'Please! Don't let's talk about the past. You're in danger, and I love you. Oh, Georges, I love you so!'

'*Chérie*, forgive me! I don't blame you for what you thought, and theoretically, at least, I *was* a clerk in the

Ministry of the Interior. But I haven't been sitting at a desk in the Préfecture at Rouen, as you believed, all through the war. My work has taken me to many places, and that is why I have never been able to get back to Paris on leave. The fact is that I am a member of the *Deuxième Bureau*.'

'The Secret Police!' she breathed.

'Yes—in the anti-espionage section, and I have had much to do with the catching and shooting of numerous Nazi spies.'

'But surely the Germans would not shoot you because of that? You were only doing your duty.'

He shrugged. 'Some of us know too much about the Boche to be healthy. Besides, if our poor France is to be crushed beneath the conqueror's heel it is men like myself who will organize resistance until she shall be free again. We understand underground methods, and therefore we are much more dangerous than any ordinary patriot. The Gestapo know that, so they will leave nothing undone to hunt us down and kill us.'

'But nobody knows you were in our Secret Service. Even I didn't know, so how could they possibly find that out?'

He frowned. 'There's a fair chance that by assuming another identity I may be able to keep under cover. But I've got to work quickly. You see, by this time the Gestapo will have taken over at the *Sûreté*. There are hundreds of files there connecting me with various cases in the past, and it's most unlikely that they'll all have been destroyed or removed in the last few days during the evacuation. The Germans will lose no time in going through them, and they may be on their way to my old home now in the hope of catching me there, or trying to find out where I've got to.'

'That's why you came here?'

'Yes, I had to get out of our Headquarters at Rouen at a moment's notice. The Germans were already entering the town. I have only the clothes that I stand up in and very little money. I want you to telephone—not from here, but from a call-box. Ring up Uncle Luc and ask him to pack up the clothes and things which are likely to be of most use to me in two suitcases, then to deposit them at the Gare de Lyon and bring the cloakroom checks to me here.'

'You're going to leave Paris?' she asked.

'No. My orders are to remain here in hiding, but to carry on the fight against the Nazis by every means in my power unless a formal peace is agreed between the Allied and German Governments.'

'But I thought you said that within a few days now the French Army will be compelled to—to surrender?'

'I fear so, *chérie*. But that does not mean the final triumph of our enemies. The Norwegian and Dutch Governments have already established themselves in London for the purpose of continuing the war with all their resources outside Europe, and, although the French Army in France may be forced to lay down its arms, we shall still have our Empire and our Fleet. Paul Reynaud seems to be a man of courage, and he will almost certainly transfer his Government to North Africa with the intention of carrying on the struggle from there. In any case, my Chief's last orders, which reached me in code early this morning, were to ignore any armistice which might be agreed in France and to work underground against the enemy as long as they remain in Paris. But we must not delay. Every moment is precious. Slip out now and telephone for me, while I have a wash and try to make myself a little more presentable.'

Kissing him swiftly she stood up. Without bothering to get her hat she went on to the landing and ran downstairs.

The nearest call-box was round the corner about two hundred yards away. The street was quite deserted, as upon this grim evening of the occupation the citizens of Paris who had remained had locked their doors and were gathered gloomily within their own homes, lest by their very presence in the streets they should seem to be paying homage to their conquerors.

Georges' Uncle Luc was the Mayor of Batignolles, and Madeleine wondered if at this time of emergency he would be at the Town Hall; but she decided first to try his own home. The telephone was still working, although on a restricted service; it was over twenty minutes before she could get through. When she did it was Uncle Luc's house-keeper who answered, and the poor woman was in a great state of distress. A party of Germans had arrived at the house about a quarter of an hour before. They had spent some ten minutes questioning *Monsieur le Maire* and had driven off, taking him with them. Madeleine thanked her, endeavoured to reassure her fears, and hanging up fled back down the street towards her own apartment.

When she reached it Georges was just coming out of the bathroom, his dark hair now smooth, his clothes brushed, and looking much more like his normal cheerful self than when he had first arrived.

Breathless from running up the stairs, Madeleine panted out her news, and Georges' face immediately became grave.

He was not greatly attached to his uncle and only rented a room in his house for convenience as a permanent place to keep his most cherished belongings and to sleep in on his occasional visits to Paris. There had, in fact, been a certain coldness between them for some time past, on account of a divergence of their political opinions.

'I don't think the old boy will come to any harm,' he said after a moment, 'because he's a member of the *Croix de Fer*, and the Nazis are sure to endeavour to establish good relations with our Fascists, as they're the most likely people to give them the co-operation they will need to keep order in Paris, It's a possibility that they're pulling in all the mayors as a temporary measure, or to give them their instructions collectively. On the other hand, there's just a chance that the Nazis went to Batignolles in the hope of finding me there, and that they've taken Uncle Luc off to question him.'

'He doesn't know that you're here, though,' said Madeleine, striving to reassure herself; 'and even if he did he wouldn't give you away, would he?'

'Not deliberately; but he has no idea that I work for the *Deuxième Bureau*, and the Germans wouldn't be fools enough to tell him that if they caught me they meant to kill me. They'll probably put up a plausible yarn about wanting to see me on some formality, and the old boy might fall for that. If so, he'd give them certain addresses where they might look for me; and this one among them. I'll have to throw overboard any idea of recovering my clothes and just drift round as I am until I can get others. In any case, it isn't safe for me to stay here any longer.'

Going up to him she put her arms round his neck and exclaimed: 'Oh, my darling! I've seen you only for such a little time! But of course you must go if there's the least chance that they might come here—and go at once. At once!'

For a moment they remained embraced while he kissed her very tenderly; then she said: 'You'll manage to let me hear from you, won't you? You must, chéri. I shall be half-crazy with anxiety.'

He nodded. 'I'll do my best, but you mustn't worry if you don't hear for a few days.'

'Perhaps, later on, I can help you in your work?'

'I don't want to involve you in that. It will be dangerous.'

'I don't care.'

His quick smile came again. 'To hear you say that comforts me more than anything that anyone could say on this tragic day. It seems almost as though our poor France has been like a man afflicted with blindness who is stricken down by some brutal unseen enemy; yet, thank God, there are still some of her children who can see clearly. Those of us who can must never waver in our faith, and whatever the cost to ourselves fight on until France is once more free.'

'I will fight with you, Georges,' she smiled up at him. 'You know that, don't you? To the bitter end—if need be.'

He stooped his head and kissed her, then letting her go he moved towards the door.

'Wait!' she called after him. 'You said that you had very little money. I have some here. Wait, and I will get it.'

She had just remembered that, in addition to the nursing fees and a handsome present which Gregory had given her, she had the *mille* notes which he had thrust into her hands to ensure Kuporovitch a decent burial. Hurrying into her bedroom she got her bag, and she had no hesitation in taking the notes, as well as her own money, from it. In times like these the living were infinitely more important than the dead, and she felt too that Gregory himself would approve her action.

As she came back into the sitting-room she saw Georges' face intent with listening, and a second later she caught the tread of heavy feet upon the stairs. Halted in her tracks, she stood there, grasping the banknotes in her hand, her mouth half-open. The door-bell rang.

Georges swiftly waved her away and drew an automatic from a holster that was strapped under his left armpit. The bell rang again; then a voice came:

'Madeleine! Are you home? It is Luc Ferrière.'

With a gasp of relief she started forward to open the door, but Georges grabbed her by the shoulder and hauled her back. In her relief at learning that it was his uncle she had forgotten that Uncle Luc had been taken from his house by the Germans and so might not be alone.

For a moment there was a deathly silence, then outside a gruff voice muttered something. The sound of shuffling steps came clearly, then a thud as a heavy boot crashed against the lock of the door; the wood splintered, and it flew wide open.

A group of black-uniformed German S.S. men stood there; with them was Uncle Luc. One of the men pushed him inside, and the rest made to follow.

'Stand back!' shouted Georges. 'Stand back, or I fire!'

Uncle Luc was a tall, fair man with a narrow head; he wore a bowler hat and pince-nez. He waved his hands vaguely in protest.

'Georges, my boy: please do not do anything foolish. Put away that gun. It is not permitted for French citizens to carry arms any more in Paris; but do not be afraid. The officer here and his men only wish to question you.'

The blood had drained from Madeleine's face. She stared at the elderly mayor for a second. Suddenly she burst out:

'You brought them here! How could you? How could you?'

He shrugged and waved his hands again. '*Ma chère* Madeleine, please do not excite yourself. There is no cause for that. They do not mean to do Georges any harm.'

'Oh, how—how could you!' she repeated, choking on her words as her terrified glance took in the armed Germans grouped in the tiny hall and Georges standing tense with his pistol levelled. But the Mayor of Batignolles seemed to have no appreciation of the heinousness of his act, and replied quite calmly:

'They called at my house in search of him, and they insisted that I should take them to various places where he might be. No one is more conscious than myself of the unpleasantness of such duties, but in my official position I had no option.'

'So you've already gone over to the enemy,' Georges' voice held a bitter sneer. 'I thought you would, but not quite so soon or so openly.'

'My boy, you are overwrought by our misfortunes and have lost your sense of proportion.' Uncle Luc drew himself up and went on with unctuous pomposity: 'We have defended our country to the best of our ability. That we have suffered defeat is no fault of ours, and it behoves us all now to co-operate with the invader for the sake of keeping order. We must accept our defeat with calm and dignity. Yes, calm and dignity—that must be our watchword in this tragic hour. Come, Georges, be sensible and put down that pistol.'

The German officer, a Schwartz Korps major, was standing just behind Luc Ferrière. He was a blue-chinned, knobbly-faced man, and in his hand he held an automatic, but he addressed Georges in stilted French politely and even in a friendly tone.

'*Monsieur*, the advice which your uncle gives you is excellent. I beg of you not to make our duty more unpleasant than it need be. My orders are to bring you in for questioning. If you will come with us you will have nothing to fear. Put your weapon on the table behind you, please.'

Madeleine's heart was beating so fast that her breath came in little gasps. What would Georges do? He had said so definitely that if the Germans once caught him they would shoot him. Knowing that, would he surrender and allow himself to be taken away, or would he make a fight for his life here and now? If he did, how could she help him? The four S.S. men were all armed and one of them had a tommy-gun resting on his hip.

'Come now,' said the major. 'We waste time.'

Georges moved his pistol slightly to cover the man who held the tommy-gun, since the officer was partly protected by the fact that he was standing just behind Uncle Luc.

The major spoke again: 'I do not wish to take harsh

24

measures, but I shall have to do so if you refuse to obey me.'

'If you only want to question me you can do so here,' Georges said abruptly.

'That will not do,' the officer signed to his men, and the fellow with the tommy-gun took a step forward.

'Halt, or I fire!' cried Georges, and his voice now rang with menacing determination.

There was a moment of tense silence, then it was broken by Madame Lavallière's shrill tones as she cried from her bedroom:

'What is it, Madeleine? What is happening out there?'

Instinctively they all looked towards her bedroom door, and at that instant Madeleine had an inspiration. From the kitchen window of the apartment the wire cables of a small goods lift ran down into a courtyard in the centre of the block. If Georges could only get to the window and climb out of it while she flung herself in the path of the Germans he might be able to swarm down the cables and get away before they could reach the window to shoot at him. She had no means of conveying her plan to Georges in detail, but he knew the geography of the apartment well, and she felt certain that a hint would be enough. Turning, she sprang forward, and grasping the handle of the kitchen door, flung it wide open.

Madame Lavallière's voice came again.

'Madeleine! Madeleine! Why do you not come? What is going on out there?'

Her cries were half-drowned by an order shouted in German by the major. His men raised their weapons and came rushing forward. The tommy-gun began to spit fire and suddenly a deafening series of explosions shook the room.

Georges fired twice, hitting the man with the tommy-gun. He gave a stifled curse, stumbled and fell. Dodging round the table, Georges leapt backwards and reached the kitchen door. He had hardly done so when there was a second crash of shots, as the other S.S. men, firing over their fallen companions, let fly at him with their automatics.

The reports were deafening. Blue smoke eddied from the barrels of the guns, and for a moment Madeleine could see nothing clearly. Georges' pistol cracked again, but he had

25

now fallen back against the jamb of the door, and she knew that he was badly wounded. Slowly he slid to the floor, but his hand still gripped his gun, and he made one last effort to raise it.

Madeleine threw herself forward in a desperate attempt to cover him with her body, but Uncle Luc seized her and dragged her aside to prevent her being shot. As she strove to break free she swivelled round just in time to see the major level his pistol, pointing it downwards at the prostrate Georges. He fired at point-blank range, and where Georges' left eye had been a second before there appeared a ghastly black hole, from which a trickle of blood was running.

Madeleine gave a piercing scream and fell to the floor in a dead faint.

Hours later that night Madeleine Lavallière knelt, dry-eyed and still stunned, at the foot of the bed in the narrow spare room of her apartment. On the bed Georges now lay rigid in death.

In the interval Luc Ferrière, shocked out of his stupid complacency, had roused the neighbours and with them performed the last rites for his nephew. A white sheet now covered the torn body and disfigured face; around the still form tall, tapering candles which burned with a steady flame were set, and a crucifix reposed upon its breast. In the living-room outside Madame Bonard and another woman were sitting up, but the distraught girl had refused their endeavours to persuade her to lie down. She had insisted that she must watch and pray through the night by her dead fiancé's side.

At last, as the early dawn was creeping through the closed shutters to make the candlelight wan and pale, something stirred inside her. Great spasmodic sobs began to tear her breast, then tears brought relief to her over-burdened heart; but with tears of sorrow tears of bitter, burning anger were mingled, and as she prayed she now cried aloud:

'Beasts! Murderers! Assassins! O God, give me the chance to avenge this wrong. Support me. Strengthen me so that I may never tire, until—until France shall be free of this pollution which—which Thou hast seen fit to inflict upon our soil,

No matter what becomes of me! But before I die let me have vengeance for this—this brutal death that my dear love has suffered. Vengeance I beg of Thee, O Lord! Vengeance! Vengeance! Vengeance!'

2

City of Despair

In the days that followed, Madeleine knew little of France's agony. Her own tragedy was so near, and her mind so numbed by the horror and shock of having seen her lover butchered before her eyes, that she hardly took in the bulletins which came, hour by hour, over the now German-controlled Paris radio.

The French Army was still falling back. The Government had retired, so it was said, first to Orléans, then to Tours. The Germans meanwhile proclaimed a fresh series of shattering blows, and their panzer columns were reported to be advancing almost without opposition through Châlons and Saint-Dizier towards Chaumont and the Plateau de Langres, thus cutting off the great garrisons in the Maginot Line from the Main French Armies of manœuvre.

Georges' funeral took place on the morning of the 15th, and on Madeleine's return from it her mother endeavoured to rouse her, but her hysterical outburst of weeping during the previous night had given place to a hard, unnatural calm, in which she spoke only when addressed and then in no more than monosyllables.

Had Georges' death occurred during normal times she would have had numerous friends to comfort her, and some of them would certainly have insisted on taking her away, at least for a time, from the actual scene of the tragedy; but two-thirds of the population of the capital had fled before the advancing Germans. The remainder still kept to their houses, temporarily overwhelmed with the catastrophe which had fallen so swiftly upon them; unable to make plans for the future and as yet too absorbed with their own anxieties to rouse themselves in an effort to discover what had happened to their acquaintances.

Madeleine too was at present quite incapable of making any plans for the future. Her blue eyes seeming abnormally large from the unnatural pallor of her face, and dressed in the deepest mourning of unrelieved black, she moved mechanically about the small household tasks of tending her mother and cooking meals. There was no shortage of food so far, and in her few expeditions to the local shops she saw no evidence that the Germans were behaving with the brutality with which they were credited. The few that she saw appeared to be in a high good humour, either driving about in cars or strolling in small groups and pausing to look in the well-filled windows or to photograph buildings of historic interest, as nearly all of them carried cameras. Most of them were young, pink-faced and rather stupid-looking. They had more the appearance of sightseeing country-bumpkins than that of the brutal and licentious soldiery of a conquering army.

It was on the afternoon of the 16th that Madeleine was first roused into exchanging more than monosyllables with anybody. On coming upstairs with some things that she had bought for supper she ran into a young man on the landing who was just coming out of the apartment opposite her own. He was a tall, dark fellow, with brown spaniel-like eyes, a little hairline moustache and short side-whiskers, which gave him rather the appearance of a Spaniard.

As she reached the landing he looked awkwardly away from her and flushed with embarrassment. She sensed that he must have heard of her tragedy and was momentarily at a loss as to how to greet her; so she said at once:

'Why, Pierre, what a nice surprise to see you! So many of ones' friends seem to have disappeared in these last terrible days.'

'I know,' he murmured; 'and for you things have been far worse than for most of us. Poor Georges—I cannot say how terribly sorry I am.'

'Please—let's not talk of it,' she said quickly. 'It's too near— too painful. But tell me about yourself.' As she spoke she unlocked her door, and he followed her inside.

He gave a rueful smile. 'About myself there is not much

29

to tell. I was lucky to get back with a whole skin, and now I shall try to paint again. God knows if anyone will have the money to buy pictures, but I suppose we'll all manage to scrape along somehow.'

Pierre Ponsardin was an artist of some promise but few means; yet, after being called up, he had managed to continue to find the rent for the apartment on the other side of the landing, which served him both for home and studio, as when he had first taken it he had had a big window cut in the mansard roof, which gave the main room an excellent north light. He had known Madeleine for some time and had fallen in love with her, but when they had first met as neighbours she had already been engaged to Georges; so he had never had any opportunity of disclosing his passion. Madeleine's intuition had told her long ago that he had more than a friendly interest in her, but she had never betrayed the least sign of realizing that; and as it was several months since she had last seen him his very existence had almost faded from her mind.

With Pierre, on the contrary, separation had even intensi-fied his feelings about her. For such a sensitive and fastidious man life in the Army had proved a veritable hell. The coarse food, the discomfort, the dirt, the bullying of the N.C.O.s and the often brutal ragging of his fellow-soldiers had proved more soul-destroying to him than a prison sentence would have been to any habitual criminal. During these months of utter wretchedness one of his few consolations had been to gaze in secret upon a miniature that he had painted of Madeleine, which still hung by a ribbon round his neck under his shirt; and now that he saw her again in the flesh all his old passion for her welled up with renewed force.

Actually, he had hardly known Georges, so he had no great reason to be distressed about his death. In fact, when he had first heard of it he had, not altogether unnaturally, been forced to conceal his excitement at the new hope that it gave him now that Madeleine was free again; but he was much too good a psychologist to rush his fences and had no intention of showing his hand for the moment.

Instead, to take her thoughts off Georges and the vast tragedy which was engulfing France, he told her something of Army life, but he was careful not to present it as he had found it himself, from fear that she might think him a milksop. He spoke with admiration of his officers and of what good fellows his brother privates had been. While feigning a certain modesty, he related one or two imaginary adventures in the firing-line before the Battle of France was opened, which put him in a good light, and said what fun they had had in the periods when his regiment had been relieved from active duty and they were able to hold concerts and sports. He had been talking for some time when a little frown crossed Madeleine's brow, and she suddenly asked:

'How comes it, Pierre, that you are not with your regiment still?'

He shrugged. 'What would you? You must have heard how our Generals let us down. We would have fought to a finish had we been allowed to do so; but all the time it was retreat—retreat—retreat. And two days ago it became obvious that the Generals did not mean us to fight at all.'

'But—the main French Army is still fighting somewhere south of Paris,' she protested.

He shrugged again. 'Perhaps, but the Army, of which my battalion formed a part, was in the north, near Amiens, and I doubt if we could ever have got back so far.'

'You doubt it! But did you not try?'

'Well—yes; but you have no idea of the confusion. The roads were choked with refugees. We were often hours late in reaching each fresh rendezvous. The orders we got contradicted one another, and so it at last became every small unit for itself.'

She stared at him: 'Do you mean, Pierre, that you ran away?'

He laughed a little awkwardly. 'Hardly that! But the German advance was so swift, and we never knew on which side of us we would find them next. It became obvious to all of us that without proper orders and with the Army already in a state of disintegration we could no longer hope to influence the course of events. It was the same everywhere, from what I hear, and I doubt if the Armies in the south will be able to hold out for more than a day or two longer.'

'But they are fighting still, and you are not with them,' she

31

insisted. 'You are here, in Paris, and in civilian clothes. Why?'

He fingered his small moustache. 'Naturally it is difficult for you to understand, Madeleine, but have you realized what will happen to all men in uniform when the collapse comes?'

She shook her head.

'They will be disarmed and herded into concentration camps. If we ask for an armistice the fighting will stop, but the fighting forces will not be released and allowed to go home until a formal peace is agreed; and that may not be for months. If our Government decides to go to North Africa and fight on it may not even be for years. The Germans are short of food themselves, so they won't have much to spare for their prisoners. Thousands of our soldiers will die from semi-starvation and the appalling conditions in those camps. Would you have had me surrender myself to such a fate when I had a chance to escape from it? Surely not?'

'Georges' death may have made me hard,' she said slowly, 'but I can't help feeling that it was your duty to remain with your regiment, at least until an armistice had been declared. Afterwards, it would have been another matter.'

'Then it would probably have been too late to escape.'

'Perhaps; yet you lay all the blame for our defeat upon the Generals. How could they be expected to turn the tide of the invasion if all France's soldiers had behaved as you have done?'

'But many of them did,' he protested. 'What was the sense of fighting on when anybody who was there could see for themselves that the High Command had broken down and the battle was already lost? We did our best, but when there was no more that we could do the men in my unit held a meeting, and we all decided that the sensible thing was to try to save ourselves. How the others fared I don't know, but in Beauvais I managed to buy a suit of overalls and get a place on the roof of the last train going through to Paris. I lay doggo in the suburbs for a couple of days, then walked in last night, and, personally, I think I'm darn' lucky to be here.'

Suddenly Madeleine stood up. 'You are a coward and a deserter!' she shouted, banging the table with her small fist, 'Get out! Get out!'

He came slowly to his feet, a look of pained surprise on his good-looking face. He would have given anything now to have had the last ten minutes over again, so that he could have invented some plausible and praiseworthy reason for his having suddenly appeared again in Paris in civilian clothes. But in his own mind he had seen his conduct as not only logical, but rather commendable. After all, he had exercised considerable ingenuity in succeeding in getting away while the bulk of his fellow-soldiers must almost certainly be caught; but he realized now that he had made a hopeless mess of things, and he was so upset at the idea of having shamed himself so completely before the girl that he loved that he could only wave his elegant hands in a futile gesture and stammer:

'But, Madeleine, you don't understand how things were.'

'Get out!' she repeated between clenched teeth. 'Get out! Before I hit you for the coward that you are!'

With a helpless little shrug and the dejected look of a beaten dog he lowered his brown eyes before her blazing blue ones and walked slowly from the room.

For some minutes after his departure Madeleine stood there, positively seething with indignation. So that was how France had fallen into this miserable plight. Instead of defending her, as they should have done, her soldiers had thought only of their own skins. Whole units, such as Pierre Ponsardin's, had just abandoned the fight once they had found themselves in difficulties and made off, each man as quickly as he could, for their homes.

After a little she calmed down, and realized that she had perhaps been rather unjust to Pierre. He was not a strong, courageous man like her dear Georges, but an artist with all an artist's hatred of fighting and violence. If the other men of his unit had run away there was certainly some excuse for him, but the whole sordid tale filled her with an incredible sadness, and she suddenly burst into a violent fit of sobbing.

When she recovered she felt better and realized that her talk with Pierre had done something to her. Before, she had been like a body without a spirit, but his cowardice had raised in her the first emotion of any kind which she had felt since Georges' death and her vow of vengeance beside his body. In some strange way she felt as though a spring inside herself had been released and that she had become quite normal again, so that she could take up once more the affairs of daily life,

That evening her mother noticed the change and, although she refrained from any comment, was much comforted by it.

On the following morning, June the 17th, the radio announced that everyone should listen-in at eleven o'clock, as Marshal Pétain would make an important announcement. At eleven Madeleine sat at her mother's bedside, and together they heard the voice of France's elderly hero, the one-time Victor of Verdum. He asked for calm and dignity among all the people of the French nation, whether they were in territory already occupied by the enemy or not. He spoke of France's great weakness through her fallen birthrate, which had made it impossible for her, after being deprived of the support of the Allied Armies in Flanders, to resist the invader.

He went on to say that, having fought an honourable fight with an honourable enemy, he had the previous night asked, as one soldier to another, of the German Commander-in-Chief that honourable terms should be given to France in order to avoid further, now useless, bloodshed.

When he had finished Madame Lavallière looked across at her daughter and said slowly: 'So this is the end. A sad end for us, but at least the women of the world will be glad that the men have come to their senses and stopped killing one another.'

'You are wrong, *maman*. This is not the end—only the beginning,' Madeleine replied swiftly.

'What do you mean, child? The Marshal said that he had asked for honourable terms. That means an armistice. The "Cease Fire" will sound at once, and in a few weeks there will be peace, and that will be much, however hard the terms that the enemy impose on us.'

Madeleine shook her head. 'But you don't understand. It is only the Army in France which is surrendering, not the whole French Empire.'

'Are you sure of that?'

'Of course. Georges said that the Army here might have to lay down its arms, but that the Government would go to North Africa and continue the struggle from there. Pierre said the same thing only yesterday.'

'You may be right, *chérie*,' Madame Lavallière sighed wearily, and they fell into an unhappy silence, from which they were only roused some ten minutes later by the front-door bell. When Madeleine went to answer it Pierre was standing there. He looked very sheepish, but he managed to blurt out: 'Well. I suppose you've heard the news?'

'Yes,' she nodded. 'It wasn't altogether a surprise, but it's happened more quickly than one expected.'

'That's true,' he said slowly. 'But you heard what Marshal Pétain said—we fought an honourable fight, and were only defeated because there were too many for us. No one could possibly accuse Pètain of cowardice, and I—well, I thought that, now you've heard the real truth in the Marshal's own words, you—you might not take such a black view of me.'

She stretched out her hand and laid it on his arm. 'Poor Pierre! I'm afraid I was rather hard on you yesterday, but lately I—I've been through so much, you know.'

'Of course!' A quick smile lit his face. 'I understand perfectly, and if you'd seen the refugees on the roads and everything, you'd have realized that we simply hadn't got a chance.'

'Let's say no more about it,' she smiled back a little sadly. 'Things are going to be grim enough for all of us in Paris without old friends quarrelling.'

'Yes, I'm afraid they are,' he agreed; quite cheerfully now that he had re-established himself in her good graces. But next moment he put his foot into it again by adding: 'Still, that won't be for very long. We'll have to pay a pretty heavy indemnity, I expect, but once that's agreed and the peace is signed the Germans will clear out.'

She looked at him with a puzzled frown. 'But there is no question of peace, and cannot be, for months or perhaps years yet. You yourself said that the French Government would go to North Africa and carry on the war from there.'

'I said they *might*,' he admitted, 'but that was yesterday, and the Marshal didn't mention anything of that kind in his broadcast.'

'Why should he? He spoke only of asking for honourable terms for the Army in France.'

'Perhaps,' Pierre shuffled uneasily. 'But if you're right it means that we shall be prisoners here at the mercy of these brutes for years while the British and our own people outside France try to starve them out.'

'Of course! Did I not say that things would be grim here? What else did you expect? Surely you realized that yesterday, when you suggested that our Government might go to North Africa?'

'Well, to tell you the truth, I hadn't had much time to think about it then.'

'Surely you would not have them throw their hand in altogether?' she asked sharply.

'*Mais non, mais non!*' he exclaimed, just a trifle too quickly. 'For myself, I am all for fighting on, but it does not lie with us. It depends what Pétain and the rest of them decide in Bordeaux.'

In spite of his glib assurance, Madeleine felt absolutely certain now that he would have much preferred a total surrender, so that, whatever humiliation France might have been made to suffer in loss of territory or prestige, he might the sooner resume his normal life again of painting a few pictures whenever he got hard up, and spending the rest of his time talking and drinking with his friends in the art clubs and bars.

She was not angry with him, only a little contemptuous of his weakness, as she said quietly: 'You're making a big mistake if you think that we're going to get rid of the Boche so quickly now that he has got to Paris. You must excuse me now, Pierre. I'm sure that I heard *maman* calling me.'

She had not heard her mother, but at that moment she did not feel like talking to him any more, because she did not want to be rude again; it was a convenient excuse to close the door and get rid of him.

That evening, just as she and her mother had finished supper, they had another visitor—Georges' Uncle Luc. Madeleine had seen him at the funeral, but had not spoken to him since they had met in that very room and she had fainted at the sight of her stricken fiancé. She now went deathly white and made a motion as though to reclose the door, but Uncle Luc removed his little bowler hat from his tall, narrow head with a courteous, old-fashioned bow and asked her permission to enter, upon which she felt that it was quite impossible to shut him out.

Once inside, he inquired after her mother, saying that he

had come to see them both, and asked if Madame Lavallière would receive him.

Madeleine waved him to a chair, and, her face still drained of blood, went in to speak to her mother. Tied to her bed as she was, Madame Lavallière was used to receiving visitors in her room and she at once began to tidy herself, while reasoning gently with her daughter.

'*Ma petite*, I know how distasteful Luc Ferrière's visit must be to you. Naturally you feel that it was through his stupidity that poor Georges met his death; but you must endeavour to be reasonable. We have known the Ferrières for many years, and in times like these old friends must not quarrel. Try to remember that this visit is probably even more painful for him than it is for you, as almost certainly he has steeled himself to come here and express his regrets for what happened. You have a generous heart, my child. Now is the time to be magnanimous and forebearing.'

Only that morning Madeleine had been enunciating the self-same doctrine to Pierre, so she nodded dumbly and braced herself for the interview.

When the Mayor of Batignolles was shown in, having greeted Madame Lavallière, he perched himself on the edge of a hard chair, placed his bowler hat upon his bony knees, and removing his pince-nez started to polish them.

After coughing twice he began in a pompous voice: 'No doubt you will have guessed the reason for my intrusion. In these sad times none of us can afford to harbour hard feelings against our neighbours, and, although of course no fair-minded person could possibly attach any blame to me for the shocking event which occurred here a few nights ago, I felt it would be a gracious gesture on my part to express to you both personally my deep distress in our mutual bereavement. You will, I am sure, not have overlooked the fact that Georges' death is a sad blow to me as to yourselves—in fact, he was my favourite nephew, and nothing could possibly have induced me to bring those Germans here had I had the least idea of the violent act that they contemplated.'

As he mouthed his pretentious phrases Madeleine could have struck him. She knew that he and Georges had never had anything in common and that for the past two years they had barely been on speaking terms. Georges had only kept his room in his uncle's house because he was always so busy and occupied it so rarely that he had felt it too much trouble to move elsewhere, and the old man had only allowed him to retain it because he loved money and was loth to sacrifice the useful rental which he received from his mainly absentee tenant. Her eyes were narrowed and the corners of her mouth twisted down in an ugly sneer, but fortunately he could not see her face as she was standing at the foot of her mother's bed, his back half-turned towards her.

'Of course, my dear Luc,' Madame Lavallière was saying in conciliatory tones. 'Please do not distress yourself. Madeleine and I perfectly understand that what happened was no fault of yours. How could any of us foresee that those brutes would shoot the poor boy down when he refused to go with them?'

'Ah! There you have it!' he held out a long nicotine-stained finger to mark his point. 'If only Georges had listened to reason. If only he had gone quietly the poor fellow might be with us now. Really, you know, although one hates to say it, he brought his tragic end upon himself.'

That was too much for Madeleine. 'How can you?' She burst out. 'How can you say such a thing? They meant to take Georges away and shoot him. I know they did! He told me so. He took the only chance he had, and at least before he died he succeeded in ridding the world of one of these filthy Germans.'

Luc Ferrière turned to her and slowly shook his head. 'My poor child, I freely forgive your outburst because you are still overwrought. I can see that I should have allowed a longer time to elapse before calling upon you; then you would have been more yourself. But, in view of the news which we all received this morning, I felt that perhaps it was particularly appropriate that I should choose this evening for my endeavour to bridge any misunderstanding which may lie between us. With Marshal Pétain's declaration and by his wise decision this terrible war is now over. Within a month or so at the most the world will have peace again.'

Madeleine was biting her lip, so before the girl could burst out afresh Madame Lavallière turned quickly to their visitor.

'The request for an armistice does mean an end, then, to the fighting everywhere? The Government, after all, are not going to transfer themselves with the Fleet to North Africa?'

'No, no!' exclaimed the Mayor in shocked surprise. 'Thank goodness sane counsels have prevailed. Such a move could only prolong the war indefinitely and bring endless misery to us all. *Monsieur le Maréchal* spoke for the Empire, as well as for France, when he asked for an armistice.'

'Are you—are you absolutely certain of that?' Madeleine whispered.

'Of course! I have it officially. The terms of the armistice are not yet agreed, but there is no question of hostilities being continued in any portion of the French Empire.'

'But that is shameful!' Madeleine cried. 'We have immense resources outside France, and for us to throw our hand in altogether like this is the worst possible treachery to our Allies.'

Luc Ferrière shrugged his lean shoulders. 'Be reasonable, Madeleine. Of what do our Allies consist? Norway, Belgium, Holland—all those countries are beaten already. Their armies are defeated, and although their Governments have fled to Britain, what can a handful of exiles possibly do there against our late enemies?'

'There is still the British Empire,' said Madeleine hoarsely. He gave a little cynical, high-pitched laugh.

'Surely, my dear, we have learnt our lesson in that direction? In two wars now the British have used us for their own selfish reasons to bolster up their top-heavy Empire. But in the recent campaign they revealed themselves in their true colours at last. After fighting in Belgium for a fortnight, they left us in the lurch, and scrambled home as quickly as they could. Now that our wise leaders have seen that peace is more valuable to the world than massacring thousands of men for platitudes, Britain will sue for peace within a week.'

'I wonder?' said Madeleine slowly. 'Perhaps they let us down but I don't think they did so intentionally. To have done so just wouldn't have made sense. Perhaps they're not strong enough to fight alone, but they've still got their Navy, and they're such queer people—even Napoleon said that they never know when they're beaten.'

Luc Ferrière's nasal laugh came again. 'That was a long time ago. The British were different then. They hadn't got soft from too much prosperity.'

Madame Lavallière raised herself a little on her pillows. She was desperately afraid that at any moment Madeleine and the Mayor of Batignolles might begin to quarrel violently, and her eye lighted on the clock. With sudden relief she stretched out her hand to the wireless beside her bed and turned the knob, as she said:

'It's just time for the British news bulletin. Madeleine speaks excellent English and she will be able to tell us what they have to say themselves about Marshal Pétain's speech this morning.'

Luc Ferrière nodded. 'I too know quite enough English to understand what they say on the wireless.'

The announcer was already speaking. A German station was trying to jam the B.B.C. with music, but the jamming was not very effective, and they heard him say that before the news listeners would hear the Prime Minister, The Right Honourable Winston Churchill.

Madame Lavallière endeavoured to pick out a sentence here and there. Luc Ferrière sat with downcast expressionless face. Madeleine, standing at the end of the bed, gripped its edge with ever-rising excitement until the last great declaration of defiance made music in her brain.

'What has happened in France makes no difference to British faith and purpose. We have become the sole champion now in arms to defend the world cause. We shall defend our island, and with the British Empire around us we shall fight on, unconquerable, until the curse of Hitler is lifted from the brows of men.'

'There!' she cried triumphantly, as the dogged, courageous voice ceased; and for her mother's benefit she translated the last sentence into French. 'They will fight on, unconquerable, until the curse of Hitler is lifted from the brows of men. You heard that, Monsieur Ferrière—you heard it! Now what have you to say?'

He spread out his hands and gave a little pitying smile. 'The old lion may roar, but he has lost his teeth. The English Channel is not the barrier that it used to be. Now that great fleets of aeroplanes can be sent against the island Hitler and his Luftwaffe will make short work of Churchill.'

For a moment all Madeleine's hopes were dashed once more. What he had said of the English Channel seemed so true, and if once the Germans could make a landing, covered by their great Air Force, how could the little British Army, which had already lost most of its equipment at Dunkirk, possibly stand up against all the armoured millions that Hitler could launch against it?

Luc Ferrière was speaking again. 'You see now how stupid it is to cherish these wild ideas that it is possible any longer to defeat the might of Germany. Since that is so, it becomes the duty of all to accept the situation and turn our energies to recovering from the effects of the war as quickly as we can. Our own political system has failed lamentably, and however much our propagandists may have taught us to dislike Hitler we cannot escape the fact that with his vision and great ability he has rebuilt a new, strong Germany in a remarkably short time. No doubt he has his plans for a full reconstruction of Europe, and to endeavour to thwart him would only be to bash our heads against a solid wall. Germany offered her friendship to France before the war in an attempt to keep her out of it. Very foolishly we preferred to sacrifice ourselves to the interests of Britain; but that is all over now—a folly of the past, which should be forgotten. We must accept our defeat with clam and dignity—I think I used those words the other night, and our great leader used them only this morning. Then by giving our full co-operation and goodwill to our late enemies we may hope . . .'

'You—you really mean that you're prepared to help the men who killed Georges!' gasped Madeleine. 'You can't! It's horrible! Utterly horrible!' And with a little cry of despair she ran from the room.

Monsieur Ferrière sadly shook his narrow head. 'Poor little one!' he murmured. 'I am so distressed for her; but she is still quite young. She will live and learn that we older ones are right.'

Having kissed Madame Lavallière's hand and thanked her for receiving him, he let himself out.

In her bedroom, with her face buried in the pillows,

Madeleine lay sobbing out her heart. To her the Mayor of Batignolles' attitude seemed utterly incredible; yet she knew that he not only represented official France, but also a great section of French opinion. Her mother, although she had said little, had obviously sided with him. Then there was Pierre. He too, although a young man, so obviously preferred surrender at any price to the risk of death, mutilation, or even discomfort. Far away across the English Channel Churchill was still roaring defiance at the common enemy of all mankind; but what could he and the British do now that France had deserted them? Were all Frenchmen cowards that they should have refused his appeal to fight on? No, that was impossible; there were Frenchmen who would still risk everything for the true honour of France. Georges would have done so had he lived. He had told her that he had secret orders to stay in Paris and operate from underground against the enemy, whatever might happen, until a full and proper peace was signed. There must be others like him. She herself would never, never submit to the Germans and treat them as friends. As long as she lived she would look upon them as the brutal beasts they were and hate them from the very bottom of her heart. Yet where could she find those who felt the same? She felt so desperately alone.

It was just then that the door-bell pealed. Checking her sobs with an effort she quickly attended to her face and went to answer it. On the threshold there stood a middle-aged doctor, under whom she had worked on various occasions and who was a visiting surgeon at the Hôpital St. Pierre.

'I hope you'll forgive my calling at such a late hour,' he said, 'but I've come to see you about your Russian friend.'

For a moment she stood with her mouth open. In the terrible stress of the events of the last few days all thought of Kuporovitch had passed from her mind, and she now remembered her promise to Gregory to see that his friend received a decent burial.

'I'm so sorry,' she said. 'I ought to have called at the hospital long before this to make arrangements for the funeral. I suppose you're anxious to have him removed from the morgue. When did he die?'

The doctor smiled. 'He didn't die. Why, I can't think. His

skull must be made of steel to have survived the injuries that he received; but he lived through the night after you brought him in, and the following day, as his heart seemed perfectly sound, we decided to try a trepanning operation. I'm happy to say that it's proved extremely successful.'

'But how marvellous!' she exclaimed. 'I'm so glad! I must come round to the hospital tomorrow morning to see him.'

The doctor hesitated. 'Well, as a matter of fact, Mademoiselle, that's just the point I came to see you about. It will be a long time before he's completely recovered, but he seems to have the constitution of an ox, so he's already off the danger list, and the Germans have commandeered practically every bed we've got for their wounded. You know how impossible it is to shift them once they've made up their minds about a thing, and they wouldn't give us any time at all. We only heard late this afternoon, and the orders were imperative that we should have one hundred and fifty beds cleared before midnight, whoever we threw out. We've been making frantic arrangements to remove the patients all the evening, and, of course, most of them can be transferred to their own homes; but this Russian has no home, and all the other hospitals in Paris are in the same overcrowded state as ourselves. I hope I'm not wrong, but I gathered that you were more or less responsible for him, so the fact of the matter is that I've brought him along to you. He's in an ambulance downstairs.'

Madeleine was so surprised that she hardly knew what to say. Her mother's apartment was a very small one, but there was the little spare-room.

'You see, if you can possibly take him in,' the doctor hurried on, 'it would be a great blessing, because as a professional nurse you would be able to look after him; but quite frankly, if you can't I'm at my wits' end to know what to do with the poor fellow.'

'But of course I'll have him here.' Madeleine said at once. In such circumstances it would not have occurred to her to refuse to accept a stranger, at least for a few days until some other arrangements could be made, and Kuporovitch was already something more than a mere acquaintance from the very fact that she had been with him when he had met with his frightful accident.

43

While the doctor left her to go downstairs she hurried into the little spare-room and quickly prepared the bed. A few moments later the ambulance men brought Kuporovitch in on a stretcher. White bandages now covered the whole of the upper part of his head, and his black eyebrows stood out more than ever in startling contrast to his pale face. He was unconscious, and so a dead weight, but the orderlies helped her to get him into bed. The doctor felt the Russian's pulse, declared himself satisfied, gave Madeleine certain instructions and, promising to look in the following morning, wished her good-night.

When they had gone she stood for a few moments looking down at the broad, stocky figure which now occupied the bed upon which her dear Georges had lain in death only three nights before. There was nothing particularly handsome about the Russian's face, but even in sleep it had a tremendous rugged strength and determination.

As Madeleine stared at him she was suddenly conscious of a new thought. This man was Gregory's trusted friend. Even from the very little which she had heard them say to each other, she had learned that the two of them were inveterate enemies of the Germans. Kuporovitch had told her himself that morning when they had had drinks together in the Rue Royale that he would stick at nothing to kill any Nazi.

For the first time since Georges' death Madeleine smiled naturally. In this helpless, unconscious figure that lay motionless as a corpse beneath the sheets she knew that at last she had found an ally. He was now as weak as an infant and the flame of life in him still burned very low, but she would nurse him back to health and strength to aid her in her vengeance. She was alone no more.

3

The Man Who Should Have Died

She was with Kuporovitch again the following morning when he opened his eyes, but as she bent over him there was no trace of recognition in them. The first glimmerings of consciousness had only returned to the injured man for a short time on the previous afternoon, and it would be some days at least before he would be able to attempt to speak or lift a finger for himself. The main thing was that he should get as much sleep as possible and never be disturbed unnecessarily. French medicine places more importance upon rest than the passion for washing patients which is a great feature of English nursing; so Madeleine made no attempt now to lather her patient with soap and water, but, fetching some broth which she had already heated on the stove, she poured a few spoonfuls of it between his almost colourless lips, and he soon dropped off to sleep again. The only thing she could not manage was to move her heavy patient, when necessary, alone; but Pierre willingly agreed to come in and help her with this night and morning.

Madame Lavallière's reactions on being told about their unexpected guest had been extremely mixed. With a selfishness which was to some extent pardonable in a cripple she habitually regarded all problems as they affected herself. At first she rather resented the intrusion, as her financial resources were very limited and the future so uncertain. There was no guarantee that the French Government would now be able to continue paying the pensions of people like herself in German-occupied France, and if Madeleine was tied to the apartment for a considerable period nursing the Russian she would be unable to undertake any paid work which might offer outside.' However, when Madeleine pointed out that she still had the six thousand francs which Gregory had left her for the Russian's burial and that this money could now be used for his keep, Madame Lavallière began to take a better view of the matter and to consider the advantages which might accrue to herself from it. As long as the Russian was unable to care for himself Madeleine would be prevented from taking other work, which meant that she would have her daughter's companionship. Then, once the Russian was convalescent she would also have his company, and that, in view of the loneliness she had suffered for many months, was a pleasant change to which to look forward.

Kuporovitch had been brought to the apartment on the Monday evening, and the week that followed seemed to drag by, while all France waited in miserable suspense to hear the result of the armistice negotiations. On the Tuesday Hitler and Mussolini met at Munich to agree on the terms. On the Wednesday the French plenipotentiaries left Bordeaux. On the Friday the terms were presented to them at Compiègne. With his usual love of the dramatic and as a shrewd move to enable the German people fully to savour their revenge, Hitler had decreed that the French should accept the terms in the same railway coach in which Marshal Foch, Haig, Wemyss and the other Allied plenipotentiaries had sat on that grey morning of November the 11th, 1918. General Huntziger and the other Frenchmen appointed by Bordeaux took the seats which had been occupied by the defeated Germans; von Keitel then read the preamble to the terms.

That occupied less than half an hour. When it was done Hitler abruptly got up and contemptuously left the carriage, followed by all the rest of his Staff, except General von Keitel. There were to be no concessions and no arguments. The French must swallow the terms whole, or the conqueror would occupy the rest of France. As he stalked from the clearing the German engineers were already defacing and destroying the French memorials to their honoured dead of the last war. That night the French plenipotentiaries telephoned the terms to Bordeaux. On the Saturday they were accepted.

Much doubt still existed as to what attitude would be adopted by the overseas territories of the French Empire, and many rumours were rife. On the Sunday General Mittel-hauser, who was commanding in Syria, declared his intention of continuing hostilities. In Morocco, Senegal, the Cameroons and Jibuti various Generals stated that they meant to fight on with Britain.

On the Tuesday combined forces of the British Navy, Army and Air Force made raids along the French Channel coast; on the Wednesday the British Government declared the blockade extended to France, and at the end of the week they officially recognised General de Gaulle as the leader of all Free Frenchmen. There no longer seemed any doubt that the British were fully behind Churchill and meant to fight to the last ditch; but on the 30th a portion of the armistice terms were disclosed by the announcement that the Germans had completed their occupation of the whole of the northern and western seaboard of France right down to the Spanish frontier. So ended for France the tragic month of June.

Rumours of continued resistance in various parts of the French Empire were still rife, but it was apparent now that the prestige of Pétain, Weygand and Admiral Darlan was having its effect. They had taken the line that unity was all-important, as the only way in which the mother-country could be saved from being completely ravaged was by full compliance with the armistice terms; and these stipulated that the French Forces throughout the whole Empire should lay down their arms. Numerous appeals were made to this effect in broad-casts by the French leaders, and the German-controlled Paris radio lost no opportunity of hammering home the point.

Madeleine's only contacts in those days were Pierre, the doctor's visits to Kuporovitch and her brief calls at the local shops. The few people with whom she talked all sympathized with the plight in which the British found themselves, but held the view that France must look after herself. Then on July the 4th there came the, to them, astounding news that the British Fleet had attacked the French Fleet at Oran, sinking or putting out of action a number of France's largest warships and killing or wounding many hundreds of French sailors.

An immediate revulsion of feeling against Britain set in. Even before that many people had sought to explain away the defeat of the French Armies by the failure of the British

47

to break through from the north and rejoin the main French Forces on the Somme. To cover their own shortcomings the French politicians and military commentators had suggested in many newspaper articles that the British had virtually run away from the enemy and that their evacuation from Dunkirk had been much more hasty than it need have been. Now, with the news of the bombardment of their Fleet, which they regarded as an act of the most vile treachery, French opinion almost universally swung away from their ex-Ally. The German propagandists were able to make splendid new capital out of the affair for their old argument that the British had never cared a rap about France but used her only as a catspaw. Even Madeleine could not understand this apparently unprovoked attack, as the German radio was now jamming the B.B.C. broadcasts, so she was unable to hear the British explanation as to why they had been compelled to take such drastic action.

On the 4th of July the Pétain Government broke off diplomatic relations with Britain, a move which had the full support of the now embittered Parisians; and their anti-British feeling was still further aggravated a few days later when the news came through that their latest battleship, the *Richelieu*, the pride of the French Navy, had been torpedoed and put out of action at Dakar.

It was now three weeks since Kuporovitch had been brought to the Lavallières' apartment. At first he had lain almost comatose for days on end, but gradually a little strength had begun to flow back into him. He still had to lie full-length, but for the past week he had been able to talk a little and was fully conscious of all that was going on around him.

It was not until July the 11th, the day upon which President Lebrun resigned, thus formally bringing an end to the Third Republic, and, having formed a new Government of twelve Ministers, Marshal Pétain assumed the powers of a Dictator, that the Russian had rallied enough strength to ask what had happened to him. Madeleine told him about his accident, then gave him a brief account of the events that had followed and of how France was now out of the war. He made no comment, as he still had some difficulty in talking clearly, but

48

she could see from the expression in his quick eyes that he understood all she said.

In the early stages he had experienced little pain, but as he began to recover he was afflicted with the most agonizing headaches, and the only thing that seemed to bring him some relief was for Madeleine to sit on the edge of his bed and hold one of his hands in hers. She knew that in that way some people have the power of taking pain from others, but she experienced no suffering as a result of it herself and simply assumed that from the clasp of her hand he was able to draw a certain fortitude which enabled him the better to endure the dull, throbbing ache which so often tormented him.

Pierre continued to come in and help her when she had to move him, and one day towards the end of July he came upon them unexpectedly, while she was sitting on the edge of the Russian's bed, holding his hand.

The young artist said nothing at the time, but afterwards, when he and Madeleine were together in the sitting-room, he suddenly burst out:

'You—you haven't fallen in love with this fellow, have you?'

'Good gracious, no!' she laughed. 'Whatever makes you think I might have done that?'

'Well, you were sitting on his bed just now, holding his hand!'

'My dear Pierre, there's nothing in that. He says that it helps him bear the pain when he has these appalling headaches, so I often do it.'

'That's not his reason. It's because he's in love with you!' Pierre exclaimed truculently.

'What nonsense! You're imagining things!'

'Oh no, I'm not! Anyone could tell that who saw you together. He never takes his eyes off your face whenever you're in his room. If you take my tip you'll watch your step now that he's getting a bit stronger and stop this hand-holding, or the next thing that'll happen is he'll be trying to kiss you.'

Madeleine had never even thought of Stefan Kuporovitch in that way before. Georges' death was still much too near for her as yet to feel the least interested in any man; even Pierre's tentative compliments and admiring glances during these weeks had passed her by almost unnoticed. But now that he made this definite allegation she suddenly became conscious that she had known it all along. Ever since Kuporovitch had been strong enough to take a renewed interest in life he had shown all the symptoms which she recognized from past patients who had fallen for her.

She did not know if she were glad or sorry. If it were likely to complicate their relations it would be a bore, and she knew that he was in his late forties, so of an older generation. For her part, even if Georges had not been constantly in her thoughts still, there could be nothing between the Russian and herself. On the other hand, like any healthy girl, Madeleine liked admiration, and in these dark days when so many of her friends had disappeared it was comforting to think that she had a normally strong and capable man like Stefan upon whom to lean. Pierre, she knew, was eager enough to give her his affection, but she had never had much confidence in him as a support in times of stress, and she knew only too well that if the war continued many unpleasant situations might have to be faced in the grim weeks that lay ahead. However, she had no intention of disclosing her thoughts to Pierre; so she said:

'*Mon ami*, you're letting your imagination run away with you, and I'm in no need of advice. I've had plenty of experience in handling patients who would like to become amorous, but in this case I'm sure there will be no need for me to employ it. What is more, it is none of your business if I hold the poor fellow's hand or not.'

He shrugged. 'Oh, well, don't be offended. I wouldn't even have mentioned the matter except that I'm so fond of you and don't want to see you bothered. I *am* frightfully fond of you—you know that, Madeleine, don't you?'

'Of course I do!' She laughed lightly, laying a hand upon his arm. 'You've been a splendid friend to me, and I'm sure that you know that I'm fond of you.'

He caught her hand and an eager glance came into his dark eyes. 'D'you really mean that, Madeleine?'

She withdrew her hand quickly. 'Certainly I do; but please, Pierre, don't put any wrong construction on what I said. I've nothing to give to any man except friendship, now.'

He nodded. 'I don't mind waiting. Later, perhaps, you'll

feel differently. Look here, now that Kuporovitch is better, what about coming out for a little dinner and to do a cinema this evening?'

It was over six weeks since she had been out of the house at night, and she hesitated for a moment. 'Ought we to, with the Germans here?'

'Why not? They're behaving quite decently; there have been awfully few cases of their interfering with anybody.'

'I know, but I didn't mean that. Somehow it doesn't seem quite right to go to places of amusement during the occupation.'

'Oh, I don't know. There's no point in cutting off one's nose to spite one's face, and, after all, they may be here for months yet. It would be silly to coop ourselves up indefinitely.'

'I suppose you're right,' Madeleine agreed after a moment. 'All right then. I'd like to come. Will you come across for me about seven o'clock?'

That evening he took her to Emil's in the Rue Ventadour just off the Avenue de l'Opéra. It was not one of the famous places patronized in normal times by the wealthier visitors to Paris, but one of those really excellent French restaurants in which Paris abounds, having its own specialities and a good solid clientèle of middle-class French people, to whom good eating is almost a religion.

The cooking now suffered somewhat from the shortage of butter and lack of cream, which was beginning to be generally felt in Paris; but as yet there was still no appreciable shortage of food or wine. Prices, however, had advanced considerably, and Madeleine was horribly shocked when she saw the size of Pierre's bill, as she knew that he was not rich. With a little grimace she told him that she would not have had so many dishes if she had realized how expensive everything was.

Smiling across at her, he replied that he did not mind a bit, because it was such a pleasure to take her out and see her enjoying herself again. Then he went on to explain why it was that prices had risen so steeply.

The Army of Occupation was under the strictest discipline, and there had been no cases of looting at all. They paid for everything they wanted, but, in actual fact, the whole of Occupied France was being looted systematically and with diabolical cunning. The Germans had now pinned the franc to the mark at the rate of twenty francs to one mark, and all the French shopkeepers, hotel proprietors, etc., were compelled by law to accept the German soldiers' marks in payment for goods or services. The pre-war rate had been about six francs to the mark, so the new valuation meant that the Germans were able to buy anything that they wanted at less than a third of its proper price, and, of course, in most instances this was far below what the unfortunate French traders had originally paid for their goods wholesale.

To make matters worse, now that France was bearing the cost of the Army of Occupation, Hitler had decreed that his troops should receive a special occupation-bonus which had the effect of more than tripling their pay. In consequence, all the German soldiers had money to burn and were forcing their worthless paper right, left and centre upon their wretched victims in exchange for goods, which they either consumed in gigantic quantities or sent off in huge parcels to their relatives in Germany. Never before had such an ingenious and devilish system been devised for despoiling and bankrupting the people of a conquered nation.

In self-defence the French had been forced to raise their prices wherever possible, hence the size of Pierre's bill. But the Germans were already getting wise to this, and new measures were being taken to institute price-control, so that this systematic beggaring of a nation with its own money, demanded on the excuse of maintaining an Army of Occupation, might go on unhindered.

As Madeleine listened she positively seethed with rage. There were several parties of Germans in the restaurant. They were all drinking champagne and guzzling down a succession of rich dishes. Previously she had been careful to keep her glance averted from them, but now she stared with ill-concealed hatred at the nearest group of soldiers, and if looks could have killed the food they were eating would have choked them. Seeing her fury, Pierre hurried her out into the street; but she had not recovered her equanimity until they reached the Auber Palace in the Boulevard des Italiens, where they meant to see the latest René Clair.

The film was a good one, but the show was spoilt for

Madeleine and many others in the audience by the news-reels that followed, as these, of course, were now selected by order of the German censors. Marshal Goering, who had recently paid a visit to Paris, was shown entering the Hôtel Crillon, which had been taken over as the German Headquarters; and later laying a wreath on the grave of the Unknown Soldier at the Arc de Triomphe. As he had come to Paris largely for the purpose of initiating the new campaign for a *rapprochement* with the French, the fat Marshal was saluting and smiling most genially at everyone. The ceremony seemed to Madeleine a horrible piece of hypocrisy, although, like most people, she quite wrongly credited Goering with a greater respect than his fellow-gangsters for the brave soldiers of the last war. But the thing that made her squirm was another reel in which Laval and a number of other French politicians were shown openly fraternizing with a number of German officers.

One or two people got up and left. Madeleine would have liked to do so too, but Pierre showed no sign of moving, and she did not wish to spoil his evening: so she sat on and they saw the second picture—a rather indifferent comedy—after which they went home, as the Paris cinemas were now being kept open as late as in peace-time, and the René Clair film was coming on again.

When they got back she told Pierre how much she had enjoyed herself, although she was not really quite certain if she had or not. She had certainly enjoyed her good dinner and the René Clair film, and it had been a very pleasant change to go out again after all this long time; but Pierre's account of how the Germans were bleeding her country white with their useless paper money, and to see them lording it everywhere and ordering French people about, caused a fresh intensification of her bitterness against them.

June had been a month of tragedy and July a month of suspense, while Paris seemed to hold her breath in fearful anticipation as to the possible results of her captivity; but in August, with certain exceptions, things almost seemed to have gone back to normal, and everywhere people were picking up the threads of their lives again. Rations had been severely cut, and the big stocks of clothes and tinned foods were now rapidly disappearing from the previously well-stocked shops,

The sight of the grey-green uniforms in the streets was a constant reminder of the presence of the enemy, but good order was maintained in the city, and its inhabitants no longer feared for their lives or security; so Paris breathed again.

In spite of German jamming, the Parisians still managed to get most of the British news over their radios, and by early August it was abundantly clear that Britain, if at present quite incapable of materially harming Hitler through lack of arms, had very definitely settled down with grim determination to making the arms, which would at least enable her to defend herself in no mean manner.

For some seven weeks the war had lapsed into a state of almost pre-blitz unreality. Perhaps the Germans were too astonished by the magnitude and swiftness of their success to be able to exploit it fully; or it may have been that their passion and genius for achieving one hundred per cent efficiency in their organization before making any major step had for once betrayed them into devoting priceless time to preparations which, had they continued to prosecute the war with the utmost intensity without waiting to perfect their future plans in every detail, could have been used to infinitely more advantage; but at last they swung into their stride again, and the long-expected attack, which everyone on the Continent anticipated would administer the *coup de grâce* to Britain, was launched.

4

Those Who Fight On

From the 8th of August onwards a large part of every news bulletin was devoted to the doings of the Luftwaffe. For a fortnight it concentrated upon Allied shipping and the nearest British ports. Dover harbour was reported as blocked with wrecks, and all the Thanet towns as in ruins. Then the Germans carried raids much farther inland, attacking all the air bases in south and south-eastern England, and penetrating as far as London.

Each night these triumphs were announced over the radio with impressive figures of British planes destroyed both in aerial combat and on the ground. In spite of British counter-claims, it seemed to the people of Paris that this was the beginning of the end of their ex-Ally. It was common know-ledge that the Germans were massing a great Army of Invasion all along the Dutch, Belgian and French coasts, and clearly they were only waiting until they had driven the numerically inferior R.A.F. from the skies before despatching the great flotillas which would carry the irresistible panzer divisions across to England. The friends of Britain could only watch and pray.

Stefan Kuporovitch was by now rapidly regaining his strength. As soon as he had recovered his powers of thinking and talking clearly he had expressed the keenest interests in all news, and, having nothing to occupy him, decided to improve his scanty English, so that he might hear at first hand as much of the B.B.C. broadcasts as escaped the German jamming. For the purpose Madeleine bought him a Russian-English primer and dictionary, and each evening, as she spoke English well herself, she gave him a lesson. His concentration on the subject and the fact that he could spend hours on it each day without interruption enabled him to make rapid progress, so that in quite a short time he was able to understand most of the broadcasts and converse with Madeleine in passable English.

By mid-August he was allowed to get up; by the end of the month he was able to dress himself unaided and walk about the apartment. He now spent a portion of each day sitting with Madame Lavallière, and she took a great fancy to him. While, in fact, being an extremely shrewd realist, he appeared to have all the irresponsibility and lack of care for the future of the traditional Russian. He never tired of talking, and he laughed a lot, making light of the many little hardships which were now beginning to be felt by the Lavallières as a result of the Occupation.

He told them that to know what hardship really meant they should have lived in Russia during the years immediately following the Revolution. As a young man he had been a Czarist officer, and it was in those days that he had been used to visit Paris on his leaves. Only the confusion of the Civil War and later a passionate admiration for Marshal Voroshilov had caused him to throw in his lot with the Bolsheviks.

That he had managed to avoid a firing-party and attain the rank of General in the Soviet Army was ample testimony of his extraordinary ability in steering a course through the troubled water of Russian political intrigue; but, although he had so skilfully backed the right people at every turn of the wheel, he was at heart a reactionary, and in secret had always disliked the Soviet régime. For years he had seized every chance to make illegal purchases of foreign *valuta* against the day when, with this hoard of dollars, pounds, francs, marks and lire to support his old age, he would be able to get out; and Gregory Sallust's coming to the Castle of Kandalaksha, far away upon the White Sea, of which he had been Governor at the time, had given him his longed-for opportunity.

He was now no longer suffering so acutely from headaches, as Madeleine knew very well, since when he had a bad one she could always see the pain of it reflected in his eyes, but he pretended that he was, particularly in the evenings, as that

56

gave him an excuse for long sessions of holding her hand. She did not mind that in the least, and it rather amused her to see him pretend that a headache was coming on, only to forget it completely ten minutes later for a good half-hour; then suddenly to remember for a short while that he was supposed to be in pain and stop laughing rather guiltily. He now made no secret of the fact that he adored her, but he made no attempt to kiss her, as Pierre had predicted he would, nor did he make any other advance. She was glad of that, although it struck her as rather strange, since he spoke with the utmost freedom and evident relish of the innumerable affairs he had had with an infinite variety of women in a long life which seemed mainly to have been devoted to fighting and amorous adventures.

But she soon guessed the reason for the great circumspection which he exercised with regard to herself. He had his own particular code of chivalry. She had nursed him back from the shadow of death to health and strength with unremitting care and patience. Therefore he placed her in a class apart. Nothing would have induced him to embarrass her for a single second by attempting to make love to her while he was still a guest under her roof, in spite of his at times almost overpowering desire to do so. Outwardly, at least, he appeared perfectly content simply to be with her, and often they would sit up far into the night while her entertained her with a seemingly endless flow of amusing reminiscences.

Pierre's assistance in moving the invalid was now no longer necessary, but he continued to look in every day and often joined them at their simple meals, bringing his own rations. At first Madeleine had feared that his jealousy of Stefan would cause trouble between them, but the Russian was such a gay and charming person that, almost despite himself, the young artist was won over to a cordial liking for him. Pierre too had now become as bitterly anti-Nazi as the others, since the presence of the Germans in Paris was affecting him personally.

During the month of July he had worked hard on two pictures, and when they were finished had taken them along to Emile Martin's *Galerie* in the Rue Bonaparte, where his work was usually displayed for sale. A week later Monsieur Martin had rung him up to tell him apologetically that he had been compelled to part with them to a German officer for a handful of paper marks. At their proper price the two pictures would have kept Pierre for the best part of three months; as it was, they had only fetched barely sufficient to keep him for three weeks. Naturally, he was furious at the way in which he had been cheated of the full results of his work, and even more resentful about the future for himself that the incident foreshadowed. Few Parisians could any longer afford to buy works of art, so artists must now depend upon the Germans for such sales as they could make, but at the prices the Germans were paying this meant that Pierre would have to work at least three times as long hours as he had done previously and slave from dawn to sunset every day of the week to earn even a bare living.

Another thing which was now embittering all Parisians was the huge number of German civilians which in recent weeks had flooded into the French capital. Towards the end of July half the wealthier population of greater Germany seemed to have woken up to the fact that Paris was now open to them. Thousands of German officers and S.S. men had sent for their wives, daughters, and sweethearts, and thousands upon thousands more German civilians of all ages and both sexes had descended, of their own initiative, upon Paris.

Once there, they had begun a positive orgy of buying—silk stockings, hats, furs, models, jewels, wine, scent, cigars, toilet soaps, beauty preparations, and above all tinned foods of any kind that they could lay their hands upon. For a month past the shops had been as crowded as in an autumn sales week and the wretched shop-girls were absolutely worn out from attempting to serve an unending stream of fat, pimply German *Hausfrauen*, all arrogantly demanding instant attention, and quarrelling to the point of violence with each other over lengths of material and garments, which they snatched from the counters and rows of hangers. The locust flight was easing now, but it had left the great Paris stores and luxury shops almost bare.

This licensed sack of Paris had naturally increased the rancour of the French against their conquerors, because it affected them personally, striking deep at the pockets of the traders, both great and small, and at the standard of comfort to which all but the poorest sections of the community had long been accustomed. It was now only possible for them to get meagre supplies of the most simple things, such as salad oil, fresh fruit, eggs, soap flakes and toilet paper, with the greatest difficulty, while the delicacies which they loved were obtainable only at fantastic prices through the black markets which were springing up everywhere.

Yet this sudden dearth of everything also had the effect of intensifying anti-British feeling. German propagandists and their French collaborators never tired of pointing out by radio and Press that all the ills which were afflicting France were attributable to her ex-Ally.

It was urged that if the wise counsels of such men as Bonnet, Laval, Baudouin and other pro-Fascist leaders had been heeded France would have taken the hand of friendship which Germany had proffered in 1939; but she had foolishly preferred to reject it and sacrifice herself to the interests of Britain, who, as ever, had been unprepared to defend her own bloated Jew-controlled Empire. Then there was the now old story of the British having begun their preparations for evacuation three weeks before the final decision was reached in France, and having gone home directly the really serious fighting started. It was conveniently forgotten that the British Army had been under the French High Command, that Gamelin had ordered it forward into Belgium and that it had been forced to retire only because its position had been rendered untenable by the French collapse hundreds of miles farther south at Sedan.

Churchill's refusal to allow the bulk of the R.A.F. fighter squadrons to cross the Channel during the critical phase of the Battle for France, and the attack on the French Fleet at Oran, were also constantly dug up, but the main point upon which the Nazi propagandists were tireless was that the British decision to fight on was now the sole cause of all that France was suffering.

As long as the British remained obdurate no proper peace could be established, and until that happened Germany could not withdraw her Armies of Occupation. Almost unarmed as the British were, and with every one of their Allies already knocked out, how could these madmen conceivably hope ever to defeat Hitler? Therefore, it was argued, for humanity's sake, they should have had the decency to throw in their hand and bring an end by a negotiated peace to the nightmare which was now afflicting all the people of Europe.

This feeling became so strong in Paris that great numbers of the French openly gave their support to Laval's policy of co-operation with the Germans, in the belief that the only way out of their own miseries now lay in bringing about Britain's complete defeat as speedily as possible.

By the beginning of September Kuporovitch was well enough to go downstairs, and each afternoon he went for a short walk, at first round the colonnades of the Palais-Royal and later, when he was stronger, in the Jardin des Tuileries and up the Champs Elysées, with Madeleine. The weather was excellent, and being out in the open air on those sunny September afternoons caused him to achieve a great bound forward in renewed vitality, so that towards the middle of the month he declared himself once more fit for anything. It was on the 19th he impulsively announced that to celebrate his full recovery they must go out that very night to dinner, and she smilingly agreed.

It was nearly thirteen weeks since his accident, and in all that time he had not had a meal in a restaurant, so he insisted that they should go somewhere really good. She suggested the Vieux Logis, a place famed for its Alsatian dishes, which was situated up on the heights at no great distance from the Sacré Cœur. Only a limited number of taxis were still running, but having walked as far as the Opéra they managed to get one and then drove up the famous hill that such countless thousands of people of all nations had mounted in happier days to nights of gaiety which ended only with the dawn.

But the Vieux Logis had nothing in common with a Montmartre boîte or the larger, more celebrated, places such as the Bal Tabarin, the Moulin Rouge, Café de l'Enfer or L'Abbé Telême. It was a fair-sized raftered room, having the appearance of an old barn which had been converted into a restaurant. There was no band, but a quiet sedate air reigned, appropriate to the serving and enjoyment of good food. It was only about half-full, but some of the more discerning German officers had discovered even this quiet haunt, and groups of them occupied three tables.

Having ordered their meal, they examined with amusement a gigantic pear, pickled in spirit, inside a water-carafe, which was on a nearby window-ledge. Obviously, it could not have been pushed through the narrow neck of the bottle, so the only explanation of this phenomenon was that the pear had been inserted, when quite small, and the carafe tied on to the branch of the pear tree until the fruit had reached its amazing size, through having grown in what would have amounted to a miniature hot-house of its own.

Madeleine had just remarked with a sigh that she wondered how long it would be before people had the leisure to devote to growing such oddities again when she noticed an elderly priest sit down at a table behind Kuporovitch and directly facing herself. There was nothing very remarkable about the priest, save that he was an exceptionally small man, and his lovely silvery hair, which, as he wore it quite long, made a strange contrast to his bronzed, wrinkled little face.

Restaurant meals were now restricted by law to one main dish, but the more expensive places were still able to provide a good selection of side-dishes. The *hors d'œuvre* at the Vieux Logis proved excellent, and they followed them with a partridge *en casserole,* cooked in peasant fashion with young cabbages, carrots, turnips, onions, mushrooms and beans. They then had *crêpes Suzette,* and Stefan insisted that they should finish up with *pâté de foie gras.*

This admirable meal was made ten times more enjoyable by the fact that for weeks past they had lived upon the most simple fare, and that it was washed down with a bottle of 1923 Chambertin. With their coffee they drank some old Alsatian Kirsch, and they were both in the highest of good humours when, to their intense annoyance, a wireless was suddenly turned on full blast.

The Germans had decreed that all news bulletins were to be given in every public place in the city, and it was one of the things which grievously aggravated the French that if they happened to be in a café or restaurant at the time the news came on they were compelled to listen to it whether they wanted to or not.

With evident relish the announcer gave the most gory

details of the Luftwaffe's latest activities. For the past two nights great fleets of German bombers had been over London. It was stated with sickening hypocrisy that this was in retaliation for night raids made by the British against the Rhineland and Berlin. Thousands of tons of explosives had been dropped so that during the first night's attack the docks and a great portion of the East End of London had been set ablaze. The fires had been so extensive that they were still burning when the German airmen arrived over their targets on the second night to spread further devastation. In one breath the announcer declared that, unlike the brutal British, the Germans had confined themselves to military objectives, yet in the next he stated that a great portion of London now lay in ruins and the casualties inflicted were known to be immense.

Both Madeleine and Stefan knew that it was dangerous to comment upon the news in public places, as great numbers of Gestapo men had been drafted to Paris, and there were, in addition, innumerable French pro-Nazis who to curry favour with the administration were reporting criticisms of the régime. Yet, as Madeleine thought of the thousands of innocent people who must have been burnt to death or crushed beneath falling walls in this holocaust she could not refrain from saying under her breath: 'The swine! The filthy swine! If there were a God in Heaven He would strike that fiend Hitler dead!'

Kuporovitch shrugged. 'Perhaps He will in His own good time.'

She clasped her hands until the knuckles showed white. 'Oh, Stefan! Why can't we do something? There are hundreds of us to every one of them. If we were only determined enough and didn't mind risking our own lives, we could overwhelm these beasts in a single night. They're not human. There's nothing honourable about them, as there has been about soldiers in past wars. They're soulless vermin who ought to be exterminated. If I had the chance I wouldn't hesitate to kill . . .'

She suddenly broke off in quick alarm. The little priest was standing just beside her. She had not seen him move, yet there he was and placing his small brown hands on the table, he bent down to say very quietly: 'My child, I hope that you will permit an old man to give you a word of warning. You might easily be arrested and thrown into a concentration camp if any ill-disposed person had overheard what you have just said.'

As she had spoken hardly above a whisper she could not imagine how anyone at another table could possibly have caught her words, but he gave her a reassuring smile.

'It is true that I only understood you because I am a lip-reader; yet quite a number of people have mastered that art, particularly detectives, so in these days when you talk in whispers in any public place you should guard your tongue.'

'Thank you, Father,' she said. 'I'm grateful to you for your warning.'

'Not at all, not at all;' he suddenly stretched out a hand and, grasping the back of a chair from a nearby table, went on: 'Have I your permission to join you for a moment?'

Taking their consent for granted, he sat down and continued: 'No one is actually facing any of us now, so if we speak softly we shall run no undue risk. You have ample reason for hating our enemies so bitterly?'

Madeleine swallowed hard, sipped her Kirsch and said: 'My fiancé was murdered by these fiends before my eyes on the very first day of the Occupation.'

There was a short pause, and she heard him murmur: 'I know it, my child. Poor Georges!'

His words electrified her, and she turned to stare at him in amazement, but it was Kuporovitch who spoke. He had been quick to realize that this might be a trap and their uninvited guest a police-spy; so his voice, though low, was pregnant with menace as he said:

'If you know of Mademoiselle's tragedy, it is clear that you accosted us deliberately just now. Who are you?'

'There is no cause for alarm,' replied the little priest swiftly. 'If I had meant to denounce you as anti-Nazis I could have done so without coming to your table. Georges Mercier was a friend of mine and we worked together.' He turned back to Madeleine. 'I wonder if you are aware why the Nazis shot him?'

'It was because he was a member of the *Deuxième Bureau*,' she whispered, 'although I had no idea of that until he came

63

to me for help, a few hours before he was murdered.'

He nodded. 'Georges was one of the most discreet of all our agents, but since he told you of his real work just before he died perhaps he also told you of his last orders?'

'Yes. They were to remain in Paris, to ignore any armistice which might be entered into with the Germans, and to continue to operate against them until a proper peace was actually signed.'

'That is so; and a few of us were more lucky than poor Georges, so we are still able to carry on the work for the true France which will yet survive this nightmare.'

'Are you, too, then, a member of the *Deuxième Bureau*?' Kuporovitch asked.

'I was. In one sense I still am, although the *Bureau* itself was evacuated with the rest of the Government, so that it is now in Vichy, and it no longer has any official status in German-occupied France.'

Madeleine was smiling now, and her eyes were bright with a strange elation, as she murmured: 'But you're carrying on in secret. How I wish that I, too, could do something—any-thing—to help strike a blow against these blond beasts who are defiling our whole world.'

The little man nodded his silvery head. 'I hoped that you would feel that way, and the time will come when the help of a stout-hearted girl like yourself may prove invaluable. But, first, we must build up a proper organization and we shall need many like you.'

'There must be thousands,' Madeleine declared with conviction.

'I'm sure there are,' his shrewd dark eyes, set in many wrinkles, bored into hers; 'but the difficulty is to find those thousands whom you can trust among the tens of thousands who are now untrustworthy because they can no longer see clearly. Pro-German propaganda has so distorted the views of the great mass of the people. They are weary of the war and all their sufferings, so they no longer have the ability to look very far into the future. Most of them even hope now that Britain will be speedily defeated, as their wishful thinking leads them to believe that would mean a new settlement which within a few months would enable them to resume their normal

lives. I am an old man, and for many years it has been my
business to probe as far as possible into the future; so I believe
that I see clearly. In my view, France can never rise again,
or ever know real freedom, until Hitler and all that he stands
for are destroyed.'

'You're right,' cut in Kuporovitch abruptly. 'Even the
defeat of Britain won't materially alter your situation. As
long as Hitler is the master the French people remain a race
of slaves.'

'Certainment! Therefore, it is for those of us who see the
truth to preach a secret crusade. Wherever opportunity offers
we must do so, among people whom we feel we can trust, but
who at present do not realize the truth—or are fainthearted.
We must be very, very careful, because we should do no good
to our country once we were dead or in a concentration
camp; but even in the smallest things we should leave nothing
undone which will help to hamper the German war effort.
In such ways each one of us can help to bring nearer the
day of a British victory, which means our own release from
what otherwise will be a lifelong captivity.'

Madeleine thrilled to his softly spoken words. Here at last
was the chance for which she had been waiting and longing
all these weeks. There was a moment's silence, then she asked:
'How did you know who I was before you came to our table?'

His small brown face lit up with a sudden smile. 'I had
often heard Georges speak of you as a girl of character. When
I learned how he had been foully done to death in your apartment I put you down in my mind at once as a possible recruit
for the organization which I am forming.'

'Why, then, did you not get in touch with me before?'

'Unfortunately, many of my old colleagues have gone over
to the enemy, so whenever I'm in Paris there is always the
danger that I may be recognized and followed. I have only
been in Paris three times since the collapse, and on the second
I took steps to identify you, but I did not wish to risk compromising you by calling at your apartment. To-night, I
happened to be in the Place de l'Opéra when you picked up
your taxi, although I don't suppose you noticed me. Once
more my ability for lip-reading stood me in good stead. It
was just the opportunity for which I had been waiting; I

caught the address you gave the driver and followed you here.'

Kuporovitch leaned forward. 'Even so, you were taking a big risk, my friend, since you could have had no guarantee that my feelings against the Nazis were similar to Mademoiselle's.'

The little man smiled again. 'I am not without my sources of information. I know that Mademoiselle has been nursing you in her apartment for many weeks, so it was hardly likely that you would betray her. Besides . . .'

He broke off abruptly, as the Russian gave a low laugh. 'You're right about that, and you can count me as in this thing too. Thanks to Mademoiselle's care, I'm now fit again and ready for anything. As an old soldier, I need no teaching how to handle arms or explosives. When the time comes you have only to tell me what to do and I will do it.'

Their companion had been staring into a mirror opposite to him, and in it he could see a good portion of the restaurant, to which his back was turned. Leaning forward again, he began to speak in an even lower voice than before.

'My friends, I warned you that we were playing a very dangerous game. I fear that even by speaking to you here I may have been the cause of bringing trouble upon you. I have just seen a man who used to work with me but has gone over to the enemy. Our eyes met in that mirror, and, in spite of my disguise, I'm certain that he knew me again. He is seated behind me, three tables away and a little to my left. He is wearing a suit of mustard-coloured check and has a heavy black moustache. You, Mademoiselle! Don't let your eye rest on him, but glance casually round the room and tell me what he is doing now.'

'He left his table just after you began to speak,' replied Madeleine, 'and has gone over the telephone box near the door.'

'It is as I feared,' their small friend said, but he kept his voice low and unhurried. 'Some minutes at least must elapse before he can get the police here, but he may try to waylay me as I go out. If there's trouble the police will pull you in for questioning, because he has seen you talking to me. You will say that I'm a complete stranger to you and that I planted myself at your table uninvited. While I was here I questioned

66

you persistently on your reactions to the news of the bombing of London. That will fit in with the sort of thing that they think I might be doing—just getting a cross-section of opinion by accosting strangers wherever the opportunity offers. You can add that you resented my planting myself here, but were too polite to pack me off about my business. Such a story will avoid your entering into long explanations and having to tell any lies, in some of which you might be tripped up. Stick to that, and it's almost certain that the police will release you after an hour or two.'

'He has got his number and is speaking now,' Madeleine interrupted anxiously.

'*Merci, mademoiselle*. It is time for me to go then; but there's one thing that I must ask you both. If you're to be of the maximum help to me later on, it is important that the police should not get your names on their books as suspects; you had better give false names and addresses. If you're found out you can always say that you did so because you were scared. Later, I will send you instructions, and you must trust anyone that comes to you who says that they have a special devotion to St. Denis, the patron Saint of France. Now, be of good courage and don't worry about me. I am very capable of looking after myself.'

He stood up then, and Madeleine watched him, her hands clasped tightly under the table, as he collected his black wide-brimmed hat, paid his bill, smiled good-night to them, and walked with an aged, slightly shambling gait towards the door.

Kuporovitch could not see the doorway without turning round, but he knew that he must restrain his curiosity. Pouring himself and Madeleine another ration of Kirsch, he lifted his glass and smiled across at her. 'It's been a grand evening so far. May it end well for all of us; but, in case things go wrong, I'd like you to know, Madeleine, that I love you more than any woman I've ever met. Give me the tip when the fireworks are about to start.'

5

Transportation to Death

Madeleine's hand was trembling slightly as she raised her glass in reply.

'I've known that you love me for a long time, Stefan, but let's not talk of that now. Oh, God! I do hope that he succeeds in getting away.'

Kuporovitch's dark eyes twinkled. 'Excitement makes you even more beautiful. The flush upon your cheeks now is superb, and for myself the very thought of going into action again is as good as a magnum of champagne. But, tell me, since I dare not turn round, how is the little fellow getting on? Has he reached the door yet?'

Madeleine had been holding her breath and she released it sharply.

'The detective has just stopped him. He bars his path. They are talking together.'

In an agony of suspense she watched the two men at the far end of the long barn-like room. Actually, they exchanged perhaps no more than half a dozen quick short sentences, but that conversation seemed to her to go on interminably. Suddenly she gasped and lifted her hands in front of her face.

The detective had attempted to seize the little priest by the shoulder. Evidently their friend had been prepared for such a move and was already covering his interrogator with a pistol concealed beneath his cassock. Two shots rang out in quick succession. The detective's eyes opened to their fullest extent and began to roll in their sockets. He clutched his stomach with both hands, let out a quavering wail and slumped to the floor. Instantly, half the people in the restaurant came to their feet; a babel of excited shouting arose and everyone craned their necks to see what was happening.

At the very moment of the shooting two uniformed policemen had appeared in the doorway. They rushed forward to seize the little priest. Quick as a cat he eluded them, dodging swiftly between tables. A German officer made a grab at him as he sped by; another pulled his automatic from its holster and took aim. Springing up, Kuporovitch grabbed the glass carafe containing the huge pear from the nearby ledge. Lifting it high above his head, he heaved it with all his force right across the room into the midst of the group of Germans.

The weighty bottle crashed right in the centre of the table among the crockery and glasses. The officer with the gun fired, but the flying missile had upset his aim and, instead of finding its intended mark, the bullet struck the shoulder of a peroxide blonde who was fraternizing with another German officer some tables away.

The whole restaurant was now in a state of pandemonium. The blonde girl began to scream hysterically. With a speed and agility more in keeping with a young athlete than a man of his years, the priest reached the far end of the restaurant and sprang upon an empty table. The two policemen were half-way down the room, excitedly waving their batons as they charged towards him. Kuporovitch rushed forward to try to intercept them, but they were on the far side of several tables, and by the time he reached the lane they had taken he was too late.

The priest turned for an instant and fired at the officer who had shot at him. The bullet hit the German fair and square in the middle of the mouth. He crashed back on to the table among his companions, choking horribly and streaming with blood.

Kuporovitch was now forcing his way through a struggling mass of people who had panicked and were rushing towards the door from fear that in the *mêlée* they might get shot. Madeleine turned to shout encouragement after the Russian. Two more shots crashed out, fired by another German. They were followed by the tinkling of smashed panes of glass in one half of a window at the far end of the room. As Madeleine swung round she saw that the curtains had been wrenched

69

back; the little priest had made good his escape through the open half of the window.

While one of the policemen scrambled through in pursuit the other jumped on to the table and began to blow his whistle. Between shrill blasts he yelled excited orders that no one was to leave the room. More police soon appeared upon the scene and some semblance of order was restored.

The Nazi who had been terribly wounded in the face and the French detective were removed in an ambulance. The senior German officer present then began a violent harangue to the French police, demanding the arrest of everyone in sight, with a view to wholesale reprisals for the wounding of his junior. An inspector sought to placate him by a hurried assurance that everybody should be taken into custody, and ten minutes later police vans arrived, into which all the French diners, the proprietor and his waiters, were herded.

Kuporovitch, having rejoined Madeleine, had not let the grass grow under his feet. By steady and almost uninterrupted drinking he had finished the entire bottle of Kirsch and was well on his way into a bottle of cognac which he had removed from a nearby table after the diner who had been seated at it had fled in panic. His capacity for liquor being immense he was by no means drunk, but now extremely cheerful. As they bumped their way down the hill in the prison van he told Madeleine, with the glee of a wicked child who is not deliberately dishonest, that so far he had had an absolutely magnificent evening which had cost him nothing, as in the excitement nobody had asked him to pay his bill.

The next few hours, however, proved anything but amusing. First, on arriving at the *Sûreté-Générale,* the names and addresses of all the people who had been brought in were taken. Madeleine, bearing in mind the instructions she had received, gave hers as Antoinette Mirabeau, of 47 Rue Meslay, this being the name and address of a cousin of hers whom she knew had left Paris at the time of the evacuation. The girl had been on the telephone, so the address could easily be checked up. Kuporovitch was in no position to fake such an alias, so he gave his name as Ivan Smernov and said he was a White Russian who had lived in Belgium for a number of years, but had come to Paris at the time of the invasion. He added that, like many refugees, he had no permanent address but moved from one lodging-house to another, or on fine nights slept out in the open according to the state of his funds.

The yarn was a thin one, but it was the best that he could think of at the moment, and at that time there were still thousands of homeless people who had come from the north drifting about in Paris. If he had been arrested in the street it might quite well have passed, but it was hardly likely that a homeless refugee would have been dining in an expensive restaurant, and the inspector obviously regarded the answer with suspicion.

One by one the little mob of people who had been brought in were released, as it was obvious that none of them had any connection with the priest and the shooting that had occurred. At last only Madeleine and Stefan were left, and their anxieties were by no means lessened when, instead of being sent through the door after the others, they were taken upstairs.

While two *gendarmes* remained on guard with them the inspector rapped on a door, and on receiving a muffled call to enter went in, closing it behind him. It was then they noticed that under the large 'No. 104,' which was painted on the door in white, there was pinned a visiting card which read: 'Wolfram Schaub, Major, S.S.', and they realized with renewed trepidation that they were to be examined by one of the Nazi officers who now controlled the French police. After a moment the door was opened again, and they were led in.

Madeleine suddenly went white as a sheet and dropped her handbag. One of the French *gendarmes* politely stooped to pick it up for her, but in stooping herself she gained just a moment in which to make a wild endeavour to get back her composure. Major Schaub, the lean chunky-faced man in the black uniform of the German S.S. guards, who sat behind the desk, was the man who had come to her apartment on that unforgettable night of the occupation and fired the final shot which had driven the last flicker of life from her dear Georges.

Half fainting from a mixed emotional stress of hatred and fear, she waited in an agony of suspense to see if he would recognize her. If he did, her alias as Antoinette Mirabeau

71

would be torn to shreds. Her association with both Georges and the little priest, on top of the false name she had given, would be more than enough to cause the Major to believe that she was already up to the neck in some anti-Nazi conspiracy. Even the faintest hope of release would be gone and she would find herself in an internment camp before morning.

Her every effort was needed to retain an outward semblance of calm and prevent her limbs from trembling. As in a daze she heard the French inspector's report, but she dared not look up for fear of meeting the Major's eyes and seeing recognition dawn in them. When the report was finished the Nazi began to shoot staccato questions at the prisoners in excellent French, and she was now compelled to raise her glance. His hard blue eyes bored for a second into hers, then with a faint smile of appreciation they flickered downwards, taking in her figure. The look was an insult, as it stripped her naked where she stood, yet she was hardly conscious of it from the sudden surge of relief that she felt. He had looked in her eyes, but he did not remember her. Major Schaub showed great annoyance when he learned that the prisoners had undergone their first examination together. In swift, sarcastic phrases he rated the French inspector soundly, telling him that he did not understand his business and that such examinations should always be carried out separately, since there was more likelihood of the prisoners making contradictory statements.

To see the French inspector snarled at and insulted in front of his men so infuriated Madeleine that she temporarily forgot her own precarious situation, which enabled her to answer the questions that the Major snapped out promptly and with spirit. Kuporovitch, who was still completely ignorant that the Major had seen Madeleine before, which now placed her in special peril, answered with calmness and dignity. Both of them flatly denied that they had ever seen the little priest before and stuck firmly to the story that he had come uninvited to their table and made rather a nuisance of himself, by seeking to draw them into adverse criticisms of that night's news bulletin.

The inspector had turned up Mademoiselle Antoinette Mirabeau in the telephone book and checked the address that

72

Madeleine had given. When she was questioned about her family and occupation she gave the answers in every case without a trace of hesitation, because she was able to reply just as though she were Antoinette, and when she said that she was a teacher of music that tallied with the fact that the Rue Meslay was just round the corner from the Conservatoire.

The Russian's answers, on the other hand, were by no means so satisfactory. His case was also aggravated by the fact that one of the German officers had stated that it was he who had flung the water-bottle containing the pear which had landed in the middle of their table, evidently with intent to injure one of them. This Kuporovitch stoutly denied, and luckily for him the inspector's notes read to the effect that the officer had *thought* that Kuporovitch had thrown the bottle, because it had come spinning through the air from his direction. Both Madeleine and Stefan seized on this to assert that the officer must have been mistaken, but the suspicion still lingered.

Asked how he supported himself, Kuporovitch said that he had brought his savings with him out of Belgium, and as evidence of this produced the several thousand francs which still remained of his money from his pocket. Then, when it came to the question as to what his relations were with Madeleine, he showed uncanny shrewdness. So far, she had managed to maintain a fairly clear bill, whereas he was evidently subject to much permanent suspicion from the fact that he was a foreigner with no permanent address. He saw at once that the less connection there appeared to be between them the better it would be for her, and he felt it wiser to jeopardize her reputation than her safety; so after a well-acted little show of reluctance he said:

'Well, if you insist, *monsieur*, I really hardly know *Mademoiselle* here. The fact is that I'm a very lonely man, and she, too, perhaps is lonely, because although she was a stranger to me until this afternoon she graciously allowed me to speak to her while she was walking in the Jardin des Tuileries, and later permitted me to take her out to dinner.'

The S.S. man's hard face relaxed into a sudden grin, and he looked Madeleine up and down with an appreciative glance. 'So that's how it is,' he said quietly. 'Well, I admire your choice, and I must say it's hard luck that you've been deprived of the pleasant ending which you doubtless anticipated for your evening with this young lady. Still, I'm by no means satisfied about you.'

While the questioning had been in progress a short, dark French detective in plain clothes had come into the room and stood there listening intently. Suddenly he addressed the Major.

'If I may recommend, *Herr Major*, I would suggest that we let the woman go. Now that the food situation is becoming so difficult any number of our young women are willing enough to be picked up by a stranger for the sake of a good dinner, and evidently this is a case of that kind. We have nothing against the girl on our records, and we require all the room we have in our prisons for more serious cases. They're terribly overcrowded as it is.'

The Major nodded. 'Yes, I think you're right, Lieutenant Ribaud, but I don't think that we should release the man without further investigation.'

'As you wish, *Herr Major*,' replied the Frenchman. 'But we are already overburdened with work as it is, and he's probably no more dangerous than the majority of these homeless people who're wandering about the city. These White Russians have no particular cause to enter into a conspiracy against the régime, but they're all more or less undesirables, so I would suggest that since he is a vagrant without domicile we should expel him to Unoccupied France. That, at least, will mean one less mouth to feed, and once he's out of our territory he won't be able to do us any damage even if he wishes to.'

'That's a very good idea,' the German said at once. 'All right then. Release the woman and have the man put across the frontier.'

Major Schaub gave a curt nod of dismissal to Kuporovitch and favoured Madeleine with another lecherous leer. The inspector stepped forward, and they were both marched out of the room.

The decision was a sad blow, both for Madeleine and Stefan, and they were denied even the consolation of taking a proper farewell of each other, since in front of their captors they had to keep up the appearance of being no more than casual acquaintances who had met the previous afternoon.

74

When they had been taken down to the entrance-hall Stefan kissed her hand gallantly and said with a lightness that he was far from feeling that he hoped they would meet again in happier times.

She pressed his fingers and nodded dumbly, fearful of speaking lest she betrayed her emotion. Having nursed him back from death's door through all these tragic weeks, she naturally felt a special interest in him, but it was not until she was on the point of losing him altogether that she realized how much the jovial Russian's companionship had meant to her. In a vague way she had realized that once he was fully recovered he would probably move from her mother's apartment. But in the uncertainty of the times no one in Paris was inclined to make any plans for the future, so she had never actually visualized his leaving and what his departure might mean to her; and, now, overnight, through sheer ill-luck, their separation had been decreed before she had even had time to get used to its possibility. With a heavy heart she turned away and went out into the grey street, while he was led down to the basement and locked into a cell.

For five days Kuporovitch was kept a prisoner. He was given scanty and uninteresting but sufficient meals, and, although he questioned his warders frequently, they could give him no idea as to how long he might be confined there; so he could only assume that it was not convenient for the authorities to send him into Unoccupied France at once and that he must wait upon their pleasure.

On Sunday the 15th he was taken upstairs and out to a waiting car, in which there were two *agents de ville*. The car drove off, and as soon as it was outside Paris took the road to Melun, continuing on through Nemours, Montargis, Gien and Nevers to Moulins, which they reached late in the afternoon. It was here that the new frontier had been established, dividing Occupied from Unoccupied France. At the barrier Kuporovitch's captors handed him, together with a packet of papers, over to other police officers who were under the control of the Vichy Government. He was then marched away to a large barrack-like building on the outskirts of the town and locked up in a small room with barred windows for the night. The following morning he was taken out again, put in another police car, and driven the remaining fifty odd miles to Vichy.

The famous spa on the banks of the River Allier was crowded to overflowing. Normally it has a population of only some 17,000 people; now, as the capital of Unoccupied France, it was called on to house not only the headquarters of the Civil Ministries, of the fighting services, the prisoners of war and refugee organizations, and the Diplomatic Corps, but also the thousands of hangers-on and stray people of every nationality who were trying to get jobs, news of missing relatives, or permits, either to return to their homes in Occupied France, from which they had fled before the invader, or to leave the country.

It had no doubt been chosen on account of its many luxury hotels, which in times of peace accommodated the great numbers of wealthy people who came from all over Europe to do the cure, as these lent themselves readily for conversion into Ministries and as quarters for the more important officials, but they housed only a comparatively small portion of the swarms of bureaucrats, police, soldiers, diplomats and refugees who now thronged the little town.

The great thermal establishment, where in pre-war days the ailing had received their massage or strolled about to the music of the band while sipping their mugs of tepid water, had now been taken over by the Forces, as, although under the terms of the armistice the French Army was to be reduced to a purely token force, its disbandment had not yet been completed, and this entailed enormous work upon the military authorities. Even shops and garages were being used as sleeping quarters, but the accommodation was still insufficient, and during the fine weather which still prevailed, many of the less fortunate were dossing down each night in the two parks and the gardens which ran along the east embankment of the river.

As the car entered the town it was compelled to slow down to a walking pace, because the people were so numerous that they overflowed from the pavements into the roadway. One of Kuporovitch's captors pointed out the Hôtel du Parc to him as the new seat of the French Government; then they drove slowly on until they reached the Hôtel International in the

Rue Maréchal Foch, which had been requisitioned as Police Headquarters.

There, Kuporovitch was taken up in a lift to the sixth floor and put into what had obviously been a bedroom. A basin with running water was affixed to one wall, and the room still contained a wardrobe and chest-of-drawers, but the bed had been removed, and by the recent placing of heavy bars across the only window the room had been converted into a cell. At midday a meal of thin soup and bread was brought up to the Russian, and shortly afterwards a bearded police inspector appeared, carrying in his hand the documents which had been despatched from Paris with the prisoner.

The inspector ran swiftly through the brief dossier, reiterating here or there a question which had already been asked and receiving the same answer that appeared in the report; but this visit seemed more a formality than anything else, and he displayed little interest in the business. Just as he was about to go Kuporovitch pointed out that there was no charge against him and asked when he might expect to be released.

'When you reach your destination, I suppose,' the inspector replied promptly.

'My destination, eh!' Kuporovitch repeated in a puzzled voice. 'So you are sending me somewhere else. But why, and where to—may one ask?'

The Frenchman gave a bored shrug. 'Since you are a Russian you will naturally be repatriated to Russia.'

'What!' exclaimed Kuporovitch. For nearly a week he had been living for the hour when, free in Vichy France, he would be able to set about recrossing the frontier in secret to rejoin Madeleine. This was shattering—utterly devastating. The very suggestion threatened his whole world with ruin. He might never see his adorable Madeleine again. Hurriedly he broke into a storm of protest.

'But you can't do that! It's impossible—unthinkable! I'm a White Russian—an ex-Czarist who has quarrelled with the régime.'

The Frenchman shrugged again. 'That is unfortunate, monsieur, but what can we do? It is everyone for himself in these days. In Unoccupied France we already have nearly ten million refugees from the North. We cannot turn our own people out, yet the territory which we control is no longer big enough to support them. As it is, the shortage of food and fuel will create the most appalling misery in the coming winter. Therefore we are getting rid of everybody we possibly can who has no proper claim to be domiciled here.'

'But to send me back to Russia would be as good as condemning me to death!' expostulated Kuporovitch.

'That would be hard indeed,' the Frenchman sighed. 'If you have friends here with influence it is possible that they might secure you a permit to remain.'

'Unfortunately that is out of the question. I know no one in Vichy. But surely *Monsieur l'Inspecteur*, an exception could be made in my case?'

The inspector shook his head. 'It would be wrong to encourage you in that hope. The orders regarding aliens are definite and urgent. You have my sympathy, but unless you can bring influence to bear it seems that your only recourse will be to endeavour to make your peace with the Soviet Government when you arrive in Russia. *C'est la guerre, monsieur,* and life is hard on all of us these days.'

When the man had gone Kuporovitch sat down gloomily to consider his position. He was intensely averse to going anywhere, even to regain his freedom, which would place many more miles between himself and Madeleine; but, had he been given a choice of evils, he would far rather have remained in prison in Vichy than be deported to his own country.

It was not even as though he was in reality a White Russian who had spent many years in exile. Had he been, there was at least a good chance that if he was prepared to give assurance of complete acceptance of the Soviet régime on reaching Russia he might have reaped the benefit of some form of amnesty, which he knew vaguely was now open to returning exiles. The fact was that up to some six months before he had been a Bolshevik General, and he had then deserted his command and fled the country. In consequence, there was no doubt about it that once he set foot on Soviet soil he would be summarily court-martialled and handed over to a firing-party the moment he was recognized.

In something nearer panic than he had felt for many years he began to consider the possibilities of escape. The bars across the window prohibited any attempt in that direction, even had he been prepared to risk his neck in a highly perilous endeavour to climb, spreadeagled like a fly from any projections which offered in the face of the building, up on to its roof; and having examined the lock of the door he found it to be a stout one, which he had no means of either picking or forcing.

At the best of times Vichy is a depressing place, as it lies at the bottom of a hollow ringed by hills, and for the next hour he sat brooding miserably in the partly furnished bedroom on this frightful decree, that would carry him a thousand miles from the woman he loved, and at the same time place his life in extreme peril. In vain he racked his brains for some ingenious story which he might spin to his captors in the hope of causing them to reverse their decision; he could think of nothing.

His agonized thoughts were interrupted by the entrance of a warder and a kittenish young man with a tripod and camera. He was told that he was to be photographed for a *carte d'identité* which would be sent with him, and this news brought his spirits down to a new low level. The journey by ship from Marseilles round to a Soviet Black Sea port was certain, in these days, to take some weeks. The French police only knew him as Ivan Smernov, and he had hit on the idea that if he thinned down his heavy black eyebrows and grew a beard on the voyage he might escape recognition by the Soviet officials when he landed and succeed in disappearing once more after they released him. But if a photograph of himself as he appeared at present was to be hung like a millstone round his neck his identification was certain. Nevertheless, it was useless to resist, so he submitted to being taken with the best grace he could muster.

Dusk was falling when the inspector came to him again and announced briefly that as a matter of routine his chief wished to see the prisoner before he was removed to the quarters where other aliens who were being deported had been confined. With surly kindness he added: 'If you've got any story to put which might induce them to let you remain in France you'd better tell it to the Colonel.'

As he was taken downstairs in the lift to the first floor Kuporovitch's brain was racing overtime. All the afternoon

79

he had cudgelled his wits without result, and now it seemed
that the sand in the hour-glass of his fate was about to run
out without his being able to make use of the little time left
to him.

Only one thought that might possibly provide an avenue of
escape offered itself. He still had over four thousand francs in
French money on him. In Russia, provided one could satisfy
their price, many officials were fairly readily bribable. That
was a custom of centuries, which had survived from the old
days, and even Stalin had found it impossible entirely to
eradicate. Kuporovitch had always heard that French officials,
too, were often susceptible to reason if their palms were
properly greased. Four thousand francs was not a fortune,
but in these difficult times it was quite a useful sum.

The inspector led him along a corridor, and having knocked
on the door beckoned him forward into a spacious sitting-
room that had now been converted into an office. The curtains
had not yet been drawn or the lights lit, so the dusk obscured
the features of the man who was seated at a big desk with his
back to one of the tall windows.

As Kuporovitch advanced towards him he prayed to all the
gods he had never worshipped to aid him now, as he felt convinced that in this interview lay his last and only chance of
escaping deportation, and death at his journey's end.

6

S O S to Gregory Sallust

'This is the man that you wished to see, *mon Colonel*,' said the inspector, saluting, and at a nod from his superior he saluted again and left the room.

Kuporovitch heaved a sigh of relief. He had feared that the inspector would remain, and he knew very well that no senior officer would accept a bribe in the presence of his junior, but now that he had been left alone with the police chief his hopes rose that he might yet be able to buy his freedom.

His eyes were now more accustomed to the dusk, and they swiftly took in everything which could be assimilated about the officer in whose hands his fate lay. The Colonel was a small man who sat with downcast head, apparently staring at his hands, which were clasped over his stomach. Then he looked up, and even in the twilight it could be seen that his face was wrinkled and monkey-like, with a pair of very quick dark eyes, as he rapped out by way of interrogation: 'Your name is Ivan Smernov?'

'*Oui, mon Colonel*,' replied Kuporovitch promptly.

Suddenly the little man chuckled and waved one hand towards a chair. 'Sit down, please, General Stefan Kuporovitch. I am so sorry that I have had to put you to so much inconvenience to get you here.'

With a gasp of surprise Kuporovitch stared anew at the small figure behind the desk. Gone were the silver curls and the black cassock, but the voice, the wrinkled face and the piercing black eyes were those of the little priest.

For a moment the Russian could hardly believe his eyes.

although he continued to strain them in the gathering darkness, but the little Colonel chuckled again:

'You recognize me now, eh?'

'Indeed I do!' muttered Kuporovitch. 'But what the devil are you doing here?'

The Colonel stood up abruptly. In a series of swift jerky movements he pulled the blinds and switched on the lights, then he replied:

'When I was asked that question in Paris the other night by one of my ex-subordinates who had gone over to the enemy I found it so embarrassing that it cost him his life; but here I do not find it embarrassing at all. This is my own office, and everybody in this building takes his orders from me. I am Colonel Lacroix.'

'Lacroix!' Kuporovitch repeated with a great sigh of relief. 'Then you are the famous Chief of the *Deuxième Bureau* and must have the power to prevent my being deported to Russia?'

'Of course.' The Colonel sat down again and pushed forward a box of cigarettes. 'I am sorry that you should have been distressed by the idea that we meant to do so, but you will appreciate, General, that my position here is one of extreme delicacy. When the collapse came I decided that I could serve the cause which we both have at heart far more effectively by remaining as a high official under the Government that had betrayed France than by going into hiding. Everyone here believes me to be entirely loyal to the Pétain Administration. That is why I could not risk having you brought straight from the frontier to my office. I had to allow matters to take their normal course in order to provide an excuse for an interview with you, such as I always have with all foreigners who are about to be deported.'

'You knew that I was being expelled from Occupied France, then?'

'Certainly. There was much that I still wished to say to you when our talk at the Vieux Logis was so regrettably cut short. It was obvious that both Mademoiselle Lavallière and yourself would be taken to the *Sûreté* for questioning, and I was anxious that no harm should come to either of you. In consequence, I arranged matters with Lieutenant Ribaud, who is entirely loyal and one of my most trusted agents.'

'Aha!' grinned Kuporovitch. 'I remember—the short dark fat man. It was he who suggested to the German major that Mademoiselle Madeleine should be released and that I should be put over the frontier.'

Lacroix nodded. 'He did that on my instructions. Had he not, they would almost certainly have detained you, whereas, as it is, they sent you here, which enables me to continue the conversation which I was anxious to have with you. But we will not talk further here, as one cannot be too careful. May I take it that you are prepared to accept my orders and follow such instructions as I may give you for the furthering of our mutual interests?'

'*Certainement, mon Colonel,*' Kuporovitch bowed. 'I should consider it an honour to serve under you.'

'Good! In that case, we will leave at once. You must be in Lyons by tomorrow morning, and there is someone that I wish to see tonight who is staying in an hotel no great way off the direct road there. My car is below, so you shall come with me, and we will dine and sleep at the hotel.' Lacroix picked up the telephone on his desk and asked for the inspector who had brought in Kuporovitch to be sent along to him.

When the inspector arrived the Colonel told him that on interrogating the prisoner he had found that the man might prove of considerable use to them on a matter that required immediate attention. Kuporovitch could hardly conceal his joy at the unexpected turn affairs had taken as he followed the Colonel downstairs and drove away with him in his car.

A glass screen prevented the military chauffeur from overhearing anything that they might say, and as soon as they were settled Kuporovitch said: 'Tell me, *mon Colonel,* how is it that you come to know my real name?'

'A mutual friend of ours told me about you in some talks we had before the collapse,' smiled Lacroix. 'You worked with him in Norway and Belgium, and it was you who got his *chère amie* away to England from the beaches of Dunkirk.'

'Ah!' exclaimed the Russian. 'You mean Gregory Sallust?'

'Yes, it was the good Gregory who told me of your adventures together, but it was only through some tactful enquiries, which I made about the Lavallières from the wife of their *concierge,* that I learned you were still in Paris. Your name rang a little bell in my mind, and I heard from Madame Bonard the story of your accident. Then I remembered that Madeleine Lavallière was the name of the nurse who telephoned reports to me about Gregory during his illness, and the whole thing fitted in.'

They were leaving Vichy and taking a road which led through the dark countryside to Roanne, as Kuporovitch asked: 'Have you heard anything of Gregory?'

'No. But it is about him that I wish to talk to you. This nation-wide conspiracy which I am attempting to organize requires a great deal of very careful planning if it is to have the maximum effect. All Frenchmen except a very few were for a time robbed of their wits from the shock of the appalling fate which had so suddenly overtaken their country. There was a time when even the most stout-hearted of us felt that Britain must give in, so that all open resistance to the enemy would be brought entirely to an end.'

'Isn't that still a possibility?' Kuporovitch said a little doubtfully. 'According to the Germans, the Royal Air Force has been almost entirely wiped out in these past few weeks, and the British cities are now taking a terrible hammering. How long will they be able to stand up to that?'

Lacroix spread out his hands. 'It is impossible to say. The situation is still critical, and at any time Britain may be called upon to face a supreme crisis, owing to a German invasion, but in other respects things are by no means so bad as the Nazis would have us believe. The R.A.F. has suffered severely, as any Air Force must which has the whole of the Luftwaffe directed against it, but these British airmen are terrific—absolutely unbelievable. Although the odds are ten to one against them it is they, and not the Germans, who are proving the terror of the skies. The reports which I receive are absolutely reliable. I am certain of that because they are checked by a dozen secret sources before they reach me, and for every British plane that the Nazis have been shooting down they have been losing five themselves.'

'*Mon Dieu,* what valour!' Kuporovitch cried, his dark eyes sparkling.

'Yes—and as yet, thank God, they show no signs of tiring.

Only yesterday, Sunday the 15th of September, a date which I believe the world will have cause to remember, the greatest air battle so far waged in history took place over London and South-East England. It resulted in the destruction of 185 German aircraft, which were actually seen to crash—not counting the scores of others which must have failed to get home or been too seriously damaged to be used again—for the loss of 30 British aircraft and only 15 of their pilots, as the others baled out and came down safely on their own soil.'

'Stupendous!' Kuporovitch muttered. 'Stupendous! Is it also untrue then that London and many other British cities have been practically razed to the ground?'

'In certain areas the damage has been very extensive, but by far the greater part of London is still standing. These Nazi swine have succeeded in killing and maiming several thousand non-combatants, of course, but it now seems certain that they have made a cardinal error in going in for indiscriminate bombing. By doing so they thought to terrify the civil population into peace riots, but in that they have failed entirely, as the British are more strongly united under Churchill than ever. The most encouraging thing about the situation is that these ferocious attacks have had practically no effect at all on the British war effort. I have it on the best authority that over ninety-five per cent of Britain's war factories have so far survived the blitz and remained totally unharmed.'

'You think there is a real chance, then, that Britain may be able to carry on the war for an indefinite period?'

'I hope so. In any case, it is this continued resistance by Britain which has now caused Frenchmen in both Occupied and Unoccupied France to form themselves into two opposite camps. Many of them see no hope of peace for years to come, except by a German victory, so they are beginning to give the Germans full collaboration. Others, like myself, who know that there can be no freedom for France until the Nazi menace has been destroyed, are now prepared to aid the British in their struggle by every means that lies in their power. Sufficient time has elapsed for everyone to think matters out for themselves and to take sides, even when they consider it wisest to keep their own convictions secret from their neighbours. But the material is now at hand from which we can recruit a great army to work in secret against our enemies.'

Kuporovitch nodded. 'An enormous amount can be done if only sufficient numbers of people are willing to adopt an active policy of non-co-operation.'

'True,' agreed the Colonel; 'but it is not sufficient merely to hinder the Nazis in small things. We must form our boldest spirits into sabotage squads, and if such squads are to inflict the maximum amount of damage upon the German Army of Occupation their objectives must be chosen in collaboration with the British.'

'So as to relieve the pressure upon them wherever possible and assist them in the fight they are waging, eh?'

'Exactly; and for that we must have as a liaison officer with the British a man of great courage, determination and resource!'

'Gregory Sallust!' said Kuporovitch quickly.

Lacroix nodded. 'Yes, it is Gregory that I have in mind, and I am anxious to discuss my plans personally with him at the earliest possible moment; but as it is out of the question for me to go to England he must come here to see me and carry my views back verbatim to his Government.'

'Can you arrange that through your agents?'

'No, that is just the difficulty. My agents in Britain continue to send me their reports through channels which it is un-necessary to specify, but they would do that in any case to the head of the *Deuxième Bureau*—whoever he was. As I have seen none of them since the collapse I do not know whom among them I dare trust with the very dangerous secret that I am now conspiring against my own Government and entering into secret negotiations with such a man as Gregory.' The little Colonel turned to Kuporovitch and rested his hand on the Russian's arm. 'That is why it occurred to me that, since you know Gregory, if I send you to England you could see him for me and bring him back to France with you. Are you prepared to undertake such a mission?'

'Nothing would please me better,' replied the Russian with a chuckle.

'Good! I can furnish you with the papers which will enable you to cross the Spanish and Portuguese frontiers, and from Lisbon you can get a plane. Unfortunately, however, you will be hung up there for some time as the airline to England is now very congested.'

'If the matter is so urgent, could you not send me direct in a fishing trawler or seagoing motor-boat from one of the smaller French ports?'

Lacroix shook his head. 'That is beyond even my resources. The whole of the French seaboard is now occupied by the Germans; but you should have no difficulty in securing a small boat in England, and it would save us much valuable time if you return to France that way.'

'Do you suggest that we should choose any lonely stretch of coast which we think suitable for our landing, or have you some special place in mind?'

'Have you ever heard of a little place on the Brittany coast called Saint Jacut de la Mer?'

'No,' grunted the Russian; 'outside Paris, I know only the Riviera of France.'

'It is a tiny village near Saint Brac, situated a mile or so from the end of a long lonely promontory that juts into the bay. A further mile beyond the headland there is a small island, which even in daylight is concealed from the village by the configuration of the ground. The waters of the bay are very shallow, so that the tide runs out for a great distance, and when it is low it is possible to walk across the sands to the island; but at high tide a fair-sized boat can put in there without danger of running aground. In the middle of the island there is a great pile of rocks, so it should be quite easy to pick out in starlight, and among them are the ruins of an old castle, a small part of which has been patched up by a peasant who earns a precarious living cultivating a few acres of soil. His name is Henri Denoual. He is entirely reliable, and the place is so isolated that there is nothing there to interest the Germans. The password which you must give Denoual on your arrival to assure him of your bona fides is easy to remember, as it is that of the name of the Patron Saint of France—St. Denis. If you land at the island at night when the tide is high he will give you shelter until morning, then take you across to the mainland and set you on the road to Paris.'

'It is to Paris, then, and not to Vichy, that you wish us to return?'

'Yes. It is unnecessary for you to run the additional risk of crossing the frontier between the coast zone and Unoccupied France; since I shall be making fairly frequent trips to Paris.'

'Very good, *mon Colonel*. Saint Jacut de la Mer is the name of the place, and Henri Denoual of the man. I shall not forget. How long do you think I am likely to be delayed in Lisbon?'

'A week at least, possibly more. Then you will have to find Gregory and make arrangements for your return journey.'

'If he has survived these bombings and is still in England that should present no difficulty. I shall go straight to his friend, the English milord, Sir Cust, who will be certain to know his whereabouts.'

Lacroix smiled in the semi-darkness of the car. 'You mean Sir Pellinore Gwaine-Cust. Yes, I was about to suggest that; but in any case it's hardly likely that you will be able to make the return trip under a fortnight. I will send word to Denoual to be on the lookout for you any night after the end of this month, but I doubt if you'll get back until well into October. And now, my friend, since I work all hours and am very tired, if you will permit me I shall snatch a short sleep.'

While the car roared on through Roanne and thence by side roads through the Beaujolais the broad-shouldered Kuporovitch sat smoking thoughtfully in one corner of it, and in the other the queer little man, hardly larger than a well-grown child, who was the great Chief of the French Secret Service, remained curled up, with his hands folded on his stomach and his chin resting on his chest.

At length they came out on to France's *Route Nationale 6*, between Macon and Lyons; then, having driven some way along it, they pulled up at a fair-sized building which stood on a lonely stretch of road and some way back from it. Lacroix roused himself and explained that this was the famous *Compagnons de Jéhu*, situated just half-way between Paris and Marseilles, at which in happier days many wealthy travellers had been accustomed to break their journey for one night when motoring to or from the Riviera.

It was a modern building in the style of an old posting-house, but its principal recommendation in normal times was its excellent cuisine and the fact that it remained quite unknown to the masses of tourists who swarm over France in the summer months. Lacroix and Kuporovitch were received by its proprietor, Monsieur le Baron Paulin, who in the years of peace had built up an excellent connection for the place among his personal friends, and ran it more on the lines of a private guest-house than an ordinary inn.

Such great numbers of people had fled from Northern France before the advancing Germans that it was estimated that only some 18,000,000 remained in the occupied territory, with the result that the smaller half of the country, ruled from Vichy, was now grossly over-populated. Every town and village was crowded with refugees.

The *Compagnons de Jéhu* had not escaped, as many of the Baron's Paris friends had taken refuge with him, but having had warning of Lacroix's coming he had managed to provide them with a room, and although he was now hard put to it to obtain supplies he promised them a good dinner. Since it was now getting on for nine o'clock they sat down to it right away, and this being the first decent food that Kuporovitch had seen since his arrest he did most noble justice to the meal.

Afterwards the Colonel disappeared for some twenty minutes to do the business which had caused him to make the journey. Then on his return, the Baron invited both him and Kuporovitch into his office, where he produced some of his now precious coffee and liqueurs for them. They talked mainly of the war and the possibility of various parts of the French Empire re-entering it against the Nazis; but Lacroix did not think that likely any longer. He said that, owing to a reshuffle of the Vichy Government which was in progress, General Weygand had given up the post of Minister of Defence in order to take command in North Africa. The Army there would prove loyal to Weygand, and Weygand to Pétain; while at home the ambitious pro-Nazi General Huntziger, who was to take Weygand's place in the Cabinet, would exert his influence there to get the Generals in other Colonies, who were of doubtful loyalty to Vichy, removed from their posts.

At eleven o'clock the two travellers went up to their room, and after Lacroix had given the Russian more detailed instructions as to what he was to say to Gregory when he reached England, they turned in.

The following morning they were up early, and having partaken of a simple breakfast drove to Lyons. Just before they reached the middle of the town Lacroix produced a packet from his satchel which he handed to his companion. It contained all the necessary papers for passing the frontier, together with French, Spanish, Portuguese and English money, and a passport made out in the name of Ivan Smernov, in which Kuporovitch was amused to see the photograph of himself which had been taken only the day before by the Vichy police. The car pulled up. The little Colonel wished his emissary the very best of luck. They shook hands warmly, and Kuporovitch got out.

As he had nothing except the clothes in which he stood his first thought was that he must buy himself a few things before going to the station to catch his train. But, as the car drove away, he stood for a moment motionless upon the pavement. It was a lovely morning, and smiling exultantly he drew a deep breath down into his broad chest.

He was free again—free; and after all these weeks of enforced inaction about to do something which might prove damnably dangerous before he was through with it, but which was well worth the doing. He could have shouted aloud in the sunshine from sheer joy.

7

Defiant London

Kuporovitch's journey to Lisbon took much longer than he had expected. The trains, like everything else in Unoccupied France, were horribly overcrowded, running only infrequently and at half speed. In normal times, having left Lyons on the morning of the 17th, he would have crossed the Spanish frontier that night, but the train took the best part of a day to crawl as far as Avignon, where, as it was going on to Marseilles, he had to change; and there was no connection which he could catch until the following day.

He spent the evening wandering round the ancient city; then on the 18th he left the towering Palace of the Popes and the famous broken bridge over the Loire behind, to roll gently through the grey-green olive groves, dotted with lemon-walled, rust-tiled houses, which make up the scene of Provence. It was nine at night before the train eventually pulled up at the little town of Cerbère on the Spanish frontier, and there everybody had to undergo two most rigorous examinations, first by the French police on leaving France, and secondly by the Spanish police on entering Spain.

As the Russian's entire baggage consisted of a rucksack and the few items which he had bought in Lyons he had little trouble with the Customs, but he had to submit to being stripped and searched as a precaution against currency smuggling. The French officials detained half a dozen people who were on the train, and the Spanish turned back over a score who for one reason or another did not fully satisfy them; but at last the remaining passengers were allowed through, and shortly after midnight herded into a large waiting-room, where they were told they must remain until the train left for Barcelona in the morning.

The Spanish train which started at six o'clock reminded Kuporovitch of his native Russia, as both the Russian and Spanish railways have a broader gauge and carriages than those of the rest of Europe. On it he had looked forward to a slap-up breakfast, but Spain was now little better off for food than Occupied France, so to his disappointment he had to make do with rolls, some very wishy-washy coffee and an orange.

By 8.30 they reached Barcelona, where he had to change again, but this time the connection was a good one, and he spent the rest of the day travelling at a moderate speed through the arid, sparsely-populated Spanish countryside towards Madrid. It was dark when he reached the capital, and once again there was no connection to take him farther on his journey until next morning.

As the train did not leave until ten o'clock he had an opportunity of driving round the Prado district before catching it, and was by no means cheered by what he saw. The city still showed many traces of the Civil War, as much of the damage from shelling and bombs remained unrepaired. It was clear, too, that the population was very far from having recovered from the effects of its bitter and long-drawn-out struggle. An air of want and hopelessness pervaded everything. There were queues outside the food-shops, and most of the poorer people were dressed in clothes that were little better than rags.

He was sorry for the Spaniards, but felt that, although they could not appreciate it at the moment, their present poverty might stand them in good stead. Any hope of a Dictator country such as Spain coming into the war on the side of Britain had been remote from the beginning, as her rulers had much more cause to feel gratitude to Hitler and Mussolini for the assistance they had rendered in establishing the régime; but at any time pressure might be exerted on Spain to join the Axis. Kuporovitch considered that no country which was already in such a state of destitution could possibly afford a war, so there seemed a good chance that General Franco, who had never been a member of the Fascist Party and was by no means rabidly anti-British, might continue to use that as an excuse to save his people from being dragged into the conflict.

All that day the train carried the Russian westward. There were further rigorous examinations on the Spanish and Portuguese frontiers, then at last, on the evening of the 20th, he reached Lisbon.

Next morning, he went at once to the French Consulate in accordance with Lacroix's instructions, but they told him that it would take a week at least before they could get him a seat on the plane leaving for England, so he had to resign himself to kicking his heels about the Portuguese capital.

Lisbon proved the exact antithesis of Madrid. Where the one had been half-dead from depression the other was hectic with a strange restless life. From the beginning of the war people of all nations had been flocking there as a safe spot to dig in for the duration. Escapists of all nations, including English, French, Germans, and particularly huge numbers of rich Jews, had made it their headquarters. When the blitz had come another hundred thousand people at least, from Holland, Belgium and France had fled to Lisbon in the hope of getting away to America; but passages were at an enormous premium and accommodation extremely limited. In consequence, the great bulk of them were still marooned there and now forced to live precariously upon the proceeds of the jewels, furs, and other objects of value that they had managed to bring with them and had intended to sell for their passage money.

It was a city of extraordinary contrasts, as the scarcity in certain commodities had already caused prices to rise to fantastic levels. The Government was doing what it could to check inflation for the protection of its own people, but the huge foreign element presented a special problem, over which it was almost impossible to exercise control. Great fortunes were being made and spent with the utmost recklessness by unscrupulous speculators on the one hand, while on the other scores of suicides were taking place each week among the unfortunates who were driven to it through utter despair and virtual starvation.

Each day Kuporovitch went to the French Consulate in

the hope of expediting his chances of a seat in an outward-bound plane, but the British were adhering most strictly to their own system of priorities, and there was nothing he could do to bring influence to bear in that direction. A week passed, and his prospects seemed little better than when he had arrived.

In Lisbon he was able to get the English news as well as the German with equal ease, and he heard all that the public ever learned of the extraordinary affair at Dakar. On September the 23rd it was announced that General de Gaulle had arrived off the West African port with a force of Free French troops and an escort of British warships. Apparently he had expected to be welcomed by the French garrison with open arms, but it proved quite otherwise. It seemed that the cat had got out of the bag before the expedition had sailed from England, so that the Vichy Government had been able to take adequate precautions. They had even had so much time to spare that they had been able to replace the Governor with a man who was rabidly anti-British and to reinforce the garrison with reliable troops taken out in six French warships which, for some inexplicable reason, the British had allowed to pass through the Straits of Gibraltar.

When General de Gaulle had arrived his compatriots had simply made rude noises at him, and when he had sent an emissary ashore to parley with the Vichy French they had promptly shot at, and wounded, the officer. Whether any landing in force had been attempted was not clear, but the British Admiral had bombarded the harbour until his ammunition was exhausted, and the expedition had to sail away again, having accomplished nothing except to provide the Germans with fresh propaganda material for widening the breach between Britain and Vichy France.

Afterwards General de Gaulle declared that he had withdrawn his Free French Forces because he could not bring himself to see his compatriots killing one another; but why he had been allowed to go to Dakar if he were not prepared to fight was a great mystery, and the British Admiral appeared to have been badly let down by his superiors at home. Kuporovitch, who, largely owing to his friendship with Gregory had become intensely pro-British, felt ashamed and disgusted about the whole affair, as it had the effect of making the British a laughing-stock throughout Lisbon, and some Fifth Columnist revived the ancient tag concerning the Duke of Buckingham's ill-considered expedition in the time of Charles I, which now ran round the Lisbon bars: 'There was a Fleet that sailed to Spain, and when it got there it sailed home again.'

Meanwhile the strafing of the British cities by the Luftwaffe continued unabated; yet now that Lacroix had assured him that the figures of planes destroyed, as given by the B.B.C., were correct, Kuporovitch waited for them to be given out each night and morning with the acutest interest and anxiety. How the comparatively small R.A.F. managed to continue their magnificent resistance to the huge air armadas sent against them he still could not understand, but as a fighting man it filled him with the profoundest admiration, and on the evening of the 28th he got gloriously drunk to celebrate the news that the previous day the British had scored another outstanding success by destroying 133 enemy planes for the loss of 34 of their own, and only 18 pilots.

At last, on October the 6th, and then only because another passenger was detained at the last moment, he managed to get a seat on the plane for England. The journey was disappointing, since, even at the risk of being shot down, he had hoped that he might see something of one of the air battles; but the windows of the aircraft had all been blacked out in order that none of the passengers should have any chance of learning military secrets when over the English coast on the last lap of their journey.

The flight also took much longer than he expected, as the plane went far out into the Atlantic to avoid enemy aircraft before turning northward, but late that afternoon the Russian was safely landed at a West of England port. Once more he had to undergo a critical examination by Customs and Immigration officials, but at last he was allowed out through the gates.

It was then for the first time that he saw some of the bomb damage—ruined buildings and gaunt rafters projecting from burnt-out roofs—but the people of the town did not seem particularly concerned and were going about their business

95

as usual. To his joy he found that the English Madeleine had taught him was sufficient for him to make himself understood and long sessions of listening to the B.B.C. broadcasts had enabled him to understand the language considerably better than he could talk it. He spent the night in the depressing atmosphere of a railway hotel, but there was no air raid, and the following morning he was on the train for London.

In view of the intensive air attack which the Germans had maintained against England for the past two months, he had naturally expected that the railways would be seriously disorganized and that he would meet with even greater delays than those with which he had been faced while travelling through France and Spain; but to his amazement the express carried him with peace-time swiftness through the heart of England, made lovely now with autumn tints. His surprise was increased when the steward in the restaurant-car served him with an excellent meal, at which, compared with Continental standards, there appeared practically no limit to what he could eat; and during the whole journey he saw only one partially-destroyed building which could be attributed to enemy action. By the time he reached London he had come to the conclusion that the accounts of the blitzing of Britain must have been grossly exaggerated.

His only previous visit to London had been between his arrival in England after Dunkirk and his departure for France again less than a fortnight later, so he did not know the city well; but as he set off in a taxi from Paddington to Sir Pellinore Gwaine-Cust's mansion in Carlton House Terrace he began to revise his estimate as to the weight of the German attacks.

Although Paddington Station itself still remained unharmed at that time many buildings in its neighbourhood had suffered severely. In practically every street there were great gaps in the rows of houses, as though they had been large slabs of cake out of which some giant had hacked a complete slice. Many of the roads were roped off for short sections, so that the taxi had to wind about continually instead of taking a direct route, and on peering down the roped-off sections Kuporovitch saw that many of them were half-filled with rubble from collapsed houses, or had great craters, out of which huge broken drainpipes reared on end, and masses of wood-paving had been flung about. Here and there, still-standing frontages with blank, empty windows gaped roofless to the skies, having been burnt out with incendiary bombs; and even in the streets which were still free for traffic enormous numbers of windows had been shattered by the blast of high-explosive bombs.

At first he thought that the area through which he was passing must have suffered with particular severity from the Germans having attempted to put the railway terminus out of action, but only having succeeded in plastering the streets all round it; yet, as his taxi progressed, turning and twisting alternately through main thoroughfares and side-streets across the great shopping centre of the West End, he saw that the bombing had been entirely indiscriminate, and that the whole of central London appeared to have suffered equally from the sustained savagery of the attacks.

He noticed too that the streets were almost empty compared with when he last saw them. There was now little traffic, and the people, although still going about their work with a dogged look, were showing the strain in their faces.

On arriving in Carlton House Terrace he saw with some relief that Sir Pellinore's house was still standing, although two others quite near it had dissolved into a great heap of rubble and twisted metal, which overflowed into the roadway. The elderly butler remembered him at once, but informed him that Sir Pellinore was out and would not be back until dinner-time. He thought, however, that Mr. Sallust was still living at his flat in Gloucester Road and rang up to find out.

As so many of the telephone exchanges and cables had been damaged it took the best part of twenty minutes to get through, but at last the butler secured the number. Gregory was not in, but his faithful henchman, Rudd, took the call and said that his master was expected back quite shortly; so Kuporovitch decided to go down there right away.

His second taxi-ride gave him a further opportunity to assess the damage which had been inflicted on inner South-West London, and he now decided that the reports of the bombing had not been exaggerated at all. It was only the vast size of the capital, with its scores of square miles of buildings, streets, squares and parks, together with the fact that the Germans did not appear to have concentrated upon any particular area, which had enabled the population to carry on. Had the thousands of bombs which had been dropped been directed upon a smaller city it must inevitably have been wiped out.

At Gloucester Road Rudd received the Russian, and having installed him in a comfortable chair with a large whisky-and-soda proceeded to give him some account of the blitz.

'Well, it ain't exactly a picnic, as yer might say,' he remarked cheerfully, 'speshully when Jerry's dropping them things abaht, and yer's aht in the street, as me and Mr. Gregory is nah, every night—'im and me belonging to the Fire-Fightin' Service; but it ain't nuffin compared wiv what we 'ad to put up wiv in the hold war when we was at Ypres. Yer see, it's this way, sir. London's the 'ell of a big place, when yer comes to think of it, and I reckons little hold 'Itler bit off more than 'e could chew when 'e started in to knock it dahn. O course, I ain't saying 'e ain't done a tidy bit o' damage, and it makes us just screamin' mad when we 'as to pull what's left o' wimmen and kids aht from underneath great 'eaps of rubble; but I reckons that there American journalist 'it the nail on the 'ead when 'e wrote 'ome to 'is paper. 'E said that at the rate the Nasties are going now it'd take 'em two thousand weeks to destroy London, and 'e don't reckon 'Itler's got another forty years ter live!'

Kuporovitch's command of English was not yet sufficient to follow Rudd's Cockney idiom entirely, but he got the gist of it, and it heartened him a great deal. He was just saying how wonderfully the English railways seemed to have stood up to the crisis when the door opened and Gregory came in. He looked a little tired and was clad in a dirty suit of blue dungarees, but as he saw the Russian his lean face lit up, and he gave a great shout:

'Stefan! By all that's holy!'

'Gregory, *mon vieux*!' exclaimed Kuporovitch with equal delight, and standing up he gave the Englishman a great bear-like hug, while the grinning Rudd slipped quietly out of the room.

'And to think that I left you for dead in Paris last June!'

Gregory cried, breaking into French. 'Yet here you are in London, looking as fit as when I first met you.'

'I owe that to the nurse whom you so thoughtfully left to look after me.'

'What! That pretty little Madeleine! You old devil! I only left her the money with which to bury you. If I know anything of your way with women I'll bet that by this time the poor girl's beginning to regret your resurrection!'

Kuporovitch came as near to blushing as such a hardened sinner could, but he covered his confusion with his hearty laugh.

'No, no! The little Madeleine has nothing to regret on my account, thank God!'

'Then your recovery must be very recent.' Gregory teased him. ' "The devil was sick, the devil a monk would be; the devil was well, the devil a monk was he!" '

'No, no!' Kuporovitch protested again. 'I would not harm a hair of her lovely head.'

'Then, dammit, you must have *really* fallen in love with her!'

'I have,' Stefan confessed. 'Most desperately. But, tell me, what news of Erika?'

'She's better—practically recovered now, thank God! But she had a positively ghastly time, and for weeks after I got back it was still touch-and-go as to whether she'd ever get really fit again.'

'Is she in London?'

'No. Pellinore sent her down to Gwaine Meads, his place in Montgomeryshire, and I went with her. I was about all in myself after those terrific weeks we had between the invasion of Norway and the collapse of France. The old man absolutely insisted that I should kill two birds with one stone by helping her recovery through being with her and taking a proper rest myself.'

'I suppose you came back when the blitz started?'

'Yes, I'm still unemployed officially. Naturally, as soon as Erika had turned the corner and I was feeling more like my old self, I tried to get some sort of job. But there was no special mission upon which Sir Pellinore could send me, and my friends in the Services seemed to think that I should only be an awful misfit if they took me into one of them as a junior officer. That was pretty depressing but old Pellinore assured me that sooner or later something suitable to my peculiar talents was bound to turn up. Directly the Boches started knocking hell out of London I came back, and Rudd got me taken on as a member of his fire-fighting squad.'

'Is that a permanency? Will it tie you here?' asked Kuporovitch anxiously.

'Oh no. If something in which I could be more useful offered I could always put in my resignation.'

'Good! I'm glad of that, as I come from Lacroix with an invitation which, I think, will intrigue you.'

'Lacroix!' Gregory echoed the name almost in a whisper and with something of awe in his tone. 'Is that great little man still with us?'

Kuporovitch nodded. 'Very much so. He still holds his job but only so that he can the better sabotage collaboration between the Nazis and the Vichy French.'

Gregory's brown eyes lit up his lean face as he murmured: 'This sounds like something really in my line. I'm off duty tonight, so we'll go out and dine somewhere, and you must tell me all about it.'

Dusk was now falling.

Rudd came back to do the black-out, and Gregory added: 'Make yourself comfortable here for a bit while I get out of these things and have a wash.'

Soon after he had left the room the sirens began to wail, and gunfire could be heard in the distance.

When Gregory returned, spick and span in one of his well-cut lounge suits, he remarked: 'It's no good telephoning for a taxi. It takes ages to get on to a number in these days, but we'll be able to pick one up in the street.'

'Do they still run when an air raid is in progress?' asked Kuporovitch doubtfully.

'Good Lord, yes!' Gregory assured him. 'The London taximen are absolutely splendid. They don't give a damn for the Jerries and carry on, however bad the blitz. I only wish it was the same with all our other services.'

'What's wrong with them?' Kuporovitch inquired, as they went downstairs and out into the darkness.

Gregory suddenly began to speak with bitter fury. 'In August, through the absolutely splendid show put up by our Air Force, we demonstrated to the world that there were still prospects of Britain's emerging victorious from the war. In September the lack of resource, initiative and even common-sense displayed by some of our Civil Authorities is putting us well on the road to losing the war altogether. In the Spring before the war the people responsible for Home Security issued a thing called an Anderson Shelter, which was turned out by the thousand and distributed free among the poorer people for them to set up in their back-gardens. That was grand, but ever since the Ministry concerned has been sound asleep. Hitler might have blitzed London any day after September the 3rd, 1939, yet they didn't even start to erect street air raid shelters until the bombs actually began to fall, and, when they did, they set about it in the most crazy way.

'No attempt seems to have been made to secure designs from Britain's leading architects and military engineers in order that various types of shelter might be erected on waste-ground and tested out for blast resistance. If they had done that the most satisfactory model could have been adopted as the universal type; instead, each Borough Council is being allowed to erect any old brick structure that it likes, and some of them are so flimsy that their ends fall in if a car drives into them in the black-out.'

'I don't wonder that happens,' muttered Kuporovitch with an oath, as he stumbled over a sandbag.

'Then the Tubes!' went on Gregory angrily. 'Any fool could have foreseen that the poor wretches who had been bombed out of their homes would take refuge in London's only natural deep shelters—the Underground Stations—but the London Transport Board can have received no instructions from the Government. They even closed their stations in the daytime, every time those filthy sirens sounded.'

'What! They shut the people who could shelter in them out in the streets? But that is incredible!'

'Nevertheless, it's a fact; and it's only during the last week or two that unofficially, and entirely as a compassionate measure, the Transport Board have allowed homeless people to remain down in their stations for the night. But even now the Government hasn't taken any measures for the comfort of these poor wretches, or to ensure proper sanitation. It's a . . .'

A nearby anti-aircraft battery suddenly let off a terrific crack, and the rest of Gregory's sentence was drowned, but a moment later Kuporovitch caught his words again.

'Why the hell nobody does anything about the blitzed buildings I simply can't think. This party's been going on for over a month now, yet not the least attempt is made to tidy things up. Whenever a place is bombed and huge chunks of masonry crash down, half-blocking a street, they simply rope it off, instead of putting the unemployed on to clear away the débris and erecting a hoarding which would hide the worst effects of the mess. We've got millions of troops in this country. If they can't get ordinary labour why not bring in the Army to lend a hand? As it is, half the streets in London are either blocked by bomb-craters or have a time-bomb in them.'

'Yes, I noticed that when I was coming down here and on my way from Paddington to Sir Pellinore's,' Kuporovitch agreed. 'No attempt at all has yet been made to deal with the damage that has been done and in time that is bound to have a very bad effect on the people.'

'But that's only a small thing,' Gregory persisted. 'All the municipal services such as water and gas are getting in a hopeless state. The bombing isn't so bad, and people are standing up to it pretty well, but what does get them down is the awful inconvenience that it causes. In half the houses in London now the gas pressure is so low that one can't cook anything, or it's cut off entirely, owing to the damage to the mains; and water is even worse. Only a trickle comes out of the tap, so we're lucky if we get a bath once a week these days. That's pretty hard when one comes home black as a sweep from having been fire-fighting all night. And it's all so damned unnecessary, because things could be reasonably straightened out in no time, if only the Government would call in engineer units from the Army to mend conduits and telephone cables and so on that have been broken in the raids.'

There was a horrid droning of enemy planes overhead. Somewhere south of the river bombs were falling, but only the practised ear could distinguish them from the detonations of the heavier anti-aircraft guns. Except for an occasional A.R.P. warden the streets were deserted, but some distance along the Cromwell Road they struck a crawling taxi, and Gregory having told the man to drive to the Hungaria Restaurant they climbed into it. He was evidently intensely bitter and continued to let himself go.

'Worst of all is the way that the Post Offices are behaving. At Dunkirk the Army lost everything except its pants, and we were all told afterwards that not one moment should be lost in any form of national activity which might help to build up its strength again; yet the Post Offices all shut down the instant they hear a siren.'

'What difference does that make to munition workers?' Kuporovitch asked in some surprise.

'My dear fellow, the Post Office is the index of all commercial activity in this country, because it's the only shop in every High Street which is under Government control. If the Post Office shuts, and its staff seeks refuge in the basement, how can a private employer of labour be expected to ask his people to carry on? Countless offices and shops immediately followed this cowardly example. The custom has spread to the banks, the great stores and the factories. Even when a single raider comes over the Estuary of the Thames, all Government offices from Hendon to Croydon, with the exception of those of the Fighting Services, close down, and practically everything else, except the brave little individual traders, closes with them. You have a look around tomorrow if there's an air raid in the daytime. You'll see queues of angry people left on the pavements, who can't telephone or send telegrams, often of the greatest urgency, cash cheques at the banks, or make applications at the Labour Exchanges, or even do their household shopping. Literally millions of hours of the nation's vital time are being wasted through this criminally wicked funk and apathy in our Civil Authorities.'

'But I thought Churchill was so marvellous,' remarked Kuporovitch.

'So he is—a man in a million, God bless him! But he can't do everybody's work, and I expect he's much too busy running the fighting end of the war with the Naval, Military and Air

Chiefs to know the half of what's going on. I only wish I were a big enough shot to get ten minutes with him and tell him what the ordinary people are saying about some of their so-called leaders; then persuade him to let me loose in Whitehall with a hatchet!'

'Calm yourself, my friend, calm yourself!' purred the Russian. 'After all, it is the British way to muddle along, is it not? And in due course no doubt things will improve themselves.'

'That's all very well,' Gregory grunted, 'but if Fleet Street can do it, why the hell can't the Government?'

'Fleet Street? What have they done?'

'Why, carried on of course. I mean all the big national newspapers. Fleet Street has caught it worse than most places, and the majority of our big newspaper buildings have been hit in the past month; but they manage to get their papers out just the same. They only allowed the air raids to interfere for one single day—September the 7th, the first night of the blitz. They went to ground then like everybody else, but within twenty-four hours they had made up their minds that if the life of the country was to go on they'd got to stick at their jobs, blitz or no blitz! Although we've got no gas or water or air raid shelters worth the name, and it takes an hour to telephone and half the day to cash a cheque, we still get our morning papers as regularly as clock work.'

'That's a good show,' Kuporovitch muttered, as the Ack-Ack batteries in Hyde Park blasted hell out of the night. 'A very good show.'

'Yes,' returned Gregory. 'That's a very good show. But it's pretty grim to think of all the heroism the people are displaying while these wretched Ministers and high-up Civil Servants are letting the country die standing on its feet.'

As they ran up Piccadilly Kuporovitch remained silent. He was at first inclined to think that the strain of being out night after night fire-fighting was beginning to tell on Gregory's nerves; but when he considered the matter he realized that Gregory was the last man to get the jitters and that as there was no reason at all for him to lie about matters there must be real reasons for his intense indignation.

Bombs crumped in the distance, and the anti-aircraft

barrage continued to play its hideous tune, but by the time they reached the Hungaria Gregory had calmed down. The restaurant on the ground floor was no longer in use, but the big grill-room below it was still carrying on, and the *maître d'hôtel*, Monsieur Vecchi, who was an old friend of Gregory's, led them to a corner table in the low gallery.

'Well, how are things, Josef?' Gregory asked him as they sat down.

Vecchi's unfailing smile lit his round face. 'We must not grumble, Mr. Sallust. Many people have gone to the country but quite a lot of our old friends remain, and they still come here. We closed the big room upstairs because peoples prefer to dine and dance in basements these days; also we make arrangements for our guests to sleep here if they wish.'

'By Jove! That's a grand idea!' Gregory grinned. 'Do many of them take advantage of your hospitality?'

'A dozen or so, every night. Those who have a long way to go to their homes; but for the rest we still manage to get taxis. What would you like to order for your dinner?'

As Gregory was entertaining a Russian he decided on a Russian meal: Vecchi's famous hot *hors d'œuvre, bortch* and chicken *à la Kiev,* all of which were specialities that he had acquired when, many years before, he had been *maître d'hôtel* at the Astoria Hotel in St. Petersburg, before the Revolution.

Kuporovitch remembered the hotel well from the days when he was a young Czarist officer, and for a few moments they talked together in Russian. Then Vecchi left them to give instructions about their dinner.

The meal was excellent, and Kuporovitch was delighted to see pre-Revolution Russian dishes again, of all places in bomb-torn London. They washed it down with a magnum of Louis Roederer 1928, and over it Kuporovitch gave Gregory details both of his convalescence and of the mission which had brought him to England.

Gregory agreed at once about the importance of establishing proper liaison with Lacroix and that it could be best done by his going to France.

While they talked they could hear now and again the dull thud of a bomb or the more staccato crack of the light A.A.

guns. Once the whole building shook as a big one landed somewhere in the neighbourhood of Piccadilly, but the band played on, and the fifty or so odd people who had braved the blitz to come out to dine and dance appeared quite undisturbed. As Gregory had been out fire-fighting both the previous nights they decided to make an early evening of it, so at eleven o'clock he paid the bill and they got a taxi.

The blackened streets now appeared completely desolate and the anti-aircraft had lessened, but the horrid droning overhead told them that Goering's murderers were still at work, trying to pick out the most congested portions of the city in which to drop their bombs. As the taxi passed Hyde Park Corner a spent shell-splinter thudded on to its roof, but they reached Gregory's flat in safety, tipped the stout-hearted taximan liberally and brought him in for a drink. Rudd had made up the bed in the spare room for Kuporovitch, and, too tired to be kept awake by the raid, soon after midnight the two friends were asleep.

The next morning they rang up Sir Pellinore, who was as delighted as Gregory had been to learn that Kuporovitch was still alive, and said that he would be very happy to see them if they came up right away.

The windows of the big library at the back of Sir Pellinore's mansion had been shattered by blast, so the fine view over St. James's Park was now shut out by sheets of weatherboard. The house was just on a hundred years old and had not a steel girder in it, but to those of his friends who had urged him to move to safer quarters the elderly baronet had replied:

'I'll not let that damn' house-painter feller drive me into some mouldy funk-hole. Think I want to die of pneumonia, eh? My old house is as comfortable as money can make it, and I've got the best cellar of good liquor in London. If the devils get me I'll at least pass out as I've always lived—warm, well-lined, and in a place of my own choosing!'

The old boy's bright blue eyes fairly sparkled when he heard about Kuporovitch's mission, and for the best part of an hour they discussed it. Then Sir Pellinore left them to go and see a friend of his who was attached to the Foreign Office. Later he brought the friend back to lunch with him, and afterwards they entered into a full council of ways and means.

The P.I.D. man knew Lacroix personally and expressed the greatest keenness to co-operate with him in sabotaging the Nazis and fermenting revolt in France. He said that he could arrange mátters with the Admiralty for Gregory and Kuporovitch to be given transport across the Channel and landed at the little island off Saint Jacut on a suitable night; but the date could not yet be fixed as they would have to go into the question of tides. The moon need not worry them as it was not full again until the 20th of October, but it was essential that the landing should take place as near high water as possible and, as nearly as could be managed, midway between the hours of sunset and dusk, in order that the boat that took them across should get the maximum amount of cover from darkness in both approaching and leaving the French coast. Before leaving, he promised to let them know on the following day the best night for making their trip.

That night the two friends dined with Sir Pellinore. Brushing up his fine white military moustache, he cursed the Nazis roundly for having interfered with his kitchen arrangements; in spite of that, they did themselves extremely well, killed two magnums of Krug 1928 and, ignoring the bombers that droned overhead, had a great yarn about the war.

On the following day a note arrived for Gregory by D.R. from the P.I.D. man to say the tide would be full at Saint Jacut on October the 15th between 11.30 and midnight. It would have been better if they could have made their landing an hour or so later, but to do that meant postponing the venture for another two or three days, and that would bring them into the period of the full moon, so they would either have to risk a rather early arrival, while a certain number of people on the coast might not yet have turned in, or put the whole business off until the moon had waned and the tide was suitable again, which was not before the end of the month.

Gregory and Kuporovitch agreed that they must not delay a single day longer than necessary, owing to the Russian's long enforced halt at Lisbon, as, even if they sailed on the 15th, it would be just on a month since he had set out from Vichy. They went to see Sir Pellinore, and it was definitely decided that everything should be fixed for the night of the 15th.

As they had six days to spare Sir Pellinore suggested that they should spend them at Gwaine Meads with Erika. Anxious as he was to do so, Gregory expressed certain qualms at leaving his fire-fighting squad while the blitz was still in progress.

'Nonsense, my boy! Nonsense!' boomed the baronet. 'You're unofficially back in the Services now, and this is your embarkation leave. Once you get over to the other side God alone knows when you'll see that young woman of yours again. There are more people still in London than there are in the whole British Army, and if they can't look after their own city they deserve that it should burn. If I had a plane and a load of incendiary bombs I'd drop the whole lot on the Home Office myself; then perhaps the nitwits who run it would wake up to the fact that there's a war on and make fire-watching compulsory. You're under my orders. They are to pack your bags and get off to Wales.'

Gregory demurred no longer and with Kuporovitch left Paddington on the night-train.

Erika was overjoyed to see them both, and for the next few days they almost managed to forget the war with all its horrors and wearisome inconveniences. The staff of the lovely old Tudor mansion had been greatly cut down, and one wing of it was now a convalescent hospital for Air Force officers; but apart from occasional German planes passing high overhead at night to bomb Liverpool, and the sight of the blue-uniformed invalids sitting about the lovely garden when the weather was fine, there were no traces at all of the war. Instead of being two hundred miles away from grim determined London, they might easily have been two thousand, and they lived on the fat of the land from the products of the home-farm.

The wounds in Erika's chest where she had been shot five months before were now entirely healed, but she was still weak from her long illness and had a rather nasty cough as a result of the injury to her lung; but she insisted that she was already as good as well again and that as soon as she was strong enough she meant to take up work which Sir Pellinore had said that he could get for her—translating the contents of German newspapers for the Foreign Office.

Little was said of the mission upon which the two men were going, and Erika made a brave show of hiding her fears from Gregory. Her illness had, if possible, made her more beautiful than ever, and Kuporovitch could see from the way Gregory looked at her that he adored her more than words could express. Although her body was still weak, her fine brain and shrewd wit were as quick as ever, and for hours at a stretch they succeeded in putting the war away from them while they laughed a lot together; yet always in the background of their thoughts was the knowledge that this was only a brief respite. There could be no real peace or prolonged happiness for any of them until the gangsters who threatened Britain and now held a hundred and forty million wretched people prisoner upon the Continent had been utterly destroyed.

At last, on the morning of the 15th, the final good-byes had been said, and Erika waved them away from the doorstep of the old manor-house, with her heart almost bursting, but no tears showing in her deep blue eyes. It was not until the car that was taking them into Shrewsbury had disappeared round the bend of the avenue of great limes that, stuffing the edge of her handkerchief between her teeth, she ran back into the house to give way to a passion of tears.

While in Wales, Gregory and Kuporovitch had received French money, French clothes of a rough-and-ready variety, *cartes d'identité* purporting to have been issued in Paris, and their final instructions; and most of the day was spent in a rather tiring cross-country journey down to Weymouth, which being the nearest port to Saint Jacut, had been selected for their embarkation. At four o'clock they reported to the naval officer commanding there. He passed them on to a Lieutenant Commander, who gave them a high tea in the mess, and immediately afterwards took them past the sentries on to a jetty, at the end of which a long, low, seagoing motor-boat was in readiness.

It was still full daylight, and dusk was not due for another hour or more, but for that time they would have the protection of the Naval Coast Patrol; and it was essential to make an early start if they were to arrive off Saint Jacut by half past eleven. The Lieutenant Commander introduced them to an

R.N.V.R. lieutenant named Cummings, who was in charge of the launch. He was a fat, cheerful fellow, who before the war had been a keen yachtsman and knew the coast of Brittany well; and it was for that reason he had been selected to run them across. There were no formalities to be observed, so as soon as Gregory and Kuporovitch had installed themselves in the small cabin of the launch it cast off and with gathering speed slid out of the harbour.

The sea was moderately calm, but at the speed they were making the boat bumped a lot as she snaked through the little wave-crests, from which a constant spray flew over her. Fortunately, both passengers were good sailors, so they felt no ill-effects, apart from the strain of the constant rocking, since both of them had hoped to sleep for the best part of their six- or seven-hour journey in order that they might arrive fresh at its end; but that proved impossible, as their cramped quarters did not permit of enough space to lie down, or even to curl up in moderate comfort.

The coast of England dropped behind until it was only a grey smudge on the horizon and then became lost in the falling twilight. Gradually the stars came out, and a sickle moon came up, intermittently obscured by passing clouds. Hour after hour the launch scurried on, its diesel engine purring rhythmically. There was a great sense of loneliness there, in the little boat out on the dark waters.

For some reason he could not explain Gregory felt depressed. He thought that was due to his having so recently left Erika, yet if all went well he should be back in England quite soon, as he had been furnished with papers, now sewn into the soles of his shoes, which would secure him priority on a plane from Lisbon once he had seen Lacroix. Nothing had been overlooked in their arrangements at either end, as Lacroix could be relied on to handle the French part of the business, and if his man Henri Denoual, did his share, there should be no delay in their reaching Paris.

Even if he did not, Gregory had no doubts at all about his own ability to get there. They might have the bad luck to run into a German coast patrol, but that was unlikely since it was quite impossible for the Germans to keep an adequate watch at night along all the thousands of miles of indented coast between northern Norway and the Pyrenees. Had any considerable force attempted a landing it would soon have been detected, and in no time German armoured forces could be rushed up to cope with it, but one small boat was a very different matter, particularly as the moon would be well down at the time of their arrival. He had undertaken far more hazardous adventures before and had always felt an exhilarating excitement when about to set out on them; but somehow this time that was altogether lacking, and he had an unpleasant foreboding of which he could not rid himself that trouble lay in front of them.

At eleven o'clock the bulky Cummings came down to say that they had picked up the Brittany coast and were now making their way along it. His navigation proved excellent, as ten minutes later he fetched them from the cabin and pointed to a dark mound ahead, which rose out of the seas, vaguely silhouetted between two others against the lesser blackness of the night sky.

'There's your island,' he said. 'I've often sailed these waters in the piping times of peace, and I'd know that mass of rocks between the two headlands anywhere. Nobody seems to be about, thank God, but we'd better lay off for a bit until the tide runs as high as we can get it.'

Farther to the east they could see the beams of the searchlights sweeping the sea outside Saint Malo, and the next twenty minutes proved anxious ones as there was always a possibility that the Germans had mounted searchlights upon the headland of Saint Jacut, which might suddenly blaze out and catch the boat in their beams. If that happened it was a certainty that within a few seconds of their being spotted a coastal battery would begin to roar, and it was ten to one that they would be sunk there in the bay long before they were able to get away out to the open sea.

However, all remained quiet and no lights appeared. At eleven-thirty to the tick the boat was very gently beached on a sandy spit which ran out from the northern end of the island. Having shaken hands with the lieutenant and wished him a safe return, the two friends slipped overboard into the shallow water.

Once ashore they shook as much water off their legs as they

111

could, then cautiously proceeded inland. Soon they came to great rocky boulders, with smaller slabs between them, over which, suppressing their curses, they slipped and slithered, as they dared not show a torch, and among the piles of big rocks the darkness was absolutely pitch. The tangle of stone sloped gently upwards for about a quarter of a mile, then it became interspersed with patches of rough sandy soil. The stars were now hidden by clouds, so there was no longer sufficient light to keep the great pile of rock in the centre of the island constantly in view. For some minutes they lost their way, curving off to the left-hand side of it; but finding that the ground sloped down again they turned and headed in a new direction. This brought them to still higher ground, and soon afterwards they stumbled into a small cultivated patch.

The clouds parted for a moment and to their relief they could now just make out the ruins of the old castle. It was on the landward side of the biggest mass of rocks, but in the old days the top of its single tower would have given a sentinel an uninterrupted view over the whole bay and far out to sea. To one side of the tower a biggish portion of the ruin had a sloping roof, and this was evidently the part that Henri Denoual had patched up to make a home for himself.

As they moved silently towards it the clouds closed again, but they now caught the faint sounds of music. Approaching a little farther, they paused to listen. Evidently Denoual, or one of his family, was no mean artist, as the music was a violin solo. Going forward again, they moved round a corner of the high stone wall and saw some thin streaks of light showing the position of the door.

The ever-cautious Gregory got out his automatic and turned back the safety-catch; then, with a muttered, 'Well, here goes!' he knocked.

The violin solo ceased abruptly. There was a shuffling of feet; the door was suddenly flung wide open. The place consisted of a lofty barn, but, temporarily dazzled by the brightness of the light, they could not see any details. Gregory only knew that his dark forebodings had been justified. The room was packed with German soldiers.

8

Henri Denoual's Island

The faculty to which Gregory had owed his life on a score of occasions was not physical strength, although his lean body was as tough as whipcord, nor was it any remarkable degree of brain-power, although he was moderately well-equipped in that direction. It was much more his capacity for extraordinarily clear thinking and ability to form instant decisions.

They had walked slap into a trap. Evidently Henri Denoual had been found out by either the Gestapo or the Military Intelligence of the German coastal garrisons. It could not be coincidence that this lonely ruin, which he had converted into a home, was full of enemy troops. The island was a small one, and had there been either gun positions or searchlights mounted upon it the discipline of the German Army was far too good for these men to have left them entirely unmanned or protected by sentries. The night was still, with no sound but a quiet sea murmuring gently on the beaches. Had there been enemy emplacements anywhere among the rocks, he and Kuporovitch could hardly have failed to catch the sound of the voices or footsteps of the men on duty at them. He felt certain that the island was absolutely deserted except for the soldiers in the barn.

Therefore it could not be that Henri Denoual's ruin had simply been taken over, and these troops were employed upon ordinary coast defence duties. It *must* be that the Germans had discovered that the place was being used as a rendezvous for secret agents and had put a squad of men into it to lie doggo there each night and arrest anybody who might arrive to see Denoual.

113

It followed that it would be quite useless for the midnight visitors to try to pass themselves off as old friends of Denoual's who did not know that he no longer lived there and had come to pay him a casual call, or to pretend that they were amateur fishermen whose boat had struck a rock and sunk in the shallows, casting them upon the island. No story of that kind, however plausible, would secure their release, now that they had blundered into these Germans. They could only be there for the purpose of arresting anyone who came to the place and passing them straight on to the Gestapo.

In less time than it takes to flick on a cigarette lighter Gregory had sized up the situation and faced the fact that their only chance of escape lay in shooting their way out. Kuporovitch was some paces behind him, so there was at least a chance he might get away in the darkness.

With a shout of 'Run, Stefan, run!' he thrust forward the automatic he had been holding behind his back. As he squeezed the trigger the gun spurted with flame, and the roar of its shots shattered the midnight stillness.

The glare from the open doorway still dazzled Gregory, so he was unable to take deliberate aim. He fired into the centre of the little crowd of grey-green uniformed men who had come hurriedly to their feet as the door was flung open. One man screamed, another fell with a heavy thud; the rest scattered in confusion. But Gregory himself, standing right in the middle of the doorway, was an easy target. Some of the men had already grabbed up their weapons. A pistol cracked, and a bullet flew past his ear. Next second someone hurled a heavy three-legged stool at him. It caught him full in the chest, and he went over backwards, his pistol flying from his hand.

Yelling to his men to follow him, a young *Leutnant* flung himself through the doorway at the fallen Gregory; but Kuporovitch was not the man to leave a comrade in distress. Instead of taking advantage of Gregory's warning shout to run off into the darkness, he had swiftly side-stepped out of the lane of light streaming from the open door and drawn his gun—ready for action.

As the *Leutnant* leapt Kuporovitch fired. His bullet took

the German slap between the eyes, and he was already dead when he fell on top of Gregory. A second man sprang through the doorway, but Kuporovitch got him too with a bullet through the side of the neck, which tore open his jugular vein. Even as he clawed at the wound his life-blood was pouring from it.

The heavy casualties they had suffered in this very first minute of the fracas made the remaining Germans more cautious, and as Gregory struggled out from underneath the dead *Leutnant* he saw that the doorway was now empty. All the others had taken temporary cover behind the thick walls at its sides; but he knew that at any second they might start to fire blind at an oblique angle through it, and he was too old a hand to risk death from a stray bullet. Instead of getting to his feet, he turned over on his tummy and began to wriggle swiftly away. It was just as well that he had adopted these tactics, as he had hardly covered a couple of yards before the barrels of two tommy-guns were thrust out, one from each side of the door. With a hideous clatter they sent streams of bullets in a lateral spray waist-high across the open ground.

Fortunately, Kuporovitch had already gone down on one knee, and the second the guns opened he flung himself flat. He had barely done so when Gregory reached him. Side by side, still on their tummies, they began to wriggle backwards away from the open door as quickly as they could. They had covered some thirty yards when a head appeared round one side of the door brightly silhouetted against the light, Kuporovitch paused for a moment, rested his elbow on the ground, took careful aim, and fired. There was a loud clang as his bullet struck the German's tin hat, and the head was instantly withdrawn.

The Russian cursed softly, but Gregory whispered: 'Don't grumble! you've done damn' well so far. I thought my number was up just before you killed that *Leutnant*. Even one on the battle bowler will be enough to make that fellow keep his head in for a bit and gives us more time to get away.'

As he was speaking they had resumed their backward progress, and soon afterwards they were sufficiently far out of the line of the door to get to their feet and run for it. Instinctively they headed seaward, and a few minutes later pulled up, stumbling and panting, among the tangle of big boulders which fringed the sandy beach.

Immediately after landing them the launch had turned and headed straight out to sea on its way back to England. It had taken them a good quarter of an hour to find the ruined castle and another five or six minutes had elapsed since. In that time the powerful engines of the launch would have carried it seven or eight miles upon its homeward journey, and it must have already been too far out when the shooting started for Lieutenant Cummings and his men to have heard the sound of the shots; so both the fugitives realized that there was no hope at all of escape that way.

'We'll have to swim for it,' muttered Gregory. 'That's our only chance, but the mainland can't be much more than a mile distant.'

'You're right,' Kuporovitch grunted. 'Go ahead, my friend, and good luck to you. Unfortunately, I can't swim, but I'll cover your retreat and kill a few more of these lice before they get me.'

'If you can't swim we're staying here,' said Gregory firmly. 'I'm not going to leave you to be butchered.'

'No, no!' the Russian protested. 'What is the sense of our both being killed or captured? Besides, it's much more important that you should get away than myself. It is you that Lacroix wishes to see in Paris, not me, and great things may hang upon your meeting.'

'Maybe they do,' Gregory's voice was surly. 'All the same, I'm not going without you. But listen! I'm a pretty strong swimmer. If you lie flat on your back and keep dead still I reckon I could get you across. How about it?'

Kuporovitch shook his head. 'No, my friend. If the channel were only a few hundred feet that might be possible, but it is a mile or more. I weigh sixteen stone, and we should be as hopeless as new-born children if we landed naked on the other side, so there is also the weight of our clothes, weapons and ammunition. You could not possibly tow such a weight all that distance.'

Gregory knew that his friend was right. The effect would be too much for him and one or both of them would drown half-way across.

'All right, then,' he said. 'We'll stay here. If you remember, Lacroix told you that the sea runs right out, and that people can walk dryshod from this island to the mainland when the water's low. With luck we may be able to hide among the rocks until the tide goes out.'

'True. So there's still a good chance that I shall be able to evade capture. That's all the more reason you should make certain of your escape by swimming the channel now. Gregory, I beg of you to do so. Somehow or other I will manage to join you later on.'

'That's no good. We should never find each other. But as it was high tide at eleven-thirty the tide will be full out by half past five. It will still be dark, as dawn is not till six-thirty, and the moon's already well down on the horizon. We'll stick it out together, Stefan, and slip away as soon as the water's fallen far enough for us to wade across. We should be able to make a start round about half past four.'

'All right, then, if you insist; but for the next four hours it looks as though we shall have a pretty game of hide-and-seek between these rocks.'

Gregory laughed softly, but there was little humour in the sound.

'Hide-and-seek with death, eh? How're you off for ammunition?'

'So far I've only used one clip and I started out with a hundred rounds.'

'Let me know if you run low, and I'll pass you over my shells. My big gun was knocked out of my hand when I fell; so I've only got the little fellow that I carry strapped under my armpit. Still, it's pretty deadly at short range.'

As they whispered together they kept their ears and eyes alert for signs of the enemy. Now that they were back again on the seaward side of the old ruin they could no longer see the light coming from its doorway; but evidently the Germans had plucked up the courage to leave the building, as they could be heard calling to one another in the distance.

Suddenly a bright finger of light pierced the darkness a quarter of a mile away, then another flashed out, and the two swept backwards and forwards over a wide arc, meeting

117

in its centre. The Germans were using portable searchlights to try to locate their attackers.

For a good half-hour Gregory and Stefan crouched among the tangle of rocks, while the Germans moved up and down the south and east coasts of the island, which were nearest to the land.

Now and again the long beams travelled swiftly over the gently heaving water, and Gregory had cause to thank his stars that his decision to remain with his friend had caused him to abandon any idea of swimming to the mainland; the searchlights would almost certainly have picked him up and, without the least chance of retaliation, he would have proved an easy target for the enemy.

Gradually the searchlights grew nearer and began to flicker over the boulders towards the northern end of the island. Evidently the Germans were satisfied that they would have spotted the fugitives had they taken to the water and felt certain that they must still be hiding somewhere on the island.

The golden rays flickered on the big piles of stone, throwing them up with glowing brightness, but here and there patches of shadow still remained, made blacker by the contrast. Even in the glare of the lights there would have remained a score of safe hiding-places in each square hundred yards of rocks but for the fact that the Germans were using their searchlights with considerable skill. Every few moments the lights were switched off, the men who were carrying them moved several hundred feet, then switched them on again from a new position; in consequence, the two friends never knew from which direction the beams would suddenly flash out next.

With growing anxiety they decided to move round to the west side of the island, and crawling forward cautiously on hands and knees they covered about a quarter of a mile, while the searchlights slowly probed the black patches between the boulders at their rear, and the methodical Germans called encouragement to one another.

The game of hide-and-seek had been on for over an hour when, to their perturbation, Gregory and Kuporovitch found that half-way along the west beach the rocks abruptly ceased, giving place to an open stretch of bare shelving sand. They wriggled forward for some way across it, hoping to find another cluster of great boulders; but having covered about a hundred yards they could see no indication of rocks ahead and began to fear that they would be caught out there in the open. Halting, they held a whispered consultation, decided that it was less risky to return, and swiftly snaked their way back to their former cover.

Another twenty minutes passed, then the unhurried but devilishly systematic search-party began to approach the edge of the rocky belt in which the fugitives were now concealed. After that, they knelt in a little gully, their guns in their hands, and so tense with suspense that they hardly dared to breathe.

Both of them felt there was still a good chance that they might continue to escape observation and that the Germans would turn back when they reached the open sand to try the rocks on the south and east of the island again, or perhaps give up altogether in the belief that their attackers must, after all, have managed to swim away before it had been possible to get the searchlights going. Yet the strain was grim. At any moment now one of those ever-seeking fingers of light might catch and hold them; then, within an instant, they would be fighting for their lives.

The Germans were still calling to each other, and from their shout Gregory gathered that several of the men were browned-off. They were grumbling that further search was now useless, and they wanted to turn in to get some sleep, but a harsh-voiced *Unteroffizier*, who was evidently in charge, kept cursing them and spurring them on to continue their efforts. He damned them for fools and bitterly reminded them that if they failed to account for the two spies everybody concerned would get hell pasted out of them by the High Command at Dinan when he reported the affair, which could not possibly be concealed, owing to the casualities they had already sustained.

Suddenly one of the beams flashed out only some twenty feet from where Gregory and Kuporovitch were lying flat on their faces between two great slabs of stone. The light was held high and it swept lengthways right through the tiny canyon. In an attempt to evade it they scuffled swiftly forward round the corner of a rock, but a loud shout from the man who was directing the searchlight told them that they had been discovered. Instantly the other light was also directed on the area in which they were lurking, and the Germans, who from their shouting appeared to be ten or twelve in number, rapidly closed in; but the game was not yet played out.

In their new position the fugitives were again in a black gulf of shadow, and now they both came to their feet, guns in hand, to peer over the rocky ledge. Kuporovitch's big pistol cracked. There was a yelp from the man who held the nearest light, and it disappeared as he stumbled and fell.

The second that Kuporovitch fired the Germans began shooting from all directions at the flash of his pistol, but he and Gregory had ducked down again, and the bullets spattered harmlessly among the rocks.

'Well done!' Gregory exclaimed. 'If only we can shoot out both their lights we'll get out of this fix yet.'

But unfortunately, although Kuporovitch had aimed for the light, he had only hit the man; so it was not smashed but had fallen on the ground, from which it was swiftly retrieved by one of the fellow's comrades, who began waving it wildly back and forth across the rocks behind which the fugitives crouched.

As the firing subsided Gregory poked up his head again and sent three bullets cracking in the direction of the second searchlight, but the pistol he was now using was too small for accurate range at such a distance. The only effect of his shots was to bring another burst of fire from tommy-guns and pistols.

Next moment he caught a slithering noise upon the stones behind him. Swivelling round he was just in time to see a dark form scrambling over the nearest boulder. His little gun spat again. The German gave a whimpering moan and collapsed almost at his feet.

Knowing that a wounded German can be very nearly as dangerous as an unwounded one, Gregory leapt upon the man. Grabbing him with the left hand round the throat he clubbed his little pistol in his right and brought it down with all his force on the fellow's skull.

It was just as well, as the man was still grasping an

automatic rifle, and had he been left there at such close range he would certainly have succeeded in putting a dozen bullets into their backs. Dragging the rifle from the man's now limp hands, Gregory cautiously stood up and let fly with it at the searchlight nearest to him. It suddenly went out, and a scream of pain told him that he had also got its bearer.

Bullets were now spattering all round him, but disregarding them for a moment he swivelled the rifle towards the other light. He was just too late. A shouted order from the N.C.O. came even as he turned, and the light was switched off before he could draw a bead on it.

The firing petered out. For the next few moments there was a sinister silence. Gregory and Kuporovitch crouched back and back, straining their eyes into the darkness, and expecting at any instant that they would have to face a mass attack from the whole force of their enemies. It did not mature. Twice they thought they saw moving shadows and fired their pistols, but with no result. Then there came a sharp whizzing noise in the air, and something fell with a clang and a faint plop within a few feet of them. Both of them caught their breath. They felt certain that the Germans, having come to the conclusion that to take them alive would prove too costly, had now decided to blow them to bits with hand-grenades.

The moon had set and the banks of heavy cloud had rolled away. Overhead the stars were shining in an almost clear sky, but in the crevices between the great tangle of stones it was impossible even to see a white hand stretched out before one's face, much less to locate the small bomb that had fallen in their immediate neighbourhood. Throwing themselves flat on their faces again, they could only pray that it was not actually in the gully which they occupied, and that when it exploded the great boulders on either side of them would protect them from its jagged fragments.

In fearful suspense they waited there, each instinctively counting the seconds as they dragged by; but no explosion came. Instead, another missile hurtled over and bounced from rock to rock before coming to rest in their vicinity. A third and a fourth landed near by. A full minute had passed, yet the first had still not exploded. Perhaps it was a dud, but even if it were the second should have gone off with a blinding flash and deafening roar before this. Kuporovitch could feel a small pulse throbbing swiftly in his forehead and Gregory held his breath until his lungs were almost bursting.

At the same moment they suddenly became conscious of the same thing. Their eyes were beginning to water and smart. Both being old soldiers, the truth flashed upon them. The missiles that had clattered upon the rocks were not hand-grenades filled with high-explosive, but small canisters containing tear-gas.

Within another few seconds their eyes were irritating so much that it needed an intense effort of control not to rub them. As lachrymatory gas is much heavier than air, and they had been lying at full length, they had already caught the worst effects of it. With rage in their hearts they knew now that nothing but immediate treatment could save them from temporary blindness. The filthy stuff was prickling on their shaven skins. Although they shut their mouths they had to breathe, and as they stumbled to their knees they drew in great breaths of it through their nostrils, which caused them to sneeze and cough violently.

They were weeping now as copiously as bitterly wronged children. Tears streamed down their faces, and, try as they would, they simply could not keep their eyes open to see what was happening round them. Even when the remaining search-light flashed out again they were only conscious of it as a blur of light pouring down upon them. A moment later they caught the sound of heavy metal-shot boots clinking upon the smaller stones. Both of them began to fire wildly, but strong hands grabbed them from behind, and they were forcibly disarmed.

As they were seized by the cursing but triumphant Nazis they could only wonder if they would be handed over to the Gestapo, or if their captors meant to butcher them at once as a reprisal for the Germans that they had killed that night.

9

Hitler Youth at Play

The doubts of Gregory and Stefan as to the treatment they were likely to receive from their captors were soon resolved; within five minutes both of them had made up their minds that they would never live to see another dawn.

They were still blinded by the tear-gas, which rendered them incapable of even dodging the blows aimed at them, and the men who had caught them were in a most evil mood. Nearly half their original number had been either killed or injured, and they were obviously determined to take full vengeance on the two spies who had led them such a bloody dance.

The two were cuffed, kicked and beaten by the cursing Germans, who now set upon them from all sides, and they would certainly have had their brains battered out on the rocks there and then had not the N.C.O. exercised all his authority to restrain his men; not with any thought of mercy, but, as he kept bawling to them, because the night was still young and they'd be fools to deprive themselves in a few minutes of the material for hours of good sport. Gradually, the violent manhandling to which the prisoners had at first been subjected lessened, as the N.C.O. succeeded in restoring some sort of order. In a rasping voice he then decreed that they should be frog-marched up to the castle.

How they survived the ordeal neither of them afterwards knew. With their arms straining in their sockets from the weight of their bodies, so that it seemed they must be dragged out, they were bumped and hauled, first across the smooth sand, then over the rough higher ground up to the centre of the island. They could not protect their faces, which were constantly scraped and cut against stones or lumps of earth and by the coarse grass. That hideous progress seemed unending, and, stout-hearted as they were, both of them were screaming for mercy before it was over.

At last they were thrown, bruised, battered and bleeding, on the wooden floor of the big room that Henri Denoual had patched up into a home for himself. For a time they lay there groaning, too far gone now to respond to fresh kicks from the jeering Germans grouped round them. Even these sweet-natured and highly cultured products of the Hitler Youth Organization found that they could get no more fun out of their victims for the moment, so turned away to tend their own hurts and cleanse their weapons.

The effects of the tear-gas were now wearing off, and through a mist of pain Gregory found that with his left eye, which was close to the floor, he could see a little. The other was swollen and fast shut from a savage blow he had received upon it. He dared not move from fear that at the least sign of consciousness these paladins of the New Order would set on him again with their hobnailed boots. All he could see as he lay there was one of Stefan's legs, and beyond it the booted feet of two soldiers who were sitting on a long stool.

He had no idea how long he lay like that, but suddenly he let out a gasp of shock and began to splutter violently from someone having pitched a bucketful of cold water right over his aching head. A roar of laughter greeted his wriggles, as he weakly shook the water from his hair and endeavoured to sit up. Next second there was another splash and a loud shout, as Kuporovitch received the second bucketful in his face.

'On your feet, damn you!' yelled the *Unteroffizier*. With an effort Gregory twisted round his head and, while attempting to rise, got his first sight of their principal tormentor. The N.C.O. was one of those big, stupid-looking, fair-haired animals that are so typical of the Prussian manhood.

When scientists wish to classify a skull, recovered from some prehistoric burial-ground, they draw a line from the corner of the eye-socket to the earhole. If the lower half of the skull, as is the case with all apes, is much larger than the top half, it belonged to a member of a primitive and undeveloped race; but if the jaw is small, the cranium large, and there is a bigger mass of bone formation above the line than below it, then it must have belonged to a person well advanced in human evolution and having already attained considerable spiritual and moral qualities. That rule applies with equal force to living men and women, and no amount of lying or bragging will ever conceal the fact that the lack of spiritual and moral qualities in the German race is still plain for all to see from the shape of the typical German head which may be broad and powerful, signifying vigour, determination and animal cunning, but lacks height and mass above the all-important line between the eye and the ear.

Like so many German heads, this N.C.O.'s was potato-shaped, with the smaller end uppermost, which receded, both front and behind, to an ugly rounded point, that bristled with close-cropped fair hair. His eyes were a doll-like china blue. His jaw was powerful and well-formed, but his big face had the pasty appearance acquired from years of a diet in which there is too much starchy food and too little meat.

As Gregory endeavoured to stumble to his feet the Prussian hit him sideways across the face, so that he measured his length on the floor again, and another shout of laughter went up from Hitler's brave little men.

Most of them were youngsters who could not have been much more than children when Hitler came to power. During the whole of their adolescence and young manhood they had been consistently educated into the belief that their country had for generations been the victim of the greedy aggressive older nations, and that in Hitler Germany had at last found a leader who would right her wrongs and lead her to a new prosperity. The only history that they knew had been learned from the Nazi-edited schoolbooks, which had been deliberately falsified to beget in them hatred of other races. They knew nothing at all of peacetime conditions outside their own country and were fully convinced that Germany's poverty was entirely due to the harsh terms which had been inflicted upon her at Versailles.

They had been brought up on the doctrine that Might is Right and that only by each one of them exerting his full brute strength at every opportunity which offered could the balance be redressed and Germany triumph. They had been told that they were the *Herrenvolk*—the Master-Race—but that they were far outnumbered by the non-Aryan peoples, and that only by the exercise of complete ruthlessness against all enemies of their Fuehrer could they hope to win through.

Even before the war many of them had participated in Jew-batings and the horrid brutalities exercised upon prisoners in their own concentration camps. Animals are cruel to each other by instinct, but a really merciless man can be more brutal than any beast.

At best, the higher qualities of the German race are far below those of any other European people. While for four hundred years the other nations were undergoing the civilizing influence of the great Graeco-Roman culture, which brought justice, toleration and security to countless previously barbarous tribes, the German hordes beyond the Rhine remained unconquered. They still lived in their dark forests, making a god of war, treating their women as slaves, and torturing their enemies. Even Christianity did not reach them until many centuries after it had been accepted by the rest of Europe. In consequence, despite their great abilities in the material sphere, the Germans are still at least twenty generations behind the rest of Europe in their moral and spiritual development.

And even such spiritual qualities as these young men might have had had been denied to them by Hitler, who had suppressed all teachings of higher things and, instead, deliberately fostered the brutal lust for domination which is an inalienable characteristic lying dormant in the whole Teuton race. They had been taught that mercy was only a sign of weakness in themselves, which must be rigorously suppressed, and that chivalry was a thing to mock at and to take advantage of whenever it would give them a better chance to trick and defeat their decadent enemies.

In Czechoslovakia, and in Poland, they had had innumerable opportunities to experience the perverted joy of inflicting pain. In Norway, Holland, Belgium and France they had been ordered by their officers to machine-gun refugees, old men, women and children. They had even been ordered to crush their own wounded under the tracks of their tanks, rather than halt the advance. Their hearts had turned to stone within them, and Hitler, their chosen leader, had brought out for all the world to see the real and terrible truth. Now that they were the masters of Europe, and thought that they had no more to fear, they were behaving as the brute beasts that deep down in their cold savage natures they really are.

Kuporovitch had no illusions about them, and while Gregory lay moaning on the floor the Russian stared round him at the ring of soulless jeering faces. There was nothing he could do, no hope of escape, and any attempt to do so would only have been to invite further punishment.

The Prussian sergeant was now bawling something at him, but unlike Gregory, who spoke German like a native, Kuporovitch spoke only Russian, French, and his recently acquired smattering of English: so he did not understand a word.

Suddenly the German kicked him in the stomach, and he went over backwards. With every breath driven out of his body he lay doubled, squirming with agony.

Gregory was ordered to get up again, but he remained lying where he was. Two of the men lugged him to his feet, and the Prussian began to yell at him, asking his name and what he had been doing on the island; but Gregory knew that no answer he could give would save him from what was coming to him, so he feebly shook his head, pretending that he did not understand.

After a moment the sergeant gave up and hit him again with all his might, once in the stomach and again in the face. The body blow was like the kick of a mule and the shock so frightful that Gregory vomited where he stood. The second blow caught him behind the ear and temporarily knocked him out.

More buckets of water were brought and cast over the prisoners until they revived, then the hideous game went on. Even when neither of them could any longer stand alone they were held up by their captors while the Prussian pasted hell out of them, until at last they lapsed into deep unconsciousness, from which neither kicks nor further bucketfuls of water could stir either of them.

When they gradually came to themselves once more they

were still lying on the floor, but they realized that it was morning. Daylight now filled the barn-like room, and only two soldiers were in it. Both sat propped up with their backs against the wall, one either side of the door, and they appeared to be asleep.

Very gingerly, limb by limb, Gregory stretched himself. The pain was agonizing, and he could still see out of only one eye, but he did not think that either of his arms or legs was broken. He was still wet, and very cold. After a little he felt Kuporovitch stirring near him, and turning over he whispered through his blood-caked, thickened lips: 'How goes it, Stefan?'

'All right,' croaked the Russian, 'except for my left ankle. It's broken, I think.'

Gregory began to curse under his breath. It seemed that their captors had never meant to go to the extreme lengths of killing them, so there were probably standing orders that anyone coming to the island should be handed over alive to the Gestapo. He was praying now that before the Gestapo received what was left of him he would manage to get his hands for a few moments on the Prussian sergeant. But he knew that he must not waste his energies in futile wishing, as he might yet need every ounce of strength that he could muster. He remained still then, trying not to think at all, but breathing gently and as regularly as the pain of his battered body would permit.

They had no means of measuring time, but for about an hour they lay there, gradually regaining the use of their faculties. Both silently considered and rejected the thought of escape. They knew that it would have been quite impossible to get through the doorway without rousing the two soldiers, and they were still far too weak to have either put up a fight or run any distance. They could only try to put away from them the unnerving thought that when the sergeant returned he would probably begin to torture them anew, and pray that they might be left alone long enough to regain sufficient strength to attempt their escape later should any reasonable chance offer.

There came the tramp of heavy feet outside. The two soldiers in the doorway roused themselves and stood up. The sergeant stamped into the room followed by two more of his men. Pausing for a moment, he stared down at his prisoners, then gave Kuporovitch a vicious kick.

'Ouch!' grunted the Russian, pulling back his injured leg.

The sergeant aimed a second kick at Gregory, but the latter saw it coming and swiftly wriggled aside.

'So there's still some life in you!' muttered the Prussian morosely. 'If it hadn't been against my orders I'd have wrung both your necks, but the Gestapo wouldn't thank me for handing them a couple of corpses. Up you get, damn you! The boat's here, and I'm taking you over to the mainland.'

As he spoke he turned abruptly away, evidently expecting to be followed, and the two prisoners painfully dragged themselves upright. Owing to his twisted ankle, Stefan could not walk, so Gregory pulled his friend's arm about his shoulders, and as best they could they shuffled out into the morning sunshine.

Although they were still half-dead from the beating they had received, the fresh air did them both good, and for the first fifty yards they felt a vestige of new strength creeping back into their tortured bodies, but they were not permitted to enjoy that for long.

The Germans, now feeling like a little morning sport, began to drive them on at a quicker pace than they could properly manage with Kuporovitch only able to hop along on one foot. From shouts and curses their captors resorted to blows and painful jabs with the long hunting-knives that they carried. The beach was only some half a mile distant, but now as they staggered panting down the slope it seemed as though they would never make it. Twice they fell, provoking gusts of laughter from the licensed murderers in grey-green uniforms; but they stumbled up again, and at last, gasping and perspiring, reached a rowing-boat, which had been lightly beached on the sandy shore.

The sergeant and two of his men got into it, but he waved Gregory back as he was about to help Kuporovitch aboard. To the renewed mirth of the others, he declared that it was not for the German *Herrenvolk* to soil their hands with menial labour when there were members of the slave-races present to do it for them. The two prisoners were to push off the boat.

Kuporovitch leaned against its prow, bearlike and sullen, not understanding what had been said. Gregory understood perfectly well, but pretended not to until he was left no option through the other soldiers who were remaining on the island demonstrating with gestures and more kicks what the prisoners were expected to do. It was no good inviting further chastisement through appearing mulish, so Gregory nerved himself for the effort, and leaning his shoulder against the gunwale of the boat, heaved at it, while Kuporovitch, standing on one foot, leant his weight as well.

The boat was stoutly made and heavy. It would not budge, but the sergeant seemed in no hurry. He and his two companions sat in the boat smoking and grinning, while the other men stood round on the beach, enjoying this edifying spectacle of two exhausted, bloodstained, crippled men panting and sweating as they heaved at the weighty boat.

They would never have managed to launch it but for the fact that the tide was nearly at full again, and the still-rising water took an increasing share of the weight. At last it began to move. 'Come on!' panted Gregory. 'One more effort, Stefan!'

Kuporovitch exerted all his great strength, and the boat slid forward, but as it went, caught off his balance on one foot, he stumbled and fell headlong with a great splash into the shallows, which brought forth a huge shout of laughter.

Wet, bedraggled, and half-fainting, they clambered into the boat and lay there for a moment panting in her bottom; but their ordeal was not yet over. 'Up you get, slaves!' roared the Prussian. 'What do you think you're doing there? It's not for men of the Fuehrer's Army to row scum like you ashore. Get out the oars and put your backs into it!' His men made his meaning plain by thrusting the hafts of the oars towards them.

Dragging themselves up, they slumped on to the thwarts, got the clumsy oars into the rowlocks, and limp, gasping, dripping with perspiration, began to paddle shorewards, while the sergeant roared at them for ever greater efforts. They saw now that it was well over a mile to the mainland, but the Prussian was not steering in that direction. He was holding the boat on a course parallel to the shore.

At first they thought that this was just a fresh devilishness to inflict further suffering upon them, but as the boat progressed they remembered the description which they had been given of Saint Jacut, and that its little harbour lay round the point some distance up the farther creek, which meant that there lay before them an agonizing pull of two miles at least.

Kuporovitch could only exert pressure with one foot, and after pulling for a few moments Gregory knew that two of the fingers of his right hand, which had been numb since he had come round, must be broken. With every move back and forth pain racked their bodies, but the potato-headed gangster in the stern would give them no respite. It seemed that they had been rowing for an age, and that their backs were actually breaking under the strain, when they rounded the headland and entered the wide mouth of the creek.

The boat was hidden now, both from the island and from the little harbour which was still farther round the bend, and owing to their position in the boat, the two wretched galley-slaves could not see that, half a mile ahead of them, the fishing fleet of Saint Jacut, consisting of some six or eight small vessels, had just put to sea and was heading in their direction.

As they laboured on, the sweat now coursing down in rivulets through the caked blood on their swollen faces, they remained quite unaware of the approaching fishing-smacks until the fact of the sergeant altering course twice in rapid succession caused them to look round. They were well in the middle of the channel, but the smacks were spread out right across it, so they would have to pass between two of them. Since they were fairly close together, it seemed that the sergeant could not make up his mind on which side to pass the nearest of the smacks, which was now coming under full sail straight towards them.

A moment later the Prussian began to shout and heave with all his might upon the port tiller-rope. As the nose of the boat swung round Gregory stopped rowing, and straining the sore muscles of his neck once more, again looked over his shoulder. One glance was enough to show him that they were in serious trouble. Two of the heavy smacks appeared to have left their course, and with a full wind in their sails were converging upon the rowing-boat. The nearest was no more than twenty yards distant.

In the bows of both the smacks French fishermen were shouting and gesticulating, but in neither case were they apparently prepared to haul down sail or alter the course of their vessels. The Prussian was now standing in the stern of the boat shaking his fist at the Frenchmen and screaming profanities in German, but his experience with boats was probably small, as he seemed to have no idea of how to get out of the way.

Gregory, who had spent several years of his boyhood as a cadet on H.M.S. *Worcester*, and still retained from those days the rudiments of managing small craft, was extremely puzzled by the seemingly incompetent handling of the two smacks that were bearing down upon them. They had ample room to manoeuvre in, and by putting about their tillers either could easily have sheered off on another tack, yet these Breton fishermen who were most excellent sailors, stood shouting and waving their arms as though they were completely helpless.

Suddenly it flashed into Gregory's tired brain that Henri Denoual's friends among the fisherfolk might know that his place on the island was used at times as a secret rendezvous and had now been taken over by the Germans. Perhaps this was a deliberate attempt at rescue. In any case, it looked now as though a collision was inevitable, and that at least would offer a chance of escape. Letting go one of his oars, he grasped the other with both hands and pulled it in, intending to use the butt as a lance against the Germans.

But they, too, evidently now suspected a plot. While the sergeant, grabbing the tiller-ropes again, frantically endeavoured to steer the boat, which was now rapidly losing way, between the two oncoming smacks, the other two soldiers, half standing up, had drawn their automatics. Kuporovitch, too, was fully alive to the possibilities of this unexpected situation. With a single heave of his great arms he had tossed one of his oars upright and sat there grasping it, but dared not bring it crashing down on any of the men in the stern as they had him covered.

The two German privates were thrown off their balance, and with splendid timing Kuporovitch let go his oar. It came crashing down, catching one of them with a dull thud on the shoulder. He let out a yell of pain, and his pistol dropped from his nerveless fingers.

Recovering himself, the other German fired at Gregory, just as he thrust with the butt of the oar at the fellow's chest. Had he fired a second earlier at that short range Gregory would have been riddled with bullets, but one of the fishermen, seeing his peril, had thrown a rope bumper with excellent aim. It caught the German in the face, his arm jerked upwards, and the spate of bullets from his gun sped harmlessly over Gregory's head.

At that instant there was another rending crash as the second smack rammed the boat on its other side. Crushed now between the two larger vessels, part of its planking was stove in, and it rapidly began to fill with water.

His blue eyes blazing in his pasty face, the Prussian sergeant had been about to launch himself on Gregory, but the second impact sent him sprawling backwards across the tiller between his two comrades. Thrusting them aside, he dragged out his gun, while screaming in one breath that he'd shoot both the prisoners and in the next that he would have every man, woman and child in Saint Jacut executed as a reprisal for this sabotage.

The boat was now sinking under them, stern first, owing to the greater weight of the three Germans who were massed there. Kuporovitch endeavoured to stand up, but his injured ankle gave way, and he fell back with a moan into the bows. Then as the boat tilted its bow was carried upwards, so that two of the fishermen leaning over the side of their smack were able to grasp him by the arms and drag him aboard, just as the boat went down, leaving the others struggling in the water.

In those few violent seconds while the three Germans were all in a heap in the stern of the rapidly filling boat Gregory could easily have scrambled aboard one of the smacks, but he deliberately refrained from taking the chance to make good his escape. His eyes were riveted upon the sergeant. He meant to kill the swine personally, even if he died for it himself.

He was terribly weak and very near collapse from the frightful time he had been through. The Prussian was a much younger man, fresh, taller, armed and as strong as a horse. The odds were terribly uneven, but Gregory had one advantage—a quickness of brain which far outclassed the Prussian's, and an unscrupulousness which even his enemy, try as he might, could not excel.

The German fired twice before he went under. Gregory ducked and both bullets missed. As the boat tilted he stood there, waist-high in the water, grinning fiendishly down upon his enemy. He caught one glimpse of the man's face before it splashed beneath the surface, and the stupid blue eyes were now filled with a horrible animal fear. But Gregory had no thought of mercy, or even that he was most probably throwing his own life away by going in, weak as he was, to a death grapple with his brutish foe. Stretching out his hands, he flung himself forward right on top of the sinking Prussian, and they went under together.

In spite of all the individual acts of stress and violence which had taken place, from the first certainty that a collision could not be prevented to the sinking of the boat had barely occupied two minutes. At one moment Kuporovitch was vainly striving to stand in the raised-up bow of the boat, and the next he was on the deck of one of the smacks propping himself up against its side between two Breton fishermen.

The boat had now gone right under and showed only as a wavy outline below the little lapping crests. Gregory and the sergeant had disappeared; the two other Germans were flapping about in the water. The one whose shoulder Kuporovitch had injured was already in difficulties. Yelling for help, he splashed his way to the side of the smack and thrust up his sound arm to grasp the small anchor which was dangling over the bow of the vessel. One of the fishermen near Kuporovitch grabbed a boathook, pushed it down towards the man, and hooked it into his uniform near the collar.

'*Danke, Danke!*' gasped the German, but his thanks were premature. When the boathook was firmly fixed the fisherman muttered something in patois to his companion. The other swung a mop-handle he was holding over the side and banged the German sharply across the knuckles with it.

134

From hope and relief the young Nazi's face suddenly changed to ungovernable terror. A second hard crack over his fingers forced him to let go of the anchor, then the man with the boathook, instead of hauling it up, thrust it down, forcing the German under the water. For two or three minutes he was held there, while the bubbles of his life's breath caused little eddies upon the surface; then the two fishermen drew him up and threw his drowned body down into the hold as though it had been that of a dead rat.

The other soldier had struck out strongly for the shore, but he was not destined to reach it. The second smack got under way again and gave chase. When it came up to within a few yards of him, one of the fishermen in it cast out a heap of fishing-net, which fell on the German's head and unrolled in the water around him. Next moment he was enmeshed with his feet and arms caught in the clinging net, and unable to strike out freely any longer. For a moment he struggled wildly and almost got free, but another bundle of nets was thrown out, which half-buried him and carried him right under. The fishermen gave him time to drown, then he too was hauled on board, and his limp body flung face down in the hold.

Meanwhile, Kuporovitch was hardly conscious of these things, owing to his acute anxiety for Gregory. It now seemed an age since the boat had sunk, yet neither he nor the Prussian had so far come to the surface.

As Gregory went under he knew that he had not the strength to strangle his powerful opponent, and he did not mean to be dragged down with him if he could help it. With his left hand which was still sound, he grasped the sergeant by the collar, then he straightened his right thumb and with all his force plunged it into the brute's left eye.

There was no scream, since by that time they were both a good six feet under the water, but he felt the violent jerk of the Prussian's body, and the great hand that was clutching at his shoulder suddenly lost its grip.

For a full minute Gregory thrust and thrust with all the power of his strong right arm and rigid thumb, while they went down, down, down together, the Prussian squirming under him. Then there was a bump, as the man's back hit the

135

bottom. Had the water been deeper Gregory would have been able to get away, but his own impetus carried him forward right into the arms of his now stationary enemy.

Although two of the fingers of Gregory's right hand were useless, his instinct was to withdraw it, as his enemy's arms closed about his body in a deadly hug. In another second he had realized that his one chance of escape now lay in paralysing his enemy before his own lungs burst, and that the only way for him to do that was to get the point of his thumb right into the Prussian's brain. With maniacal force, and knowing that his life depended on it, he thrust and thrust again.

Suddenly the man's arms relaxed, slipping sideways from Gregory's shoulders, and he was free. Pushing the corpse from under him, he stood up and, cleaving the water with his arms, strove to rise to the surface. It was only then that he became conscious of a new peril. His feet and legs were nearly buried up to the knees in the mud at the bottom of the creek.

The deep breath that he had taken before going down after his adversary was now used up. His lungs were straining for fresh oxygen, but, flail his arms as he would, he could not jerk himself free from the clinging slime. For a moment he struggled violently, straining every muscle, but without result. Then he knew that he was trapped and must die there.

10

The Enemies of Antichrist

For a few seconds Gregory went dead-still, gathering all his remaining force together for one last effort. In his early struggles to free himself he had dragged first at one foot, then at the other; but as one had come up a little the other had only gone down farther into the clinging ooze. Fighting off his panic, he strove to think clearly, knowing now that his strength could not save him, but his wits still might. Almost instantly it came to him that if only he could get one foot out and place it on the dead German's body he might be able to drag the other free.

Exerting his overstrained muscles to their uttermost and flinging his body sideways, he strove to wrench out his right foot, but the slime seemed a living thing, with the grip of a giant octopus. With despair creeping into his heart he knew that his strength was ebbing and that his effort had failed.

His lungs were bursting. He could no longer control his jaws. A big bubble came out of his mouth, and the muddy water gushed down his throat.

He had always heard that drowning was a pleasant death, but had no cause to think it so. The water brought no relief, and the pains in his chest were more agonizing than ever. It was too late now to curse his own folly in preferring personal vengeance upon this brutish lout, who lay dead in the slime beside him, to life and all the glorious things it offered. The game was up. He would never again know the joy of Erika's caresses, the thrill of a new adventure, the feel of a hot bath and a comfortable bed after a long hard journey, or the cool richness of a beaker of iced champagne. He was going to die there for the pleasure of having killed a stupid oaf and make food for fishes on the bottom of a little creek which was no more then twelve feet deep.

At that thought his wildly whirling brain conceived the notion that the Breton fishermen had seen him go in and that when he did not come up would try to find him; but in a flash he knew that such a thought was only the wildest of wishful thinking. They would find him all right when the tide went out, but the water was too cloudy for them to see him standing there, and they might drag the creek with anchors and grappling irons for hours before there was any chance of one of them catching in his clothes; by then he would long since be drowned past all resuscitation.

Although his lungs were rapidly filling with water he began to fight again, yet weakly now, and his efforts to free himself were no longer controlled, but just the spasmodic jerkings of a desperate dying man. It was dark down there, but through the turgid water he saw what seemed to be a darker patch slowly weaving its way towards him. The pain in his chest became unendurable, his head was splitting, stars whirled before his eyes, then blackness engulfed him, and he lost consciousness.

Up on the deck of the fishing-smack Kuporovitch was half-crazy with anxiety. He knew that Gregory in his weakened state was no match for the hefty Prussian, and as neither of them had come up to the suface felt certain now that they must be locked in a death-grapple on the bottom. As soon as the two Bretons with the boathook had dealt with the German soldier who had tried to climb aboard, he gabbled out to them his desperate fears for his friend, and the younger of the two took a header over the side to see if he could find the missing Englishman.

After a minute he came up gasping, dived again, came up again, swam back a little nearer to the place from which the smack had drifted, and went down twice more; but his efforts proved unavailing. He shouted that the water was so dark and muddy near the bottom that he could not see more than a yard in any direction.

In the meantime, Kuporovitch had kept one eye on the other smack which was pursuing the unwounded German. He saw the fishermen cast out two bundles of nets which enmeshed the swimmer, causing him to sink and drown. He saw them haul in the first net and pull up the drowned man's body; then they began to heave in the second net. That too was taut from a weight that dragged it down, and suddenly a second body appeared on the surface.

It was the trailing-net which Gregory had seen coming towards him as a dark patch through the murk. Even as his consciousness was leaving him it had wrapped round his body, while he instinctively thrust his fingers through the spaces, clutching at it with the fierceness of a dying man. His unconscious grip had held, and the way of the heavy boat going under sail through the water above had wrenched him from the muddy death-trap.

As soon as the two boats could be brought together Kuporovitch boarded the second. The men had just cut Gregory clear of the net, and he lay there on the deck—a loose sodden heap, with water slowly trickling from his mouth. One of the bronzed Bretons, a tall bearded man, who appeared to be their captain, was examining him. He said that he looked pretty far gone, but they would do their very best for him, and turning him over on his stomach they set to work to give him artificial respiration.

For a long time Kuporovitch sat there on a coil of rope while the fishermen worked on Gregory in relays. He was still far too anxious to know whether life could be restored to his friend to bother about future plans, but the bearded captain gave him an outline of what they proposed to do.

The gravest penalties for all concerned in the sabotaging of the Germans could only be escaped if the affair was represented as a genuine accident. Therefore it must be reported at once. It was for this reason too that they had been careful not to disfigure the two German soldiers while they were in the water. Their drowned bodies were being sent back by one of the smacks to be landed with deep expressions of regret and handed over to the mayor of the commune until the German authorities could collect them. In the meantime, the rest of the fleet would proceed to sea, so that no one on shore should see the escaped captives; they could be landed when the fleet returned that night, and darkness would give them good cover.

It was over an hour before the men working on Gregory could report that they had some real hopes for him, but his heart was strong, and soon after they announced that it was now only a matter of sticking to the job until they got him round. At last his eyes opened, and delighted Stefan was able to kneel down and give him a bearlike hug.

Now that he knew Gregory would live the Russian became acutely conscious again of his own hurts and extreme fatigue, which in his great anxiety for his friend he had almost forgotten. Gregory was carried below to be wrapped in hot blankets, and Kuporovitch was helped down after him. The fishermen made up two bunks, a steaming mug of cognac toddy was brought to each of them, and no sooner had they swallowed it than they fell into the deep sleep of utter exhaustion.

When they were roused it was night again. At first they were so stiff and ached so badly in all their limbs that they could hardly move, but the fishermen gave them another go of hot toddy, then helped them to dress and up on to the deck, where Gregory had his first chance of expressing his thanks to their captain and his concern that the Germans would take swift reprisals on account of the rescue.

The bearded Breton smiled in the starlight. 'That is a risk we must take, but I don't think you need worry overmuch. Our greatest danger was that one of the Boches might escape to give a true account of what happened; but all three of them are dead, so there is no one to contradict our story, which will be that they handled their boat badly and that its sinking was entirely an accident. The two bodies, which were landed at mid-day, bore no marks of violence, and by the time the third is recovered it will probably be hardly recognizable.'

'But what about us?' Gregory hazarded. 'They're certain to want to know what happened to their prisoners.'

'As far as we are aware, you were both drowned too. The currents in the creek are tricky, and, as you know yourself, it's very easy for a man who goes under to get bogged in the mud at its bottom. Out of a boatload of five there's nothing very remarkable in the fact that only two bodies should have been recovered.'

'They'll think it odd, though, that not one of the five was rescued or managed to swim ashore.'

'Yes, I fear they may, but as they cannot possibly prove anything it will be difficult for them to formulate a charge against us. At all events, that is a risk that I and my friends take willingly for the pleasure of having snatched two of Henri Denoual's friends out of the clutches of these swine.'

'What happened to Denoual?' Gregory asked.

'They arrested him when they first came to the island about ten days ago. I saw him when they brought him ashore, and the fiends had beaten him even worse than they beat you. His poor face was almost unrecognizable, and one of his arms was broken, but his torment was not over, as word reached us that they had taken him into Dinan and handed him over to the Gestapo.'

'You know the work upon which he was engaged?'

'Yes. A number of us used to help him in it by smuggling his visitors ashore at night and taking them to the old farmhouse where we are going to send you.'

'How did you learn that they had caught us?' Kuporovitch enquired.

The brown-faced Breton smiled again. 'We saw the lights and heard the shooting on the island when we were out fishing last night, so we knew that somebody must have fallen into the trap. This morning I arranged with my friends that we should have our little fleet standing out in the creek all ready to intercept their boat when they came ashore, if they had any prisoners in it.'

As they had been talking the smack had been nearing the land under a gentle breeze, and now the sail was lowered, bringing her to rest in a small bay. A rowing-boat, which she had been trailing behind her stern, was pulled up alongside. Having thanked the captain and his crew from the bottom of their hearts, Gregory and Kuporovitch got into the boat with two of the fishermen, who rowed them ashore. On reaching the beach one of the Bretons remained with the boat while the other showed them the way to a steep track which led upwards through the darkness.

The going was slow, as Kuporovitch could not put any weight on his left foot, but the other two supported him. After ten minutes' climb they reached flat, grassy ground on the top of the cliff, and turning east a little, headed inland,

It took them over half an hour to cover about a mile, but they then struck a winding single-track road, and having made their way along it for a further five minutes they reached a lonely coppice, at the side of which a big hay-wagon could be vaguely seen in the starlight.

Their guide and a farm hand who was with the wagon exchanged a few brief sentences in Breton patois; then the fisherman handed over his charges, wished them luck and left them to return to his boat.

The farm hand pulled aside some of the hay in the back of the wagon and showed his two passengers a large hole that had been hollowed out at the bottom of the great sweet-smelling mound of fodder, all ready for them. When they had crawled into it, feet first, he covered the entrance with enough hay to conceal them, but lightly packed so that they could get sufficient air to breathe through it. Then he climbed up on to the seat of his wagon, and set off at a slow but steady pace down the hill.

Enough hay had been left on the floor of the wagon to make a comfortable couch, and although Gregory and Stefan had slept all through the afternoon and evening they were still far from recovered from their terrible ordeal of the preceding night. The gentle jolting of the wagon proved soothing rather than irritating, so after it had covered a mile or two they both dropped off to sleep.

They were wakened by its halting with a slight jerk, and for a moment they wondered where they were. Then, as memory flooded back to them, anxiety came with it as they heard a guttural German voice and guessed that the wagon had been pulled up at some control-post, where any rigorous examination must result in their discovery.

During the next few moments they remained very still, not daring to move a muscle. The scent of the hay gave Kuporovitch an almost uncontrollable desire to sneeze, but he managed to suppress it. After what seemed an interminable time, but was actually no more than sufficient for a few questions and answers between the German sentry and the farm hand, the wagon-wheels creaked, and they moved on again.

For a further three-quarters of an hour they lay, rocking

gently in the close, scented darkness, then the wagon halted once more; but this time they heard a cheerful shout from the wagoner, which was answered by other genial French voices. The screen of hay was pulled aside, and they saw that it was still full night, but a big red-faced man in corduroys was standing there holding a lantern, so that they could see to scramble out.

The red-faced man was accompanied by a plump apple-cheeked woman and a lad of about sixteen. They were evidently farm people, and as Gregory's eyes got accustomed to the light he saw that the wagon had pulled up in a farm-yard, three sides of which were enclosed by house and barns. The farmer introduced himself as Jacques Queraille and, with the wagoner helping Kuporovitch, led them over to one of the farm buildings. The lower part of it was a big barn, but the upper part, which they reached by a steep wooden stair-way, proved to be an apple-loft, where the year's crop was in process of being sorted, the larger fruit to be sent into market and the smaller to be made into rich red Brittany cider.

On both sides of the loft there were long tiers of what looked like shallow bunks, made of wire-netting, supported on frames of wood. It was on these that the apples had been laid out to dry, and in several places the bunk-like wire shelves were screened by pieces of sacking.

Mère Queraille exclaimed in horror when she got a proper sight of the battered faces of her two guests, which were still caked in dried blood, and she hurried off with her son to fetch basins of hot water and bandages. Meanwhile, her husband produced straw palliasses, coarse pillows and blankets from a small room at one end of the loft, and, pulling aside some of the sacking screen, proceeded to make up two beds on the wire-netting.

On Mère Querailles's return the painful business of treating the injuries began. Like most good farmers, Queraille knew something of anatomy from his experience with animals, and, having examined Kuporovitch's ankle, he declared that it was not broken but badly sprained. Cold compresses were put on the swelling, and it was tightly strapped up: Gregory's fingers were set and bound in splints, their other cuts and

143

abrasions were bathed, cleaned and bandaged, then they stretched themselves out on two of the wire shelves. The sacking screens were replaced, so that no one casually entering the loft would have any idea that two men were sleeping there, and the Queraille family wished them good-night.

Their sleep in the hay-wagon had been quite a short one, so they were ready enough for more, and very soon dropped off again, not to wake until full light of morning was filtering in on them through the screens of sacking.

As soon as they wakened they began to take a fresh stock of their injuries and found that they were in exceedingly poor shape. Apart from Gregory's fingers and Stefan's ankle, the faces of both of them were terribly cut and swollen, and they had the most hideous purple bruises on a dozen different parts of their bodies. They knew that they were very lucky to be alive at all, but even so it annoyed them to think that for some days at least they would be fit for nothing. To move at all was torture, and both of them were running temperatures.

They were still commiserating with each other when they heard footsteps on the wooden stairs, and peeping from behind their screens saw that it was Madame Queraille who had come to visit them. She was carrying a heavy tray with a steaming breakfast, but neither of them felt very much like food at the moment, although it was now many hours since they had eaten.

When they told her how wretched they felt she redressed their hurts and left them there in the restful semi-darkness of the loft to doze or sleep again.

In the afternoon she returned with some hot broth and a fat, shrewd-faced Roman Catholic priest, who introduced himself as Father Xavier. While they were sipping the broth he told them that he had heard about the frightful manhandling they had received and their subsequent rescue, and he congratulated them upon having got away with their lives. He then asked if they were willing to tell him their reason for landing in France.

Kuporovitch said: 'We both have a special devotion to Saint Denis, Father, and wish to kneel again before his shrine in Paris.'

144

'I thought that might be the case,' smiled Father Xavier, 'but it was possible that you had private reasons for landing on Henri Denoual's island. I, too, have a special devotion to Saint Denis, so it will be a pleasure for me to make arrangements for your journey.'

'We're very anxious to reach Paris as soon as possible . . .' began Gregory eagerly.

'No doubt, my son, no doubt,' the priest cut him short in a soothing tone, 'but Mère Queraille here tells me that neither of you is fit to travel. With the help of the good God I think that I can get you safely to Paris, but it is only sensible that before you face new exertions you should have regained at least a reasonable degree of your strength. Therefore, for the time being, I have decided you will remain here, where there is little danger of your being discovered, and you can be well looked after.'

He spoke with such quiet firmness that they knew argument was useless. They knew, too, that, anxious as they were to see Lacroix, they would be little use for anything until they had recovered from the worst effects of the mauling they had been through.

Father Xavier went on gently: 'You will stay here for a week at least, but more probably it will be ten days before I consent to your removal. Now, while you remain lying down' we will offer up a short prayer of thanksgiving for your deliverance and for your speedy recovery.'

With Madame Queraille beside him he knelt down on the floor of the loft and for several moments prayed most earnestly for France, for all who served her, and that God might strengthen the hearts and the limbs of all those, wherever they might be, who were striving for freedom from the emissaries of hell who had brought such misery and oppression upon the peoples of Europe.

Having finished, he produced two little holy medals and hung these round the necks of the invalids. Then he left them.

For the next week the two sick men did little but sleep and rest. The jovial but slow-spoken farmer looked in occasionally to see how they were getting on; his wife, who was much more talkative and a dear, motherly soul, brought them plain, well-cooked meals each morning and evening and treated their hurts.

By the eighth day of their stay in the apple-loft all their minor injuries had ceased to trouble them. Gregory could use his fingers again, provided he was careful not to strain them, and only Kuporovitch's ankle remained as a serious handicap to any new activity, although he could now get about quite swiftly with the aid of two sticks. Much as they liked each other's company, both of them were beginning to get distinctly bored with their enforced confinement, and knowing the urgency of the work that there was for them to do they were most anxious to proceed on their journey. It was, therefore, with considerable relief that on the afternoon of the 24th they heard the voice of Father Xavier as he came up the wooden stairs behind Mère Queraille.

He greeted them kindly, examined Kuporovitch's ankle and gave them a good looking-over, immediately after which Gregory asked him if it would be possible for them to be sent on to Paris that night.

The Father said that he would now delay them no longer than necessary, but a couple of days would be required to make adequate arrangements before they could set out.

At first, Kuporovitch had thought that, just as the Little Father of the Vieux Logis had turned out to be Colonel Lacroix, so Father Xavier was another secret agent who was using the cassock as a disguise; but the prayers with which the Father had terminated his first visit had clearly shown that he was actually a Catholic priest. To the Russian it seemed strange that any man who was so deeply religious should concern himself in worldly affairs which at first sight had no bearing on religious matters, and he asked the priest what had caused him to take an active part in the anti-Nazi conspiracy.

Father Xavier looked a little surprised and said: 'For you to ask that, my son, shows that you cannot be fully aware of the evil thing which we are fighting. This war is not like the last, or any of the old wars, where one country fought another only for territorial gain and self-aggrandisement. It is a vast civil war, in which the people of all countries have taken sides and each group is seeking to force an ideology and way of life upon the other group, which is unwilling to accept it.

'In the last war all Frenchmen were for France, all Italians for Italy, and all Germans for Germany—the German clergy, for example, both Catholic and Protestant, were whole-heartedly behind their Government—but that is by no means the case today. The Nazis and the Fascists have started a new religion, in which there is no God but the State. It had already been accepted in peace-time by varying proportions of the population in every country, and now, by force of arms, the Dictators are endeavouring to secure its acceptance throughout the whole world. If they succeed mankind will not only lose their political liberties, but also their right to worship God in the manner of their own choosing. It is not only the Jews that Hitler persecutes, but men of every creed who refuse to bow the knee before him. Should he ever succeed in achieving final victory the reign of Antichrist will ensue. The Nazis' state has no place for Christianity in any form, and if Hitler once became all-powerful he would close every church and chapel in Europe, as he has already closed the synagogues.

'For eight years now German children have been deprived, as far as it lay within the Nazis' power, of proper religious instruction. In a Hitler-dominated world there would be no baptism in the name of God, no confirmation, no Holy Communion, and *Mein Kampf* would be the new Bible. How could I, or any right-thinking priest, remain a pacifist knowing that my faith, and the faith of all Christian men and women, whatever their creed, must die unless Hitler-Antichrist can be destroyed?'

'Of course, you're right, Father,' Gregory agreed; 'but the pity of it is that so comparatively few people seem to realize that. Many of our clergymen at home in England are splendid fellows and have done magnificent work during the air raids; but many more particularly among the higher-ups, don't seem to have the faintest idea yet what we're really up against.'

Father Xavier shook his head sadly. 'I am grieved to hear that. Here, praise be to God, it is very different. Our Breton people have always been stalwart children of the Church, and all of them know that not only their liberty but their Faith is at stake in this hideous conflict. In the whole of Brittany,

147

outside the towns, I'm certain that there's not a single man or woman who would betray you, and when you were rescued by the fishermen of Saint Jacut you must have seen for yourself how gladly they were willing to risk anything for the sake of helping the enemies of Hitler. The people here look to their priests for leadership, and of what use is a priest to his flock in times like these if he does nothing but stand in his church on Sundays to celebrate a few Masses? It is only proper that we should not only comfort the people in their afflictions but use any wits which God may have given us to direct the fight for the overthrow of the legions of Evil.'

'We've been terribly worried about those good fellows at Saint Jacut,' Gregory said. 'I do hope the Germans haven't carried out any reprisals on them.'

'No,' smiled the Father. 'The Good God does not leave those who pray to Him for protection unanswered. There are many drownings at sea in these days, and the morning after your rescue the bodies of two sailors were caught by the fishermen in their nets. They were able to take these ashore and, as they were past recognition, pass them off as the bodies of you two, saying that they had dredged them up from the creek. The Germans were very suspicious about the "accident" and meant to hold a full enquiry, but they had no real evidence, and on the production of these two bodies they decided to consider the affair as closed.'

They talked on with Father Xavier for a little about the war, then, promising to arrange for their journey to Paris as soon as possible, he left them.

Two afternoons later, on Saturday 26th, they were warned by Mère Queraille that they were to leave that night. Soon after dark Father Xavier arrived with a tall, thin, grey-haired woman dressed in a dark blue uniform, whom he introduced as Madame Idlefonse, explaining that while France was in the war she had driven an ambulance for the Army, and that now she still drove her ambulance upon more secret business.

She was a quiet, practical woman, and she told them at once that one of them would have to play the part of the patient and the other of the hospital orderly who would sit inside the ambulance. It was best that whichever of them spoke French the more fluently should act as orderly. That fitted in very well, as Gregory's French was almost good enough for him to pass as a Frenchman, and, since Kuporovitch's ankle was still bound up, he was already equipped for the rôle of patient. Madame Idlefonse provided the one with an orderly's white linen suit and the other with thick flannel pyjamas; then they were left to change.

When they had done so, carrying their own things made up in bundles, they followed the others downstairs. In the barn they all knelt in prayer, and Father Xavier asked a blessing on their journey; then the goodbyes were said, the two friends expressing the deepest possible gratitude to the Querailles for having hidden and taken such good care of them.

It was not until some days later that they learnt that on October the 20th, three days after they had reached the farm, an order had been promulgated throughout the length and breadth of Occupied France that the death penalty would be imposed upon any French subjects found harbouring British nationals; but these stouthearted Bretons had never breathed a word about it lest they might embarrass their guests.

The sky was overcast, and the moon, now a week past full, not yet risen. Kuporovitch was thinking only that with luck he would soon see Madeleine again. Gregory had known Paris in its heyday and he had not seen it since its fall, so his thoughts were a little sombre as the ambulance took the dark road to the dark city.

11

Coffin for One

When they drove out of the farmyard a gentle rain was falling, but Madame Idlefonse kept the ambulance going at a good steady pace in spite of the slush and bad patches which occur every few miles on all French roads. Occasionally they struck long stretches of *pavé* which slowed them down a little, as its bumpy surface played the devil with even a well-sprung vehicle like the ambulance; but, apart from that and stopping every hour or so to smoke a cigarette and stretch her legs, Madame Idlefonse drove on into the night as though she were part of her well-regulated machine. Between twelve and one in the morning she told them through the driver's hatch that they had accomplished half their journey and were running into Alençon.

Just outside the town she drew up at a small all-night café, and, although there was little choice in the refreshments it offered, the hot weak coffee and tough crusty rolls that they secured were very welcome. After half an hour's rest, Madame Idlefonse declared herself ready to resume the journey, and they drove on to Chartres, where they stopped again to fill up with petrol. At half past six in the morning they passed through Versailles, which was just waking to a rainy depressing day, and soon after seven they reached the heart of Paris.

When the ambulance pulled up and Gregory got out he saw that they were in a street that he did not recognize, on both sides of which were old-fashioned, tall, narrow houses. Madame Idlefonse, who still appeared remarkably fresh in spite of the many hours' hard driving she had put in, told him to ring the bell of the house opposite, and the door was opened to him by a pretty girl in nurse's uniform.

Immediately she saw the ambulance she smiled at him and, having asked him to wait a moment, fetched a tall dark young man in a white linen jacket similar to the one which Gregory was wearing. The two of them then went out to carry in Kuporovitch on his stretcher for appearances' sake, although he could have perfectly well got up and walked.

Throwing himself into the part of a stretcher-case, Kuporovitch closed his eyes tightly and lay with his mouth open, feigning unconsciousness. The nurse directed them into a waiting-room on the ground floor, where they transferred him from the stretcher on to a sofa. They took the stretcher back to the ambulance, and with a wave of her hand Madame Idlefonse drove away.

On re-entering the house the tall young man disappeared into the back of the premises, and the nurse asked Gregory to remain in the waiting-room with Kuporovitch while she told the Matron of their arrival.

It was evident that the place was a nursing-home which was being used by Lacroix and his friends for cover, and Gregory mooched idly round the uninspiring room looking casually at the covers of the out-of-date periodicals spread on the table and the rather depressing black and white prints of the Victorian period which hung on the wall. His back was turned to the door when he heard it open. Next second Kuporovitch, who had opened his eyes once they were left alone, gave a huge shout of delight, and swinging round Gregory saw that the Matron was none other than Sister Madeleine.

Springing up from his sofa Kuporovitch seized both her hands in his and kissed them wildly, while with equal surprise and delight she was smiling upon him as though he were a favourite child who had just come back to her after a long absence. Gregory stood grinning in the background, and when the Russian's transports had somewhat subsided he shook hands with his ex-nurse, as he said:

'What a grand surprise to find you at the end of our journey!'

'It's a lovely surprise for me, too,' she laughed. 'I was warned to expect two new "patients" this morning, but I had no idea who they would be.'

'And to think that you are the Matron here!' chuckled Kuporovitch. 'When the nurse went to fetch you I expected to see a brisk, middle-aged lady with grey hair and pince-nez.'

Madeleine laughed again. 'Yes, I'm afraid I'm a bit young for the part; but, you see, this place isn't really a nursing-home, although we run it as much like one as we can. It was Colonel Lacroix's idea, and although he now has quite a number of helpers who can act as nurses and room-maids, he thought it important that the Matron at least should be someone with a professional knowledge of nursing, and I happen to be the only woman available to fill the bill.'

'It was a darn' good idea.' Gregory nodded. 'You can fake all the temperature charts and talk plausibly about the various ailments from which your patients are supposed to be suffering if the police pay the place a visit at any time.'

'That's it,' Madeleine agreed, 'and so far it's worked very well. You see, most of our people do their work at night and need to sleep at least a part of the day in any case, so a nursing-home offers them just the right kind of cover. Ten out of my fifteen rooms are in use now, and nearly every night most of their occupants are out on a job; but in the daytime, if any Quisling paid us a visit, he would find all my "patients" neatly tucked up in bed with bottles, bandages and basins arranged tidily beside them.'

'If we'd been here for the past ten days we could have given you some pretty authentic colour,' Gregory grinned.

Her face suddenly filled with concern. 'Yes, you both look as though you'd been through an awful time. I've been terribly anxious about you, and I can hardly wait to hear about your journey. Come up to my room—it's much more comfortable there, and I expect you're hungry too, but breakfast should be ready soon.'

At the back of the house on the third floor Madeleine had a pleasant little sitting-room of her own. The rest of the house was cold, as fuel was now becoming appallingly short in Paris, and gas was only allowed to be used for cooking; but she had a small oil-stove, and they warmed themselves round it.

Twenty minutes slipped swiftly by as they told her of their crossing from England, and she related how the day after she and Kuporovitch had been arrested Lieutenant Ribaud had called on her to reassure her that when the Russian reached Vichy he would find himself in friendly hands. A week later Ribaud had called again to let her know that Kuporovitch had been sent on a special mission from which he might not return for some weeks, and to fix up another meeting for her with Lacroix. Soon afterwards arrangements had been made for the opening of the nursing-home, and from that time on she had been kept at it without a break, helping in the secret work that meant so much to her.

Kuporovitch enquired after Madame Lavallière, and Madeleine said that her mother was as well as could be expected, although with the approach of winter she was now suffering severely from the increasing cold and poor food. Madame Bonard was looking after her again, just as she had in the days when Madeleine used to go out as a professional nurse, but she managed to visit her mother for an hour or so two or three times a week.

There was a knock at the door, and on Madeleine's calling 'Come in!' Gregory saw the tall, good-looking, dark young man who had helped him with the stretcher enter the room. It was Madeleine's old neighbour, Pierre Ponsardin; but, having had his eyes shut when he was carried in, Kuporovitch had not seen him, and Pierre had thought the Russian really unconscious. Laughing now, they greeted one another.

Pierre was introduced to Gregory, and having congratulated them on having made the trip to Paris safely he said that he had only come up to let them know that breakfast had been on the table for the past ten minutes. He had already had his and left them to go about his work.

When he had gone Madeleine explained to Stefan that after his arrest Pierre had been a great comfort to her, and that since there could be no doubt of his personal loyalty to her, and hatred of the Nazis, she had roped him in as a good man for the post of male attendant at the nursing-home.

They then went downstairs to a dining-room in the basement where the best part of a dozen people were gathered, already eating the morning meal. Two of the women were in nurse's uniform; the rest, mostly men, were in ordinary clothes and formed the bulk of the patients, for whom breakfast was really supper, as they had just come in

153

from their night's operations and were about to go to bed for the day.

Madeleine did not introduce her new "patients" to the others, and during the meal they both observed that the conversation was kept strictly general. No one even hinted at the work upon which they were secretly engaged, and when they spoke of the war at all it was only in the light of the latest news in the papers and news bulletins.

When they had finished breakfast Madeleine took her new charges up to their rooms, which were side by side on the fourth floor. During their beating-up on the island both of them had lost the rucksacks they had been carrying, so neither had a scrap of luggage, but she provided them with pyjamas, dressing-gowns, and even shaving tackle, as she kept a store of such things, as well as a large wardrobe of secondhand clothes, in order that any of Lacroix's agents who frequented the place could be provided with a complete change of costume in any emergency.

Gregory asked when they would be able to see the Colonel, and Madeleine replied: 'He only visits us about once every ten days, because there's no disguising his exceptionally small figure, and every visit he makes to Paris exposes him to special danger of recognition by those of his ex-agents who are no longer trustworthy. Your safe arrival will have been reported to him by tomorrow, so he may turn up any time after that; in the meantime, I'm afraid you'll have to amuse yourselves as well as you can.'

For the next few days Gregory and Kuporovitch read and slept a lot, only leaving their rooms to take their morning and evening meals in the basement, or to sit with Madeleine when she was off duty. That was never for long spells except in the evenings, as although the nursing-home was a phoney one, appearances had to be kept up, the patients' beds made, their rooms cleaned, and the catering attended to. The work was not unduly hard, as she had three fake nurses, a cook, who before the collapse had been a famous hostess, and Pierre to help her, but the house was a large one, and there always seemed a dozen little jobs in it waiting to be done.

Kuporovitch was more in love with her than ever, but the times when he could get her to himself were few. Gregory did his best to help his friend by providing such opportunities, whenever the chance came his way, but Madeleine herself nearly always made some excuse to avoid them, as in spite of her fondness for the Russian she felt a strong aversion to the idea of letting any man make open love to her.

It was late on the afternoon of October the 31st that the inmates of the home were thrown into a sudden state of apprehension. As a precaution against a surprise raid by the police, a trusted electrician had wired every room in the building with a secret alarum. Near the door in the front hall an inconspicuous button which was raised a fraction of an inch above the surface of the floor had been inserted in the parquet. If anyone placed their foot on it a tiny electric bell tinkled in every room, not sufficiently loudly for anyone in the hall to hear it, but quite loud enough to warn all the patients and nurses that strangers were entering the house, and possible danger threatened. This device gave ample time for any patients who were in another's room or doing anything which they would not normally have been doing as invalids to get back to their own beds and prepare themselves for a visit.

At the time Gregory was sitting with Kuporovitch idly discussing the news in the afternoon papers. Immediately the bell tinkled he jumped up, tiptoed softly back to his room, slipped off his dressing gown and settled himself in bed. For the best part of twenty minutes he lay there, wondering what the devil was going on downstairs; then the bell tinkled again, and he knew the danger was over.

Soon afterwards Madeleine came upstairs and told them the cause of the alarum. That afternoon she had been to visit her mother, and to her intense annoyance had found Luc Ferrière with the old lady. The Mayor of Batignolles had naturally asked her what she was doing these days, and on Lacroix's instructions that, except in an emergency, it was always less dangerous to tell the truth than a direct lie, she had replied that, young as she was, she had had the good fortune to receive an appointment as the matron of a nursing-home.

He had congratulated her and expressed his interest, asking about her patients. The answers to his questions had presented no great difficulty as a fake case history of each of the agents who was using the home had been carefully thought out in advance, but she had changed the subject as soon as possible, and then endeavoured to outstay the Mayor.

It seemed, however, that he had time on his hands, so at last she had been compelled to say that she must go, and he had suggested driving her home, an offer which she could not decently refuse. There were few private cars still running in Paris now, but owing to his official position, the Mayor had been granted a small petrol allowance which was sufficient for him to maintain a runabout. In it, his lanky figure crouched over the wheel, and, still wearing his absurd bowler hat on his long narrow head, he had run her back through the almost deserted streets.

In front of her house she had thanked him for the lift and quickly made to say goodbye, but to her annoyance he had wriggled himself out of his little automobile and asked if he might come in for a moment to see something of the home that she was running. Fearing that to refuse might have aroused his suspicions she thought it best to bring him in—hence the alarum which had been given to all the patients.

'Do you think he's got a hunch that you're mixed up in something, or was it just idle curiosity?' Gregory asked.

'Idle curiosity, I'm almost certain,' she replied. 'He's the type of man who loves to poke his nose into everything; but I showed him the waiting-room, the operating theatre, the dining-room downstairs, which I told him was for the staff, and two of the bedrooms which were empty, but ready to receive patients. He was full of smarmy flattery about everything and went off quite happily. The only danger is that he said he must try to send me some patients. Of course, I had to thank him and say I hoped he would, but it's going to be a most frightful nuisance if he does.'

'It would be an inconvenience, no more,' Stefan strove to reassure her. 'They would have their own doctor, and we should have to be on our best behaviour during his visits, but any patients would be confined to their own rooms. You could do the dressings that are required yourself, and they might be in the house for weeks without learning anything at all of what really goes on here.'

'Yes, I suppose so,' Madeleine agreed; 'but it's certain that

Luc Ferrière is collaborating with the Nazis, so it's unfortunate that he should have found out about this place at all.'

It was the following evening, just about black-out time, that Gregory, when doing his windows, which were at the front of the house, was surprised to see a motor hearse drive up. As he watched, four black-clad mutes removed a coffin from it, which they carried to the front door.

He knew that from time to time one of the secret freedom-fighters who lived in the home was wounded in a clash with the police, and that if they could manage to get back they became genuine patients whom Madeleine looked after personally until they were recovered from their injuries; but he felt certain that she would have told him if one of them had returned the night before so badly wounded from an affray that he had died during the day. However, it was an unwritten rule that none of the inmates of the home should deliberately question one another as to what went on there, so, having drawn the curtains, he thought no more about it.

Five minutes later Madeleine arrived to ask him and Kuporovitch to come downstairs to the first-floor room at the back of the house which was used as the staff common-room. Outside it two of the mutes were standing, and the two others were down in the hall. On entering the room they saw that the coffin was reposing on the floor, but it was now open, and Colonel Lacroix was sitting quietly at the table.

After they had greeted one another with the greatest heartiness Gregory said: 'What an ingenious idea, *mon Colonel*, to have yourself taken about Paris in a coffin! That's a disguise which it would defeat the ingenuity of even the Gestapo to penetrate.'

A quick smile lit up the little Colonel's monkey-like face. 'Yes, it serves most admirably, particularly for my visits here. Even the best nursing-homes sometimes lose their patients, and it provides excellent colour for our neighbours to see a coffin carried in and out of the place now and then.'

Gregory sat down opposite him, and Kuporovitch took another chair as he said with a smile: 'No doubt you've heard about our somewhat adventurous journey.'

'I have indeed, and you were both lucky to escape with

your lives. We owe you a great debt for bringing Gregory over.'

Kuporovitch shrugged. 'That's nothing. I'm only sorry that it took so long. I left Paris on the 16th of September, you may remember, and here we are on November 1st. Nearly six weeks for a trip from Paris to London and back is pretty poor going, but I assure you that the delays were absolutely unavoidable.'

'I fully appreciate that,' Lacroix said quickly, 'but such matters will, I hope, be easier in future. I'm happy to be able to tell you that things have been going well here in your absence. It's still early days to contemplate any major operation against the Nazis, but our movement grows in a most encouraging fashion. France is very far from dead. We now have people pledged to support us in every town of importance in the country, and hundreds of villages as well, both in Occupied and Unoccupied France.'

'That's splendid,' murmured Gregory, 'but the greater the numbers the greater the danger. Forgive me if I suggest that it might be a mistake to move too quickly before all these good people have been fully tested as to their loyalty.'

Lacroix nodded. 'In a general sense I agree. But, apart from a few headquarters establishments, such as this, where my principal agents cannot do their work efficiently without to some extent coming in contact with one another, I'm working on the cell system. In the provinces we're forming groups of five, who at the worst could only betray one another; and in each group the leader only is in contact with five other leaders, and so on. From time to time I now issue general instructions which percolate right through the movement, giving our members guidance as to how best they can hamper the Nazis from day to day without drawing any special suspicion upon themselves. Soon I hope to initiate carefully planned acts of sabotage; but for that we shall need arms, explosives and money.'

'To get arms and explosives to you is going to be one hell of a job,' Gregory said thoughtfully. 'Only your Mediterranean coast is open now, and even there, unless your organization is much more advanced than I imagine it to be, the difficulties of running the stuff through the Vichy-controlled Customs would be immense. To be honest too, I very much doubt if the British Government is in any position to spare arms at the moment. We lost such masses of stuff at Dunkirk that the major part of our regular army had to be entirely re-equipped, not to mention the needs of the new militia divisions and the hundreds of Home Guard units that we've been raising.'

Kuporovitch leant forward and with a sinister gesture drew the side of his hand across his throat. 'I should have thought, *mon Colonel*, that you already had all the arms in France that you wanted—for the taking.'

Lacroix nodded. 'You mean by garotting German sentries and making off with their weapons? Yes, a certain amount of that sort of thing is already being done, but I don't want to encourage it too much for the moment. If the number of Germans murdered increases to an alarming extent they will take counter-measures. They'll start rounding up all the ex-soldiers and fit men into concentration camps, and that would deprive me of my most stalwart fighters when the time is ripe to launch a full-scale revolt.'

'I take it nothing of that kind would be justified for a long time yet?' hazarded Gregory.

'No, no! Many months must pass before the privation that the French people will have suffered through the winter can prepare them to back such a movement wholeheartedly. It may even take a second winter to drive them to real desperation, and it is of the first importance that we should not spoil everything by acting precipitately.'

'In that case, the question of arms is of no great urgency.'

The Colonel frowned. 'As you point out yourself, the running of arms into France presents a difficult problem, so we can only hope to smuggle through small quantities at a time. When we are really ready it is my intention to stage a new Saint Bartholomew's Eve, on which all the Nazis in the country will be murdered in their beds, or hunted to death like the rats they are. But to carry through such a coup successfully I shall need great numbers of men and weapons. I have little doubt that the movement will spread, and that when the time comes plenty of stout-hearted men will be available, but to provide arms for them all means many months of systematic smuggling. I already have a few safe channels in the south through which the goods could be shipped, and that is why I wish you to take the matter up with your Government without delay.'

In that case, I'll put your request forward immediately I reach London,' Gregory agreed. 'I've no idea what the British Government will be able to let you have, but they must have pretty big stocks of explosives on hand, and you'll need that for carrying out acts of sabotage, long before you're in a position to arm all your people for a general rising. Anyhow, you may be certain that they'll spare you anything they can and increase the supplies as time goes on. You'll have to let me know, though, full particulars about the channels you suggest and the names of the consignees on whom we're to make a start.'

'Good! Before your return I will give you all details. Now, about money. This question is of far greater urgency, and one in which I hope your Government will be able to give us immediate assistance. You will appreciate that we have absolutely no official funds at all. We started from scratch; just a handful of my friends and myself, and unfortunately none of us are rich men. We each put up what we could to cover general expenses, and all those who have joined the movement contribute what they can; but many of the best of them are already in hiding, so they cannot get at any private funds they may possess, or earn any money. They must be supported, and there are constant outgoings in the shape of rentals for headquarters such as this, upkeep, bribes, travelling expenses, and so on. We have been lucky in receiving several handsome donations from wealthy people, mainly elderly women who can do little themselves but wish to make their money fight; yet such occasional gifts are quite inadequate if we are to expand the movement until it is large enough to be a real menace to our enemies.'

'I quite understand that,' Gregory replied at once. 'As you're aware, I have no official position whatsoever, but I feel confident that the British Government would never allow the activities of the French freedom-fighters to be hampered through lack of adequate finance. It would be extremely risky, though, for me to endeavour to bring back from London

160

any great sum of cash on my person. Have you any ideas as to how it could be conveyed to you safely?'

'Yes, I have managed to get a good friend of mine appointed to a post in our Embassy at Lisbon now; so if you, or any British agent, could get the money that far, which should not be difficult, he would do the rest.'

These main points settled, they began a more general discussion of the European situation. In the past ten days there had been great diplomatic activity. On October the 22nd Hitler and Laval had met to discuss Franco-German collaboration. On the 23rd, accompanied by his Army and Air Force Chiefs, Hitler had travelled to the Franco-Spanish frontier to talk with General Franco. On the 24th, under conditions of the greatest secrecy, Hitler had met Pétain with a view to forcing yet further concessions personally out of the old Marshal. There had also been fresh tension in the Balkans, which had culminated on October the 28th in Hitler meeting Mussolini in Florence, and the Italian Forces in Albania invading Greece.

The Greeks had been driven some way back from their own frontier, but they were said to be putting up a stout resistance. Authentic news was still scarce, but Lacroix, who was in a better position to know than most people, expressed the opinion that, although the Greeks were comparatively ill-armed, now that they had been called upon to defend their own soil they would give the Italians some very hard fighting before the country was overrun.

General de Gaulle had landed in the French colony of Gabon on the previous Sunday, and although fighting was reported to be in progress there considerable numbers of the garrison had come over to him. As Lacroix was a great friend and admirer of the General's he was particularly elated by this first success of the Free French Forces, and the others congratulated him upon it.

They had been in conference for about an hour, and Lacroix was giving Gregory all the information he could regarding the German preparations for the invasion of Britain, when to their consternation the alarum bell tinkled.

All three of them came to their feet, and the Colonel said swiftly: 'I have yet to give you those details, Gregory, about the arms-running and the delivery of money in Lisbon. The four stout fellows who are acting as mutes will be coming in to fetch me, and it may not be safe for me to return here tonight; but it will take them some minutes to get the coffin downstairs. Quick! Slip up to your rooms, get your clothes on, then follow me out of the house as though you are mourners. If you are questioned the body is that of your old friend Professor Fresnais, the ethnologist.'

He was still speaking when Madeleine and two of the mutes came hurrying into the room. She was calm, but a little pale, as she said: 'It's the police, but they don't seem ill-disposed. Nurse Yolanda and your other two men are keeping them occupied for the moment down in the hall.'

Lacroix was already getting into the coffin, and no sooner was he lying at full length in the satin-lined shell than the mutes seized the coffin-lid, placed it over him and began to screw it down.

Gregory and Kuporovitch, meanwhile, were scurrying quietly but quickly upstairs. In frantic haste they tore off their dressing-gowns and began to pull on their clothes. Barely two minutes elapsed before they were ready. Their underclothes had been tucked in anyhow, and their ties and collars were still undone, but each had a muffler round his neck and a heavy overcoat over his clothes, so that to outward appearances they were fully dressed. Thrusting the automatics with which Madeleine had furnished them from the secret armoury of the home into their pockets, they met on the landing.

Tiptoeing down to the first floor, they saw that the four mutes, now carrying the coffin, had just reached the hall. Madeleine was walking behind it, and the unwelcome visitors, who consisted of an inspector and three *agents de ville*, stood respectfully aside with bowed heads as it was carried towards the door.

Side by side, looking suitably mournful, Gregory and Kuporovitch came down the last flight; but the inspector stepped forward and said: '*Pardon, messieurs*, where are you going?'

'We are about to follow our poor friend Professor Fresnais on his last journey,' Gregory replied sadly.

'I regret, *messieurs*,' the inspector's voice was courteous but firm, 'that, I cannot permit. We have reason to suspect that this house is used for subversive activities, and it is now surrounded. I have orders that no one is to be allowed to leave.'

Gregory's face showed only shocked surprise, but he was now acutely anxious. Things were evidently much worse than they had first believed. Fortunately, owing to the careful routine which Madeleine maintained, everything in the home was in apple-pie order. There was little chance of the police finding anything they could bring a charge upon, unless they happened to recognize one of the "patients" as a man that they were after. The great thing was that Lacroix had safely passed through the net. The four mutes, shouldering the coffin, were already out in the street, and the motor hearse was backing towards them.

These thoughts had raced through his brain as he took the last two steps downstairs. Instantly he began to protest, although only as a matter of form, since he now felt certain that Kuporovitch and himself would not be allowed out of the house until the police had completed their investigation.

Madeleine was outside on the pavement. She, too, now realized that this was no formal visit, as, even in the semi-darkness, she could see that a little knot of *gendarmes* had been posted on either side of the house, a little way down the street.

As she stood there uneasily watching the mutes slide the coffin into the back of the hearse she caught the wail of a klaxon horn. A large car came hurtling round the corner and drew up within a few yards of the house. Madeleine's heart missed a beat. Major Schaub jumped out of the car, followed by two other S.S. guards.

He did not appear to notice her, but his glance swiftly took in the hearse, the mutes and the inspector and the others, who were standing in the open doorway of the hall.

'What's going on here?' he barked in staccato French.

The inspector came forward and saluted. 'It is the funeral of Professor Fresnais, *Monsieur le Major*. He died last night from weakness after a severe operation. There are two men here who wished to follow the hearse to the cemetery, but I have detained them.'

'You have done rightly,' said the Major. 'As for the hearse, we can let that go. Our business is with the living, not with the dead.'

It was at that moment that, swinging on his heel, he came face to face with Madeleine. Even in the half light his recognition of her was instant.

'*Ach, so!*' he exclaimed, his eyes narrowing. 'Surely you are the pretty girl who is willing to provide Russian refugees with a little amusement for the price of a good dinner. Mademoiselle Mirabeau was the name, if I'm not mistaken. So you have become a nurse! I must say the uniform suits you! But the last time we met you were pulled in for having been in conversation with an anarchist who shot a French detective. And now I find you as a nurse in a home which is under suspicion as a rendezvous for saboteurs. This is most interesting!'

Suddenly he swung round again. The hearse was just on the point of moving as he called out: 'Halt there! Halt!' And pulling out his pistol he sent a warning shot over the head of the driver.

The hearse pulled up with a jerk. At the sound of the shot the French inspector and his men came running out on to the pavement. Gregory and Kuporovitch, knowing now that there was real trouble ahead, followed.

Major Schaub walked up to the back of the open hearse and tapped the coffin-lid with the barrel of his automatic. 'I have heard of tricks being played with coffins before,' he said coldly, 'and I am not now prepared to accept the statement that this one contains the body of a dead professor.'

The mutes had left their stations beside the hearse and gathered round him. With a sudden flourish of his gun towards them he rapped out: 'Take it back into the house! I wish to see what's inside it!'

12

The Unexpected Snare

The doorway of the nursing-home stood open and was now empty except for Nurse Yolanda. The inspector and his men had all come out of the house and stood grouped together on the edge of the pavement. Kuporovitch had stepped up to Madeleine and, taking her by the arm, drawn her back a little. The Russian did not want to start anything himself, but he was determined to put up a fight rather than allow Madeleine to be arrested. With his right hand he firmly grasped the automatic in his pocket, which had its safety-catch off and was ready for instant use.

Night had come now. The light from the doorway of the nursing-home lit the scene, but the ends of the street were obscured in darkness. The infringement of the black-out regulations, the hearse, the S.S. men, and the French police had attracted the attention of numerous passers-by. They now formed a small crowd at either side of the doorway but some way back from it, consumed with curiosity yet fearful of being involved.

Gregory had followed the inspector out of the house, and he now stepped forward off the pavement. He had heard Major Schaub's order to the mutes that the coffin was to be carried into the home and opened, and he knew that all other considerations must be disregarded in an attempt to prevent that.

He had seen the small groups of police posted further down the road, but in the immediate vicinity there were only the inspector, the three *agents de ville* and the three S.S. men. As the four mutes were not really mutes at all, but Lacroix's people, Gregory felt certain that they would be armed. There were also himself, Kuporovitch, and the driver of the hearse, so the odds were exactly even—seven against seven.

He knew that if a fight started it would be a desperate business, since all fourteen would be firing at one another at pointblank range. It was a certainty that several of them would get killed, and probably some of the bystanders would be injured. Madeleine and the other inmates of the home would also have to be sacrificed, as in any attempt to get the hearse away there would be no time to get them away with it; so they would be arrested afterwards. But it had not taken Gregory two seconds to sum up the situation clearly and form his decision.

Lacroix was the very heart and soul of this great and growing conspiracy which in time might break the Nazi stranglehold on France and thus play a huge part in bringing the war to a successful conclusion. That was the thing that mattered above all else. If Lacroix was captured, even if the whole movement were not broken up entirely, it would set it back by many months. At all costs that must be prevented. Whoever else fell a victim to shots or capture, an attempt had to be made to save the all-important brain of the movement.

Stepping off the pavement, Gregory walked quietly up to Major Schaub and said in excellent French: '*Monsieur le Major,* if you will think for a moment you will realize that you can't do this sort of thing.'

'Why not, *monsieur*?' said the Major icily, staring at him in surprise.

'Because it's not decent,' Gregory replied firmly. 'How can you expect us French people to collaborate with you if you insult our dead?'

'I do not insult your dead!' retorted the Major. 'I simply require that this coffin should be opened in order that I may inspect its contents before it is despatched to the cemetery— or wherever they propose to take it at this late hour.'

Gregory glanced round at the four mutes, endeavouring as best he could by his glance alone to warn them that he meant to make trouble; then he said: 'Am I not right, *messieurs*? To disturb the newly dead by wrenching off a coffin-lid is to insult them.'

Before any of the men could reply Major Schaub cried

166

angrily: 'To hell with that! We're wasting time. I intend to have this coffin opened. Come on, you men! Get that coffin back into the house, or there'll be trouble for you!'

Gregory had purposely come up very close the the Major while he was speaking to him—so close that he was not only within easy striking range, but the German had no room to use his gun. Suddenly, without the slightest warning, Gregory brought his left knee up with all his force into the Major's crutch. An instant later, as the Major's mouth opened and he swayed forward slightly, Gregory hit him with all his force under the chin; he fell crashing into the roadway.

The sight of the assault acted like a signal. The four mutes, the inspector, the *agents de ville*, the two remaining S.S. men and Kuporovitch all jerked their guns from pockets or holsters.

As the Major fell Gregory sprang into the open back of the hearse alongside the coffin, yelling at the top of his lungs: 'Drive on! Drive on!'

His shout was half-drowned by a ragged burst of firing. Kuporovitch shot one of the S.S. men through the head. Bullets from the guns of two of the mutes hit the other in the body, but not before the shots from his automatic had brought one of them, gulping blood, to the ground.

The inspector and his men came late into action. They knew it to be their duty to support the Germans, but had a natural reluctance to fire at the Frenchmen who were gathered round the hearse. Their indecision gave Kuporovitch his opportunity. His one concern was to save Madeleine. Thrusting aside one of the *agents de ville* who stood in his path, he dragged her back through the open door of the nursing-home and slammed it to.

Next moment shots crashed out again. The inspector knew that he would pay for it with his own life if he allowed Gregory and the mutes to get away with the murder of the Nazis. The hearse was now in motion, and the three remaining mutes, clinging on behind, were twisting themselves up into it. Raising his old-fashioned revolver, the inspector fired at them. Two of his men followed his example. The other had run to the door of the nursing-home and was banging loudly on it. One of the mutes was hit and let out a yell of pain. The glass in the side of the hearse was shattered and came clanging down among its struggling occupants. Gregory was underneath, but he wriggled free and pulled his gun.

As the hearse sped away they returned the fire of the *agents de ville*, and one of them fell reeling into the gutter, Major Schaub lay stretched out where he had fallen, still unconscious. The two other Nazis and the dead mute made ugly twisted heaps beside him.

The *agents de ville* were now giving chase, firing as they ran. The bystanders were shouting and scurrying for the nearest cover, fearful of being wounded, but a brawny workman thrust out his foot and tripped the inspector before diving into a nearby alleyway. As Gregory's swift glance took in the scene he searched anxiously in the semi-darkness for Madeleine and Kuporovitch, but he could not see them. He could only hope that they had managed to make good their escape in the confusion.

At the far end of the street the group of police were now coming into action. A sergeant bravely stood right in the centre of the road, calling at the top of his voice on the hearse to halt. Its driver drove straight at him, and he only managed to leap aside just in time. His companion sent a ragged volley at the hearse as it sped past them. A flying splinter of glass cut Gregory's cheek, but next minute, almost on two wheels, the hearse hurtled round the corner.

For a few moments the hearse raced through the darkened streets that Gregory did not recognize. Then it roared past a tall archway outside which there was an empty sentry-box, and he realized that beyond the dark courtyard lay the Elysée Palace, the official home of France's Presidents. Swinging to the right the hearse dashed down a side turning into the Champs-Elysées. Here it turned right again and headed up the broad thoroughfare towards the Arc de Triomphe, ignoring all traffic lights and speed limits. Three minutes later they rounded the arch and careered wildly down the Avenue Foch, until at its end they entered the Bois de Boulogne.

Only then did the driver begin to moderate his pace. A few hundred yards farther on he turned off the road down one of the thickly wooded rides of the great park, the use of which is prohibited to motor traffic. Then, when the hearse was well screened by the trees, he pulled up.

Without a moment's delay two of the mutes began to unscrew the coffin-lid while the third held a torch. As soon as the lid was removed Lacroix scrambled out of the satin-lined shell. He had heard the shooting through the ventilation holes concealed in the sides of the coffin, which had been specially constructed for him, and he asked at once what casualties his men had sustained.

'They got Alexandre,' replied one of the mutes, 'and Raoul here is wounded in the shoulder; but the rest of us are all right.'

'How about the people in the home?' asked Lacroix.

'The Matron and the thickset man who was with her got back into it and slammed the door.'

'Thank God for that!' murmured Gregory. 'The inspector said the house had been surrounded, but Kuporovitch is a cunning old fox. With luck he may be able to get them out through the garden.'

'Anyhow, your friend got one of the Nazis,' commented the mute. 'Poor Alexandre and I accounted for the other.'

'Good!' said Lacroix. 'Things might be worse then, but we have no time to lose. Already a general call will have been sent out from Police Headquarters for this hearse to be halted wherever it may be seen. We were lucky to get as far as this without being held up, but on all the routes leading out of Paris the Germans have strong road controls armed wih machine-guns. We must abandon the hearse at once and disperse in the hope of getting through separately on foot.'

'Where will you make for?' asked Gregory.

'For Vichy. Once we can reach the frontier of Unoccupied France there are a dozen places in which we can cross it unknown to the authorities. For myself and my men I have few qualms, but about you, Gregory, I am anxious. It is important that you should get back to England as soon as possible. If you proceed with one of us to Vichy you may meet with grave delays. It is better, I think, that you should go home by the direct route that I had already planned for you.'

'That's all right by me,' Gregory agreed. 'You have only to give me directions. But before we part you must let me have those particulars about shipping arms and your man in Lisbon.'

Lacroix glanced round his bodyguard. 'I wish to talk alone with my friend here. You will leave us for a few moments. Take up your positions about fifty yards away; so that we are not surprised if one of the police cars which now must be searching for us happens to turn in along this drive.'

When the men had scrambled out of the hearse Lacroix produced a small pad and fountain-pen from his pocket. While Gregory held a torch the Colonel wrote swiftly upon the paper, then he tore off the sheet and handed it over, as he said:

'It would be a bad business if you were captured with that on you, so you must memorize these particulars at the first opportunity, then destroy them.'

Taking a cardboard covered booklet from another pocket he handed that to Gregory, as he went on: 'That is the passport I had faked for you. It is in the name of Lucien Rouxel. Now, about your journey: you'll go tomorrow morning to the office of Dormey, Jamier et Fils in the Rue de la Roquette, which is near the *Cimetière du Père Lachaise*. They are haulage contractors who are working for the Germans. Ask for Monsieur Adolphe Dormey, show him your passport and tell him that you are a night watchman who seeks employment. He will then arrange for you to be smuggled through in one of his lorries either to Boulogne or Calais. At whichever place you arrive I now have good arrangements. The lorry-driver will put you in touch with someone who has managed to conceal a motor-boat under a deserted wharf in one of the small harbours along the coast. German troops are now thick as flies in that area, but, thank God, the women of France do not lack courage, and many of them are becoming very skilful at distracting the attention of sentries when required to do so for their country's sake. Fortunately, the moon is in its dark period, so with the help you'll be given you should have no great difficulty in getting away from the coast. The boat will put you aboard the first British ship that it meets and return either the same or the following night. Is that all clear?'

'Monsieur Adolphe Dormey of Dormey, Jamier et Fils,

Rue de la Roquette,' Gregory repeated. 'Yes. Then with any luck I'll be back in London early next week.'

Time was precious if Lacroix and his men were to be well away from Paris before morning. To each of them the little Colonel gave the number of the underground route they were to take; then, having shaken hands all round and wished one another luck, the little group of conspirators abandoned the hearse, striking out in different directions through the night-enshrouded woods.

Gregory was by no means certain in what part of the Bois he was, but he kept as straight a course as possible between the trees, and through the little glades where in happier times thousands of Parisian families were wont to picnic on fine Sundays, and countless pairs of lovers have lingered far into warm summer nights, until he came out in an open space at the edge of the lakes. There he recognized the silhouette of a building which was thrown up against the night sky as the Pré-Catalan Restaurant.

He had often dined there in the old days and danced within the circle of coloured fairy-lamps that hung from tree to tree in the garden, or enjoyed one of the shows at the open-air theatre, but now the laughter and the music were still, the whole place dark and deserted.

Having found his bearings he headed south-west, and after a quarter of a mile's walk came out of the Bois at the gate opposite the junction of the Boulevard Suchet and the Boulevard Lannes. Pausing there for a moment under the shaded traffic-lights, he took out the passport that Lacroix had given him and had a quick look at it. The Colonel had evidently gone through hundreds of photographs, as the one selected was of a man not at all unlike himself, and it was certainly as good as the average passport photograph, which in nine cases out of ten is little more than a caricature of its owner. Noting that he was supposed to have been born at Montélimar and had been given the occupation of commercial traveller, he put the passport back in his pocket, crossed the road and proceeded at a brisk pace down the Avenue Henri Martin until he reached the Palais du Trocadéro.

One of the now infrequent buses was just getting under

way there, and he hopped on to it. The bus carried him across the Pont d'Iéna, past the Tour Eiffel and the Invalides, into the upper part of the Boulevard St. Germain. At the corner of the Boul Mich he got off and walked through several side streets until he found one of the many small inexpensive restaurants which abound in the Latin quarter. It was still only just on eight o'clock, so he ordered himself a modest meal from the meagre bill of fare and a carafe of Vin Rosé to wash it down.

He was acutely anxious about Madeleine and Kuporovitch, but he knew that it would be an extremely risky proceeding to go back to the nursing-home in the hope of finding out what had happened to them, and that in any event he must not do so before he had thoroughly mastered the notes that Lacroix had given him, in case he was caught with them still on him.

The little restaurant, which in better days must have known generations of jolly students making merry with their girls, now had a sleepy, half-dead atmosphere, as though it were in a small provincial town. The great University of Paris was closed, and the studios were empty except for a handful of half-destitute French artists. On this evening the restaurant's entire clientèle consisted of three woebegone-looking diners besides Gregory, so he was in no danger of being overlooked. When the waitress had served his food he was able to study Lacroix's notes at leisure, reading them over again and again and photographing them upon his brain; by the time his meal was finished he felt quite certain that every detail of them was firmly fixed in his mind.

Having finished his wine, he screwed the paper upon which the notes were written into a squill, lit a cigarette with it and let it burn out on his plate, afterwards breaking up the ashes. He then paid his bill and went out into the street.

As the night was moonless it was now very dark, but the slope of the ground gave him his direction, and he headed north. On reaching the Seine he walked along the quay where the second-hand booksellers hold their street market from open boxes set up on the stone balustrade, crossed the river by the Pont Neuf and made his way past the Louvre along the Rue de Rivoli until he reached the bottom of the Champs-

Elysées. Having proceeded up it a short distance he turned left into the maze of narrow turnings beyond the Elysée Palace, in one of which he knew the nursing-home lay.

After a quarter of an hour's search he found it, and looking neither to right nor left walked rapidly along the side of the street opposite to the home as though he were in a great hurry to get somewhere. As far as he could see, no one was about, but that was no guarantee that watchful eyes were not peering from some darkened window. Halting abruptly at a house that was actually facing the home, he pressed the bell and waited anxiously, praying that it would be answered quickly.

After a moment the doorchain rattled, and the door opened a crack. With a quick 'Pardonnez-moi!' Gregory gave it a strong push, which almost sent the person behind the door off their balance; then stepping into the entrance, he shut the door firmly behind him.

In the dim light of the hall he saw that a neatly dressed elderly woman had answered his ring, and her eyes were now full of fear, as she crouched back against the wall.

'Please don't be afraid,' he said gently, in the voice that he could make so charming when he wished. 'I shan't keep you a minute, but I should be most grateful if you could give me a little information.'

The woman recovered her composure and said: 'What is it you wish to know, monsieur?'

'I want to hear all you can tell me about the trouble which occurred at the nursing-home opposite this evening.'

Again the fear came into her eyes. She shook her head quickly. 'I am sorry, monsieur, I cannot help you. I saw nothing.'

'I'm afraid that won't do,' Gregory said more firmly. 'The sound of the shooting must have brought you to your window. I'm not a police officer, so you needn't be frightened that I'll cart you off to the police-station and force you to act as a witness. I just wish to know what happened for my own reasons.'

The woman continued to shake her head and repeated tremulously: 'I know nothing, monsieur—nothing.'

Gregory was loth to threaten anyone so frail and un-

173

protected, but he positively had to find out what he could for his own peace of mind and in case he could still be of assistance to his friends. Taking out his pistol he just showed it to her, as he said:

'Come, *madame*! Either you or someone in this house must have seen what happened, and I am determined to learn all you know. Perhaps it will encourage you to talk if I tell you that I am one of those who are fighting to restore freedom to France; but now I have told you that you must understand that should you attempt to betray me by shouting for the police it will cost you your life, and you see that I am armed.'

A new expression came into the woman's eyes, and she drew herself up. 'In that case, you may put away your pistol, *monsieur*. I will willingly tell you all I can.' She then described the fracas much as Gregory had witnessed it himself, and went on to tell that after the hearse had driven away the police had smashed in the door of the home and raided the building.

He asked anxiously if they had come away with any prisoners, and she nodded. 'Yes, *monsieur*. I cannot say exactly how many, but they took the young Matron whom I know by sight, two of the nurses and three men.'

Gregory described Kuporovitch as well as he could, but the woman would not identify the Russian from his description, and there was no more information that she could give.

Having thanked her he went out into the street and walked swiftly away in the opposite direction to that from which he had come; but something of the spring had gone out of his step, since he now knew beyond doubt that poor Madeleine was in the hands of the Gestapo, and as it was quite unbelievable that Stefan would have deserted her, he, too, must either have been captured or killed.

For a time he walked the dark streets at random, wondering if there were anything he could do about it, but he at last came to the conclusion that any attempt at rescue would take many days, if not weeks, of cautious investigation and skilful planning, while it was of the utmost urgency that he should return to London with as much speed as possible in order to secure for Lacroix the money and arms upon which the salvation of the whole of France might depend. There could be no question as to his duty, so with great reluctance he tried to put the thought of his friends out of his mind, and began to search for a small hotel where he could spend the night.

Finding himself in the Rue la Boétie, he suddenly remembered that there was a cheap hotel in it which he thought was called the *Britannique,* where once long ago he had spent a night after a terrific week in Paris that had left him almost on the rocks. After ten minutes' search he found it, paid for his room in advance as he had no luggage, and went straight up to bed. It was still early, but his long walk had tired him, and he was extremely depressed about Madeleine and Stefan, so he undressed right away; then, to take his thoughts off his friends, he began to recite over and over again in his mind the particulars that had been written out on Lacroix's page of notes, until he fell asleep.

The room was stone-cold, and the bedclothes were not sufficient to keep him really warm, so he passed an uneasy night, and there was no hot water available for him to have a bath in the morning. Having disposed of an unappetizing breakfast of coffee, made mainly from chicory, and brownish-looking rolls, he left the hotel and got himself shaved at the nearest barber's. He then walked as far as the Madeleine and took a bus along the Grands Boulevards to the Père Lachaise cemetery. Soon after nine o'clock he had found the rather dingy office of Dormey, Jamier et Fils.

On going in he found himself facing a seedy-looking clerk, who peered at him from round the corner of a frosted glass partition. Politely removing his hat, Gregory asked for Monsieur Adolphe Dormey.

The clerk gave him a queer look, and without replying moved away. A moment later he came back with a big, fair, florid man, who gave Gregory an ingratiating smile and asked what he could do for him.

Gregory did not much like the look of the man, but he smiled in reply, and said: 'I have the pleasure of addressing Monsieur Dormey?'

'But no, *monsieur*,' replied the big man. 'I am his partner. Jules Jamier. If you will tell me your business I shall doubtless be able to attend to it for you.'

175

'I'm sorry,' said Gregory, 'but I wish to see Monsieur Dormey on a personal matter.'

The florid Monsieur Jamier shrugged his shoulders. 'I regret, *monsieur*, but my partner is down at our works at the moment. However, if you will come in I will send for him.'

Having ushered Gregory through a door in the glass partition into an untidy office where a pretty fair-haired girl was typing at a table, Monsieur Jamier waved him to a chair and said: 'Be seated, please. It may take us a little time to get Monsieur Dormey from the works. But perhaps you will tell me your name so that the messenger I send can give it to him.'

'My name is Lucien Rouxel, and I come from Saint-Denis,' Gregory replied, sitting down.

With a brief nod Monsieur Jamier walked out of the office and into another beyond it, closing the door behind him. A moment later Gregory could hear him telephoning, but not sufficiently clearly to catch what was being said.

Suddenly it struck him as strange that Jamier should be telephoning when he said that he would send a messenger for his partner, and that special instinct that had often served Gregory so well before warned him now that he was in danger.

He shifted uneasily in his seat, uncertain for once what course to take. If he had fallen into a trap there was still time for him to escape from it; but if his suspicions were groundless, and he left the office precipitately, how would he be able to contact Monsieur Dormey? And without Monsieur Dormey's help he would be stranded in Paris, not only with no means of reaching the coast but with no knowledge of whom to try to contact when he got there. It was a most unpleasant predicament, and he had just made up his mind that he must stay there and face matters out when he noticed the fair girl looking at him curiously over her typewriter.

On a sudden impulse he leaned forward to speak to her, intending to ask if Monsieur Dormey was really down at the warehouse, but she stopped him by placing a finger quickly on her lips. Then she thrust into his hand a slip of paper upon which she had just been typing something.

With fresh perturbation Gregory glanced swiftly at the slip, and read: 'Three days ago the Germans took Monsieur Dormey

176

away, and Monsieur Jamier is now 'phoning for the police.'

Gregory put all his gratitude into one of his most charming smiles and, handing the slip back, stood up. At that moment the powerfully built Monsieur Jamier marched back into the office, and still wearing his false ingratiating smile took up a position between Gregory and the door to the street.

13

A Friend in Need

Gregory knew he dared not waste a moment. Evidently Jamier was a French Quisling who had either betrayed his partner or, when Dormey's activities had been discovered, willingly agreed to co-operate with the police by detaining any stranger who might ask to see Dormey on private business. The unpleasant smirk on Jamier's florid face was enough to show that he had not been forced to undertake the betrayal of his partner's associates through threats to himself, but was thoroughly enjoying the business. As he stood there with his feet planted wide apart, it was clear that he meant to prevent any attempt which Gregory might make to leave the office, and by now the police cars and Gestapo men must already be on their way to collect the fish which had blundered into the net.

As Gregory had a loaded automatic strapped under his left armpit he knew that as a last resort he could shoot his way out, but he was most loth to do so unless it became absolutely necessary. The sound of the shots would rouse the neighbourhood and make him the instant quarry of a general hue-and-cry. His wits were working overtime for some means of getting out of the trap with the speed that was essential, while at the same time creating as little commotion as possible.

Producing his cigarettes, he lit one, then half-turning, he dropped the lighted match behind his back into a waste-paper basket that stood beside the typist's desk.

'How long do you think Monsieur Dormey will be?' he asked Jamier calmly.

'Five minutes—ten at the outside,' replied the bull-necked

178

Frenchman. 'I'm sorry I have had to ask you to wait even for so long.'

'Oh, not at all!' Gregory shrugged. 'I'm in no hurry.' But he was anxiously wondering now if the lighted match had caught the paper in the basket, or just gone out, and he dared not turn round to see if his ruse was working. If it was not he was now only wasting precious seconds; but half a minute later he saw the expression on Monsieur Jamier's face alter.

'Something is burning!' the Frenchman exclaimed. 'It is there, behind you! I can see smoke!'

'*Mon Dieu!*' cried Gregory, whipping round to find that the contents of the wastepaper basket were well alight.

Picking it up, he turned with it belching flame and smoke, towards the Frenchman—then held it out with an expression of consternation, as though he did not know what to do with it.

'Water!' cried Jamier. 'Water!' And made to dive for his inner office, but Gregory shouted:

'No, no! open the door so that I can throw it into the street.'

Taken off his guard, the Frenchman stood aside and pulled the door open. Gregory dashed through it, still carrying the flaming basket, but when he reached the entrance of the building, instead of hurling the blazing mass into the gutter, he ran straight on with it down the two steps, and turning left headed towards the cemetery. Having covered ten yards, he threw the basket into an ashcan, which was standing on the corner of an alleyway. Jamier had reached the doorstep of his office, but he made no attempt to follow Gregory, expecting him to come back. Instead, once Gregory was rid of his fiery burden, he dived into the alley, having obtained a good twenty yards' clear start.

He heard a faint shout behind him as he raced on towards a maze of narrow courts. Twisting swiftly in and out among them, he was soon able to pull up into a walk with the gratifying knowledge that he had already eluded any possibility of successful pursuit.

Nevertheless, as he walked on he was extremely worried. The life-line by which he had hoped to reach England in the course of the next few days was now cut. For the second time Lacroix's arrangements had unexpectedly broken down.

179

Gregory did not blame the little Colonel for that, as he understood the immense difficulties with which Lacroix was faced. In Europe the war was no longer a question of Frenchmen fighting against Germans, so that one might reasonably count upon the aid of any Frenchman that one met. As Father Xavier had so logically pointed out, the Second World War was not a national war at all—it was a civil war, being waged between two great groups of people, each of which wished to force the ideology that it favoured upon the other; and a good half of the French, particularly in the towns, had now gone over to the enemy.

Even families were divided against themselves, and in a business such as that of Dormey, Jamier et Fils there was nothing astonishing about the fact that two partners should have taken opposite sides, and one be prepared to betray the other. In the France of these days no one could be trusted with any certainty, because so many of the French were now seeking preferential treatment for themselves by helping the Gestapo. On the other hand, there were equally large numbers, particularly among the poorer people, who were still willing to take big risks if they could assist the Nazis' enemies, and Gregory was highly conscious that, had it not been for the little typist who had so gamely tipped him off, he would by this time have been either dead as the result of a shooting affray, or on his way to prison.

The whole situation was incredibly tricky, and, he felt, in some ways more difficult than when, during the early months of the war, he had been acting as a secret agent in Germany itself. There at least he had known that every hand was against him, whereas here one might be double-crossed half a dozen times a day through the temptation to trust people who appeared to be friends, but were, in fact, secret enemies. The more he thought about it the more he realized the extraordinary finesse, subtlety and courage required for the task that Lacroix had set himself, and admired the little man's guts for having taken it on.

Gregory's most urgent concern was to pick up the broken threads of the underground line that would get him to England. It was quite useless for him to proceed to Calais or Boulogne without further information, as Monsieur

Dormey's lorry-driver was to have put him in touch with the people there who would ship him across, and he had not the faintest clue as to who they might be. It occurred to him then that, although Dormey had been arrested, the lorry-driver might still be free. If he could get hold of him, even if the man could no longer take him to the coast, he would be able to tell him whom to contact if he could get there on his own. His next thought was that if he could get hold of the little typist she might be able to give him the lorry-driver's name, and he soon saw that this, in fact, was his only hope of getting it. If she could not help him he was completely stumped.

His hurried progress through the succession of courts and alleys had brought him out in the Avenue Philippe Auguste, and he was now heading towards the Place de la Nation. Realizing with fresh concern that by this time the police would have secured a detailed description of him from the treacherous Jamier, he decided that he had better get out of the area as quickly as he could. Hopping on a bus, he let it take him as far as the gates of the Bois de Vincennes, and getting off there he entered the park.

It was still before ten o'clock, and the earliest hour at which he could hope to catch Monsieur Jamier's typist was midday, when nearly all French business premises close for lunch. To return to the Rue de la Roquette at all meant that he would be running into considerable danger, but that had to be faced. In the meantime, he had the best part of two hours to kill; so he amused himself as well as he could by wandering about the Bois.

On this grey November day it was by no means a cheerful spot, and its depressing effect was heightened by the fact that the great French Colonial Exhibition of 1931 had been held there. The main Exhibition buildings were still standing, now dreary, weather-stained and deserted.

As Gregory walked slowly down the Grande Avenue des Colonies Françaises, on either side of which stood the once colourful and splendid pavilions—exact copies of Moorish mosques, Algerian palaces, Indo-Chinese pagodas, and above all of the many-spired temple of Angkor-Vat—he thought sadly of the departed glory of a once great France. Gone were the stalwart negroes in their red *tarbooshes* from Equatorial Africa, the Moroccan Zouaves, with their white turbans and baggy scarlet trousers, the little yellow Tonkinese, the blue-jacketed Spahis and the khaki-clad Foreign Legion. They were now scattered, humbled, clinging precariously to their territories, their ancient Motherland in captivity and broken by disunion, unable to see any certain future for themselves.

Turning gloomily away, Gregory strolled down to the lake, but the memories it recalled only added to his depression. When he had last been there he had dined with a very lovely lady in the restaurant at the lake's edge, and they had formed two of a crowd representing all that was brightest and gayest in the carefree Paris of that day. The food and wine had been the best that France had to offer, the band had played soft music, and as they had talked upon that most fascinating of all subjects—themselves—they had watched the myriad rainbow lights flickering among the fountains and waterfalls, turning them into sheets of liquid azure, emerald and gold. Where, he wondered, was the beautiful Clotilde now? And how little he had thought on that happy evening that when he next stood there it would be as a hunted man, in a crazy, ruined world.

Turning again, he strode rapidly away until he came opposite the great Château with its tall, strong-walled dungeon; yet that again reminded him of France in her happier and greater days. Catherine de Medici had lived there once, and her Florentine necromancer, René, had cast his horoscopes and spells in the topmost chamber of the tower. The gallant Henri of Navarre, the Grande Conde, Mirabeau, and a score of other great Frenchmen had been held captive there; but in their time France had been the first Power in Europe, unsurpassed for her culture and her chivalry, whereas now she was decadent, dying the unhappy prey of the Quisling maggots who were eating out her entrails for their own private gain.

At last the time came for him to leave the park, and, catching another bus, he returned in it to the Place Voltaire, which lies halfway along the Rue de la Roquette. Now that it was near midday there were many more people about, so he felt that while moving among them there was comparatively little chance of his being recognized on his bare description. After traversing a few side turnings he once more reached the end of the alley down which he had bolted, and having bought a paper from a newsvendor he stood just inside the entrance of the alley, pretending to be absorbed in it, while actually keeping a sharp eye on the doorway of Messrs. Dormey, Jamier et Fils, twenty yards down the street.

He had been there about ten minutes when he saw the blonde typist come out, and to his relief she turned in his direction. Stepping back into the alleyway, he waited for a moment, then as the girl passed he called softly: 'Mademoiselle, one moment, if you please.'

Looking round with a start she recognized him at once, and on his beckoning entered the alley. Turning beside her, he led her a little way along it until they were hidden from the street by the nearest corner. Then he halted and began to thank her for the warning she had given him.

'It's nothing,' she interrupted him quickly, 'but you should not remain about here—otherwise they will catch you yet. The police are still in the office, and when they arrived they were furious with Monsieur Jamier for having let you get away.'

'I had to come back,' he told her, 'to ask you what has happened to Monsieur Dormey.'

'I told you. He was arrested by the Nazis three days ago. Poor fellow—I'm sure that brute Jamier betrayed him. Jamier is an Alsatian and half-German by birth. If I hadn't my living to earn, and things weren't so difficult in these days, I wouldn't remain in his employment for a single second.'

'You're a brave girl, mademoiselle,' Gregory smiled; 'and I know that I can trust you. Monsieur Dormey's arrest has placed me in a great difficulty, as he was to have provided me with secret transport to the coast. Do you by any chance know the name of the lorry-driver who was in his confidence?'

'Hélas, monsieur,' she sighed, 'that I am sure, must have been Guillaume Truchet, who was arrested on the same day. I knew nothing of Monsieur Dormey's affairs except that he was a patriotic Frenchman who hated the Nazis with all his heart; so I fear that I cannot give you any information at all which might prove of help.'

It would have cheered Gregory to talk with this pretty

friendly girl a little longer, and she was obviously willing; but he knew that to do so would be to bring her into danger if anyone happened to recognize him while he was in her company; so he shrugged and smiled resignedly.

'Well, there it is. I must do the best I can on my own. Thank you a thousand times for the warning you gave me.' Then with old-fashioned chivalry he took her hand and kissed it.

She murmured: *'Bonne chance, monsieur.'* Then they parted, the girl to return to the Rue de la Roquette, and Gregory to plunge deeper into the maze of alleyways again.

Having worked back to the Place Voltaire, he made his way north with the idea of having a look at the big railway stations that lay up on the heights.

When in doubt or difficulty he was a great believer in the old precept: 'First things first.' And by hook or by crook he now had to get back to England under his own steam. He certainly would not accomplish that by moping in Paris, and, although he had not the faintest idea as to how he could cross the Channel when he reached it, clearly the first step was to make for the coast. To go by train was obviously the quickest way, if that was possible, but he had grave doubts as to whether it was, and these were confirmed after he had spent some twenty minutes slouching about, but with his eyes very well skinned, in the Gare de l'Est and the Gare du Nord.

Cautious enquiries at both stations confirmed his impression that it was no longer possible to travel in Occupied France without a special permit, and he could see from the numbers of *gendarmes* and Germans at the platform barriers that there was little chance of getting on to any train without one.

He next spent three-quarters of an hour investigating the outsides of the great goods yards, with the idea that he might be able to smuggle himself out of Paris in a railway wagon. But all the gates were well guarded, and, although he felt confident that by waiting until night he could have got into one of the marshalling-yards, from such a centre as Paris it would be quite impossible to tell in the darkness in which direction any goods train which he jumped would be going, and he had no desire to find himself in Switzerland or Germany.

Feeling hungry now, he went into a small restaurant outside the Gare du Nord and had a meal which was dull but adequate, and while he ate he systematically ran over in his mind the various methods by which he might possibly travel to the coast.

Unless he was recognized from his description at one of the police posts on the outskirts of Paris there was nothing to stop his walking, but that would prove a long business; in addition, he had always believed that his brain had been given to him to save his feet, and was constitutionally opposed to any form of unnecessary exercise. He could, of course, buy a push-bike, but that again meant days of most uncongenial effort. The purchase or hire of a car was entirely out of the question, as the Germans were rationing petrol most strictly, and the few remaining people who were allowed to run cars had to have special permits. He could attempt to lorry-hop, but that meant exposing himself to the inquisitiveness of the drivers, and it was certain that any passenger entering the coast zone on a lorry would be subject to suspicion.

It was then he remembered that an hour or so earlier, on his way up to the Gare du Nord, he had crossed the broad Canal St. Martin, which penetrates deep into the heart of Paris, and that in it there had been numerous barges. He knew the North of France well, and was aware that it is furnished with an exceptionally fine network of canals, which serve practically every town of importance and link up with those of Belgium. It seemed reasonable to suppose that the Germans would be keeping a much less close watch on the slow-moving canal traffic than on that of the roads and railways, particularly as it did not run direct towards the coast. A moment later he saw too that the idea possessed the additional advantage that on the coast itself the Germans' watchfulness was certain to be most highly concentrated in the neighbourhood of the French Channel ports, as these were nearest to England, so that if he could get into Belgium he would stand a better chance of getting away in a boat from one of the smaller harbours there.

When he had finished his uninteresting meal he set off up the Rue de la Fayette, at the extreme northern end of which lies the Bassin de la Villette, the great internal port of Paris's barge traffic, where the cargoes from or to the industrial north are discharged or made up.

This is a part of Paris that visitors rarely see—a grimy workaday world in which there are no fashionable *toilettes*, and two sous are rarely spent where one will do. Across the cobbled street from the Bassin there was a long line of bars, small eating-houses and the food-shops where the bargees laid in their stocks of supplies before setting out on a fresh voyage. The food-shops were now almost empty, but the sordid little cafés were still doing a fair business, and even at that hour of the afternoon were half-filled with weather-beaten horny-handed men, sitting over their bocks or syrups and spitting occasionally on the pavement.

Had Gregory been wearing his London clothes he would have been the certain focus of comment in such an assembly, but, knowing the value of inconspicuousness on any secret mission, he had left England in old duds specially chosen for the purpose. These had by no means been improved by the rough handling he had received since, so he might quite well have been taken for a workman.

Knowing that the whole success or failure of his scheme lay in his finding the right type of bargee for his purpose, he spent the best part of two hours in sitting about several of the cafés, where he entered into casual conversations with a number of the men and stood drinks here and there as occasion offered. One thing which cheered him considerably was the fact that these brawny fellows were much more out-spoken than any casual acquaintances that he might have picked up in a smart bar would have dared to be. The Quislings and Gestapo spies were out for much bigger game than these simple workmen, so none of them feared arrest on account of the frank expression of their opinions. As always, in French cafés of every class, politics was the principal subject of conversation. In the course of the afternoon Gregory heard a dozen apparently heated, but actually quite good-tempered, disputes between various groups of men who were either pro-British in sympathy, or wanted the whole war over and were in favour of a new deal under the Nazis.

At last he made his choice of a slow-spoken, middle-aged

fellow, whom he had already learnt was setting out with his barge for Lille the following morning. The man had kind, honest blue eyes, and there was something about him that suggested a quiet courage and fine self-assurance. Unlike most of the others, he did not gesticulate violently as he talked, but his reasoning was clear and logical, and he did not seek to conceal the fact that his sentiments were one hundred per cent. pro-British.

When the little groups broke up Gregory walked out of the café beside him, and they turned together along the quay. For a moment neither of them spoke; then, when they were out of earshot of the others, Gregory said: 'Could you take an extra hand on your barge tomorrow? I've got some money, and I'm quite willing to pay my way.'

The man turned and regarded him gravely, then he said. 'You're English, aren't you?'

'Yes,' said Gregory quietly. 'How did you know?'

The man smiled: 'Oh, just something about you. I'm English myself, you see!'

'Really!' Gregory looked quickly at him again.

'Yes,' he went on, breaking into English. 'Relic of the old war, that's wot I am, mate. I was caught in the St. Quentin show—March '18—you remember? But a French family hid me from the Jerries, an' after the war I married the daughter, settled down and lived 'ere ever since.'

'Good Lord!' Gregory laughed. 'I was in that show, too. What division were you in?'

'The 36th—the Bloody Hand of Ulster was our divisional sign; but I was a gunner, and they were mostly London chaps. Who'd have thought, then, that we'd have this bleeding business all over again, eh?'

'Yes, who'd have thought it?' Gregory agreed. 'Anyhow, it looks like my lucky day. It's only fair that I should be frank with you, though. I've been over here on a job of work, and I'm on the run from the Nazis. I've got to get back to England somehow and . . .'

'You've bitten off something an' no mistake.'

'I'm afraid I have, particularly as I've lost touch with the friends who were to smuggle me across. Still, it'd be a big help if you could get me as far as Lille.'

187

'Course I will, and thundering glad to do it! These last few months 'ave bin fair 'eart-breaking, an' I wouldn't miss the chance o' putting one over them Nazis for a 'undred quid. Bert Wheeler's my name, and I'll eat my Sunday pants if I don't get you safe up ter little ole Lille.'

With this splendid break all Gregory's depression of the morning vanished. Bert took him along to his barge and introduced him to 'the wife', a plump and still good-looking Frenchwoman. She was as pro-British as Bert himself, and on being told the situation made Gregory heartily welcome. The three of them went ashore again to buy provisions for the journey, as Aimée Wheeler explained to Gregory that, scarce as things were in Paris, they were even worse in the provincial towns such as Compiègne, Noyon, St. Quentin, Cambrai and Douai, through which they would pass.

Gregory insisted on paying for everything, and by telling the story that they wanted a few delicacies to celebrate an anniversary, for which money was no object, he succeeded in persuading a number of the shopkeepers to produce luxuries from under their counters which his new friends would not possibly have been able to afford. At seven o'clock they returned to the barge, laden with their purchases, and an hour later Mrs. Wheeler produced for them a really excellent dinner from her little galley in the stern of the vessel.

Afterwards Bert gave them a concert on his accordion, and it was only with the greatest difficulty that Gregory dissuaded him from playing 'Tipperary', 'Roses of Picardy', 'Old Soldiers Never Die', and at the end 'God Save the King'; upon all of which he started without warning. Gregory was made comfortable in a small box-like cabin up in the bow, and he went to sleep that night thanking all his gods that he had found this splendid couple to help him on his way.

At sunrise the following morning the barge chugged out of the Bassin on its way north, and the next four days were a little oasis of happiness and calm for Gregory in the desert of nerve-racking uncertainty through which the track of his life was once again set. Hour after hour the barge steadily nosed its way along canals and rivers, through the peaceful countryside in which there were few traces of war, and he was amazed to see how little damage had been sustained by most of the towns and villages through which they passed; but that, he knew, was to be accounted for by the fact that the German invasion had been carried out with such extraordinary rapidity that in many places the French had never stood to fight.

They reached Lille on November the 7th, and Gregory knew to his regret that the time had come when he must part from Bert and Aimée Wheeler. They flatly refused to accept any money from him, but, having noticed that these simple friends who had shown him such unfailing kindness and good cheer had only a cheap alarum clock in their cabin, he went ashore and bought the most handsome timepiece he could find in the town to present to them as a souvenir of his voyage.

Not wishing to involve Bert in any danger, Gregory had refrained from even discussing possible plans for a continuation of his journey, but when he returned from his shopping expedition with the clock under his arm he found a lean, gaunt-looking fellow with Bert in the cabin of the barge.

Speaking in French, Bert introduced the gaunt man as Hugo Gilleron, another barge-master, who was a friend of his, and announced with a happy wink that Gilleron had agreed to take Gregory on from Lille to Bruges when his barge had completed loading the following day.

Gilleron proved to be a quiet, uncommunicative man, and it later transpired that as he had no wife he had formed the habit of silence from long days spent alone on his barge, with only a young lad to help him. He was, however, bitterly anti-Nazi, as in their advance during the preceding summer the Germans had machine-gunned his old mother, his sister and her child, shooting all three of them to ribbons before his eyes, when they had been struggling along the road in a column of refugees.

Gregory gladly accepted the Frenchman's offer, then took him and the Wheelers ashore for drinks and as good a meal as they could get that evening. Next morning he took his final leave of the Wheelers, and, having transferred his kit, which consisted only of a few things that he had bought in Paris, to the other barge, resumed his journey early in the afternoon.

Lille is only a few miles south of the Belgian frontier, and

Gregory had good reason to be anxious about crossing it, as there was no Belgian visa on the French passport with which Lacroix had furnished him, and if he was found concealed in the barge it was certain that he would be arrested.

However, Gilleron reassured him by saying that the Customs people on the frontier rarely bothered them now that the Germans were the masters everywhere and the border little more than a line on a map; but he took the precaution of hiding Gregory in an empty boiler which was part of his cargo. Actually, the frontier officials did no more than take a brief look under the hatches of the barge, not even troubling to come down into its hold; so half an hour later Gregory was able to emerge and resume his comfortable corner on the afterdeck, where he could survey the placid water through which they rippled and the flat, grey November landscape, with its poplar-lined roads, that made up the Flanders scene.

The fare that Gilleron provided was rough-and-ready after the buxom Aimée Wheeler's excellent cooking, but Gregory, who was no mean amateur cook, took charge of the culinary arrangements and, as was his custom when in the quiet phases of any campaign in which he was involved, slept a great part of the time between meals to average up those hectic periods during which, for long stretches, he might get no sleep at all.

On the afternoon of the 11th they reached Bruges, and, having made Gilleron a handsome present, Gregory stepped ashore, once more faced with the grim problem of how, without further help, he was to make the final, and far the most difficult, stage of his journey.

14

The Vein of Luck Runs Out

As every hour counted Gregory decided that he would not
spend the night in the lovely old Flemish city, but make his
way at once towards the coast. He thought it likely that the
more lonely stretches would probably be barred to civilians,
but that a big town like Ostend could hardly be cut off
altogether from the interior.

He soon found that he was correct. A motor-bus service
was still running, and having made tactful enquiries of the
driver it transpired that no special permits were required for
people going into the great Belgian seaside resort. In consequence, he made the fifteen-mile journey in just under an
hour, and at half past four was set down on the Plage.

Bruges had not been badly blitzed, but Ostend had suffered
heavily, and, although he was turned back by a policeman
from entering the dock area, he got quite near enough to it
to see the R.A.F. had done terrific damage to the harbour
works. The buildings round them and a number of masts
sticking up out of the water told a tale of direct hits on Nazi-
controlled shipping.

He still had no idea how he should manage the incredibly
difficult feat of getting across to England; but without the
least grounds for it he felt just as optimistic and cheerful as
he had felt pessimistic and depressed before he and Kuporovitch had landed on Henri Denoual's island. Perhaps that was
partly due to the splendid break he had had in picking up
Bert Wheeler in Paris, and Bert's then having fixed the
journey from Lille to Bruges with Gilleron for him. But he
somehow had a definite hunch that he had struck a lucky
vein and that it would continue.

On passing a large café on the waterfront he decided to go in and think the situation out over a vermouth. He had hardly given his order when, on looking round, he saw seated alone, a few tables away, a tall, thin man whose face was vaguely familiar. Gregory's first instinct was to cover up and get out of the place as quickly as he could, as in enemy territory anyone who might know him was a potential danger. Before he could even move he saw to his consternation that the man had already recognized him, as he had got up from his table and was coming over. The only thing to do now was to face matters out and hope for the best, although he had a sudden sinking feeling that perhaps he had been over-optimistic about his luck holding, only a few minutes before.

With a little nod the man sat down, and said in a non-committal voice: 'I had no idea that you were still in Belgium.'

At the sound of the man's voice Gregory suddenly remembered who he was and where he had seen him before. He was the Comte de Werbomont, and Gregory had last seen him when he was acting as one of the Gentlemen-in-Waiting to King Leopold.

Feeling more confident now, Gregory smiled and said in a low voice: 'I haven't been living here. I got away all right, but I returned to France a few weeks ago. Now I'm trying to get back to England, and it's only fair to warn you that you may get into serious trouble if I happen to be caught while you're talking to me.'

De Werbomont shrugged. 'I don't think you're in any danger at the moment, and, as you know, we Belgians are prepared to do anything we can to help an Englishman. The fewer people one trusts in these days the better, so I shall perfectly understand if you prefer not to discuss your plans, but if there's any small assistance which I can render please don't hesitate to ask it.'

Gregory smiled rather ruefully. 'That's very good of you, Comte. As a matter of fact, I'm in a very difficult position. I have no plans at all. Everything was fixed up for me to be smuggled out of France, but unfortunately the arrangements broke down. I made my way here from Paris by barge in the hope that the Belgian coast would be less strongly patrolled than the Channel ports and that somehow or other I might succeed in getting across from some little place along the coast here.'

The Comte raised his eyebrows. 'I'm afraid you're going to be disappointed. Any idea of stowing away in a ship is entirely out of the question, now that all traffic of every kind is cut off between England and the Continent. Frankly, if I had to make such a trip I shouldn't have the first idea how to set about it.'

'How about the fishing fleets?' Gregory asked. 'The Germans need all the food they can get; surely they let the fishermen carry on? I've plenty of money, so I could afford to pay any good sportsman handsomely if he'd run me over.'

'There's no hope of that. Ever since the collapse the Germans have had no use for their artillery other than employing it on coast defence; the whole coast positively bristles with batteries of every description. The fishing fleets are never allowed out more than two miles in daylight, and a most careful watch is kept on them, so if one of them attempted to break away it would be sunk within five minutes.'

'How about at night, though?'

'Whenever the trawlers go out at night a strong guard of German soldiers is placed on each vessel to ensure its return.'

'That makes things pretty tricky,' Gregory grinned, 'but there must be lots of small sailing-yachts along the coast; perhaps I could manage to pinch one and get over that way.'

De Werbomont shook his head. 'They were all commandeered months ago and have been concentrated in the larger harbours where it would be quite impossible for you even to get on board one, let alone take it to sea.'

'It looks as though I'll have to make the trip in a rowing-boat, then.'

'What!' exclaimed the Comte. 'You would risk trying to cross to England in an ordinary rowing-boat! From Ostend to Dover is getting on for eighty miles. There are dangerous cross-currents in the Channel. Once you were tired from rowing you would certainly be carried off your course, and that would make the distance to be covered very much longer. It's doubtful, too, if you would be able to get far enough before daylight to avoid being spotted and machine-gunned by the patrolling German aircraft.'

'Yes, it's admittedly one hell of an undertaking. But I've got to get back somehow, and there doesn't seem to be any other way. I've a feeling though, that I'm in a vein of luck at present, and I'm prepared to chance it if I can get hold of a boat.'

'Even that is not going to be easy. With their usual thoroughness the Germans have listed all the small craft that they have not commandeered, and keep a constant check on them.'

'Hang it all! There must be some old tub tucked away in a boat-house that they've overlooked and which would serve the purpose.'

De Werbomont hesitated for a moment. 'As a matter of fact, I have a collapsible canoe packed away up in my attic, but . . .'

'There!' exclaimed Gregory. 'I told you that my luck was in. That is, if you'll be kind enough to let me have it.'

'Of course—if you wish.' The Belgian smiled a little doubtfully. 'But, as I was going to say, it's only a plaything that we used for bathing in the summer. My son once did a river trip in it down the Meuse, but it isn't the sort of thing in which one could hope to cross the Channel.'

'Why not?' Gregory enquired. 'If it's the ordinary type of collapsible canoe, made of struts and canvas, the fore and after parts are covered in; so it's much less likely to get water-logged than an open boat.'

'That's true,' agreed the Comte, 'and the fact of its being smaller would make it less likely to be sighted from the air; but it's much too frail to stand up to any heavy pounding if you meet rough weather.'

'That's on the knees of the gods, but for once in my life I'm dead certain that my luck's in.'

'All right then. Since you're determined to attempt this crazy voyage we'll see what can be done to launch you on it.'

Having paid the bill they set out westward along the Plage. There were few people about other than small groups of German soldiers taking an evening stroll on the sea-front. No short-distance buses were running now, so they had the best part of a two-mile walk before them; but at length they reached the Comte's villa, which lay right on the shore, on the extreme fringe of the town.

He was living there alone with a single manservant who did for him, as both his big house in Brussels and his country estate had been taken over by the Germans; and, as he told Gregory, he found it less depressing to live almost as a hermit in this little week-end seaside villa than in lodgings in the capital.

It was dusk by the time they reached the villa. and Frédéric, the Comte's man, had already done the black-out, about which the Germans were extremely strict in the coastal area.

Going straight upstairs, they got the collapsible canoe out of the box-room, but as Gregory saw it his heart sank a little. It really was a most flimsy affair and had already seen rough usage. One of the struts was broken, and in places the canvas was coming away at the seams.

'I'm sorry,' said the Comte unhappily. 'I'm afraid it's no good after all. It's a long time since I've seen it, and I had no idea it was so dilapidated.'

'It certainly won't do as it is,' Gregory agreed, 'but since the structure is intact we might be able to patch it up.'

Frédéric, who had come up to help them get it out, said quietly: 'That should not be difficult, *monsieur*. We have all sorts of odd bits and pieces down in the garage which could be used for the purpose; but it will take a little time.'

It was clear that there was no prospect whatever of Gregory's making his attempt that night, so they went down-stairs, and while de Werbomont told Gregory about a book that he was writing on the cultivation of vegetables, to occupy his lonely life, Frédéric cooked them a simple, but excellent dinner.

At first Gregory feared that by accepting the Comte's hospitality he might bring him into danger, but de Werbomont said that Ostend was too big a town for the Germans to keep any exact tally upon the people who were living there. They paid domiciliary visits to every house and flat from time to time, but only about once a month; and as they had been over the villa only three days before it was most unlikely that it would be searched again for another week at least.

All through dinner they had had to keep their overcoats on,

as on the edge of the North Sea there it was very cold, and the Germans had cut off all heating facilities except a low allowance of gas for cooking. De Werbomont told Gregory, too, that unfortunately he could not offer him a bath. He then went on to speak of the intense hatred which the Belgians felt for their conquerors and of how they all prayed for a British victory.

Gregory nodded sympathetically. 'Of course, we realize in England that King Leopold did not represent the feelings of the Belgian people when he surrendered, although everybody felt pretty mad about the way that he had exposed the flank of our army to the enemy.'

The Belgian's face suddenly went pale, and Gregory realized that for once he had been unusually tactless, because if he had paused to think he should have guessed that de Werbomont was probably an ardent Royalist.

'How can you possibly believe such a baseless slander?' the Comte said swiftly, his grey eyes flashing. 'The Belgian Army fought to the absolute limit of its endurance, and the King played his part most nobly.'

'Perhaps we'd better not discuss it,' said Gregory, in an effort to get off the painful subject; although he had his own ideas, having actually been present at the surrender.

'But if you hold such a view we *must* discuss it,' de Werbomont insisted. 'You were only in at the last act of the tragedy, whereas I saw it all, and know the facts. Our poor King was made a scapegoat by those treacherous French. At the time it was quite understandable that English people should have believed that scurrilous broadcast by Monsieur Reynaud. But you have seen how the French have behaved since, and surely that must have opened your eyes? Both the King and Lord Gort were under the command of General Gamelin, and it was he who, after the break-through at Sedan, ordered them to retire from the strong line which they should have held to open country where they were virtually defenceless. King Leopold protested but he was overruled, and, in consequence, the Belgian Army was almost annihilated.'

'There I entirely agree,' replied Gregory. 'All our people who were in Flanders say that the Belgian Army fought with the greatest gallantry under the most difficult conditions, but that hardly explains why the King should have surrendered without one word of warning to Lord Gort.'

'But, my friend, you do not know the facts. For four days before the surrender the King had kept Lord Gort informed that the Belgian Army was in ever-increasing difficulties and could not hold out much longer. He gave the same information to the French, and many hours before the actual surrender took place he sent messages to all parties of his intentions. I saw them despatched, so I know. The French Government received warning. We have the testimony of our General who was liaison officer with them for that. Your Government in London also received warning, but unfortunately communications were so dislocated that the warning sent to Lord Gort never reached him, and London could not get in touch with him either. The only people, therefore, who could have warned him, but did not, were the French High Command; and that was no fault of the King's.'

'I see,' Gregory murmured. 'In that case he has been terribly misjudged in England. Mr. Churchill asked at first that judgment should be suspended, but even he, a week later, announced in the House of Commons that we might form our own conclusions on the evidence available.'

'Yes, the damage was done then, I admit, and, of course, the Germans made good use of it for their propaganda. All Belgium was horrified to hear how your press and politicians had stigmatized our dear King as a rat and a traitor.'

'You must admit that the evidence was pretty damning,' Gregory said mildly, 'because the other monarchs whose countries had been overrun—such as the King of Norway and the Queen of Holland—took refuge in England when their armies could fight no longer, in order that they might establish Governments in London and rally the whole resources of their peoples, outside Europe, to continue the struggle against the Nazis; but King Leopold, who could perfectly well have taken an aeroplane or a destroyer to England, voluntarily gave himself up as a prisoner and most valuable hostage to the enemy.'

'But you do not understand,' de Werbomont banged the table with his fists. 'Our monarch is different from others in that, under the Belgian Constitution, on the outbreak of

197

hostilities in Europe he automatically becomes the Chief of the Belgian Armed Forces. In order to get the last ounce of fight out of them he even issued a proclamation some days before the collapse, definitely stating that they must resist to the last man, and, whatever their fate, he would remain with them.'

'That certainly makes a difference,' Gregory admitted; 'but, Constitution or no Constitution, it seems to me that any monarch owes a higher duty to his people as a whole than to any portion of them. Therefore, when the Army could fight no more he was quite justified in ordering their surrender, but he, as the head of the State, should have left the country to form a rallying-point for all his people outside it to continue the struggle against the enemy with the greatest possible intensity.'

'But you are wrong—wrong—wrong! Outside Europe Belgium's resources are not very considerable, and his Ministers who sought to persuade the King to come with them are doing all that can be done in that direction in his stead. On the other hand, Belgium itself is a great industrial country, and by remaining here the King can continue to fight to far better effect.'

'I'm afraid I don't see that, in view of the fact that he no longer has any power and is a prisoner.'

'It is just because he *is* a prisoner that he still wields such enormous power over his people. He has absolutely and categorically refused all collaboration with the Germans, and that example by the King sets a standard for the whole country. We have many rich manufacturers here, and if they had no leadership, certain of them might weaken and allow themselves to be bribed and browbeaten into assisting the German war effort. As it is, every Belgian man and woman knows that they will be incurring the gravest displeasure of the King if they lift one finger to help the enemy. They are prisoners. He is a prisoner, too, but he is still our King, and no person of any standing in the country will go over to the enemy so long as King Leopold remains adamant.'

'I see,' said Gregory slowly. 'In that case all of us in England have terribly misjudged him. It's only to be hoped that time and the truth will clear him of these unfortunate imputations.'

The Belgian smiled and leant forward earnestly. 'His name will go down in history as stainless as that of his great father. Very fortunately, all the documents, with complete proof of his integrity, are already safe in London, and the restoration of his name to honour is a sacred cause with the whole Belgian people.'

Owing to the cold, they did not sit talking for very long, but de Werbomont showed Gregory to a comfortable bedroom, where under plenty of coverings he spent the best night that he had had for some time.

Next morning they got the collapsible canoe down to the garage, which was empty, as the Comte's car had long since been commandeered; but there was a small working-bench at one end of the garage and a miscellaneous assortment of paints and gear.

The Comte proved quite useless at such work, but Frédéric was very helpful, and Gregory's natural ingenuity enabled him to devise means for not only making the necessary repairs but strengthening the canoe considerably. Having cut some pieces of wood to the required length they inserted them as extra struts, then used an old sunblind for patching the canvas where it had rotted, and carefully covered the edges of the patches with rubber solution. For the dual purpose of making it both more watertight and less conspicuous they painted it all over with a mixture blended to a dull green and broke up its outline by two broad strokes of purple which cut across its covered-in bow and stern.

It was evening again by the time they had finished, and although Gregory had hoped to set out that night Frédéric pointed out to him that he would be much wiser to give the paint twenty-four hours to dry; so he slept again under the hospitable de Werbomont's roof.

On the 13th they spent their time devising everything they could think of which might add to Gregory's chances of a successful voyage. In order to buoy up the boat, if it became waterlogged, Frédéric collected all the empty bottles that he could find, and having corked them, firmly wedged them as tightly as he could into the pointed bow and stern. They also sewed a number of cork table-mats into an old sheet so that when Gregory was within a reasonable distance of the English coast he could throw the sheet out and trail it in the water, where, as a big patch of whiteness, it might catch the eye of a British airman and result in help being sent out.

Like many wealthy Belgians, de Werbomont had laid in a good stock of tinned food at the time of the crisis, but he now willingly parted with some of his hidden reserve to provision the canoe. Bottles of water, a bottle of brandy, a torch, cigarettes and matches were also put aboard, an old carriage lamp was rigged up on the stern, and Frédéric succeeded in buying from one of the local fishermen a sou'-wester and an old suit of oilskins.

After dinner that night they waited anxiously until their neighbours had gone to bed, although this precaution was scarcely necessary, since the Belgians, as a whole, were much more pro-British than the French, and very few of them indeed were playing the part of Quislings.

Owing to the lack of proper heating, the population was going to bed early in these days, and even the German garrison, apart from the sentries on night duty, finding little amusement in the hostile town, preferred their barrack-rooms and messes to going out at night; so at half-past ten de Werbomont declared that he thought the coast was now about as clear as it would be at any time during the night.

Frédéric went out as a scout and, after having had a good look round the beach, came back to report that all was well, except for the danger that they might run into one of the German patrols which moved along it at irregular intervals; but that was a risk which had to be taken whatever time they set out.

De Werbomont then led the way down to the beach, while Gregory and Frédéric followed, carrying the now weighty canoe.

For the season of the year the sea was moderately calm, but even so quite biggish breakers were frothing on the shore, and it looked as though the little craft might easily be swamped before they could get it launched.

After a quick debate Gregory got into its cockpit just on the tide line; then, when he had thanked the other two and they had wished him luck, as a big wave came creaming in they ran him out through it till they were nearly waist-deep in the water. With a few swift strokes of his double paddle he sent the canoe leaping towards the next big breaker, just before it broke. For a second the boat rose almost perpendicular in the air, then it tilted forward, rushing down the farther slope, and he was off.

The first hundred yards proved a heavy strain. He had to keep the canoe head on to the incoming waves, otherwise, had one caught it sideways, it would have overturned, then been rolled back and dashed to pieces on the shore. But after a breathless fight he reached deeper water, and although the waves were just as big the strain of fighting them became considerably less.

He had little fear of going under, as the canoe was as buoyant as a cork. Even if it capsized it was virtually unsinkable, so he would be able to cling on to it for as long as his strength lasted; but whether he had the stamina to make the journey was another question.

The moon was only four days from full, and while he had been making his preparations he had dreaded that it might be too bright for them to dare risk carrying the canoe down to the beach. Its light would have made them visible at quite a distance to any prowling Germans; but luck had favoured him again, as the sky was overcast, and not a glimmer of the moon could be seen.

On the other hand, he had to some extent counted on it for setting his course, and he would now have to rely entirely upon the little pocket compass with which de Werbomont had provided him; yet he dared not flash a torch to see it so long as he was near the coast, and for the first half-hour he had to make his way purely by guesswork.

It was only when he risked a first quick flash to look at the compass that he began to realize to the full what he had taken on. The tide had already swung him round, and he found that he was proceeding parallel with the coast. After that, holding his torch low, he flashed it down on to the compass every few minutes, as he soon found that if he did not do so he constantly lost his sense of direction. As far as possible, he endeavoured to maintain a steady stroke, knowing that the one thing he must not do was to exhaust himself too quickly. In the camouflaged boat he felt that he would be really unlucky if the Germans spotted him, provided he could cover a fair distance before morning, but he knew that to reach England safely would require every ounce of his endurance.

After he had been out for about an hour and a half he heard the hum of planes in the darkness overhead. Only a matter of seconds later there came the crash of falling bombs behind him; the R.A.F. were making one of their raids on Ostend harbour.

The first bombs had hardly fallen before the German anti-aircraft batteries opened up, and looking back he saw that the whole coast was now fringed with the long pointing fingers of searchlights, which swept the sky, groping for the raiders, and lit up the sea with a pale gleam for miles around. Mentally he wished the raiders luck and at the same time blessed them as he now no longer had to waste time and lose way every few moments while looking at his compass.

For the next twenty minutes he put his back into it and paddled straight ahead. Gradually the din behind him subsided; then the searchlights went out, plunging him again into complete darkness on the black waters.

Soon after one the sky cleared a little, and the moon became visible intermittently through breaks in the heavy clouds. Again he felt that his luck was in. The light was not sufficient for such a small craft as his to be sighted at any distance from a German patrol boat, but he had carefully worked out the position of the moon at various times for that night, so he was able to set his course by it, and once more prevent the loss of way from looking at his compass so frequently.

Hour after hour he ploughed on through the gently heaving sea with a steady rhythmic motion, resting for short periods now and again, but never long enough for the boat to be swept far off its course. About five o'clock he took a longer spell, and made a light meal of some biscuits and lukewarm coffee laced with cognac, which Frédéric had put into a bottle for him.

The moon had now set, and he paddled on for another couple of hours in darkness, then it gradually lightened until the grey streaks of dawn came up in the east. A little after dawn a wind got up, and this gave him considerable concern, as it was blowing at an angle across his bows, which meant that he could no longer stick to his even stroke and had to paddle much more strongly with one arm than the other to keep the nose of the canoe headed in the right direction. As the wind increased it became a devilish fight to prevent the little craft from being swung right round and driven far off her course.

Gregory was tired now; the muscles of his back ached, and his hands were beginning to blister. The wind, too, was whipping at the wave-caps, so that a constant spray lashed over the boat, stinging his face, covering it with salt brine and getting into his eyes.

Morning had come, and he was as much alone as if he had been in the centre of the Atlantic Ocean. Owing to the fact that his head was only a few feet above sea-level, his horizon was very limited, and as the canoe shot down into the troughs of the waves he could often see no more than a few yards ahead; but when it swished up on to a crest he could catch a momentary glimpse of the heaving seas all round him for a considerable distance. He was out of sight of the Belgian coast, although he had not the least idea how far he had managed to get from it, and he was in two minds as to whether he wanted to see a ship or not, as he knew that in any case he must still be a very long way from England, so the odds on its being British or Nazi were about even.

At nine o'clock he abandoned the uneven battle for a little while he fed again, but it irked him bitterly that every moment he rested the canoe was now drifting sideways with the wind and undoing some of the heavy labour he had put in. When he began to paddle again another thing that worried him was that he had no means at all of judging what progress he was making while the sea continued to be so choppy. For all he knew he was only barely countering the effects of the tide and the wind, so that unless they lessened all his efforts might serve no better purpose than to keep him in the same position for hours, or even days, on end.

In the middle of the morning three British planes flew over, but he knew that they were much too high to see him, so he did not even bother to get out his cork-floated sheet, and in a few moments they had disappeared from view. Just after midday he saw a long pencil-shaped Dornier, which was flying at a much lower altitude. As it came towards him he feared for a moment that he might be spotted and machine-gunned, but its pilot must have seen something that interested him farther north, since the aircraft suddenly veered off in that direction. He was bitterly cold and had constantly to resist the temptation to take too frequent nips from the bottle of brandy, but he did not feel the least hungry and had to force himself to make another meal early in the afternoon, because he knew that it would help to keep his strength up.

About half-past three he sighted a destroyer. From her design he felt certain she was British, and he put on a terrific spurt in a wild endeavour to cut across her course. But even her apparently leisurely speed carried her along at far too swift a pace for him to get anywhere near her, and, although he waved his paddle and shouted at the top of his voice, owing to the fact that he was so low in the water she passed without her lookouts having seen him.

As it neared five o'clock his anxiety increased. The winter day was closing in, and it looked now as though he would have to spend a second night at sea. Even in a rowing-boat that would not have been quite so bad, as there he would at least have been able to stretch his limbs and warm himself a little by violent exercise; but in the tiny canoe he was imprisoned from the waist down, and had been sitting now in exactly the same position for close on nineteen hours. From time to time he was getting bouts of cramp, and he felt another night would be almost unendurable.

It was the realization of this that caused him to light the carriage lantern which had been rigged-up just behind him. By doing so he deprived himself of the option to form a judgment as to whether any ship which might come on the scene were British or German before hailing, and in the latter case hoping to remain unobserved. If anyone saw the light at all and decided to investigate, it would be pure chance whether they proved friends of enemies; but he felt that the risk had now to be taken. If a Nazi ship picked him up it was hardly likely that they would shoot him out of hand, whereas, chilled to the marrow and desperately tired as he was, he felt that if he was not picked up at all there was a good chance of his dying of exposure.

As twilight deepened the wind went down a little, so he took the opportunity to have another rest, and laying down his paddle glanced behind him. He could have fainted for sheer joy. The same destroyer that he had seen earlier in the afternoon had evidently turned in her track, as she was now heading back towards him, and less than a quarter of a mile distant.

Getting out his sheet, he draped it on one end of the paddle and began to wave it wildly, almost upsetting the canoe. Next moment there was a faint shout from the destroyer, and he knew that he had been seen. He had been right about his vein of luck; it had held out after all.

The destroyer hove to, a boat was lowered, and the frozen Gregory helped aboard. For a little time he could not even stand upright, but when the Lieutenant-Commander came down off the bridge to question him he was getting back the use of his legs. Having given an account of himself, he was taken down to the ward-room by a sub-lieutenant, who gave him a good stiff drink and lent him a pair of dry trousers. He soon learnt that the destroyer was a unit of the Dover Patrol, and that, although he was a considerable way north of the course he had set himself, he had managed to place the best part of thirty miles between the Belgian coast and himself before he was picked up. The destroyer was now beating back to Dover, and to his great satisfaction it put him ashore there shortly after ten o'clock that night.

He still had the special identity card with which he had been furnished by the P.I.D. man sewn up in the sole of his left shoe; so on opening up the seam with a penknife he was able to produce it and satisfy the Security officials as to his bona fides, upon which he was allowed to leave the dock.

For over three months now Dover had been in the front line of the air blitz, and the town had suffered heavily in consequence. but a number of its hotels were still carrying on. It was too late for him to proceed to London that night, even if he had been in a fit state to travel, so he secured a room at the nearest.

The hours that he had spent in the warm ward-room of

205

the destroyer had more or less restored him to himself, but he was still immensely tired, so he stayed up only long enough to put through a trunk call to Erika to let her know of his safe return to England. Then, revelling in the thought that his luck had held up to the very last, he pulled off his clothes and almost fell into bed.

Next day he caught the morning train to London and arrived at Carlton House Terrace in time to lunch with Sir Pellinore. Over it he gave full particulars of his hazardous trip, then wrote down for the Baronet the details that Lacroix had given him regarding the secret shipment of arms to France and the name of the trusted man in the Vichy Consulate at Lisbon to whom the big sums that Lacroix required to finance his movement were to be sent.

Sir Pellinore congratulated him most heartily upon his lucky escapes and spoke very cheerfully of affairs in Britain as they stood on this, the 15th of November. He was greatly elated that on the 6th President Roosevelt had been elected for a third term, and said:

'Mind you, we've got plenty of good friends in both the Democratic and Republican Parties, but as far as the war is concerned it would have been the very devil for us if Roosevelt had had to leave the White House. As you probably know, when a President goes out in the United States it means that the whole Administration changes from top to bottom, and however keen the new men might have been to help Britain it would have meant at least three months before they had had time to go into everything and really get the hang of their jobs. That would have slowed everything up tremendously, whereas with the old lot remaining put the whole machine will continue to turn over to our benefit without any pause at all.'

'How's the bombing been?' Gregory asked.

The Baronet laughed. 'We've beaten the devils, my boy—anyhow, for the time being. The public doesn't realize it yet, but the first Battle for Britain is over, and I'm as certain as that I like my champagne iced that this stupendous R.A.F. victory will prove the turning-point of the whole war.'

'Do you really mean that the raids have stopped, then?'

'Oh no! We still have one now and again, but they've done

mighty little damage in the past fortnight, and it's already been officially agreed that October the 31st was technically the end of Goering's big show. Between August the 6th and October the 31st 375 Royal Air Force pilots were killed and 358 wounded. As against that, 2,534 German aircraft were totally destroyed and another, 1,996 severely damaged. To put 733 British pilots out of action cost the Nazis over 4,500 of their first-line planes. Those figures are official.'

'God! What a victory!' Gregory exclaimed .'It should rank in history as another Thermopylae, where the six hundred Spartans held the whole of the Persian hosts. Still, on purely selfish grounds I'm mighty glad that it's eased up. Although I slept last night at Dover, I feel as though I could sleep for a month, so I can do with a quiet night tonight.'

That afternoon he telephoned Erika again to have a much longer conversation, and, although she was overjoyed to know that he was safe and well, the edge was taken off her happiness by the news that Stefan Kuporovitch and the French girl, of whom he had talked to her in such glowing terms, had both almost certainly fallen into the hands of the enemy, and that Gregory's hopes of seeing them alive again were extremely slender.

Early in the evening he went to his club and spent a few pleasant hours having rounds of drinks and swopping yarns with a number of his friends who were still in London. Having dined there, he afterwards went straight back to Gloucester Road. The flat was empty, as Rudd was on duty that night with his fire-fighting squad, so, having mixed himself a night-cap. Gregory got into bed.

He had not been there for five minutes before the sirens went. At their banshee wailing he cursed faintly, hoping that the raid would not be a bad one, but determined whatever happened to stay in bed. For about twenty minutes he listened to the anti-aircraft guns and the uneven rhythm of the German night raiders somewhere high over the roof-tops.

Now and again a bomb crumped in the distance; then one fell much nearer which shook the whole house. He heard the next one coming. It made a long whistling sound, and the whole place rocked, as it exploded with a roar. Like all old soldiers, Gregory loathed being bombed and never sought to disguise from himself that he was slightly frightened, but reason always came to his aid at such moments. He invariably kept telling himself that with the millions who were still in London, and the few hundred casualties which occurred, even in the worst raids, the odds were extraordinarily big against his being hit.

As he lay there his cynical sense of humour was tickled by a sudden thought of how ironical it would be if, having in the past months survived so many dangers, he should be killed by a bomb in his own comfortable bed, now that he had at last succeeded in getting safely back to London.

Even as the thought crossed his mind another bomb whistled down. As it exploded with a terrific crack he clenched his hands instinctively; then he caught the rumble of masses of bricks, as a nearby house collapsed like a landslide into the street.

Another moment passed, then he suddenly saw the ceiling above him crack. It gaped wide open. The two halves parted and started to swing down as though they were on hinges. Then the whole thing seemed to dissolve in clouds of dust and smoke as a bomb burst above his head. Next second he was whirled midst flying bricks, plaster and fragments of smashed furniture into an awful soul-destroying darkness.

15

Into the Lion's Jaws

Stefan Kuporovitch hung like a sack over the branch of a tree. With a painful effort he opened his eyes, but he was in complete darkness and for a moment he had no idea where he was or what had happened to him. Then, all that had occurred before he had lost consciousness slowly filtered back into his bemused brain.

The nursing-home had been raided while he and Gregory were in conference with Lacroix. The little Colonel had been smuggled out of his coffin. Just as the mutes were getting it into the hearse Major Schaub had appeared on the scene and demanded that it should be opened. Gregory had done what was undoubtedly the right thing in precipitating a gun-fight rather than allow their chief to be arrested. There had been a wild *mêlée*, in which a score of shots had been exchanged, and Kuporovitch himself had shot one of the Nazis through the head. Then he had dragged Madeleine back through the door of the nursing-home, slammed it to and bolted it.

Someone had said that the house was surrounded by the police, so, instead of making for the courtyard at its back, he had rushed Madeleine and Nurse Yolanda upstairs, with the idea of getting them away over the neighbouring roofs. Just as they reached the attic the trap-door in its ceiling had opened and a French policeman came plunging down the ladder.

Kuporovitch had shot him, but a volley of shots had then come spattering down from the man's companions who were still out on the roof; so Kuporovitch had rushed the two girls out of the room again, locking its door behind him. As they hurried downstairs they heard the sounds of fighting below, which told them that the police had already broken in through either the front or back of the house and were in combat with some of Lacroix's agents, who had been caught down in the dining-room. Kuporovitch had then pushed his two charges into a back bedroom on the second floor.

On looking out of the window he had seen no movement in the courtyard, and judged it possible that the police who had been detailed to approach the house from behind were now inside. It immediately occurred to him that if they were engaged in the fight that was raging below, and his own party could only get down to the courtyard, they might escape by way of it.

Dragging the sheets and blankets from the bed, with the aid of the two girls he had knotted the ends of the bedclothes together so that they formed a stout rope. Within three minutes of their entering the room they had one end of the knotted bedclothes tied firmly to the bed and the other dangling through the window within a few feet of the courtyard.

Madeleine had insisted that Nurse Yolanda should go first, and the pretty little nurse had swarmed down hand over hand, reaching the ground in safety. Madeleine followed, but was not so lucky. In their haste to make their improvised rope one of the knots had not been sufficiently tightly tied. When she was half-way to the ground the rope parted just below the window-sill, and she fell the last six feet.

It was already semi-dark, and as Kuporovitch stared down he had not been able to see very clearly; but enough to relieve his apprehensions for the moment, as through the grey murk of the winter evening he saw Madeleine pick herself up, and knew that she could not have hurt herself very badly.

Next second his heart had leapt to his mouth again. Dark forms had suddenly come running from the back of the house and with excited shouts seized upon the two young women. For a few seconds the Russian had remained there, leaning right out of the window. He dared not fire, as in the scrimmage it was just as likely that he would have shot one of the girls as either of their attackers; yet he knew that his only hope of rescuing them now lay in getting down to the courtyard. As the rope had parted just below the window-sill there was only one thing for it: the nearest branches of a big elm tree which grew in the courtyard were no more than ten feet distant from the window out of which he was leaning. Climbing up on to the sill, he launched himself with clutching hands into the now scanty autumn foliage, hoping that he would be able either to grab a branch or that some of them would at least break his fall before he reached the ground.

As he plunged forward he had felt the twigs scratching at his hands and face; then a terrific blow on the head as his forehead came into violent contact with the upper part of the tree-trunk. Stars and whirling circles had flamed for a second before his eyes, as he crashed downwards through the darkness, then he had been brought up with a terrific jolt that had driven the breath out of his body, and passed clean out.

When he came to he realized that he had fallen on to one of the main branches of the big tree and was still hanging there. Owing to their struggle with the girls, and the semi-darkness, the police had evidently not seen him when he had been leaning out of the window, or witnessed his jump from it into the tree. As they could not have known how many people there were inside the home to start with, there was no reason at all for them to search for him, and they had evidently gone off with their prisoners, imagining that they had netted the whole bag, while he was suspended in the tree unconscious.

He had the grandfather of all headaches from the blow against the tree-trunk which had knocked him out, and his middle was terribly bruised and sore from its violent contact with the big branch over which he was dangling. Very gently he raised himself up until he was spread at full length along it, wriggled back to the tree-trunk and cautiously lowered himself to the ground.

Sitting down there, with his back propped up against the tree while he recovered a little, he began to consider what he had better do.

Madeleine had undoubtedly been arrested, and by now was probably in a cell at the *Sûreté* or some other prison. The thought that she might be shot or sent to a concentration camp was absolute agony to him, and he knew that he must act quickly if he was to have any hope at all of rescuing her.

Having seen the hearse dash off, he felt reasonably confident that Gregory and Lacroix had got away, so his first thought was to set off for Vichy to secure the Colonel's aid. But he had no papers which would enable him to pass the frontier between Occupied and Unoccupied France, and he realized at once that, lacking these, and with the difficulty of obtaining transport, it would probably take him days to make his way to Vichy; and even when he got there he might find that Lacroix had been captured after all. In any case, time ruled out that idea.

His next thought was to try to get hold of Lieutenant Ribaud. As he was still acting under the Nazis he should be able to find out where Madeleine had been taken and, as Lacroix's principal agent in Paris, would undoubtedly give all the help he could. Perhaps he might even be able so to arrange matters that Madeleine could be rescued with a minimum of risk to herself and her rescuers.

Having decided on his line of action Kuporovitch got to his feet and tiptoed softly towards the house. A considerable sum of Lacroix's money was kept by Madeleine in a secret hiding-place in her room against emergencies, and it seemed foolish to leave it there if there was any chance of getting hold of it.

The back door was not locked, and pushing it gently he crept inside. The passage was in darkness, but a light showed in the front hall, and he caught the sound of voices before he had advanced more than half a dozen paces. Evidently the police had left some of their people there to seize any of the agents who might come to the house, unaware that it had been raided. As he still had his pistol, in other circumstances Kuporovitch would have gone forward; but as Madeleine's only hope now lay in his remaining at liberty he decided that at the moment he had no right to risk being captured, or a fight in which he might get shot. Turning round, he tiptoed cautiously back again, out into the courtyard and through an alley which led from it to a small side street a hundred paces from the back of the house.

It took him some ten minutes to find a telephone-box, but having got on to the *Sûreté* he was put through to the Lieutenant almost at once.

'I'm afraid my name would not convey anything to you,'

he said, 'but I have some important information which I should like to give to you personally, if it is possible for you to come out and meet me somewhere.'

Ribaud was too wise a man to ask any embarrassing questions from such a caller, and he replied: 'I cannot get away from my office for about three-quarters of an hour, and after that I have a dinner appointment at which I must not be late, but I could see you for a few minutes, if you can arrange to be somewhere in the neighbourhood of the Palais Royal at a quarter to eight. How about the Café de l'Univers, which is right opposite, and adjoins the Hôtel du Louvre?'

'That would suit me admirably,' said Kuporovitch, and rang off.

Well before a quarter to eight, he was seated at one of the tables near the door inside the café. Soon afterwards he saw the short, tubby French detective come in, and made an inconspicuous signal to him.

At first Ribaud did not recognize Kuporovitch, as he had only seen him once before for a few moments in Major Schaub's room on the night that he had been arrested; but as he sat down the Russian's startling black eyebrows, which made such a sharp contrast to his grey hair, unlocked a cell in the detective's memory.

'So you got away,' he said, beckoning to the waiter to take his order.

'You knew about the raid, then?' Kuporovitch said softly, when the waiter had left them.

'Yes—I've just come from helping in the examination of some of our friends who were brought in.'

'I take it Madeleine Lavallière was among them?'

'Yes.'

'I thought as much,' nodded Kuporovitch sadly, 'but how did you guess that I was one of the people who were using the home?'

'I guessed it,' smiled the detective. 'The fact of a stranger who gave no name ringing me up at such a time, and then to find that it was you, Madeleine Lavallière's old friend, was quite enough. How did you manage to get away?'

Kuporovitch told him, adding that as the police were still in the house he hoped that some measures could be taken

213

to warn those of .ts occupants who had not been caught in the raid.

'As far as is possible that has already been done, but was it that only about which you wished to see me?'

'Partly that, but also on Madeleine's account. I hope to God that those brutes are not ill-treating her!'

'No, she's all right for the moment, as she is still in the hands of our own police. But I wouldn't care to be in the shoes of any of these poor friends of ours when they're handed over to the Gestapo, as they will have to be.'

'Can you do nothing to prevent that?'

Ribaud shook his head. 'Unfortunately, no. All of us must stand on our own feet. We know what we're risking when we enter upon the work upon which we are engaged. If we're caught that's just too bad, but no other member of our organization must jeopardize himself by endeavouring to help friends who have fallen by the way. That is an order. Of course, if I could do anything without endangering my own position—just as I got Madeleine released before when there was no serious charge against her, and yourself put over the frontier—I would willingly do it; but it is necessary that we should place our organization before sentiment. As our Chief's principal hidden ear in the police service of Occupied France, it would be criminal in my own case to do anything which might cause myself to become suspect.'

Kuporovitch nodded. 'I quite understand that, but my case is somewhat different. I'm just a foreigner who hates the Nazis and wishes France well. I have been playing my part among the French freedom-fighters with the greatest willingness; but now the safety and the life of the woman that I love are involved, and my first duty is to her. I am prepared to face any risk for the smallest chance of getting her out of the hands of the Gestapo. Can you suggest to me any way in which I might set to work?'

'I only wish I could'—Ribaud spread out his hands—'but their police system is virtually watertight. These Germans have an absolute genius for organization, and, God knows, in the last few years the Nazis have had plenty of practice in seeing to it that their prisoners don't escape. She will undergo preliminary examination here, then in the course of a few days she will probably be sent to Germany; but night and day she will be under guard. I fear your chances of saving her are extremely slender.'

'At least you can tell me where she will be imprisoned while she remains in Paris,' said Kuporovitch; 'or will she be kept at the *Sûreté?*'

'No. She will be transferred with the other women who were captured this evening to the *Cherche-Midi*. It is an old prison, and they are using it again now for female political prisoners.'

'And Major Schaub?' asked the Russian. 'Can you tell me where he lives?'

'He has a room at the Headquarters of the Army of Occupation in the Hôtel Crillon.'

'You feel reasonably certain that Madeleine will not be moved from the *Cherche-Midi* for the next few days?'

'Yes; but if you care to ring me up at any time I can always let you know if she is still there or not. Just ask me if the cigarettes have come in, and if I say they have not arrived you'll know that she has not been shifted. If, on the other hand, I say that they have, you can suggest a time and place at which you propose to collect them, then I'll meet you there and let you know what they've done with her. You must forgive me now, but my dinner appointment is for eight o'clock, and it is important that I should be on time.'

When the Frenchman had gone the Russian paid his bill and left the café. Crossing the road, he walked past the Théâtre Français up the Rue de Richelieu, until he came to a little restaurant, and, entering it, he endeavoured to revive his spirits a little with as good a dinner as he could get, while he thought over possible plans.

By the time he left it he was feeling scarcely less depressed, but he had the germ of an idea, and, turning it this way and that in his subtle brain, he set about finding some place where he could pass the night. It occurred to him that he would be less likely to be asked awkward questions about his having no luggage if he slept in a Turkish Baths, so he went into a café and made enquiries from a waiter. The waiter told him that the Hammam was quite near by, in the Rue des Mathurins, and gave him directions to it, although remarking that he had no idea if it were still open.

The Hammam was still open, but only for massage, as the shortage of fuel in Paris now made it impossible to keep the steam-rooms going. As Kuporovitch was cold, tired, and bruised about the body, he would have given a lot for a hot bath of any kind, but that being out of the question massage was better than nothing, since it would serve to stimulate his circulation and ease the strained muscles of his stomach.

Having undressed, he found that it was now black and blue from where he had fallen across the bough of the tree, but he told the masseur that he had tripped in the black-out and come crashing down across a low stone balustrade. After the man had been working on him for three-quarters of an hour he felt very much better. About half past ten, wrapped in blankets, he turned in, and, in spite of his gnawing anxiety about Madeleine, passed a reasonably good night.

As is so often the case, his brain continued to work for him while he slept, so when he reconsidered his plan the next morning he found that his fragmentary ideas had now fallen into place; but as a first step to carrying them out he required at least a ton of coal, and coal was now virtually unobtainable in Paris.

On leaving the Turkish Baths he telephoned Ribaud from a call-box and made known his requirement. Then, in order to cover the detective against anyone who might be tapping his line, he said that he had very stupidly made a bet the night before when he had had one over the odds, that by hook or by crook he would get hold of a ton of coal, and he must do his best to win it.

Ribaud played up to the line given him, laughed a lot at the rashness of the bet, chipped the Russian about having got tight, then said that he might try a Monsieur Lavinsky of 29, Rue Buffon, near the Gare d'Austerlitz. Lavinsky was a black market operator, and Ribaud indicated in guarded language that if Lavinsky refused his help Kuporovitch should exert pressure on him by telling him that the police knew what he was up to and would take action against him unless he was prepared to oblige Lieutenant Ribaud's friend.

Kuporovitch got a bus which took him over the river and

along the quays of the south bank; and getting off at the railway station soon found Lavinsky's office. Lavinsky proved to be a fat little Jew, who, judging by the size of his warehouse, and the samples of many kinds of scarce goods which littered his office, was doing a considerable business. When Kuporovitch asked him for a ton of coal he almost threw a fit, rolling his eyes up to heaven and throwing out his short tubby hands with a despairing gesture.

'A ton of coal!' he cried. 'Why do you not ask at once for a ton of gold? It would be just as difficult to get and hardly more expensive. Besides, you must know that it is rationed, and that to sell a single knob to anyone without a permit is now a serious offence against the regulations.'

Fixing him with his brown eyes, which could go so hard on occasion, Kuporovitch replied: 'Let us not waste time, my friend, in talking hot air about difficulties and regulations. I know that you have the stuff, and I am quite prepared to pay you black market prices for it. What is more, I wish to borrow a horse and wagon from you so that I can deliver it myself.'

'But you are crazy!' the Jew expostulated. 'I am an honest trader, who has his own customers to consider, and never would I handle anything by way of the black markets.'

'Well, you're going to this time,' said the Russian firmly. 'I was talking this morning with my good friend Lieutenant Ribaud . . .'

The Jew's eyes suddenly narrowed. 'You are from the police, then. I guessed from your accent that you were a German, monsieur, and, of course, I will help you if I must; but I assure you that in the ordinary way I would never dream of going against regulations.'

Kuporovitch did not correct the Jew's wrong assumption about his nationality, as it gave him an even bigger pull, but said: 'Lieutenant Ribaud informs me differently. In fact, if we cared to do so, we could bring quite a number of charges with heavy penalties against you; but if you'll do as I wish I don't think it likely that the police will bother you.'

Lavinsky had gone perceptibly paler, and he now began to rub his hands together as he stuttered out his anxiety to be of service. But when they got down to the price of the coal, in spite of his obvious fright, he proved a stubborn bargainer. Kuporovitch had to part with two thousand francs, which was nearly half his total reserve of cash, as the price of a single ton of very indifferent coal.

He then told Lavinsky that he wanted the coal loaded on to a cart with a horse already harnessed up, so that he could drive it away when he called again at four o'clock that afternoon; he added that he also wished a man or boy to accompany him and, later, to bring back the empty cart.

He now had only a few things to buy while he killed time until the day was sufficiently advanced for him to make his bid to rescue Madeleine; so he walked slowly through the Jardin des Plantes and up the sloping street towards the Luxembourg, stopping at various shops to make his purchases. These consisted of a small brown handbag, a white linen jacket, such as barbers wear, which he managed to find after visiting several second-hand shops, and a number of items such as scissors, clippers, brush, comb and towels, which are the implements of the barber's trade. He then bought some rolls and some very indifferent sausage-meat which was mainly bread, and took them into the Luxembourg Gardens, where he sat down on a bench to make a picnic meal. Had he but known it, Gregory was that morning also killing time, in the Bois de Vincennes; but unfortunately neither of the two friends had the faintest idea where the other had got to; so, instead of being able to meet and cheer each other up, they had perforce to wander about alone and in considerable anxiety about one another.

At last the time came for Kuporovitch to make his way back to the Rue Buffon. On his arrival there he demanded a blank delivery slip, then Lavinsky led him out into the yard, where a loaded coal-cart with a young boy beside it was already waiting. Having handed over the two thousand francs the Russian proceeded to get himself up like a coal-heaver by tying an apron of empty sacks round his still sore middle, draping another like a pointed hood on his head, and smearing his face lightly here and there with coal-dust. The little Jew was eyeing these manoeuvres with the utmost curiosity, so Kuporovitch went over to him and said in a husky whisper: 'This is Gestapo business, so keep your nose out of it, or you'll find yourself in trouble. If you attempt to follow me, or have me followed, you'll be getting a free ride to Dachau.'

With a nod to the boy, who clambered up on to the back of the cart, Kuporovitch mounted to the driver's seat and, flicking his whip, drove the coal-cart out of the yard.

At a slow walk it trundled through the streets of Paris until they reached the tradesmen's entrance of the Hôtel Crillon. Pulling up, he got down, and, leaving the boy to look after the horse, slouched across the pavement to the hotel doorway, where he told the goods porter that he had a ton of coal for him.

The man said that he knew nothing about it, so Kuporovitch shrugged and replied: 'All right, then, I'll take it away again. If you don't want it there are plenty of people who do.'

'No, don't do that,' said the man hastily. 'I expect my boss forgot to tell me that a load was being delivered this afternoon. He's off duty now, but I'll show you where to put it.'

As Kuporovitch was about to follow the porter inside a German sentry stepped forward and roughly motioned him back, upon which the porter said: 'You stay out in the street, chum. No one's allowed in here except the staff. I'll go down and unlock the cellar, and if you watch along the pavement you'll see me push up the lid of the manhole; then all you'll have to do is to shoot the stuff down out of your sacks.'

The Russian was in no way dismayed, as he had felt certain that no one would be allowed inside the headquarters of the German Army of Occupation except such members of the hotel's original staff as had been retained for convenience, and that these would be under close supervision. A few minutes later he saw the lid of a manhole about fifty yards away tilt up out of the pavement, and walking along to it he lifted the lid right out, while beckoning to the boy to lead the horse and cart nearer.

Squeezing himself through the hole, Kuporovitch found that he was in a roomy cellar, where several tons of coal had already been heaped up against one wall. The light was on, and the porter was standing there. Pointing to the heap he said:

'You'd best shovel it up on to that when you've got it down so as to keep the space under the manhole clear. I'll have to

219

lock you in, as these Germans are strict as blazes, and I'd find myself in a concentration camp if you so much as poked your nose out into the passage. Shall I sign for it now or come back when you've finished?'

'I expect they keep you pretty busy, so you may as well sign now,' Kuporovitch muttered, taking from his pocket the printed slip with which he had made Lavinsky furnish him, and a stub of pencil.

The porter signed the slip and locked the door behind him; then, climbing out of the manhole, Kuporovitch set to work to unload the wagon and shoot its contents down into the cellar. Having got it down, he shovelled it on to the big heap. The whole job took him best part of an hour and a half, as he had calculated it would; so by the time he had done darkness was already falling.

He now had to get rid of the boy and the cart, and he knew that this was a weak link in his plan, as if the boy was a Quisling and reported either to the porter or Lavinsky that he had left the amateur coal-heaver behind all sorts of unpleasant possibilities loomed ahead; but the Russian had been able to devise no other way of getting rid of the cart than to bring someone with him, and he could only rely on a judicious blend of bribery and fear to ensure the lad's keeping his mouth shut.

Wriggling out of the hole again, he said to the young *gamin*: 'Your master doesn't know where I am delivering this coal, and I don't want him to. He's certain to ask you when you get back, but I suppose you wouldn't mind telling him a fib, if I make it worth your while—eh? How about a hundred francs to say that we took the coal to the Soviet Embassy? You can tell him if you like that I'm not a German, as he thought, but a Russian.'

'A hundred francs!' chirruped the lad excitedly. 'That's all right by me, mister, if I ain't getting into any trouble.'

'You won't—provided you keep a still tongue in your head. But there are queer things happening in Paris these days, and life is pretty cheap. I mean to stay behind here, and my friends know what I'm up to. If you breathe a word of that you'll get a knife in your back one dark night; so you'd better be careful.'

220

The boy let out a frightened whistle, but he eagerly grabbed the hundred-franc note that Kuporovitch held out, and as the cart drove away the Russian was fairly satisfied that he had little fear from a betrayal in that direction. Lowering himself again through the coal-hole, he drew its lid back into place after him.

When making his plan Kuporovitch had imagined that if he could only get into one of the hotel cellars he would have access to the rest of the building, but that had not proved to be the case at all, as the porter had locked him in. However, one swift glance at the door had been enough to show him that in this case it was very much less of an obstacle to his plans to be locked in than to be locked out, as the cellar door had one of those old-fashioned square iron box locks, which was affixed to its inside where he could easily get at it. After taking off his coal-heaver's sacking and cleaning his face as well as he could with lick and his handkerchief, he went over to make a proper inspection of the lock.

The slot into which the tongue of the lock disappeared was only affixed to the door-jamb by two rusty screws. Among the implements which were lying about in the cellar was a wood-chopper, and having forced its edge under the slot a good heave was sufficient to drag the screws out of the dry wood. There was nothing to hold the door to but its latch, so he could go out into the passage whenever he wished.

Picking up his small bag, he gently eased the door open and listened intently. Hearing faint footsteps in the distance, he closed the door again, and waited patiently until their owner had passed; then he opened it once more and gave a swift glance either way down the corridor. No one was in sight, so he stepped out, drawing the door to behind him.

As he did not know the geography of the building he had no idea what he would come to, whichever way he turned; but keeping his dirty hands concealed as well as possible, he set off at a brisk walk along the underground passage towards the side of the hotel that overlooks the Place de la Concorde. His luck held good, as before he had encountered anybody he spotted in a side passage the very thing for which he was looking; a lift. Slipping into it, he pressed the top button and was swiftly carried up to the sixth floor.

Knowing that the one thing which might arouse suspicion was if he should be seen tiptoeing around, or looking this way or that as though he did not know his way about, he stepped boldly out and walked along the corridor, as if in a great hurry. A German orderly passed him without a glance, and twenty paces farther on he saw a door marked '*Bains*', which, again, was what he was looking for. On trying the handle he found that the room was not occupied, and, going inside, locked the door. Walking over to the fixed basins, he turned on the hot-tap and grinned to himself delightedly. As he had supposed, whoever else went without hot water in Paris, the German General Staff certainly would not. Turning on the bath, he proceeded to undress.

For the next half-hour he thoroughly enjoyed himself as he wallowed in the warm water, which eased the still strained muscles of his middle, and it tickled his sense of humour to think that, all unknown to the Nazis, one of their most inveterate enemies was making use of their quarters with impunity.

Having dried himself on his hand-towels, he shaved and dressed again, but this time put on the white barber's coat, packing his own in the bottom of his bag under the towels and hairdressing implements. He then left the bathroom as boldly as he had entered it, feeling greatly invigorated and refreshed.

His next problem was to find Major Schaub's room. He dared not go downstairs to the main hall and ask for it at the chief hall-porter's desk, as it was almost certain that a German would have been installed there, who would realize at once that he was not a member of the hotel staff; and as he could not produce any form of special pass he would promptly be put under arrest. He thought it unlikely that the Major's room would be up on the sixth floor, as that would be devoted mainly to orderlies, while junior officers would be accommodated on the fifth, and the real big shots of the German General Staff would have their rooms on the first and second. The probability was that an officer of the Major's rank would have a room on the third or fourth, and he decided to try the fourth floor first.

Going down to it in the lift, he knocked on the first door

222

he came to, opened it, and smiled broadly at an officer who was sitting half-dressed on the bed, as he said: 'Pardon, *monsieur*, I thought this was Major Schaub's room. I have come to cut his hair.'

The officer flung a curse at him, but in a surly voice added the information that Major Schaub didn't live along that corridor.

Bowing himself out, Kuporovitch tried another room, round the corner and some distance from the first. It was locked. He tried another. That was locked too. In the next a blue-eyed lieutenant was lying reading on his bed. He said quite pleasantly that he didn't know Major Schaub and asked what regiment he was in.

'He's a Major of the *Schwarz Korps*,' replied Kuporovitch quickly.

The young man grinned. 'You can bet he's got a good room, then. The S.S. people get the pickings everywhere. You'll probably find him down on the second floor.'

Thanking him politely, Kuporovitch went down two floors and tried again. In the first unlocked room that he came to a shaven-headed Colonel was working on a large chart, spread out in front of him on a table.

'Major Schaub?' he said vaguely, with his mind evidently still on his work. 'Let's see. He's not on this wing. I think his room is in the long corridor that runs the whole length of the front of the building—somewhere about two-twenty to two-twenty-six.'

Bowing himself out once more, Kuporovitch tried two-twenty-four. The room was occupied by a soldier-servant who was busily polishing the buttons of an officer's *feldgrau* uniform greatcoat.

'You got the number wrong, Frenchy,' he said, looking up. 'Major Schaub's in two-eighteen.'

With a sigh of relief Kuporovitch closed the door and went along to two-eighteen. He knocked twice, but there was no reply, and on turning the handle he found that the door was locked. Pocketing his gun, he made his way to the nearest lavatory and, locking himself in there, sat down to wait.

At intervals of about twenty minutes thereafter he slipped out and tried the Major's door again, but he had no luck until his fourth attempt, when in answer to his knock a sharp voice called: 'Come in!'

Kuporovitch opened the door and stepped inside. The tall, chunky-faced Major was in his shirt-sleeves, standing in front of his dressing table. Turning round, he said with a quick frown: 'What the devil do you want?'

Transferring his bag to his left hand, Kuporovitch pulled his gun out of his pocket, pointed it at the Major, and replied:

'You! Put your hands up!'

'*Gott im Himmel!*' exclaimed the Major suddenly recognizing him. 'If it isn't that damn' Russian! How the hell did you get in here?'

'That's none of your business,' Kuporovitch snapped. 'Put your hands up, or I'll fill your stomach full of lead!'

The German went a little pale, but did not do as he was ordered. He even managed to raise a faint smile, as he said: 'Don't be a fool! If you let that thing off you'll bring a score of people running and be dead as mutton yourself before you know it.'

Kuporovitch shrugged. 'I *should* be a fool if I *didn't* realize that. It's you who are the fool, *Herr Major*, because *you* do not realize that you're facing a man *who does not mind if he dies*. At the moment I have nothing to live for. However, I'm here to see if we can't alter that. If you're prepared to do as I tell you I shall then have something to live for again. If not, then neither of us will leave this room alive.'

Major Schaub, in fact, was no fool at all, and his swift brain had already put two and two together. Ignoring Kuporovitch's pistol, he sat down on the bed and said: 'Then you've come here about that pretty little French girl you're interested in, eh? The one you'd been dining with the first time we met, and you know that we pulled her in again last night. Not on suspicion this time, though: she's facing a charge of conspiracy against the Third Reich.'

'Whatever charge you've made against her—if she ever has to face it, you'll be dead first!' the Russian replied quietly. 'Have I made myself clear?'

'Quite clear,' nodded the Major. 'You've managed to bribe or smuggle your way in here with the idea of threatening me with death unless I'm willing to give you an order for the release of your girl friend?'

'Exactly.'

'Well, I'll tell you here and now that you're not going to get it. If you set no value on your skin you can shoot me if you like. If you do you'll be shot yourself before you get ten yards down the corridor, and that won't do your girl friend any good. Still, I've no wish to be shot; so if you like I'll make a bargain with you. Go as you came, and I'll give you five minutes' start; but that's all I'm prepared to do. Now take your choice!'

Kuporovitch realized that his bluff had been called, but as he was a completely ruthless person he had by no means exhausted the possibilities of the situation. Flicking over the safety-catch of his pistol, he walked quietly up to the Major and said: 'It's a pity that you're not prepared to be reasonable.' Then, without warning, he suddenly swung the hand that held his gun so that it struck the Major hard on the side of the face.

As the German's mouth opened to let out a yell Kuporovitch dropped the gun and leapt upon him, burying his thumbs and fingers in the Major's neck and forcing him back upon the bed.

Wolfram Schaub was a strong man, but he was no match for the weighty Russian. In vain he tore frantically at the choking fingers until red circles began to spin in the blackness before his eyes; then his adversary picked him up bodily and banged his head twice against the bedroom wall. Dazed by the blows, and with his cheek bleeding from a nasty cut where the pistol had gashed him, he collapsed in a limp heap.

Three minutes later Kuporovitch had him trussed up with the blind-cords and lightly gagged so that he could mutter, but not shout. Then, propping his enemy up on the bed against the wall, the Russian stood there, grinning with diabolical satisfaction at his handiwork.

'Now,' he said, 'must I show you some of the tricks that the Cheka used to practise on their Czarist prisoners, or will you sign the order that I require?'

Schaub shook his head.

'All right then. We'll see just how much guts you really have. There was nothing particularly brave in calling my bluff just now. You knew very well that I should not be such a fool as to shoot you and bring half the Nazis in this huge rabbit warren running with their guns; but I have never believed that the Germans are a courageous people. The Russians, now, are really brave, and so are the British. It is one thing which the two races have in common—both of us are used to losing battles, but we fight on just the same, because we refuse to acknowledge it when we are beaten. That is why neither country has ever been defeated in a major war.'

The Tartar streak in Kuporovitch had now come to the surface. Time had ceased to exist for him, and the fact that he was alone in the citadel of his enemies had passed from his mind as he went on: 'Even in the First World War you never broke the spirit of us Russians. It took two Revolutions, six months apart, before we were forced out of the game. But you Germans are different; like all other European races, there have been times when your country has been overrun and you have been compelled to sue for peace. You are great fellows—as long as you are victorious and fighting people who are not so well armed or organized as yourselves; but once things begin to go against you it's a very different story. You throw your hands up in the air and yell *'Kamerad*!' Now, will you sign the paper that I want from you, or must I give you a little of the medicine that you have been giving to other people?'

Again the Major shook his head.

'As you wish,' Kuporovitch grinned. 'Quite honestly, I'm going to enjoy this, because I dislike you Nazis, and I've been waiting to get a crack at one for quite a little time. I wonder if you ever heard of a young woman called Paula von Steinmetz?'

On the Major making no sign Kuporovitch continued: 'The little Paula was a friend of mine. She made a most delightful mistress, but whenever I think of the life you filthy Nazis forced that poor child to lead it makes me almost physically sick. Honest marriage suits some people, and recently I've come to feel that even in my own case there is much to be said for it. Free love I do not mind. What would we healthy fellows do without it? Prostitution is fair enough in a world that has not yet learnt to organize itself better. But you devils had Paula's brother in a concentration camp. By a threat of torturing him to death you forced her to give herself to Norwegians and Dutchmen and Belgians—in order that she might recruit Fifth Columnists for you—and that I do not like at all. This comes to you from Paula.'

As he spoke the last word the Russian hit the Major a savage blow in the mouth with his clenched fist, but he did not stop there. He proceeded to lam into him, right, left, and centre, until both his eyes were closed, his face half pulp, and he was writhing in agony from terrific punches in the solar plexus.

Breathing a little heavily, Kuporovitch at length let up, helped himself to a cigarette, lit it and began to look through the drawers of the Major's dressing-table until he found some sheets of official paper and a fountain-pen. Then he turned round and undid the now blood-soaked towel which he had used to gag his victim.

Schaub was still conscious, as, despite the ruthless ferocity of his attack, Kuporovitch had been careful not to strike him any blow that would have knocked him out. Taking him by the shoulder, the Russian dragged him up into a sitting position and shook him roughly, as he said:

'Do you want a little more, or are you prepared now to do your stuff?'

The Major spat out a loose tooth, mumbled a stream of blasphemies, then murmured: 'All right, you hell-hound. You win! But as sure as my name's Wolfram I'll get even with you for this—before you're much older.'

'The future will take care of itself,' replied Kuporovitch, untying the German's hands, and pushing him over to the dressing-table where he had set out the pen and paper. 'No monkey-tricks now,' he added. 'I know that Madeleine Lavallière is in the *Cherche-Midi,* so I want an order from you to the Governor of the prison to hand her over without questions to anyone who may present that paper to him. If you try to double-cross me I'll get back here somehow and skin you alive.'

The S.S. man had no more fight left in him. He wrote out the order, signed it, and handed it to his captor. Kuporovitch put it in his pocket and said:

'I'm not giving you the chance to raise an alarm until I'm out of this place. Get back on the bed now; I mean to tie you up and gag you again.'

Obediently Schaub lay down and rested his aching head on the pillow; but before Kuporovitch inserted the gag in his mouth he managed one malicious twisted smile, as he snarled:

'You think you're mighty clever, don't you? But he who laughs last laughs longest. The paper that I've written for you is all in order, but the Gestapo Chief at the *Cherche-Midi* would never give up one of his prisoners to a complete stranger, just on an order signed by me. He'd only do that if it were presented by one of our own people or a French official of some standing. So you see, as far as you're concerned, it's only a piece of wastepaper. I'll tell you another thing. My batman will find me here tomorrow morning. Directly I'm free I'm going to do a job which will hurt you much more than you've hurt me. I'm going along to the *Cherche-Midi* personally to re-examine Madeleine Lavallière. I don't mind if she talks or if she doesn't talk, but during our examination I'll have her nails torn off her hands and feet, and her eyes put out. Now think that one over, damn you!'

For answer Kuporovitch gave the Major one more heavy blow, this time an uppercut under the chin, which knocked him right out. Yet he was acutely worried now. He had a horrid feeling that Schaub had not been lying and that the paper he had been at such pains to get might, after all, prove valueless, and there was nothing more that he could extract from the German. Having tied him up and gagged him, he picked up his little brown bag and left the room, locking the door behind him.

Stepping into the lift, he went down to the basement, nodded casually to a man whom he found there waiting for it, and without a backward glance hurried down the passages until he reached the coal-cellar. Entering it, he pulled off his white coat, put on his ordinary one, collected his overcoat from a corner where he had left it, and pushing up the cover of the manhole climbed out into the street.

He had hardly reached it when a frightful thought struck him. Schaub had said that his soldier-servant would find him in the morning, but it was not yet eight o'clock; so it was almost certain that the servant would visit the room to tidy it up before the Major's normal time of going to bed. He saw then that Schaub had naturally refrained from mentioning that for fear that if his attacker knew that he was likely to be released within the next hour or so he would have killed him to make certain of his silence.

Kuporovitch wondered then why the hell he hadn't killed the Major, while he had the chance. For a moment he contemplated going back to do so, but a few seconds' thought was enough for him to realize that he had been extraordinarily lucky to have spent the best part of two hours in the headquarters of the German Army of Occupation without once being challenged or asked for a pass that he had not got. To go back again would be to tempt the gods. Dismissing the idea, he began to run down the street, now half-crazy with the knowledge that it would almost certainly be useless for him to present the order for Madeleine'a release that he held, and that through his own act he had brought about the possibility that within an hour or two Schaub would arrive at the *Cherche-Midi* to have her dragged off to the torture chamber.

16

' Set a Thief ... '

As Kuporovitch hurried away from the Crillon his brain was
in a whirl. He now felt certain that Schaub was right and
that even on his signature the Gestapo Chief at the *Cherche-
Midi* would never release a prisoner to an ordinary civilian
who could produce no special credentials; yet how in thunder
could he persuade or force a Gestapo man to co-operate with
him?

It occurred to him that if he could find one walking un-
accompanied in a quiet part of the city he might attack him
without warning in the blackout, stun and strip him of his
uniform; but he threw out that idea almost as soon as he
thought of it. His French had always been good, and now
after the months he had spent in Paris it was extremely fluent;
but his German was so limited that he knew no more than a
score of expressions and stock phrases. To present himself at
the *Cherche-Midi* in a German uniform when he was unable
to speak the language, or understand it, would have been
sheer madness.

His next thought was that he might attack a French
gendarme or *agent de ville;* but it seemed highly doubtful if
the Gestapo would trust an ordinary French policeman with
one of their prisoners, and he might search the streets of Paris
all night without coming across a French police officer of
lieutenant's or captain's rank. But that led to the idea that he
might be able to borrow a uniform from Ribaud, so going
into the nearest call-box he rang up the *Sûreté*.

The lieutenant was not in his office. To his dismay, Kuporovitch learnt that the detective had gone out on some special

work and was not expected back until the morning. All the odds were that by the morning it would be too late, and this blow to his hopes made the unfortunate Russian more agitated than ever.

Endeavouring to calm himself so that he might think more clearly he left the box and tried to recall Schaub's words exactly. After a little he felt certain the Major had said that the Gestapo would only release Madeleine to one of their own people or a French official of some standing, and it was then for the first time that he glimpsed a possible way out of this terrible situation.

He had never met Luc Ferrière, but he had often heard Madeleine speak of him. Ferrière was the Mayor of Batignolles, and the mayor of an important district in Central Paris must certainly rank as a high French official, particularly as all mayors are also magistrates and have considerable powers with the police. Somehow or other, Monsieur Ferrière must be roped in to assist in Madeleine's release.

Instinctively, Kuporovitch had been hurrying in the direction of the *Cherche-Midi*, but he now turned about and dived into a Metro-station that he had just passed, taking a ticket to the Place Malesherbes, near which he knew the Mayor lived.

On coming up from the underground at the other end he made a few enquiries and within twenty minutes of having first had his idea he was standing on the Mayor's doorstep. The door was opened to him by the Mayor's housekeeper, and to his immense relief he learned that Monsieur Ferrière was at home. He said that he did not know the Mayor, but had to see him on most urgent business. A few moments later he was shown into a small study, where Ferrière, wearing two dressing-gowns, one on top of the other, as a protection from the cold, was seated with a large stamp album open on a desk in front of him.

While in the Metro Kuporovitch had considered how best to tackle the Mayor, and he had come to the conclusion that, if possible, it would be far better to trick him into giving his willing co-operation than to force him to it against his will, as in the latter case he was much more likely either to refuse his assistance altogether or betray them if some unforeseen circumstance arose. Recalling, too, that only that morning Lavinsky had mistaken him for a German, owing to his slight accent, he decided that he would, at all events, at first endeavour to convey the impression that he was German to Monsieur Ferrière without actually stating that he was. In consequence he greeted the Mayor affably, and said:

'I trust, *Monsieur le Maire,* that you will forgive me for intruding upon you at this hour, but I have come direct from German Headquarters at the Crillon to see you on urgent business.'

'In that case, no excuse is needed,' smiled the tall, thin Mayor, standing up and waving Kuporovitch to a chair. 'I am always happy to give the authorities my co-operation at any hour.'

'I felt sure that would be so,' Kuporovitch went on, 'and I come to you with regard to Mademoiselle Madeleine Lavallière. I don't know if you've yet been informed of it, but she was arrested yesterday evening.'

The Mayor nodded, falling completely into the trap, and giving himself away to Kuporovitch in a manner that was entirely unexpected. 'So your people took my tip and investigated that nursing-home she was running. I felt certain it was phoney when I visited it two days ago.'

Kuporovitch was thinking: So that's the way it was. Madeleine and the others owe their arrest to this dirty traitor's visit. By God! He shall pay for it before we're through with him!

But his pleasant smile remained unaltered as he said: 'The authorities are most grateful to you for your help, *Monsieur le Maire.* It was good work to break up this nest of spies and saboteurs; but they are not content to stop at that, and it has occurred to them that if they release some of the conspirators but keep a watch on them, they in due course, may lead us to other groups of which we as yet have no knowledge. It has been decided to release Mademoiselle Lavallière for this purpose. I wonder now if you would care to place the Gestapo in your debt still further?'

'But of course,' the Mayor spread out his long knobbly hands. 'If there is anything that I can do you have only to suggest it.'

'Very well then. This is the proposal. If Mademoiselle Lavallière is released without apparent reason, firstly, she may be suspicious and on that account refrain for a long time from contacting any of her associates; secondly, it will not be easy to keep a watch on her the whole time without her becoming aware that she is under supervision. You are a responsible French official and you have known her for a number of years. Saying that you had heard of her arrest in the ordinary way, it would not be unnatural if you endeavoured to use such influence as you possess on her behalf. The authorities would naturally listen to anybody in your position, and they might perhaps be persuaded to release her if you were prepared to go guarantee for her good behaviour and have her to live in your house under your personal supervision.'

'Ha, ha! I see!' exclaimed the Mayor. 'A clever move, that! She would then believe that there was no danger in her resuming her activities, while all the time I should be able to report to you regarding her movements.'

'Exactly,' beamed Kuporovitch. 'May I take it that you are prepared to give your help?'

'But certainly.'

'Good then. I fear, though, I shall have to ask you to go out and get her at once, because speed in this matter is of the first importance. There must have been a number of people who were using that nursing-home who do not yet know that it has been raided. If Mademoiselle Lavallière is freed tonight, it is almost certain that she will try to get in touch with as many of them as she can to warn them about going back there. With luck, you may be able to get for us the telephone numbers which she uses immediately she returns here with you.'

'In that case, I will set off immediately,' agreed the Mayor. 'It will not take me five minutes to get my outdoor clothes on, and I have a small car in which I can go and fetch her. But what about the order for her release?'

'I have it here,' replied Kuporovitch, producing the order from his pocket and handing it over. 'It remains now only for me to thank you on behalf of the authorities and to urge you to lose not a moment, as the sooner you can get Mademoiselle Lavallière back the sooner she may put us on the track of some of her fellow conspirators.'

Kuporovitch would have given a very great deal to have been able to accompany Ferrière to the *Cherche-Midi,* and he positively loathed having to part with the precious order. But in the new set-up which he had so skilfully engineered it would have wrecked his whole story if, now that he was posing as a Gestapo agent who had set Ferrière on to spy on Madeleine, he should allow himself to be seen by her in the Mayor's company; so having wished him a most cordial good-night he left the house.

Outside he walked about a hundred yards down the street and took cover in a darkened doorway, and from this post of vantage he kept an anxious watch. Five minutes later he saw the Mayor come out, and he followed him down the street to a small garage, from which after a short interval Ferrière drove away in his little car.

Kuporovitch then returned to the Mayor's house and rang the bell again. When the old housekeeper came to the door he gently pushed his way through it and closed it behind him, as he said: '*Madame,* before *Monsieur le Maire* returns, I should like to have a few words with you.'

As she stood back he went on: 'It is not always possible to give full explanations as to measures which it is sometimes necessary to take in these difficult times. Please be assured that I have no intention of harming you; but, in order to ensure your silence, I must now tie you up and gag you.'

While they had been speaking he had taken his gun from his pocket just so that she could see it; now he put it back again, and his voice was so gentle that the elderly woman showed no alarm.

Shrugging her shoulders with a little helpless gesture she said: 'I have no desire to be shot, *monsieur,* so I shall not try to resist you.'

'That is very sensible,' he smiled. 'Would you prefer to remain a prisoner in the kitchen or in your bedroom?'

'That depends on how long I must remain tied up,' she replied.

'All night, I fear, and before leaving you I should like to make you as comfortable as possible.'

She sighed. 'We had better go up to my room then.' And turning she led the way upstairs.

234

Knowing that Ferrière kept no servants other than his housekeeper, Kuporovitch had not anticipated any great difficulties in carrying out this portion of his plan. It had been a hundred to one on the house being empty except for her, and she had shown good sense in not seeking to resist him; but it would have been distasteful to have had to employ force against an elderly woman, so he was pleased that matters were going so smoothly.

On reaching her room she lay down on the bed while Kuporovitch tied her ankles and her wrists in front of her. He then lightly gagged her with a silk handkerchief and drew all the bedcoverings over her so that she should keep as warm as possible. He was just about to bid her good-night and leave the room when his glance happened to light upon a little packet of newspaper clippings on her dressing-table, and in the headline of the topmost one the name 'de Gaulle' caught his eye.

Picking the clippings up, he glanced swiftly through them, and soon he saw that they were of various dates from papers issued in the past few months, but that each was concerned with General de Gaulle's activities. This struck him as strange, seeing that he was in a pro-Nazi household, so going over to the bed he loosened the woman's gag and said to her:

'May I enquire, *Madame,* the reason for your interest in General de Gaulle?'

For the first time a spirit of fight showed in the woman's eyes, as she said: 'I don't know who you are, and I suppose you're one of these Nazis; but all the same you might as well hear the truth for once. General de Gaulle is a great man, and he represents the real spirit of France, however much people like Monsieur Ferrière may kowtow to you. The time will come when the General will land here with the English, and you'll get much more than you bargained for.'

'If those are your views, *Madame,*' said the Russian, 'may one ask why you've continued to serve such a master as Monsieur Ferrière?'

She made an expressive grimace. 'One must live, *Monsieur,* and beggars cannot be choosers. I have kept house for Monsieur Ferrière for twenty years, and where else would an old woman like myself find employment?'

235

Kuporovitch smiled down at her. 'In that case, I can give you some consolation for the uncomfortable night that you are about to spend. I, too, am a de Gaullist, and while I must protect myself by leaving you tied up like this you may rest assured that it is only on account of the good work and that *Monsieur le Maire* is about to spend a much more uncomfortable night than yourself.'

'Bless you, then!' she exclaimed, her lips twisting into a smile. 'If that is so, anything that I may suffer is suffered willingly.'

'Well done!' smiled Kuporovitch, and having replaced her light gag he patted her shoulder, switched out the lights and left the room.

Downstairs he installed himself in the Mayor's sitting-room, where, having switched off the light, he sat down in an armchair to wait.

There was now nothing else that he could do as the question of Madeleine's release lay on the knees of the gods, so he endeavoured to stifle his consuming anxiety as well as he could and pray that all would go well.

His dealings with the housekeeper had occupied about twenty minutes, and a further three-quarters of an hour dragged slowly by before he heard the sound which he had been so anxiously awaiting. The front door banged, and there were steps in the hall. Although he strained his ears to their utmost capacity he could not determine whether there were one or two sets of footsteps, and it required all his control to remain seated in the chair instead of rushing out to discover without the loss of an instant if Monsieur Ferrière had brought Madeleine back with him. The sound of voices raised his hopes. A moment later the light clicked on, and they both walked into the room to find him seated there with his pistol pointed at them.

Madeleine gave a cry of joy, while the Mayor gasped with amazement and consternation. 'What—what is the meaning of this?' he stammered awkwardly.

'Simply, my friend, that the time has come for me to reveal the little trap into which I led you,' beamed the Russian.

'Do you mean that you are not—not . . .'

'Exactly,' Kuporovitch purred. 'I am not, as you thought, an agent of the Gestapo. I am on the *other* side, and I simply used you to get Mademoiselle Lavallière out of prison.'

The Mayor's long hands began to flutter in helpless consternation. 'But—but, in that case, the most frightful things may happen to me. They made me prove my identity at the prison and take full responsibility for Madeleine. I signed the book for her. They will believe that I am a saboteur, who willingly entered into a plot to rescue one of their prisoners! Oh, what have you done! What have you done!'

'Nothing—so far,' replied the amiable Russian, standing up; 'except involve you in far less trouble than you rightly deserve. To-morrow morning—to-night perhaps—the Gestapo people, and a very angry Major Schaub, will come here to demand explanations. That is why we have no time to waste; but if you keep your head I don't think anything very serious will happen to you.'

The Mayor was wringing his hands and glancing fearfully from side to side as, pocketing his gun, Kuporovitch went on: 'I am about to tie you up, so that when they arrive here they will find you bound and gagged. For appearances' sake, it would be better too if I employ a little violence so that it will seem to them that you put up as good a struggle as possible. Then, when they question you, all you'll have to do is to tell them the simple truth about how I tricked you into getting Mademoiselle Lavallière released and say that when you got back here I set upon you and rendered you powerless before you had any chance to call in the police.'

Even seconds were precious, as Major Schaub might even now be at the *Cherche-Midi* or in a car following Madeleine to the house, so without more ado Kuporovitch set about the unhappy Mayor.

Seizing him by the collar, he tore it away from its studs so that it gaped open at the neck. He then knocked off the Mayor's spectacles and gave the cringing man a light but well-aimed punch sufficient to provide him with a good black eye. Having pushed him on to the floor, he bound and gagged him far more tightly than he had the house-keeper, so that when he had done Ferrière resembled a trussed turkey, with his wrists and ankles knotted up behind his back. Next Kuporovitch scattered the things off the desk and wrecked some of the lighter furniture with a few kicks, as though a violent struggle had taken place in the room. Then he grabbed Madeleine by the arm and hurried her out of the house.

On reaching the street they turned south-westward along the Rue Cardinet at a rapid pace, while Madeleine gave unstinted praise to the Russian for his splendid resource, and gasped out her intense relief at having been rescued before seeing the inside of a Gestapo torture chamber.

Kuporovitch who was in a high good humour, made light of the matter; but as they walked on towards the Bois de Boulogne, and he told her how he had managed to get the order for her release out of Major Schaub, he could not altogether conceal his anxiety about the future. They were now both hunted and homeless. It was a sure thing that by morning a description of them would have been circulated to all the hotels in Paris, so that they dared not put up at one of them for the night. It was early November, and even for the time of the year the weather was exceptionally cold; yet there seemed no alternative to spending a night in the open.

After thirty minutes' brisk walking they reached the Porte de Neuilly and entering the Bois penetrated some way into it until they found a bench in a secluded spot, where they sat down. For some time they continued to relate their recent experiences to one another in more detail and to speculate anxiously as to whether Lacroix and Gregory had got away and what had happened to the other residents of the nursing-home who had managed to evade capture.

Madeleine felt fairly certain Pierre was among these, as she had seen him dash upstairs on the first alarum, so it was unlikely that he had been killed later in the basement, and he was definitely not among the prisoners who had been taken to the *Sûreté* with her after the whole house had been searched. During the weeks that she had acted as matron at the home Pierre had been almost constantly in her company. He had served her well and faithfully, so that he was now something more than an old friend, and she had developed a genuine

238

affection for him. It comforted her a little to believe that he had probably evaded the clutches of the Gestapo for the moment; but the young artist was not a very practical or resourceful person, and it worried her considerably to think of him as a bewildered fugitive.

Kuporovitch reassured her as best he could, remarking lightly that they were in no better case themselves, and she then said something which warmed his heart as nothing else could have done:

'Yes, Stefan dear; but he is alone, and we at least have each other.'

There were so many things that he would have liked to have replied, but he knew this was no moment to give free rein to his thoughts, and without doing that he could not think of anything adequate to say, so he sat there like a shy schoolboy, completely tongue-tied.

Madeleine also seemed to have no more to say, so they stayed silent for a while, until he found that she was beginning to shiver. Standing up, he took off his overcoat and was about to drape it round her shoulders, but she protested quickly and would not let him.

For a few minutes they argued while he sought to persuade her, then she said between chattering teeth: 'No, Stefan. The cold's awful enough as it is, and you'd be absolutely frozen without your overcoat; but I'll tell you what we'll do, if you like. If we cuddle up together we shall keep a little warmer; then we can have the coat on top of us and share it.'

As they lay down on the bench Kuporovitch was trembling, Madeleine thought it was the cold, but actually it was from the happiness of being able to take her in his arms. Having made themselves as comfortable as they could with the coat pulled well up round them, she rested her smooth cheek against his rough one, and they settled down for the night.

Kuporovitch knew that in the morning they would have to face all sorts of difficulties and perils, but he resolutely put the morning out of his mind. To-night was his, even if he never lived to see another. Had Heinrich Himmler appeared in person beside him and offered him a safe conduct out of France, together with the bed of the President in the Elysée Palace for that night, he would not have exchanged it for that hard park bench with the fair face of the girl he loved so desperately pressed against his own. To-morrow was another day in which all his courage, strength and ingenuity would be exerted to keep her free from the malignant power of their enemies.

17

A Quisling Entertains

After a time Madeleine slept fitfully with her head pillowed on Kuporovitch's broad chest, but he did not sleep at all. He did not want to; every moment was far too precious for him to let it be lost even in drowsing, and during the long night he had ample opportunity to consider their situation from every possible angle. His musings at last produced a plan. Its very audacity gave him strong hopes that it might be successful; but the first and all-important step in it hung entirely upon the Gestapo's attitude to Luc Ferrière.

In the cold grey light of the November dawn Madeleine woke fully. After she had tidied herself as best she could they walked up and down to ease their cramped limbs and restore their circulation; but he said nothing of his project for the time being as he did not wish her to suffer too great a disappointment if it failed to materialize. Instead, he just told her that he had thought of a place where they might possibly remain hidden, but that he would not be able to find out for certain until about nine o'clock.

Her confidence in him was so strong that she did not even question him further, and having warmed themselves a little they sat down on a bench again until full daylight had come. They then left the Bois and, going out into the Boulevard Maillot, found a small eating-house where they were able to get a rough-and-ready, but satisfying, breakfast.

Until nine o'clock they took advantage of the steamy heat of the little place by remaining there on the excuse of reading through a paper. The news was mainly about the new Graeco-Italian war which had opened in the previous week, and the Greeks seemed to be putting up an unexpectedly strong resistance. Army leave had been stopped in Turkey, as it was feared that the war might suddenly spread right through the Balkans. Little news was given of British activities, but in small paragraphs it was admitted that the R.A.F. had bombed Naples on October the 31st and Berlin the following night, so in spite of the Germans' oft-proclaimed wiping-out of the Royal Air Force it was evidently still very much in being.

Having discussed the news in guarded tones, Kuporovitch left Madeleine in the café and went along to a call-box, from which he rang up Luc Ferrière's house. To his great satisfaction the Mayor answered the telephone personally, and Kuporovitch, having made himself known, asked him how he had got on the previous night.

Ferrière was extremely sarcastic at this unexpected concern for him, but between bursts of abuse it emerged that the Gestapo had arrived shortly before midnight, and on untying the Mayor had accepted his story; which, after all, was the truth.

Stefan ignored the angry sarcasm and, speaking with the geniality of an old friend, said he was so glad to hear that everything was all right and was only sorry that he had had to put Monsieur Ferrière to so much inconvenience. He then rang off.

On returning to the café he told Madeleine that things promised well but they would be unable to take any further steps until the coming night, so they must devise some means for passing the day.

As it was Sunday Madeleine suggested that they should go to High Mass and give thanks for their miraculous preservation. Kuporovitch willingly agreed, and, considering it wisest to keep away from the centre of the city, where the Germans were always more numerous, they decided to make their devotions at the Church of St. Augustus, near the Gare Saint Lazare. On approaching the church they noticed the statue of Joan of Arc which stands before it, and it seemed almost as though they had been directed there, as an omen that the Patron Saint of France would give them her protection.

They lunched in a small restaurant behind the station and

242

planned to spend the afternoon in the Musée Cernuschi near by, as, although all the heating in the public buildings had been turned off, it would at least be warmer indoors than out. Many of the most valuable pieces in the great Paris museums had been evacuated for safe-keeping at the beginning of the war, and since the Occupation Hitler and his colleagues had openly stolen a number of others, removing them to Germany. But as one of the lesser known museums the Cernuschi had not yet been despoiled, and most of its treasures of Chinese and Japanese art were still on show; so they spent an interesting but rather tiring three hours in the galleries.

Dusk had come again when they left the building, but they still had several hours before Kuporovitch could put the second stage of his plan into operation, so they took refuge in one of the smaller cinemas on the Boulevard de Clichy, and afterwards had another light meal. At half-past nine the Russian decided that the time had come when they might go into action.

He then told Madeleine that he intended to pay a second visit to Luc Ferrière's house. From his telephone conversation with the Mayor that morning he had good reason to believe that the Gestapo had accepted the explanation offered, but there was always a chance that either the Mayor had lied to him or that the police might now be keeping a watch on the house. If they were he would be walking into a trap, and he had no intention of taking Madeleine with him. In spite of her unwillingness to accept it, he forced her to take all the remaining money that he had in his wallet, then took her into a café not far from Ferrière's house, where he carefully gave her final instructions.

Having secured the telephone number of the café he gave her name to the waiter as Mademoiselle Olivaux and told him that she was expecting a telephone call during the next half-hour. He then told Madeleine that she was to remain there until he rang her up to say that it was all right for her to come along to Ferrière's house. If he did not ring up before eleven o'clock she was to assume that he had met with unexpected trouble, and must fend for herself that night. If he succeeded in getting away he would meet her the following morning at eight o'clock at the bench in the Bois on which

243

they had slept; but if he failed to put in an appearance there by nine she would know that he had been captured. In that event she was to telephone Lieutenant Ribaud, banking on his chivalry to stretch a point in her case and help her to get safely out of Paris; or, failing that, seek his advice as to how she could best hide or escape from the danger area without compromising him.

'Dear Stefan,' she murmured, stretching out a hand across the little marble-topped table and clasping his. 'You think of everything; but I shall be holding thumbs for you all the time, and, if prayers have any meaning, mine to Sainte Jeanne this morning will bring you her protection.'

With a last long look into her shining eyes he kissed her hand and went out into the night.

On reaching Ferrière's house he rang the bell with his left hand, and with his right grasped the automatic in his overcoat pocket, so that if need be he could shoot through the coat and would not be taken at a disadvantage should an S.S. guard open the door to him. But his wise precaution proved unnecessary; it was the old housekeeper who answered his ring.

Putting a finger to his lips to enjoin caution he whispered: 'Is *Monsieur le Maire* in, and alone?'

She shook her head, and Kuporovitch drew back a step as he enquired: 'Are the police still here then?'

'No, no! It is not the police; only a young Frenchman who arrived about ten minutes ago. I believe he's a friend of Mademoiselle Lavallière because immediately I showed him in he asked Monsieur Ferrière if he knew what happened to her.'

'I see,' Kuporovitch paused a moment. 'Is he by any chance a tall young man—dark, good-looking and with side-whiskers; rather like a Spaniard?'

'Yes, you have described him exactly.'

'In that case, I know him, so I will go in.' Kuporovitch had described Pierre Ponsardin, and felt certain now that it must be the young artist. While the housekeeper closed the front door he strode down the passage and, throwing open the door of the sitting-room, walked straight in, with his gun in his hand.

As he had supposed, the visitor was Pierre, who was surprised and delighted to see him, but it was quite otherwise with the lean owner of the house. Springing to his feet, Ferrière exclaimed:

'What! You again! Go away, go away! You will be my ruin!'

'I trust not,' said the Russian affably, 'but that depends almost entirely on whether you are willing to give me your co-operation.'

'No, no!' wailed the Mayor. 'This is too much! It is only by the grace of God that the Nazis accepted my story of what happened last night. They may still regard me with suspicion. It is enough for them to see you enter my house and leave it for them to have me shot.'

'I have no intention of leaving it at the moment,' replied Kuporovitch, and turning to Pierre he added: 'So you got away after all. Congratulations, *mon ami!* I am more delighted than I can say to know it.'

'It was a horribly narrow shave,' Pierre admitted. 'I got out on the roof and nearly ran into a group of *gendarmes,* but I was just in time to hide behind the chimney-stacks, and they missed me in the darkness. Afterwards, I managed to get down through another house farther along the street. But what's happened to Madeleine? I've been simply frantic with anxiety about her. It occurred to me that, in view of Monsieur Ferrière's official position and his being an old friend of the Lavallières', he might be able to get me some information; but he says he cannot help.'

Raising his gun, Kuporovitch prodded the Mayor with it in the stomach, as he said:

'Then this knobbly-kneed old Quisling is meaner than even I thought him. Be of good cheer, Pierre. With Monsieur Ferrière's unconscious aid we got Madeleine out of the *Cherche-Midi* prison last night. At the moment she is sitting in the Café du Rhône up the street and just round the corner to the left. Now that I have satisfied myself that there are no Gestapo people here I should be obliged if you would go and fetch her.'

'So she's safe!' cried Pierre. 'Thank God for that!' And, his face wreathed in smiles, he ran from the room.

245

The Russian could now give his undivided attention to his unwilling host. Pocketing his gun, he settled himself comfortably in an armchair, and remarked: 'We may as well begin as we mean to go on. Am I not right, *Monsieur le Maire*? It is with that in mind that I am making myself at home. It is my pleasure to announce to you that Madeleine and I, and possibly young Monsieur Ponsardin as well, propose to remain with you as your guests—probably for some weeks to come. I hope that we shall all settle down very happily together.'

'What!' screamed the Mayor, flinging up his long arms. 'Settle down! Have you in my house! To stay! With half the police in Paris after you! But you must be crazy!'

'On the contrary,' beamed Kuporovitch, 'I fancy that, all things considered, I'm extremely sane. After last night the Gestapo will certainly not imagine that Madeleine and I would venture back here; so you see, provided we do not go out, except at night, and are careful not to expose ourselves at any of the windows, we shall be safer here than anywhere else in Paris.'

'I will not have it! I will hand you over to the police!' cried the Mayor with a show of spirit.

'Oh no, you won't!' Kuporovitch grinned, tapping the pocket that held his gun. 'You'd be dead before you reached your own doorstep.'

'So you plan to keep me a prisoner in my own house,' sneered Ferrière. 'You seem to have overlooked the fact that the people in my office will come to enquire for me. Either you'll be discovered by them, or you must allow me to continue my official duties; how do you propose to stop my reporting you the moment I am out of range of that horrible weapon which you handle so casually?'

'That we shall arrange in good time, but for the moment I hope the position is clear.'

'And what of my housekeeper, Madame Chautemps? Do you think she will submit to this invasion without telling the neighbours?'

'I do,' nodded Kuporovitch. 'It so happens that Madame Chautemps is a de Gaullist.'

'*Quel horreur!* A de Gaullist in my house! What I shall do

246

without her after all these years I cannot think, but I will dismiss her in the morning.'

'You'll do no such thing; but it's most fortunate for us that this good woman should feel as most French people outside official circles do. I am confident that she can be relied on not to betray us.'

'But you cannot stay here! You cannot!' insisted the Mayor desperately. 'Think what would happen to me if later on it was discovered that I had been hiding you. The Gestapo would cut me in little pieces.'

'They wouldn't treat you any worse than they're already treating far better Frenchmen than you.'

'But I have done nothing to deserve it, and I serve France in my own way, for what I honestly believe to be her best interests. Have you no mercy?'

'No, none at all,' said the Russian quietly.

At that moment there were footsteps in the hall, and Pierre came in with Madeleine.

Kuporovitch told them of his intentions and asked Pierre if he too would like to avail himself of Monsieur Ferrière's unwilling hospitality; but the young artist shook his head.

'It's a comfort to know that there's this place to come to in an emergency, but at the moment I don't see why I should leave my old apartment. The police have no record of me at all. They didn't even see me in the nursing-home, so there's no reason why they should suspect me. It seems to me, too, that at any time this old devil may think up some way to betray you. Why don't you come and stay with me? There's not much room, but we'll manage somehow, and you'd both be safer there than here.'

'Yes, yes! The young man is right,' said Ferrière eagerly. 'Why don't you go and stay with him?'

But Kuporovitch quelled him with a frown.

'Thank you, no. Both Madeleine and I are known to the police. We are also known to the *concierge* and other people in the block where Monsieur Ponsardin has his apartment; so we should be running the gravest risk to go there, although I think he's quite right as far as he himself is concerned.'

At Madeleine's suggestion Madame Chautemps was then called in. The position was explained to her, and she was asked if she would like to leave or preferred to stay on and take the risk that later she might get into serious trouble for not having reported to the police that two people were hiding in the house.

'I'll stay,' she said at once. 'Otherwise who's to do for you? *Monsieur le Maire* can't do his own shopping, otherwise the tradesmen would soon begin to suspect that something fishy was going on; and if you get some flighty young baggage in to take my place you wouldn't be able to trust her farther than you could see her.'

'But the work will be too much for you,' interjected the agitated Mayor, 'and this is not a very large house. We couldn't make them very comfortable.'

'It's quite large enough,' replied Madame Chautemps grimly; 'and if the work proves a big burden on my old bones I've no doubt Mademoiselle will help me.'

'Of course I will!' exclaimed Madeleine. 'And thank you a thousand times for helping us.'

'It's a pleasure, Mademoiselle, now that I know you and your friends are on the right side.'

Kuporovitch also thanked her, then he said: '*Monsieur le Maire* has just set us a pretty little problem. If he suddenly neglects all his official duties without giving any adequate explanation an investigation will at once be made which would lead to our discovery; on the other hand, once he has left the house we have no means of ensuring that he won't betray us. Have any of you any suggestions as to how we could get over that?'

'Perhaps you could make him give you some form of security to ensure his behaving himself,' murmured Pierre. 'Something that you could destroy if he attempts to double-cross you.'

'An excellent idea,' smiled Kuporovitch; 'but what?'

'Take his stamp collection,' said Madame Chautemps. 'He's simply crazy about those stamps of his. He spends every night of his life playing about with them, and, although he's so mean that you wouldn't believe it about other things, he spends goodness knows what on those little bits of paper. I've heard tell that his collection is worth half a million francs.'

'The very thing!' exclaimed the Russian, and, jumping up,

248

he seized the two large stamp albums which still lay open on Ferrière's big desk.

'You can't, you can't!' wailed the Mayor, tears coming into his weak eyes. 'Those albums represent a lifetime of patient industry. How can you be so ruthless to rob me of them?'

'We have no intention of doing so,' Kuporovitch replied quietly. 'We are merely confiscating them temporarily as a guarantee of your good behaviour. If all goes well you shall have them back when we have made other plans and decide to leave your house; but if not you will never see them again, and they will be burnt to the last five kopek stamp in the collection.'

As he spoke he handed the volumes to Pierre and added:

'If we keep them here he might arrange a surprise raid in which I'm caught napping before I have time to destroy them. You'd better take these away with you, Pierre, and deposit them in a bank or some safe place. Then, if anything goes wrong with us, you'll be able to make *Monsieur le Maire* pay the penalty.'

Ferrière continued to protest and plead, but Kuporovitch saw that Madeleine was dropping with fatigue, so he cut him short by saying: 'All is fixed up most satisfactorily. I'm sure you will see the sense of holding your tongue when you leave the house tomorrow. It only remains now for you to show us our rooms.'

The Mayor was in a corner, and he knew it. With a helpless little shrug of his lean shoulders he looked across at his housekeeper, who said at once: 'We'll put Mademoiselle in the Blue Room, and the gentleman can have Monsieur Georges' old room. It won't take me long to get them ready.' And she left them.

On hearing her dead fiancés' name Madeleine went pale. It was getting on for five months now since his death, and in recent weeks she had been so fully occupied that she had had little time to brood upon it. With a sudden feeling of guilt she realized that she had hardly thought about him at all since becoming the matron of the nursing-home, but this mention of him, and the fact that she was in the house where he had lived, brought the whole tragedy back vividly to her.

Seeing her agitation, Kuporovitch walked over to the side-

249

table on which there was a decanter of brandy and some glasses. As he poured her out a stiff tot he said to the Mayor: 'While we're in your house I fear you will have to regard us as an army of occupation. We shall take what we want, and I shall give you chits for it. After all, there won't be much difference between that and the worthless marks the German Army is foisting on the French people; although actually my paper is a better bet, as I am a comparatively honest person, and if I escape death or capture until the end of the war I shall pay you in real money afterwards.'

Ferrière groaned, but made no protest, as the Russian poured out two more goes of cognac for Pierre and himself. Then he looked across at the Mayor with an amused smile and said: 'Won't you join us?'

'Why not?' sighed his victim. 'I might as well at least drink a small share of my own brandy.' It was his final surrender, and Kuporovitch knew then that they would have no more trouble with him, at all events for the time being.

When they had finished their drinks Pierre left them, it having been agreed that neither of the parties should attempt to get in touch with the other for the next few days, except in a case of emergency. He had hardly gone when Madame Chautemps came downstairs to say that the rooms were ready, and, well-satisfied with the evening's proceedings, having wished her and their host good-night, the two fugitives from the Gestapo went up to bed.

Next morning when they came down to breakfast the Mayor seemed to have accepted the situation which had been forced upon him, and his principal concern was now for the safety of his precious stamp collection. Madeleine assured him that Pierre was absolutely honest and that there was no cause to fear that it would not be returned intact to him in due course if all went well.

When he had gone out to his official duties Kuporovitch made a full inspection of the house to ascertain its resources. He had no food-card of his own, and they dared not present Madeleine's. They could not go out in daylight while the shops were open, yet they had to live somehow and might even have to face a lengthy siege there.

Monsieur Ferrière's cellar was a great disappointment as,

250

although, like all Frenchmen, he knew what was good from having been born with a natural palate, he was a very moderate drinker and never entertained. The cellar held only about three dozen bottles of claret, burgundy and sauterne, five bottles of brandy, two of Armagnac, and no champagne, liqueurs or non-French wines at all. On the other hand, a second cellar revealed that *Monsieur le Maire* had had the forethought to lay in a good supply of emergency stores, and the piles of tins and boxes comforted the Russian with the thought that they would certainly not suffer from starvation for several weeks at least.

Madeleine meanwhile had a chat with Madame Chautemps, during which they arranged to share the work of the house between them. Food was now becoming so difficult to obtain that even the possession of a ration-card was no definite guarantee of actually getting the goods, and to make certain of doing so it was often necessary to queue up early at the shops in order to get one's share before the items ran out. In consequence, shopping 'was a lengthy process, and it was decided that the housekeeper should give most of her time to it while Madeleine made all the beds and kept the house clean.

That evening they waited with some anxiety for the Mayor's return, since, in spite of his apparently philosophic acceptance of their presence, there was still a chance that he might decide to risk his stamp collection as less precious than his life— which would be in jeopardy as long as they remained with him—but he arrived back at his normal hour, showing no change of attitude from that which he had displayed in the morning.

When he saw that dinner consisted mainly of things from his hoarded stores he began to complain most bitterly, saying that the food situation would get infinitely worse before the war was over and that at this rate they would consume the whole of his stock in a month.

Kuporovitch told him not to worry, as when the hue and cry for Madeleine and himself had died down a little he would be able to go out again and somehow or other would obtain additional supplies.

The week passed quickly, as although neither of the refugees showed their noses outside the house there was plenty to do inside it, even for the Russian, who was by no means a bad cook, and had volunteered to take over the preparation of the meals.

On Sunday, November the 10th, the news came through that Libreville, the capital of Gabon in West Africa, had surrendered to General de Gaulle and the Free French Forces; so, in spite of Ferrière's anti-de Gaullist feelings, they held a little celebration at which they insisted that Madame Chautemps should join them, selecting for dinner that night some of the Mayor's most precious tinned foods and a few of the best bottles of wine from his cellar.

Now that they had been for eight days in the house Kuporovitch felt the time had come when, provided that he exercised caution, he might go out occasionally with reasonable safety. On the Monday he telephoned Ribaud and fixed a meeting for that night at the Café du Rhône, just round the corner.

The French detective was in a high good humour. He had heard three days before from Lacroix that the little Colonel had succeeded in getting safely away and that he was now back in Vichy. Gregory too had escaped, but parted from Lacroix on the night that the home was raided to make his own way back to England; and as Kuporovitch had enormous faith in Gregory's ability to look after himself this was great good news.

They laughed a lot over the way in which the Quisling Mayor of Batignolles had been pressed against his will into the service of the Free French cause, and Ribaud was pleased to hear that Pierre Ponsardin had also managed to evade capture and could be found when wanted at his old address. As they spoke of their friends who had been caught in the home their laughter left them, as both of them knew that nothing could be done to help these poor people. They must be written off just like soldiers who had fallen on the battle-field, only to be remembered with honour; but their number was not large and, according to Ribaud, their loss would have no very serious effect upon the ever-growing movement to sabotage the German war effort and eventually restore freedom to France.

On the nights that followed Kuporovitch went out on other missions. He was an old soldier and a scrounger of the first

252

water, who, considering himself at war again, had no scruples whatever about looting, now that he was living in enemy territory. His first exploit was to break into Lavinsky's office in the early hours of one morning, and he came away with a sackful of samples of black market goods that he had seen there. They used some of them later that week in another celebration dinner when the splendid news leaked through that the British Fleet Air Arm had scored a magnificent victory by torpedoing a number of Italy's most powerful warships in Taranto harbour. But in Paris that week this good news was more than offset by the knowledge that the Germans had, contrary to the armistice agreement, incorporated the French province of Lorraine into the Greater Reich and had begun forcibly to deport all French citizens from it.

Now that one-half of France was occupied, and the other in a state of uneasy non-belligerence with Germany, there were no steps at all which the French could take by way of retaliation, and the Nazis' cynical disregard for the terms of the armistice spread a gloom over all Paris. Madeleine became subject to the general helpless anger and depression, but Kuporovitch sought to console her by saying that, apart from the unfortunate folk who were actually being deported, the measure would do their own cause good in the long run, as it would show the French people more clearly than ever that no faith could ever be put in the word of the Nazis and that collaboration with them could only end in France being devoured piecemeal.

Kuporovitch's night forays mostly took him out to the nearer suburbs, as he did not like to rob the smaller shops. During the autumn nearly everyone who had a garden had dug it up to grow vegetables against the winter, and selecting the larger ones in a different neighbourhood each night he pilfered potatoes from one, greens from a second, fruit from a third, and so on. Occasionally, also, he secured a chicken or a tame rabbit; all of which good fresh food made a better contribution to the Mayor's table than two extra rations would have done, and helped them to sustain themselves against the rigours of the cold, which continued to prove their greatest inconvenience.

Ferrière's wireless was only a small one upon which they

253

could not listen to foreign broadcasts, but there had now sprung up in Paris such a thirst for outside news that, in spite of the heavy penalties announced by the Germans for listening to the B.B.C., or passing on statements made in its bulletins, practically every shopkeeper had become a channel for forbidden information, so Madame Chautemps was able to furnish them with the latest news after her daily shopping expeditions and long waits in queues.

The German aerial assault on Britain seemed to have petered out, but on November the 15th they again launched one of the biggest blitzes that they had ever attempted against London; yet the following day the underground grapevine news service showed the writing on the wall. The Nazis had lost seventeen planes destroyed against one British.

With the passing days, Madeleine began to get increasingly anxious about her mother. It was now over a fortnight since she had been to see her. The old lady knew nothing of her daughter's secret activities, but by this time would be wondering why Madeleine had neglected her for so long. In consequence, they got in touch with Pierre, and he came to dine with them.

He reported that Madame Lavallière was much as usual, except that she suffered most severely from the cold and whenever he went in to see her she was always complaining of her daughter's neglect. As Kuporovitch absolutely forbade Madeleine to go to see her, it was agreed that Pierre should tell Madame Lavallière, without giving her any details, that Madeleine had made herself liable to prosecution by the police through repeating news given out by the B.B.C., so she had had to change her address and disappear for the time being, and she might be caught if she visited her old home, although she would do so as soon as the affair had blown over.

Pierre said that Ribaud had been to see him only the previous day and told him that fresh arrangements had now been made for continuing underground work against the enemy, and that he was to go to a certain house where he would be given a number of pamphlets, which he was to distribute at night by pushing them through letter-boxes; so he would be on the job again very shortly.

On November the 20th it was announced with a great blare

of trumpets that Hungary had joined the Axis, but nobody took very much notice of that, as for a long time past it had been clear that the wretched Hungarians had very little option in resisting German pressure, once it was brought to bear upon them. As against that the Greeks were standing up magnificently to the Italian invasion, and a few days later the news trickled through that they were now advancing on all fronts.

This good news gave Kuporovitch another opportunity to indulge his love of celebrations, and in order to produce something special for the feast he put into execution a plan which he had been considering for some days. For the first time since he had been living in Ferrière's house he took the risk of going out in daylight, and late in the afternoon paid a visit to the Paris Zoo, to inform himself where the cages and compounds of various animals were situated. That night he went back again, and, having got in under cover of the darkness, he captured and killed a small roebuck, which he brought home in triumph, thus providing the household for some days with most excellent venison.

It was the morning after this exploit that the people of Paris were once more driven to fresh anger and hatred against their oppressors. Fifteen French newspapers had published accounts of the havoc caused by British air attacks on Le Havre, and all fifteen were suppressed, thus robbing the Parisians of one of their main sources of material for the eternal discussions which they loved to hold in their cafés.

On the 28th Ribaud telephoned and asked Kuporovitch to meet him in the Café du Rhône that evening. When he arrived, instead of asking him to sit down, the detective took him straight out to the car, which he was still allowed to run on account of his official duties. Once they were in it he said: 'The big Chief's in Paris again and asked me to bring you to see him at his new headquarters.'

As they drove through the almost deserted streets the detective told his companion with grim satisfaction about the death of M. Chiappe, which had occurred the day before. Chiappe had been a cunning and ambitious Corsican who had climbed to power with Laval and at one time had been Chief of the Paris Police. Lacroix, who had had to work

255

with him, had loathed him, as had Ribaud and most of his other subordinates.

Apparently the Vichy Government had grounds for distrusting the Governor of Syria and feared that he might go over to de Gaulle; so the Quisling Chiappe had been sent to supersede him. But the aircraft in which he had set off the day before had got mixed up in an air-battle between British and Italian planes, which was raging over a sea-battle off the coast of Sardinia that had resulted in the British Navy inflicting severe damage on an Italian battleship and three cruisers. The plane in which Chiappe was travelling had been shot down by an Italian pilot who mistook it for one of the enemy, and Ribaud was immensely tickled to think that this ace-Quisling whom he had had reason to hate personally had come to such an unexpected and sticky end.

They drove right across Paris and on past the Luxembourg to the Observatoire, near which Ribaud left his car in a garage; then they walked for a little distance across the Place Denfert-Rochereau to the Avenue d'Orléans and entered the courtyard of a large private house on the right side of the road.

At the doorway under the big *porte-cochère* Ribaud rang the bell, knocked twice and then rang the bell again, upon which it was opened by a man who was dressed as a servant but did not look or behave like one. He and Ribaud just nodded to each other, and the detective walked in with Kuporovitch behind him. Crossing the tiled hall, he led the Russian into a big *salon* at the back of the house, where eight or ten people were already assembled. Lacroix was among them, and he immediately came forward to greet the new arrivals.

Evidently the business of the meeting had not yet begun, and while they waited for another half-dozen people to arrive, either singly or in couples, Lacroix told Kuporovitch of his escape after the nursing-home was raided and that he hoped that by this time Gregory was back in England; but he had had no news of him. As the clock struck ten Lacroix seated himself at the head of a long table, and on the others taking seats round it he addressed them.

At first the proceedings did not mean very much to Kuporovitch, as the only person present whom he knew, other

256

than Lacroix and Ribaud, was Madame Idlefonse, and the first part of the Colonel's dissertation mainly concerned the excellent progress of the movement in the provinces of both Occupied and Unoccupied France. This was the result of a strong campaign, by means of the secret distribution of hand-bills and the pasting up at night on walls of subversive posters for strengthening anti-Nazi feeling; but Lacroix gave it as his opinion that they were now in a position to take more ambitious measures and to indulge in actual sabotage. He then asked for suggestions.

Various ideas were put forward, and Kuporovitch contributed as his quota the proposal that explosives should be smuggled into the cellars of the Hôtel Crillon and the German Headquarters blown up. Such an apparently impossible plan caused a certain amount of mild laughter until he related how he had actually got into the cellars himself, and, having done it once, saw no reason why he should not do it again; only this time, instead of delivering sacks of coal, it would be sacks of dynamite.

A big redheaded bull of a man, who proved to be an ex-Communist Deputy named Léon Baras, was all in favour of the idea, as were several of the others; but Lacroix vetoed it on the grounds that such an act would be certain to bring about the most ghastly reprisals. He pointed out that one of the great strangleholds which the Germans possessed over the French people was the fact that they still held over a million French soldiers who had been captured in the Battle for France, as prisoners in concentration camps. The Nazis were perfectly capable of butchering hundreds—if not thousands—of these unfortunate men. In his view, although lives should not be given undue value where the freedom of France was concerned, any such massacre, while causing the most bitter anger among the French people, would also antagonize them against the anti-Nazi movement, from fear that still more of their men might die as reprisals from the further activities of the freedom fighters.

He went on to say that he hoped, and had little doubt, that the time would come when the whole nation would rise to exterminate its enemies, but at present there was no sense in killing one German if ten, twenty, or even more Frenchmen were to lose their lives as a result. Therefore, as yet they must confine their activities to the sabotage of German war materials and avoid killing, except in self-defence.

The majority of the meeting expressed itself in agreement with his views and proceeded to go into details with regard to the destruction of bridges, the derailing of trains and the firing of German supply dumps. Then, after a two-hours' session, it closed, and the members departed, singly or in couples, at intervals of about five minutes.

Kuporovitch remained with Ribaud and Lacroix until nearly the last, and he spent some more time talking to a little pale-faced man, with a shock of white hair whom the others had addressed as 'The Professor'. It transpired that the Professor was the owner of the house, a distinguished chemist, and now engaged on the secret manufacture of time-bombs, to be used for sabotage.

At a little before one Ribaud and Kuporovitch made their adieux and left the house. As they went out Ribaud told the Russian to memorize the place and the way to it well, as he might be asked to attend future meetings on his own, since people were summoned in accordance with whom Lacroix wished to see at any particular time. He also reminded the Russian of the signal to secure admission; one ring, two knocks, and another ring. They then collected the car and Ribaud dropped Kuporovitch at the corner of the Rue Cardinet, from which he had to walk only a few hundred yards to Ferrière's house.

The first week in December was uneventful, except that on one night during it Kuporovitch participated in a plan arranged at the meeting by forming one of a squad of saboteurs who managed to get on board a row of barges in the Seine which contained valuable war material, and scuttle them. Pierre came to dinner again on Sunday, and Madeleine was upset to hear that her mother was suffering more acutely than ever from the cold, so that at times she even wept from it. But there seemed nothing that they could do to aid the invalid. All the fuel stores in Paris were now heavily guarded against night raids, and even Kuporovitch's ingenuity was not sufficient to devise a way in which they might heat Madame Lavallière's apartment. Gas and electricity for cooking were now cut to the barest minimum, and the only heat that any-one in Paris, except the Germans and a few officials, could get was from crowding round a stove to warm their hands when a meal was being prepared.

In vain Madeleine cursed the Nazis for the distress they were inflicting upon her bedridden mother, but none of the others could think of any way to alleviate her sufferings. Madeleine wanted to risk a midnight visit to comfort her, but Kuporovitch still would not hear of it and Pierre too said he thought it would be most unwise. He said he was convinced that in recent weeks the Bonards had gone over to the enemy, because their son had been killed in a British air raid on Calais; and it was next to impossible to get into the block without the *concierge* or his wife being aware of it.

On the night of December the 9th they heard of the British offensive in Libya, and it cheered them a lot to think that after the great peril through which she had passed Britain now felt herself strong enough to launch an attack in force against one, at least, of the Axis partners.

The following night Kuporovitch was summoned to another meeting at the house of the Professor. Fresh plans for further sabotage were entered into, and he learned from Lacroix that, although the Colonel had no news of Gregory himself, their friend must have succeeded in getting back to England, as a large sum of money had arrived during the previous week via the trusted man at the French Consulate in Lisbon. This had lifted a great weight off the little Colonel's shoulders and enabled him to give all his plans a new impetus.

During the days that followed there was great excitement over the serious differences of opinion which had arisen in the Vichy Government. Marshal Pétain defied the Germans by dismissing Laval and appointing Flandin as Foreign Minister in his place. The French Senate and Chamber of Deputies were dissolved, and a Consultative Assembly substituted for them: then Laval was arrested. Otto Abetz, Hitler's *Gauleiter* in Paris, went personally to Vichy and secured Laval's release; but he was not reinstated, and Madeleine and her friends took this as a good indication that the first signs of resistance to the Nazis were now being forced upon the Vichy Government by the will of the French people.

They were cheered too by the news of the British successes in North Africa. In their first drive they had taken 26,000 Italian prisoners. By December the 15th they were fighting on Libyan soil, and by the 16th both Sollum and Fort Capuzzo, two great Italian strongholds, had been captured.

Kuporovitch was now out every night, either as one of the leaders of the gangs of Paris saboteurs or foraging for supplies. While attempting to fire a portion of the great Citroën motor works, which had been taken over by the Germans, he was very nearly captured, but he managed to get away by scattering the inflammable liquid that he was carrying over the two guards who attacked him, instead of on the roof of the shed, which had been his objective.

The Italians had now been driven far back into Albania, and two of their divisions, caught with brilliant generalship by the Greek Chief of Staff, General Papagos, had been entirely destroyed. On the 19th the British had surrounded Bardia, and the number of Italian prisoners taken to date had risen to over 31,000. It was on the night that this news came through that Madeleine was summoned to her first meeting at the Professor's house, and as she might not have been able to find it on her own Kuporovitch was instructed to take her.

Lacroix was now making secret visits to Paris from Vichy nearly every week, and he told them that he had at last had news of Gregory, but he feared that it was not too good. Gregory had got safely home but had been caught in the heavy raid on London of November the 15th. He had been crushed under the blitzed building, and it had been thirty hours before they had been able to get him out. Fortunately his head had been protected by a fallen beam, but his left leg had been broken and he had sustained severe injuries to his body. For some weeks he had hung between life and death, but he had managed to pull through and recently had been transferred to the country, where he was convalescing; but the Colonel thought it would be several months before he was fit to take an active hand in the game again.

Lacroix had wanted to see Madeleine because he felt that sufficient time had now elapsed since the police had been hunting for her for the majority of them to have forgotten her description; and he had work for her to do. Now that the number of his sabotage squads was increasing, so too were their casualties through brushes with night-watchmen, sentries and police; so he had found it necessary to establish a genuine nursing-home where they could have their injuries attended to and remain in bed until they recovered.

She at once expressed her willingness to undertake such work, but Kuporovitch intervened to say that, although the police might have forgotten their description, if either of them were seen coming in and out of Luc Ferrière's house regularly in the daytime the neighbours would begin to wonder who they were. As they had no ration-cards for use at local shops, suspicion might be aroused through some officious gossip, which would lead to an investigation and an arrest.

The Colonel agreed, but thought that might be got over, and introduced Madeleine to a handsome white-haired woman, the Marquise de Villebois, who was running her house as a home for him.

When the situation was explained the Marquise said that she already had her own daughter and another girl, both of whom had trained as V.A.D.s in the early part of the war. They were quite able to run the house and look after the patients in the daytime; but she badly wanted a reliable night nurse, as she and the two girls were on their feet all day. The house was in the Boulevard Saint Germain, and they all agreed that if Madeleine set out after dark each night, and returned before the neighbours were up each morning, there was no great likelihood of her being recognized during her journeys backwards and forwards in the Metro; so everything having been fixed up she set about her new duties the following night.

The thought of Christmas, and to the French the even more important festival of the New Year, was now in everybody's mind; but little of the spirit of Christmas animated the gloomy captive city. The thousands of once well-stocked shops, in which the Parisians had bought their food luxuries and elegant useless trifles so casually, were now almost empty. Even wine, the very life-blood of the French people, was at a premium, and hard to come by. There were queues in every street each morning, while shivering housewives waited anxiously to see if they could obtain their meagre rations,

There was no heating in any of the great blocks, and coal, coke and firewood were as precious as diamonds.

Now that Britain had broken the power of the Luftwaffe and was actually taking the offensive in Libya, no one could see any possible ending to the war. Many people in Paris were now bankrupt and starving. Thousands of others had sons, husbands or lovers who had been in the Forces at the time of the collapse and were now in German concentration camps. Thousands more had wives, daughters, and sweethearts who were missing—just disappeared—they knew not where—in the terrible upheaval which had shaken the country to its foundations the previous summer. For days past there had been snow and bitter winds; the pavements were slippery with ice and the streets full of dirty slush. On every hand there was misery, destitution and despair.

Yet there was at least one person in Paris who thoroughly enjoyed the life he was leading. Stefan Kuporovitch was a man without a home, and for the time being Ferrière's house suited him admirably. It was roomy enough and as comfortable as they could reasonably wish, except for the cold, and even that caused him far less inconvenience than most people, because he was used to the Arctic winters of his native Russia.

He had long since made up his mind that their unwilling host set much too high a price upon his stamp collection to betray them; so, barring some unforeseen accident which they could not possibly guard against, they were perfectly safe as long as they chose to stay there. As he hated inactivity and was adventurous by nature, he got a big kick out of his nightly prowlings after supplies, or skilfully planned acts of sabotage. They had plenty to eat, and, as he had found means to supplement the contents of the cellar, plenty to drink. Above all, he was living in the same house as the girl he adored. For him the approach of Christmas meant only another excuse for one of his celebrations.

On Christmas Eve he took Madeleine to the house of the Marquise de Villebois, then paid another visit to the Zoological Gardens. The animals were not so numerous now, as it had proved difficult to get the right kinds of food to feed many of them, and the authorities had doubtless also decided that venison at this time of acute shortage was better in a pot than running about on four legs. However, on his previous visit he had marked down a handsome Chinese goose with exotic plumage. Having broken into the cage he wrung the bird's neck and, skilfully evading the night-watchman, at which art he was now a past-master, brought it home to provide them with an excellent Christmas dinner.

Pierre joined them for the meal, and, although he avoided the question of Madeleine's mother as far as he could, it emerged that she had recently been ill and that her sufferings from the cold were more acute than ever.

Madeleine wished to go to her that evening, but both Kuporovitch and Pierre flatly refused to let her, as Pierre was now fully convinced that Madame Bonard was in league with the police. He had seen her talking to an *agent de ville* on more than one occasion, and considered it a foregone conclusion that she had been told to keep a watch for Madeleine in the hope that sooner or later she would go to her mother.

Under great pressure Madeleine gave way and tried to salve her conscience by sending presents and loving messages by Pierre that night; but during the following days the mental picture of her mother—ill, lonely, unable to leave her bed and shivering with cold—haunted and tormented her. She had hoped that Kuporovitch would let her risk a visit at Christmas, and now Christmas was gone; but there was still the New Year, and she felt that she could not possibly allow that of all days in the year to pass without giving her mother the consolation of her presence. In consequence, she decided not to tell the others anything about it, so that they should have no opportunity of preventing her, and instead of going back to the nursing-home on New Year's Eve creep back at night to her old home.

So intent was she on this project that the news that Admiral Darlan had had a most important two-day conference over Christmas in Paris with Otto Abetz, and that the Germans had succeeded in burning down a large area of the city of London by the use of thousands of incendiary bombs on December the 29th, passed her by unheeded. On the evening of the 31st, carrying a special parcel of good things, which she had quite unscrupulously taken from Monsieur Ferrière's hoarded stores, she set out at eight o'clock, which was her

263

usual time of leaving for the nursing-home.

It was nearly two months now since she had been in the Rue Saint Honoré, but nothing seemed altered, as far as she could see in the frosty starlight. A bitter wind cut her face as she walked down the street, and the gutters were piled high with snow, but there were even fewer people than usual about. At this hour they were nearly all employed in eating the New Year's Eve dinner that they had managed to scrape up somehow; and it was largely on this that Madeleine counted to engage the attention of the *concierge* and his wife.

She knew that on entering the main door of the building a little hanging bell would ring; but as she was aware of its exact position she was able to carry out her plan of opening the door very gently, just a crack, then raising the point of her umbrella until it became wedged between the bell and the door. The trick worked, and she managed to get inside with only a faint jingle.

There was a light in the *concierge's* room, and the sounds of laughter. Very cautiously she stole past it and up the stairs, not daring to take the lift to the third floor. With her own key she let herself into the apartment and was surprised to find it in complete darkness.

Switching on the light, she went forward with her heart almost in her mouth, dreading, almost foreseeing, what she might find. In the bedroom her mother was lying, but not in a natural sleep. Her hands had been carefully folded across her breast, and a small crucifix had been placed upon them. She must have died earlier that day, or perhaps the preceding night before Madame Bonard came up to attend to her in the morning.

The room was positively icy. Madeleine's teeth began to chatter as she stood there, but her heart was burning with a wild anger. She knew that it was this desperate cold which the German Occupation had brought to Paris that had killed her mother. Between grief and hatred she was almost overcome as she knelt at the bedside, sobbing bitterly.

It was Pierre's voice that roused her. 'Madeleine! What *are* you doing here? You shouldn't have come. I was just on my way over to break the news to you.'

'When—when did she die?' sobbed Madeleine.

'Last night; but I didn't know about it until this afternoon. On my way out just now I saw the light, so I came in to see who was here. You shouldn't have come, Madeleine! If that old woman downstairs knows you're here she'll tell the police, and you'll be in most desperate danger.'

Even as he spoke they both heard the sound of footsteps on the stairs.

18

Unhappy New Year

'Stay where you are!' whispered Pierre, and slipping out of
the bedroom he closed the door gently behind him.

He had hardly done so when Madame Bonard and a
gendarme appeared in the small hallway.

'So it's you!' she said in a surly tone, evidently badly dis-
gruntled at having been disturbed from her New Year's Eve
dinner and made to climb up to the top flights of stairs.
'What're you up to, and how did *you* get in here?'

As she spoke the *gendarme* ran to the window and began
to draw the curtains. 'You'll be lucky if you get off with a
heavy fine for this,' he muttered. 'You must be crazy to sit
about in rooms without doing the black-out. The lights from
these top windows can be seen from the sky for miles, and
for such an offence you're liable to a prison sentence.'

Pierre realized then what had brought them up there. As
Madame Lavallière was dead Madame Bonard had not
bothered to do the black-out as usual that evening. On entering
the flat Madeleine had failed to notice that, and the shock of
finding her mother dead had prevented her from becoming
aware of it later. Down in the street the *gendarme* had seen
the lights go on and immediately roused out Madame Bonard
to go up with him while he took particulars of the culprit.

'How did you get in?' Madame Bonard repeated truculently.

'As a friend of the family I was given a key to the apartment months ago,' Pierre lied.

'And what were you doing here?' she went on.

Pierre was saved from having to reply by the *gendarme*
saying angrily: 'Don't stand there, man! Do the other two

windows—in that room behind you! There were three windows in a line, all blazing with light when I ran along the street.' As he spoke he moved swiftly towards the bedroom door.

'No, no, I'll do it,' Pierre cried hastily, stepping in front of him.

'All right, go on then!' replied the policeman, but as Pierre did not budge he suddenly made to thrust him aside.

'You can't go in there!' declared Pierre, grabbing the policeman's arm.

'Why not?' the man demanded.

'There's a body of a woman in it who died last night. We should respect the dead.'

'Fiddlesticks!' exclaimed Madame Bonard. 'It's no disrespect to the poor woman to do her black-out.' Her voice suddenly changed to a note of suspicion. 'What've you been up to? I believe there's something you don't want us to see in there.'

'Stand aside!' said the *gendarme* firmly. 'You're obstructing me in the course of my duty. I believe you're one of these Communists who're endeavouring to sabotage the régime. If you don't get out of the way I shall charge you with showing these lights and keeping them on with intent to assist the enemy.'

Pierre was up against it. He knew that Madeleine must have heard their raised voices through the door. She might have taken the minute he had gained for her to hide herself; but now that Madame Bonard's suspicions were aroused it was more than likely that once she got into the room she would open the cupboards and poke about to see if he had interfered with anything, and that would result in Madeleine's discovery. Pierre had never hit a man in anger in his life, but he loved Madeleine desperately. He could not bear the thought that she would be carted off and handed over to the Gestapo. Ribaud had furnished him with a pistol, but he was terrified of firearms and felt certain that he would bungle matters if he tried to use it.

As he stared into the angry eyes of the policeman he had an awful sinking feeling from knowing that he positively had to do something, or in another moment it would be too late.

The *gendarme* was standing within two feet of him. With a sudden inspiration Pierre made a nervous grab at the man's truncheon, jerked it out and hit him a glancing blow with it on the side of the head.

For a moment the *gendarme* was so astonished that he did nothing, but stood there with his left hand up to his head where he had been hit; then with a roar of rage he pulled out his pistol.

Desperate now, Pierre hit him with the truncheon again, this time much harder and on top of the head. The policeman's kepi took some of the force of the blow, but he staggered back, while Madame Bonard, throwing up her hands, ran out of the room and down the stairs, crying:

'Help! Help! Police! Murder!'

Before the *gendarme* could raise his gun Pierre hit him a third time, his nervous excitement lending strength to the blow. The man dropped his pistol and fell to his knees, where he remained, swaying slightly, while he mumbled threats and curses.

Staring down at him, Pierre was conscious of the frightening thought that he had burnt his boats; but he saw that his only course now was to go through with the job. Seizing the half-dazed policeman, he threw him face downwards on the floor, and pulling his arms behind his back tied his wrists with a handkerchief. He then grabbed a scarf from the hatstand and, avoiding the man's futile kicks, succeeded in tying his ankles together. Jumping up, he ran to the bedroom door, switched off the light and called to Madeleine:

'It was Madame Bonard and a *gendarme*! Your forgetting to do the black-out brought them up. I've laid him out, but she's rushed downstairs to get help.'

At the sound of his voice Madeleine stepped out of a big clothes cupboard where she had hidden herself, and said quickly: 'You knocked the policeman out! How brave of you, Pierre! Where is he?'

'Here, on the floor,' called Pierre into the semi-darkness; 'but his friends will come pounding up the stairs at any moment, and God knows how we're going to get out of here.'

Madeleine's mind had switched back to that terrible evening

six months before when the Nazis had raided the apartment and shot Georges. She had then had a short-lived hope that if he could back his way into the little kitchen while she threw herself in front of him he might be able to escape down the cables of the goods lift. In a hurried spate of words she now produced the idea to Pierre.

He paled a little. 'Those cables aren't meant to bear a big weight and they're pretty old. We'll break our necks if they give way.'

'We'll have to chance that,' declared Madeleine resolutely.

'All right, then. But let's go down by the one from my kitchen. If they find this flat empty when they get back that may give us a few extra moments; and if we lock the door they'll have to break it down.'

With a swift nod Madeleine ran into the kitchen, flung open the window and threw her hat into the sink so that the police would find a false trail and imagine that they had gone out that way. Pierre meanwhile had unlocked the door of his own apartment across the landing, and as soon as they were inside it they bolted the door behind them.

'You won't be able to come back here now,' she gasped, 'so you'd better take a few things.'

'D'you think there's time?' he asked uneasily.

'Yes, yes! But for God's sake, be quick!'

Running to his bedroom, Pierre pulled a suitcase out from under the bed and rapidly stuffed some of his most treasured possessions and more useful clothes into it, while Madeleine got his kitchen window open, and climbing out on the sill began to test the stoutest cable to see if it would bear her weight.

Suddenly she heard Pierre's voice behind her. 'Perhaps I'd better go first in case it breaks.'

With a shake of her head she rejected his gallant offer and swung herself out on to the cable. It was not very thick, so it proved difficult for her to keep a proper grip on it with her hands and knees. She had intended to go down, hand over hand, but before she was halfway the wire was slipping through her grasp. In sudden panic she clutched it tightly so that it cut through her gloves and burnt her hands, as though it were made of red-hot steel. With a moan of pain she slid the

269

last twenty feet, arriving with a horrible bump on the wooden cage at the bottom.

Dazed and faint, her hands smarting terribly, she managed to pick herself out of the snow and called up that she was all right. Then she saw Pierre's dark form against the starlight sky as he prepared to follow her.

Very fortunately she stood away from under him, as before he had lowered himself a dozen feet he, too, found himself slipping, and with one of his hands he was clutching his heavy bag. Next second, in order to save himself, he was compelled to drop it.

It landed with a terrific thud at Madeleine's feet, spilling its contents right and left in the trampled snow. Controlling the pain that she was feeling with an effort, she hastily began to collect the things and cram them back into the bag. A minute later he was beside her. In frantic haste they picked up the last few items. Pierre grabbed the bag, and they set off at a run down the dark alleyway, the snow deadening the sound of their footfalls.

By the time they reached the street at the alley's end and broke into a walk Madeleine was sobbing openly. She could feel the warm blood soaking into her gloves from the places where her palms had been torn, and the nerves were on fire from their searing contact with the steel cable. The torture was such that she was hardly even aware that she was badly bruised about the body from her fall. Pierre had come off somewhat better, as he had grabbed up his thickest pair of gloves before leaving his room, and as they were leather motor gauntlets they had served to protect his hands, except in one place where the leather had been scorched through.

Taking Madeleine's arm with his free hand he strove to comfort her as they hurried down a narrow turning that brought them to Les Halles. The great central market was shut, but as they twisted in and out among the stacks of bales and crates which lined the pavements and the streets adjacent to it they felt that they were now safe from pursuit, and Madeleine managed to regain control of herself. Heading north-west, they reached the Bourse, from which they got a bus that took them up to the Place Malesherbes, Madeleine keeping her hands in her pockets while she was in it, from fear that their bloody state should attract unwelcome attention.

When they reached Luc Ferrière's house they found that Kuporovitch had not yet gone out on his nightly prowl. On hearing of her adventures he showed a new respect for Pierre, whom in secret he had always previously despised as a weakling, and while helping Madeleine to bathe her hands he very wisely forbore from upbraiding her upon her rashness in going to her old home against his advice.

When her hands had been attended to, and Madame Chautemps had given her aspirin, and tucked her up in bed, Kuporovitch broke the news to Ferrière that he would have to accommodate another guest. The Mayor had no option but to agree, and by now he had become so used to the presence of the other two that he showed no resentment, only alarm that Pierre might be the cause of bringing the police down on the house before the night was out, which would prove the undoing of them all.

However, Pierre assured him that he was quite certain that Madeleine and himself had not been followed; and after Kuporovitch had given him a stiff brandy, which he badly needed owing to the strain he had undergone, he was accommodated in a little room at the top of the house next to Madame Chautemps' bedroom.

For the next few days Madeleine was unable to carry out her nightly duties at the Marquise de Villebois' house, and it distressed her very much that there could be no question of attending her mother's funeral; but the Mayor's household soon settled down again with its new occupant, and Pierre now went out every night with Kuporovitch as his assistant.

As a result of the bitter wrangling between the governors of France over Christmas, on the 3rd of January it was announced from Vichy that Unoccupied France would now be ruled by a triumvirate, consisting of Admiral Darlan, General Huntziger, and Monsieur Flandin, under the direction of Marshal Pétain. On the 5th the British captured Bardia with 40,000 prisoners, and on the 10th great excitement was caused from the R.A.F. having carried out their first heavy daylight raid on aerodromes and other objectives in Northern France. As usual, the Germans endeavoured to cover the matter up by lying about it, but everybody knew from the whispering campaign which now carried the B.B.C. broadcasts into every corner of the capital that the raid had been most successful and that the British had got away without losing a single aircraft.

By the following week Madeleine's hands had healed sufficiently for her to resume her duties, and Kuporovitch attended another conference at the house in the Avenue d'Orléans. On his return he was able to tell her from Lacroix that, although Gregory was out of the game, all the information the Colonel had sent by him had got safely through, as arms and explosives were now reaching Lacroix's nominees through his secret channels in the south of France.

The cold continued to be intense. Food was becoming more difficult than ever to obtain, and their situation was now aggravated by the fact that soap was running terribly short; so they could not afford to wash themselves with it more than once a day, and laundry could now only be rinsed in almost freezing water.

Their condition would have been even more miserable had not Kuporovitch continued to bring in supplies of illegally obtained foods, and towards the end of the month he had excuses to hold two of his celebrations. On January the 22nd the British took Tobruk with a further 25,000 prisoners, and on the 28th news came through that earlier in the month the Camel Corps of the Free French Forces, based in Equatorial Africa, had raided the Italian air base of Murzuk in South-Western Libya, destroying a number of enemy planes and all their facilities there.

At the end of January there were further signs of how uneasily Unoccupied France was bearing the German yoke. Marstal Pétain had written to Hitler pleading for the release of some of the French prisoners-of-war, and Hitler had replied by a refusal to make any further concessions unless Vichy would give him full collaboration; upon which anti-Vichy articles began to appear in many of the papers. On February the 2nd Admiral Darlan paid another visit to Paris for a meeting with Laval, who had now gone over openly to the Germans, but the results of the meeting were kept secret. Darlan returned to Vichy on the 4th, came back to Paris with

272

counter-proposals from Pétain on the 6th, and returned again to Vichy on the 7th. On the 9th Pétain appointed him Vice-Premier and Foreign Minister; so it was clear that he had now managed to gain control of the situation and henceforth would be the moving spirit in the Vichy Government.

In the meantime, the people of the United States were at last becoming conscious of the extreme peril in which they would stand if Hitler succeeded in defeating Britain, and the American Administration was exercising all the pressure that it could to restrain Vichy from collaboration with the Axis. On February the 5th a writ of attachment was issued on all funds held by the Bank of France in New York, and on the 8th the Lease and Lend Bill was passed.

The Greeks were going from victory to victory in their Albanian campaign and by February the 12th the Italian losses there were estimated to be in the neighbourhood of 90,000 men. But the German diplomats were now very active in the Balkans, and on the 13th the Yugoslav Prime Minister was summoned to Berchtesgaden. On March the 1st Bulgaria joined the Axis, and on the 3rd German troops were reported to have crossed Bulgaria and reached the Greek frontier.

With the capture of Benghazi on February the 6th General Wavell's brilliant campaign was brought to a magnificent conclusion, but this great soldier seemed tireless in his efforts to secure Britain's position in the Near East, despite his terribly limited resources. Italian East Africa was now receiving his attention, and the Generals under him were displaying extraordinary vigour and enterprise. On February the 25th Mogadishu, the capital of Italian Somaliland, fell to the South African Forces, and on March the 16th Berbera, the capital of British Somaliland, was recaptured; while Imperial Forces had now penetrated far into Abyssinia and Eritrea.

On March the 25th Yugoslav representatives signed a pact with the Nazis in Vienna, but the following day there were great patriotic demonstrations against the Government, and on the 27th General Simovitch effected a *coup d'état* by which the Regent Prince Paul was deposed and the young King Peter assumed power. On the same day Keren and Hara, two most important points in the Abyssinian campaign, fell to the Imperial Forces. These British victories on land were followed next day by one at sea. Admiral Cunningham caught the Italian Fleet off Cape Matapan and mauled it severely.

But in early April the tide turned against the British. The Quisling Sayid Rashid Ali effected a *coup d'état*, instigated by the Nazis, in Iraq, and the British were taken by surprise in Libya, where the Germans, who had sent over their armoured Afrika Korps to reinforce the Italians, unexpectedly took the offensive, compelling the British to evacuate Benghazi. That distant Addis Ababa was entered after an amazing forced march on April the 5th was a small compensation for these much more serious setbacks; and on Sunday, April 6th, the Nazis struck again with all their force, invading Yugoslavia.

During all these weeks Madeleine, Kuporovitch and Pierre carried on with their work. They could foresee no ending to the war, but had an absolute conviction that it could only be hastened by the sort of efforts they were making, which was a big consolation to them in view of the hard and dangerous lives that they were leading.

From time to time, all three of them were summoned to conferences at the house in the Avenue d'Orléans, and occasionally the two men had exciting moments when their plans went wrong, or they were in temporary danger of being caught, but by fire-raising, interference with railway points, and the sabotaging of shipping in the Seine, they managed to do quite a considerable amount of damage.

It comforted them, too, to know from the conferences which they attended that the secret movement was ever-growing, and that, whereas in September they had been a few lone men against a mighty enemy, they could now count upon the help and support of great numbers of the French people. Their exploits, too, had now become far less hazardous, since in an emergency there were nearly always strangers at hand who were willing to give them aid in getting away when they were pursued, or temporarily hiding them from the police.

To obtain supplies became more difficult than ever, but as the year advanced they suffered far less severely from the cold, and it was with immense relief that they saw the first budding of the trees in the Bois and the Jardins des Tuileries.

As April advanced, however, the bulletins became more and more depressing and the pro-Nazi announcers on the Paris radio more raucous as they bawled accounts of the Nazi victories. By the 9th the Germans had occupied Salonika, cutting off the Greek armies in Thrace and Eastern Macedonia. On the 10th General Rommel scored a great triumph in Libya, capturing 2,000 British prisoners, including three generals. On the 11th Zagreb fell to the Germans, and their forces reached Monastir, thereby cutting Yugoslavia off from Greece. By the 13th the British Forces in Greece were already in retreat, and on the 14th the Greeks were compelled to evacuate Koritza. Few people doubted now that the gallant Greek Army was doomed and that the British, having with such crazy rashness established a front on the mainland of Europe, would soon be driven out of it.

It was on the 16th that Madeleine and her friends were seated at supper with the Mayor, rather gloomily discussing the latest bulletins, when they heard a sharp rat-a-tat on the front door.

Luc Ferrière's lifelong meanness had stood them in admirable stead since they had taken up their residence with him. Owing to the fact that he never entertained, and had lived almost as a hermit, they were never troubled with unwelcome visitors whom the Mayor could hardly have ceased to receive had it been his custom to do so, and which would have meant their constantly going into hiding upstairs when such visits occurred.

At the sound of the knocking alarm showed in all their faces, as they had no idea who it could be.

'Into your sitting-room!' Kuporovitch whispered swiftly to the Mayor. 'No one must be allowed in here to see that there are four places laid at the table.' Then he bundled Madeleine and Pierre out of the room, and followed them upstairs.

Madame Chautemps had come out in the passage. Directly she saw that they were safely out of the way, and that the Mayor was settled in his room, she went to the door and opened it. A lean-faced man with a soft hat pulled well down over his eyes, and his collar turned up, was standing there. On his asking for the Mayor she held the door open for him to come in, and while she closed it he stood for a moment under the light in the hall.

Kuporovitch had sent Madeleine and Pierre into the nearest

bedroom, but had remained on the landing himself. He was peering over the banisters, his gun in his hand, ready for action, anxious to ascertain as soon as possible if the visitor were just a casual caller or might prove a threat to their safety.

Suddenly he gave a shout of joy and came bounding down the stairs.

'Gregory, by all that's holy! My son, my friend, my brother! What a joy to see you here!'

The lean man turned and limped forward, a gay smile lighting up his face, as he greeted the Russian with equal affection.

Kuporovitch's shout had brought the others out of the bedroom, and they too ran down to crowd round Gregory and shake him warmly by the hand.

'But how did you know where to find us?' Madeleine exclaimed after a moment.

'Can we talk freely?' he asked, with a quick glance at the housekeeper, who was still standing near the door.

'Yes, yes!' Kuporovitch assured him. 'Madame Chautemps is a de Gaullist and has proved an invaluable friend to us; but you must exercise caution in front of our host.' He pointed to the closed sitting-room door.

Gregory lowered his voice. 'I telephoned Ribaud as soon as I got to Paris, and he gave me your address. You've no idea how glad I was to know that you were still safe and sound after all these months.'

'How did you get to Paris this time?' Madeleine asked.

'Not by sea, thank you,' he laughed. 'I've had enough clandestine crossings to last me a lifetime, but I'll tell you about my ghastly trip home later on. I came over by plane last night and was dropped by parachute near Beauvais.'

'Have you had anything to eat?' Kuporovitch enquired anxiously.

Gregory shook his head. 'No. It took me the best part of the day to get here, and I brought only a few bars of chocolate in my pocket, so I'm hungry as a hunter. I hope to goodness you're not all starving.'

'I never starve!' laughed the Russian. 'Come in, my friend, come in, and we will resume our supper.'

Luc Ferrière was called out of his sitting-room and introduced. He muttered a little unhappily when he was told that his house must now shelter yet another secret guest, but Kuporovitch said that Gregory could share his room and went down to the cellar to fetch the two best bottles of burgundy remaining in it. Five minutes later another place had been laid, and they were all seated round the table laughing and talking again.

Pierre had a job to do that night, so he left them soon after the meal was finished, and Luc Ferrière went off to bed at ten o'clock; so Madeleine, Kuporovitch and Gregory were then able to talk with complete freedom. Gregory laughed a lot when he heard about how Kuporovitch had trapped the Mayor into providing them with a safe and comfortable hide-out. Then he told them of his difficult trip back to England and gave details of his own narrow escape from death in the previous November.

He had been in a ghastly state when the faithful Rudd and a rescue party had pulled him out of the ruins of his home thirty hours after it had been bombed, but that was five months ago, and he was now completely recovered, except that he still limped a little, although the doctors said that, too, would be all right in time. For the first two months or so he had suffered severely from the dressing of his wounds; but his ill luck in being blitzed had had its compensations. As soon as he was well enough to be moved Sir Pellinore had sent him up to Gwaine Meads, so that Erika could nurse him, and all through the late winter and early spring, while he was convalescing, he had the joy of being with her.

During these months Lacroix had managed to establish safe contacts with a number of de Gaulle's officers at the Free French Headquarters in London; so once Gregory had set the ball rolling his inability to continue as a link between Lacroix and the British Government had not materially hampered the Colonel's operations. But when Gregory had felt himself really fit again he had insisted upon getting back into harness, and Sir Pellinore had suggested that he should make a trip to Paris so that on his return he could put in a full appreciation of the state of things there from his own unbiased observations.

Kuporovitch then told him how well things were going and gave him an outline of some of his own more recent activities.

Madeleine had sat silent for some time when suddenly she broke in: 'I know you're doing good work, Stefan, and that lots of our other friends are too. You're all doing everything you can and risking your lives almost nightly, but what do the results amount to? Please don't think I'm trying to belittle your work, but it's seemed to me for a long time now that we're not really getting anywhere. Naturally, it annoys the Germans when you derail a troop-train or succeed in blowing up one of the plants that are making munitions for them; but these things are only pinpricks.'

'I don't see how Stefan and his friends can do very much more at the moment,' Gregory said mildly.

'But don't you realize,' she insisted, 'that these isolated acts are not really bringing us nearer to winning the war? Any damage that is done can easily be repaired within a week or two, and it can't be one-hundredth part of what the Germans are doing by their bombing of Plymouth, Coventry, Southampton, Bristol and Liverpool. Now that the Nazis are in control of practically the whole of Europe they have simply thousands of factories working for them, so even with American help it's going to be years before Britain can possibly catch up in the armaments race. Then there's the question of man-power. The British are gallant enough, but even with their Empire and the bits and pieces of Free Forces that are fighting with them they simply haven't the population ever to be able to put into the field an army which will be able to defeat the combined forces of the Germans, Italians and their puppet states on the mainland of Europe.'

'That's true enough,' Gregory agreed; 'but if we can hold the Germans in their cage by our blockade that ought to have its effect in time; and sooner or later we'll achieve the air superiority which will enable us to blast hell out of the German cities. Between them these two weapons will bring the Germans to their knees.'

'But when?' demanded Madeleine impatiently. 'Don't you see that it may take years, and that while you're slowly building up your Air Force and trying to starve out the Germans you'll be starving the people in all the countries that they've conquered, too? It was grim enough here last winter. What it's going to be like next I can't think, and as long as there is anything left to eat at all you can be certain that the Germans will take it for themselves. Surely you see that in time the spirit of the people in the occupied territories will be broken by sheer starvation, unless you can devise some means to bring them aid or stir them into revolt while there is still some fight left in them.'

Kuporovitch nodded. 'I'm afraid you're right about that; but any premature attempt at a revolt would be absolute madness. The Germans are employing a part of their forces now to throw the British out of Greece, but the numbers of the British there obviously cannot be large, and the Greeks and Yugoslavs are so ill-equipped to fight a modern war that it will be quite impossible for them to put up any prolonged resistance. Even while the campaign is in progress Occupied France is still lousy with German troops, and once it's over they would be able to use the whole of their Army, if need be, to quell any rising here. We shouldn't stand a dog's chance.'

'I don't think you'd stand much chance anyhow,' Gregory remarked, 'until the British are in a position to land regular troops on the French coast to support a revolt, and I don't think there's the least hope of that this year, or probably even next. For any such landing to be successful, quite apart from the fact that we haven't yet got sufficient supplies of tanks, our expeditionary force would need complete aerial protection, and although we've managed to beat the Luftwaffe on our own ground we're nowhere near strong enough yet to start a major air offensive.'

'Then someone will have to think up some other idea for dealing a really heavy blow at the Nazis,' Madeleine persisted; 'something which will shake them so much that there will be a chance for us to make a successful rising. I'm absolutely convinced that it is the only hope for the people in the conquered territories. If something's not done within a year at most they'll be down and out for good.'

Gregory nodded gravely. 'You mean that somehow or other we must give an entirely new orientation to the war. There's a lot in what you say, Madeleine, but how it could be done is just one hell of a problem.'

'If we could only kill Hitler that might do the trick,' she suggested. 'The Germans regard him now as a kind of symbol of victory—almost as a god. Time and again he's gone against his own General Staff; yet he's managed to pull the chestnuts out of the fire every time. His loss would prove an incalculable blow to them. It would shake their confidence in themselves and that's what we want.'

Kuporovitch shook his head. 'I'm afraid that's out of the question. The reprisals for his murder would be ghastly beyond belief.'

Madeleine's blue eyes were blazing in her white face. 'What does that matter? If only we could shake the whole Nazi machine to its foundations! If France had fought on thousands of her men would have died on the battlefields. Even if thousands of them should be sacrificed now they would be dying for their country just the same.'

'In view of the fact that we're waging Total War you're perfectly right,' Gregory agreed, 'but I'm afraid any attempt to assassinate Hitler is a hopeless proposition. He must be the most carefully guarded man in Europe. When I spoke of a new orientation of the war, though, I meant by its spreading to our advantage. For example, if either Russia or the United States came in on our side. How about Russia, Stefan? This pact between Moscow and Berlin is one of the most phoney tie-ups that have ever been entered into. Everyone knows that Russian and German interests are diametrically opposed.'

'Then why didn't the Russians come in with us at the beginning?' Madeleine asked.

He shrugged. 'The Russains didn't see the fun of pulling our chestnuts out of the fire for us, and we certainly hadn't deserved that they should. If they'd come in at the kick-off they would have had to take the whole weight of the first great German assault after the Nazis had overrun Poland. Stalin's attitude in wishing to see the Germans weaken themselves first against Britain and France was perfectly logical. But I don't think he'd like to see Britain totally defeated, because he knows perfectly well that within a year the Nazis would find an excuse to quarrel with him, and he'd either have to surrender his grain and oil-lands, which are his life-blood, peaceably, or take on the mightiest army the world has ever seen, alone. Now that the Luftwaffe has been knocked about a bit, and the Germans have had to spread themselves so much, to hold down all their conquered territories, what do you think the chances are, Stefan, of Stalin ratting on his pact with Hitler and coming in against him?'

'I'm fully convinced that there's no chance of that at all,' Kuporovitch replied with a cynical grin. 'If he'd been going to come in for the reasons which you state he would have come in during the Battle for France, when all the German Armies were fully engaged in the West. All Stalin wants is peace to continue the Five-Year Plans which in another twenty years will make Russia one of the most wealthy and prosperous nations in the world. He knows now that Britain means to fight it out, so he's sitting fairly pretty. Such a war to the death must continue for another five years at least, and both Germany and Britain will emerge from it utterly exhausted; so even if the Nazis are still in power when it's over they will no longer have the strength to attack Russia.'

'There, you see!' Madeleine exclaimed. 'You admit yourself that with things as they are the war cannot be over for at least another five years. By that time France will have starved to death. We must do something to create an entirely new situation. We simply must—it's our only hope.'

'I don't see that *we* can do anything,' said Kuporovitch glumly, 'but there's the United States.'

Gregory shook his head. 'America may come in before it's finished, but not for a long time yet, and in my opinion she's not likely to do so unless she feels that Britain is really going under. Of course, President Roosevelt and the Administration are a hundred per cent. for us. I think the majority of Americans are too, but, apart from a few adventurous fellows, they won't fight unless they feel that they've absolutely got to. It's not sufficiently realized over here either that there are still enormous numbers of people in the States who are definitely Axis sympathizers. Chicago is almost a German city. New York has its great Italian colony. Then there are the Irish, many of whom are by no means pro-British. Back in England we all feel that the President is doing every possible thing he can to help us; but he has to watch every step he takes, and it's one hell of a big job to educate the isolationists of the

Middle West up to the fact that their freedom, lives and property are just as much threatened by Hitler's bid for world power as our own. Nothing short of a full declaration of war with the employment of the United States Armed Forces could bring about the sort of change in the situation of which we're thinking, and I'm quite certain that's not going to happen for a long time.'

'Getting back to Hitler,' said Madeleine. 'If we can't assassinate him, isn't it possible for us to discredit him in some way in the eyes of his own people? For instance, couldn't you manage to get some documents faked in London which would prove that Herr Schickelgrubber is really a Jew?'

'That's a good idea,' Gregory laughed, 'but, unfortunately, we can't carry it into practical application. You see, the entire Press of Germany and all the countries which she has overrun is controlled by the Nazis. They would never allow the publication of the evidence, and to put it over by the B.B.C. wouldn't do much good, because even if it were true Goebbels would simply laugh it off as British lies and propaganda.'

'You remember Father Xavier, Gregory?' Kuporovitch remarked. 'What he said made me think a lot. You remember how he views the struggle as a war in which Christianity must be wiped out unless Hitler Antichrist can be destroyed? Surely enough has not been made out of that, and a new orientation could be given to this Civil War if the heads of the Churches preached a new Crusade—particularly the Pope. A declaration by His Holiness might even cause widespread dissension in the German and Italian Armies. I mean, of course, if the Pope was prepared to go all out, denounce Hitler from his private radio as a menace to all established religion, and call upon every Catholic in the world to give his life, if need be, in exterminating the pagan Nazis.'

Madeleine nodded. 'That would be the greatest blow of all which could conceivably be struck to bring about the sort of situation that I mean.'

'Yes,' Gregory murmured. 'That would be the real big stuff. Of course, if the Pope came out on our side like that he'd be seized and imprisoned by the Italians, but plenty of Popes have suffered for their faith in bygone days, so I see no reason at all why His Holiness should not be prepared to now,

282

In fact the stronger the measures taken against him personally the greater would be the effect of his call to battle. He's certainly no friend of the Nazis, as it is, but I expect he fears that if he raised the whole of the Catholics against them his priesthood would be massacred.'

Madeleine shrugged. 'His passivity did not prevent the Catholic priests in Poland being massacred, and the more priests who suffer martyrdom for their faith in the rest of Europe the more intense the indignation of all religious people would be. There would be risings everywhere, and the German garrisons would be butchered overnight by a furiously indignant people. It might mean a blood-bath for a week, but what is that if only it resulted in a quick ending to the war?'

'You're right again,' Gregory smiled, 'but unfortunately in this case I'm afraid we're up against Vatican politics. One must remember that Dictators are here to-day and gone to-morrow, whereas the Papacy goes on for ever, and its policy does not consider this year or next, but deals in centuries. The Pope's advisers have probably come to the conclusion that even if Hitler wins this war he will find the whole world too big to swallow, and the Nazis will bust, as a result of their conquests. In that case, after having had to go underground in Europe for a few years, the Roman Church would come into its own again, and emerge stronger than ever on account of the persecution that it had suffered. In any case, there's no way that I know of in which we can bring practical pressure to bear on the Pope, so it seems to me that we're getting outside practical politics.'

'I agree,' declared Kuporovitch, 'but how about Communism? Much could be done, I believe, if a campaign could be launched to foster Communism in the German Army. In the last war it was the spread of Communism by the German troops, who had been indoctrinated with it during their garrisoning of the territories that they overran in Russia, which contributed just as much as the British Blockade to the final collapse of Germany. I've always maintained, too, that in the present war, if Stalin did decide to come in against Germany, it would not be by force of arms. He would send over the Red Air Force with millions of leaflets, and thousands of German-speaking parachutists would be dropped to raise the

German workers against the Prussian military caste who have always been his nightmare. Of course, Stalin would not attempt anything of that kind until Germany appeared to be actually on the point of collapse and the occupied territories already in a state of revolt; but if he ever attacks Germany at all I'm certain that is the way he will do it.'

Gregory grinned. 'You've sabotaged your own suggestion by saying that he would never do it until Germany is already on the verge of anarchy. In the meantime, what hope have we got of spreading Communism in the German Army on a scale large enough to do any good?'

'I'm afraid I must leave you now,' said Madeleine, standing up. 'I must get off to my job at the nursing-home. But I do feel terribly strongly about this, Gregory, and when you get back to London please talk it over with all the cleverest people you know. It's infinitely more important than things like this little revolt in Iraq, or even the slaughter that's going on in Greece just now. Some way *must* be devised to deal a really mighty blow against Hitler and the Nazis during the coming year, or by the time that the British are really strong enough to come to the rescue of all the wretched millions in Europe it will be too late.'

When they had seen her off and settled down again Kuporovitch said with a sigh: 'Poor darling! She would give her own life without hesitation, I believe, if she could bring the downfall of the Nazis even one day nearer. It is strange to see such bitterness and fanaticism in one so young and beautiful, but her fiancé's death made a terrible impression on her, and just as I was beginning to hope that she was becoming a little less obsessed with her desire for vengeance above all else, her mother dies of cold. That, too, of course, she puts down to the Nazis, although they were only indirectly responsible. God knows I hate the brutes enough myself, but to overcome a wild beast one must keep calm, and I dread this spirit in Madeleine, fearing always that it will land her one day in some awful danger. After all, what the freedom-fighters have been doing is not so bad, and it's no good crying for the moon. This desperate urge of hers to precipitate some form of crisis is not only impracticable but damnably dangerous.'

'On the contrary, Stefan, she's right,' said Gregory quietly.

'I'm sorry to say that back in England we have far too many complacent people, who believe that just because we won the Battle of Britain last autumn we've only got to sit tight now, and in due course Hitler will bust himself.

'He won't bust himself—why should he? Since his extraordinary victories of last summer the German Army and people have been behind him as never before, and now that he controls such a vast area of territory our Blockade may still prove a nuisance, but that alone can't possibly overcome him. Whoever may have to go short of things you may be quite sure that the Germans will be the last to suffer. You can bet too that by this time their agricultural experts are hard at it all over the place planning to raise bumper crops next summer. They've masses of labour, more than they know what to do with, now that the Armies of the countries they have overrun have been disarmed and disbanded. Too many people are saying that time is on our side—it's not any longer, at least not as far as rescuing the people of Europe from their oppressors is concerned.

'That's where Madeleine has hit the nail on the head. By the time the Germans themselves are down to really short rations, so that our bombing will reduce them to a state where they find themselves properly up against it and start to squeal for peace, everyone else in Europe will have died from starvation.

'It may have been that belief which caused our Government to send troops into Greece with the idea of establishing a new front in Europe. I don't know, but in my view it was very wrong and completely futile. The few divisions that we could send can't possibly stand up against the vast weight of the German Army, so they'll only be slung out again with a further loss of prestige for Britain, and a useless sacrifice of highly trained personnel and valuable material. Total War is Logical War, and chivalry is not logic, so by the Greek adventure we are only making our position worse than it was before; but because our people have gone the wrong way to work it doesn't alter the fact that we dare not sit still. Unless the war is to drag on for ten years and end in the utter exhaustion of both sides with a peace of compromise, something has got to be done to give it an entirely new orientation.'

'I admit that you convince me,' Kuporovitch murmured. 'Here I have been too close to things, and with no one to talk to who understands the wider aspects, so as a result of the last few months I have become a cabbage. Are you very tired, or shall we talk some more? It is only by hammering these things from every angle that one sometimes gets somewhere.'

'No, I'm not tired,' Gregory said. 'These last few months I've stored up enough sleep to do on quite small doses for a while, but I'd like another drink.'

'Right then.' Kuporovitch stood up, and going down to the cellar returned with two more bottles. They talked then of the High Direction of the war, going round the world and back again, staring for hour after hour at a map which Kuporovitch had pinned up on the wall of the dining-room, as they tried to forecast what Hitler's next move might be; and assessed the chances of one country or another coming in against or with him. Both of them were extremely well informed on military matters and had a first-class knowledge of history and geography; so, allowing for the ingenuity, speed and determination with which the Nazis always struck, they were able to assess within a reasonable degree the possible result of new moves upon the vast chessboard.

It was after four o'clock in the morning when they had reached the conclusion that there was only one move on the board which would mean checkmate to Hitler within a foreseeable period, and that upon whether it was made or not hung the lives of all the millions that Hitler had enslaved.

The difficulties of creating such a situation as would force that move to be made were immense, but these two men had never allowed difficulties to deter them from any project upon which they had agreed, and when they at last went up to bed they had already decided upon the measures which they must take in the hope of bringing about the desired move.

For the next few days there was nothing that Gregory could do, as before he could initiate his plan he had to see Lacroix and secure the Colonel's agreement and co-operation, so he spent most of his time wandering about Paris talking to casual acquaintances that he picked up in the bars and getting a line on the feeling of the population of Paris for himself.

As most people had foreseen, affairs in Greece were going

badly. The small but gallant Imperial Army was being forced back by sheer weight of men and metal. All organized resistance in Yugoslavia had already been overcome, and the Greeks too were now in a bad way. On April the 22nd their Army of the Epirus, consisting of a quarter of a million men who had covered themselves earlier in the year with such undying glory in Albania, was forced to surrender through lack of supplies and being cut off from its bases.

It was on that day that Lacroix again arrived in Paris, and Kuporovitch was notified by Ribaud of a meeting which was to be held that night. A few minutes before ten, with Gregory beside him, he entered the house in the Avenue d'Orléans.

Lacroix welcomed Gregory with the utmost enthusiasm, congratulating him on his escape from death and the excellent recovery he had made. The conference then took place, and when it was over Gregory told Lacroix that he and Kuporovitch wished to talk to him in private; so the three of them went into a small library adjoining the big room in which the meetings were held, and when they had sat down Gregory put forward his proposals.

The little Colonel listened patiently, his hands folded on his stomach and his wizened face turned down in an attitude of contemplation, so that they could not see the reactions in his quick dark eyes. When Gregory had finished he looked up and said:

'There is much in what Madeleine Lavallière says, *mon ami*. We are but poor mice nibbling at the great beast's cloven hoof, and for many months to come I see no hope of our inflicting any wound that will really be felt upon it; but what you propose is a most desperate gamble. By doing as you wish I stand to lose the services of many of the best members of my organization. It is almost certain, too, that some of them, or at least their nearest and dearest in their places, would be arrested and find themselves in a German concentration camp. If I were certain that you could bring it off I would agree. Your reasoning is sound and the idea is magnificent. It would be the greatest coup in history, but the odds are too big against its succeeding. No—I cannot give my consent to this amazing plan that you have hatched.'

When Gregory had once made up his mind about a thing

287

he would never take 'No' for an answer, even from this great little man whom he admired so much. He had brought the map with him, and taking it from his pocket he spread it out on the table: then he proceeded quietly and clearly to go over the various possibilities of the future so far as they could be foreseen, just as he and Kuporovitch had done together a few nights before. In the end he produced the same conclusion: his proposal was the sole hope of bringing about the one and only move in the board which might prevent the war dragging on for years of ever-increasing horror, and save the 140,000,000 captive people of Europe from a creeping death by undernourishment and its attendant diseases.

For two hours they argued and wrangled; then at last Lacroix stood up. 'You win, *mon ami*; you have convinced me against my will. I will say that it is sheer madness, but it is our only hope, and for that reason I am prepared to gamble the lives of those who trust me and who are the principal support of our whole movement here in Paris on it.'

So, the great decision was finally taken.

19

Sabotage and Love Scenes

During the course of the winter Lacroix had been able to improve enormously his underground travel system in both Occupied and Unoccupied France, so that with the aid of his hundreds of new adherents he and his helpers were able to move swiftly and safely between Vichy and Paris, or to most other parts of the country.

For the success of Gregory's plan it was necessary that he should secure the full co-operation of his friends in London, so it was agreed that he should return there immediately; but there was no longer any necessity for him to undertake a perilous journey, trusting to his own wits and a great deal of luck to get him across the Channel. Lacroix guaranteed him swift transit to the Spanish border, and as he was carrying in the sole of his shoe papers which would ensure him priority on the Lisbon plane to London, he hoped to be back inside a week.

In consequence, he remained with Lacroix, who was returning that night to Vichy, while Kuporovitch, having wished him an affectionate good-bye, left the professor's house and made his way back across Paris to Luc Ferrière's house.

Since Madeleine had been doing night duty she had been sleeping each day from her return in the early morning until lunch-time. As soon as she was awake on the day after the meeting Kuporovitch told her that her outburst on the night of Gregory's arrival had had the effect of really starting something. They had evolved a plan, which, if it were successful, would alter the whole course of the war.

Naturally, she was most eager to hear about this great idea which had been inspired through her own burning desire to exact swift vengeance on the Nazis; but Kuporovitch said that, much as he would have liked to do so, he could not possibly give her any idea of what was intended. As it was, the freedom and lives of many of her friends must be placed in jeopardy, and although he trusted her without limit personally, it had been decided by Lacroix, Gregory and himself that on no account must they let anyone into this secret except Sir Pellinore and the people whose help it would be necessary to have in London.

She at once accepted the situation and pressed him no further; then he told her that, in order to make a start upon the part which had been allotted to him, he needed a typewriter with a special set of characters and as many different varieties of plain and hotel notepaper as she could get for him. She said that she had no idea at all where he could get the sort of typewriter he wanted, but she promised to speak to Madame de Villebois about the paper, as she felt sure that the Marquise and her daughter, who were still able to move freely about Paris in the daytime, would easily be able to obtain a good variety for him.

On discussing the matter of the typewriter with Pierre, Kuporovitch learned that typewriters of any kind were now extremely difficult to obtain in Paris, as none were being imported from the United States, the French factories no longer had the materials to make them, and the Germans had commandeered great numbers for the use of their various departments which controlled the whole national life of the people in Occupied France. However, Pierre told him where he could find several shops which normally dealt in typewriters.

That evening the Russian made a tour of the shops Pierre had suggested. Two of them he now found shut and untenanted; like so many small businesses they had been bankrupted by the Occupation. A third and fourth had nothing to offer him, and it was not until he tried a fifth, the last on his list, that he found exactly the thing he wanted, because it happened to be a type of machine which was of little use to the Germans.

Having carried it home he set to work at once to practice typing and make some rough drafts of various letters. To begin with his efforts were deplorable, but he soon got the hang of the thing, and before the night was over had managed to produce two letters which had only a few minor typing errors in them.

Thereafter he worked away like a beaver. In view of the special business upon which he was now employed it had been decided that until the great coup was either made or had to be abandoned he should give up his co-operation with the sabotage parties; so he worked most of each night and a good part of the day, indefatigably turning out letter after letter and addressing them to a number of people whose names and addresses Lacroix had given him. As the days passed his speed increased, and he rarely made a bad slip in his typing. Madeleine furnished him with all the paper he required and gradually the stack of letters, bearing varying dates as far back as the previous autumn, and done up in separate bundles for each person, grew higher in the locked cupboard where he kept them.

The news continued to be depressing, as the Germans achieved victory after victory in their Balkan campaign. On the 26th April Athens fell. By the end of the month the British had been compelled to evacuate the mainland. The Greek Army had surrendered and the Germans were in possession of the entire peninsula, as well as all the Greek islands of the Aegean from which they could so easily menace Turkey.

Many of Lacroix's most fearless helpers were Communists, so it was decided that Labour Day, the first of May, should be signalized by some special act of sabotage against the Germans.

The enemy was now taking full advantage of the great canal system of Northern France to transport goods by water from Paris, through Belgium to the German frontier; so plans were prepared for the blowing-up of certain locks which connected the various basins of the terminal barge port in North-Eastern Paris, and the big bridge which carries the Rue de Crimée over them.

All the approaches to the wharves were now strongly guarded at night by German sentries, and they had to be lured away from their posts in order to avoid the reprisals which would follow if any of them were killed. As a general rule the women of Paris showed their antagonism to the Nazis much more strongly than the men, and except in the brothels, which were now under German police supervision, it was extremely difficult for a German soldier to get a French girl even to talk to him. In consequence, the saboteurs had developed a practice of using attractive girls who were in the movement to occupy the attention of the sentries while the freedom-fighters crept past them in the darkness and laid their charges of explosives.

Several of these brave women had recently been caught, and at a meeting which Madeleine and Madame de Villebois's daughter, Jeanne, attended, fresh volunteers were asked for. As it was not possible to carry out these major acts of sabotage in which many freedom-fighters were employed very frequently, Madeleine and Jeanne did not feel that an occasional night devoted to acting as decoys would greatly interfere with their duties at the nursing-home; so they both offered their services.

Pierre was most unwilling that Madeleine should undertake such work, not only from its danger but from its nature, as it was quite on the cards that she would have to submit to being cuddled and kissed in some dark corner by a German sentry for a quarter of an hour or more. Much as she herself loathed the thought of that, she declared her determination to go through with it, as it was the best contribution which she could make to this blow against their oppressors.

The day started off badly as there were a number of labour demonstrations against the Germans. These had nothing to do with Lacroix's secret movement, and, while they were of value as showing the growing hatred of the population, they served no useful purpose at all, but led to clashes with the police in which a number of the demonstrators were injured. These minor riots, too, although easily suppressed, had the unfortunate effect of putting the Germans on their guard against graver disturbances; but it was too late to cancel the orders of the sabotage parties, and when Madeleine and Pierre set out that night they both felt an uneasy foreboding that special measures might have been taken which would jeopardize the success of the intended operation.

They formed two of a party that had been allotted the

bridge, and Madeleine left Pierre and the other men who had gathered at a small café about three hundred yards from it to go forward with Jeanne de Villebois.

The two girls sauntered along as though out for an evening stroll and willing to indulge themselves in any amusement that offered. At the end of the bridge they were challenged by two German sentries. Halting there, they proceeded to poke fun at the men, asking if they thought that two pretty girls were likely to rush upon them and disarm them.

One of the soldiers who spoke a little French said: 'So you think yourselves pretty, do you? Come here, and let's have a look at you.'

The girls moved up nearer, and, as Jeanne was also something of a beauty, the Germans at once displayed a lively interest in them.

'Perhaps you'd like to search us for weapons,' Madeleine laughed, and her invitation immediately provoked a little horse-play. The Germans were not rough, because they thought they were on a good thing, and they chipped the two girls just as any other young men might have done in a similar situation; but soon the affair took a more serious turn.

Heinrich, as the taller of the two was called, sought to lead Madeleine away from her friend to the other side of the bridge, and after a pretence of being unwilling she gave way to him. Leaning his rifle against the railings he immediately tried to kiss her, and she thought the next few moments were as hateful as any that she had ever spent in her life.

It was not that the young man himself was at all unpleasant, and in that she was fortunate, but the whole time that he was holding her tightly to him and kissing her she could not get out of her mind the things he represented. She knew that underneath he was just a soulless brute who would not have scrupled for one second to kill her if he had been ordered to do so, because for many years past he had been educated in the belief that any sort of brutality was absolutely justified, provided it was committed in the interests of Germany and the Fuehrer.

Soon, with his hot breath on her neck, he began to explore her person. She was almost sick with shame and rage, but she managed to fob him off and began to talk of their meeting again when he was off duty, and they could find a more comfortable place in which to make love.

'That'd be fine,' he grinned, 'but there's no time like the present; and you're a peach of a girl—the prettiest I've seen in all Paris. Come now!' And he pushed her roughly, for the first time, against the stone coping at the end of the bridge.

She was wondering wildly now if Pierre and the others had had time to plant their mine so that she might break away and run for it, but if she did so prematurely she might endanger their lives. The sounding of a horn had been agreed upon as the signal which they were to give when they were ready. She had not heard it but might have missed it while she was struggling with the amorous soldier, and he was muttering loud endearments in her ear.

She was grappling with him now, but even in the midst of her distress and confusion she caught a faint cry from the other side of the road. Jeanne, too, was evidently in difficulties, and Madeleine knew that her friend must be near the limit, or she would never have cried out. To do so might bring an N.C.O. or other soldiers running out of the guardhouse, which was a shed about fifty yards away along the canal bank.

Her own situation was now near desperate, as the young German had her pinned up in an angle of the stonework at the bridge's end, but Jeanne's cry gave her a second's respite. Heinrich heard it too, and stiffened suddenly, evidently fearful that he might be caught by his N.C.O. and suffer the most rigorous penalties of the iron Prussian discipline for his flagrant neglect of his duties.

'Stop!' Madeleine gasped. 'Let me go! That fellow over there is hurting my friend.' But the door of the guardhouse was not flung open, and reassured, the lusty young German, now wrought up to a terrific state of excitement, set upon her, throwing caution to the winds, determined to overcome her by brute force.

Suddenly a shot rang out from the centre of the bridge. There came the sound of shouts and running feet. On account of the demonstrations earlier in the day the Germans had placed sentries there as well as at the two ends so that if anyone should pass the latter without calling out that all was well the person concerned would fall straight into a trap. Madeleine and Jeanne had done their part, and Pierre and his friends had succeeded in getting past the two sentries the girls were engaging unseen, but they had run straight on to the others.

Next moment everything was in wild confusion. Heinrich grabbed his rifle with one hand and struck Madeleine violently in the face with the other, as he snarled: 'So you were acting as a decoy, you filthy little bitch! I'll teach you. As soon as we've sorted this I'll turn you into the guardhouse and pull your clothes off. Then the whole lot of us will take turns at having some fun with you.'

A man raced by in the darkness. Heinrich lifted his rifle and fired. The man let out a strangled scream and pitched head-foremost in the roadway. There were more shouts from the centre of the bridge. The guard was now tumbling out of the shed, and an N.C.O. was bawling orders. Half-stunned by the blow she had received Madeleine swayed and fell to her knees.

At that second there was a violent explosion about two hundred yards away. Another gang of saboteurs had succeeded in blowing up one of the canal locks. The ground shook, and pieces of debris came whistling through the air.

For an instant the light of the flash made everything as bright as day. Madeleine saw Jeanne running head down twenty yards away. A belated cart had pulled up right at the entrance of the bridge. Its driver, a burly workman, was staring down at Madeleine and Heinrich, who had grabbed her just as she had staggered to her feet. The German was too intent on preventing Madeleine from getting away to take any notice of the carter. Suddenly the burly man sprang down from his seat, and raising his whip brought it cracking down in the sentry's face.

The German let out a yell and staggered back, releasing Madeleine. The cart hid them from the other soldiers. Before Heinrich could recover, its driver had seized him by the neck and, forcing him back against the railings of the bridge, slung him into the canal.

'Run, *Mademoiselle*, run, or these devils will get you!' cried the carter; and as he scrambled up again to his driver's seat Madeleine raced away after Jeanne.

Fear lent her new strength, and she dashed down the street, her legs flying under her. A soldier sent a bullet after her which ripped her beret from her head. At the shock she tripped and almost fell, but recovered herself and raced on again. A moment later the shouting and firing were dying away behind her. She saw Jeanne ahead, still running, and putting on a fresh spurt caught her up.

The two girls dived down a side turning and dropped into a walk. Both were panting as though their lungs would burst, and Jeanne was sobbing bitterly.

'It's all right,' gasped Madeleine. 'They won't follow us as far as this—they'd lose themselves in the darkness.'

'That brute!' sobbed Jeanne. 'That filthy brute! I don't think I'll ever feel clean again.'

Madeleine took her arm. 'Yes, I don't think I've ever hated anything so much, but we had to do it, and it's all over now.'

After a few minutes they had more or less recovered themselves. A late bus took them to the Opéra, and they parted there to make their respective ways home.

Madeleine waited up anxiously for Pierre, wondering whether he had been one of the men who had been shot, or if he had managed to get away. To her great relief he reached Ferrière's house about three-quarters of an hour after herself, and he was unwounded.

Kuporovitch was upstairs in his room typing, and Luc Ferrière had gone to bed, so they had the sitting-room to themselves, and Madeleine used some of their precious supply of coffee to make them a cup apiece so as to warm them up before they went to bed.

Pierre reported that two of their squad had been shot, and one, he thought, captured, but the other two had managed to escape unharmed with him. He was in a queer restless mood and would not sit down, but walked about the room. Madeleine made light of her own unpleasant experiences, as she knew that it would only infuriate him to know what she had been through; but suddenly he burst out:

'I won't have you do this sort of thing again. It makes me positively sick to think of it. I expect you'll say that I have no right to interfere, but I have got a right. I've loved you for years—you know that! And any man who loves a girl as I

296

love you has every right to protect her from such beastliness.'

'Pierre darling,' she laid a hand on his arm as he paused beside her chair, 'I know you love me, and, of course, you hate it. The thought of that German messing me about to-night must have been even worse for you than the actual experience was for me. But try not to think of it. Every one of us must be prepared to give everything we've got for France, and if a girl like myself can be useful that way, then it would be plain cowardice for her to shirk her duty.'

'No one can accuse me of being unpatriotic,' he said abruptly. 'I've proved my love of France with the risks I've taken night after night all through this winter. You know that.'

'Of course I do,' she murmured.

'But there's a limit,' he went on quickly. 'You and I have been lucky so far—extraordinarily lucky—but our luck can't hold for ever. The British and the Germans have reached a stalemate, so it's absolutely impossible now to foresee any ending to this damned war at all. If we carry on as we've been doing we're bound to be caught. I don't mind that for myself so much, but the thought of you in a German concentration camp drives me simply crazy. You must agree that I've been patient, but it's getting on for a year now since Georges' death, and I've been watching you pretty closely. You've got over that, I'm certain of it; so I'm not going to keep silent any longer. I love you. I want to marry you. Madeleine, let me take you out of this to safety.'

'But, Pierre,' she protested, 'you couldn't even if you wanted to.'

'Oh yes, I could. I ran into my cousin, François, only yesterday. He got a special permit to come to Paris on business. His mother—that's my Aunt Eugénie—has a house at Limoges, and he said that they'd be delighted to have us live with them. It'd be easy enough for us now to cross the frontier into Unoccupied France, and . . .'

'But we couldn't, Pierre!' she exclaimed. 'We couldn't! It would mean throwing up our work here.'

'That's true,' he agreed quite mildly. 'But hasn't it occurred to you that we've done our share? We were in this thing practically from the beginning, and there are scores of other people now to carry on.'

'But Lacroix needs all the help he can get.'

Pierre shook his head. 'Try to look at it as though we were in the Air Force—any Air Force that you like, because they all follow the same plan. The airmen go in as fighter pilots, and for several months they do their stuff. Either they're killed or put out of action, or if they're lucky they score a number of victories to their credit. Then they're promoted and given jobs on the ground to instruct others. They've earned that, you see—and it's probably the knowledge that if they can shoot down enough planes and survive for a number of months, after which they'll be safe, or reasonably safe, for good and all, which helps them through their tougher spots. Well, we've done our stuff and brought down a good bag of the enemy, so there's nothing cowardly now in our leaving it to others. In Limoges we'd keep in touch with the movement, of course, and continue our work, but on safer ground. I'm not suggesting that we should chuck in our hands altogether.'

Overwrought as he was, Madeleine did not wish to excite him further, so she said: 'You're wrong about Georges, dear. His memory is still very close to me. It's hard on you, I know, but I'm not ready yet to think of anyone else that way. As for leaving Paris, I'm certainly not prepared to at the moment. I can't tell you why yet, because I don't even know myself, but I have real grounds for believing that plans are on foot to do something really big which will break the deadlock into which the war seems to have drifted. If that happens conditions may be so altered in Paris that I might feel really justified in leaving it; but until then I'm afraid we must just go on being patient.'

He grumbled a little but made no further strong effort to persuade her, and shortly afterwards they went upstairs to turn in.

Madeleine had purposely refrained from telling Stefan about the job which she had been given to do in the attempt to blow up the bridge over the canal, and when he heard about it on the following day he was gravely perturbed. Ruthless as he was in all other matters, his deep love for Madeleine made him take a very different view of sabotage activities where she was personally concerned. Apart from not asking her to marry him, he took much the same line as Pierre, suggesting that as one of the earliest workers in the freedom movement she had now done more than her share, and that arrangements should be made for her to be got out of Paris to live somewhere in Unoccupied France.

On her flatly refusing to agree he took a much stronger line and said: 'Very well, then. God knows I should hate to be deprived of your company, Madeleine, but I have much more influence with Lacroix than you. If you attempt to take on any further work with the sabotage parties I shall get him to transfer you to some job in Unoccupied France, whether you like it or not, and I'm quite sure that you would not refuse to obey his orders.'

'But surely that's unfair, Stefan,' she remonstrated. 'You would be abusing your powers in order to shield me out of a personal fondness, and that simply means that some other girl would have to do the dirty work.'

'Exactly,' he replied with a cynical smile. 'I have never hesitated to abuse anything when it suits my book; but since you have already done your part, and others have not, I don't feel that in this case I should be acting unfairly. The point is that I love you, and having made up my mind that I will not have you expose yourself to greater dangers than need be, or further unpleasantness, that is the end of it.'

Madeleine felt that she should be angry at his taking such a dictatorial tone with her, but somehow she was not. Her pride made her say that she should continue to do as she liked, but they were not called upon to have an actual showdown, since as a result of the attack on the canal locks the Germans decreed a curfew. No citizen of Paris was allowed out in the streets between eight o'clock and dawn without a special pass, and squads of police and troops patrolled the streets all night.

The order had the effect of confining the saboteurs to their homes, so for the next fortnight Pierre hardly went out at all, but Madeleine went early, just about dusk, to the nursing-home, so the other two saw comparatively little of her.

During the first week of May fresh negotiations between Darlan and Abetz, with the slimy Laval acting as a middle-man, resulted in the announcement that the German levy for the cost of maintaining an Army of Occupation was to be reduced by 25 per cent., and that the frontier between Occupied and Unoccupied France would now be opened to certain merchandise and some civilians; but it was not stated what further help Vichy had agreed to give the Germans against Britain as the price of these concessions. In the same week Imperial Forces advancing from Basra succeeded in nipping the Iraqi revolt in the bud, and the situation was restored there. Then, on the 10th, came the extraordinary tidings that Deputy Führer Hess had secretly left Augsburg in a Messerschmitt 110 specially equipped for a long-distance flight, and, after making a parachute descent, landed near Glasgow.

With intense interest the world waited to hear the reason for the blood-stained brigand having voluntarily placed himself in the hands of his Führer's enemies; but, apparently scorning the unrivalled opportunity given to them for effective propaganda, the British Government maintained a complete silence on the matter.

The curfew was lifted after a fortnight and two days later Gregory appeared again, having made a safe and speedy journey from Paris to London and back via Lisbon, during which, between trips, he had put in eight days of frantic work with Sir Pellinore and the P.I.D. people. He arrived with two big suitcases which had been smuggled through with him, and both were crammed with documents that had been forged in accordance with his suggestions in London.

He brought one piece of bad news in which Kuporovitch was interested because he knew the man concerned and hated him as much as Gregory did. *Herr Gruppenführer* Grauber, the dreaded Chief of the Gestapo Foreign Department U.A.-1, whom Gregory had captured in the South of France the preceding June, had escaped from a concentration camp in England.

However, Kuporovitch took the news that their old enemy was free again quite lightly, simply remarking: 'It's a pity that you tender-hearted British didn't shoot the swine when you had him, but I see no reason to be upset about his escape, as that sort of thing is one of the pulls which Britain has through being an island. In the last war plenty of Germans

300

managed to escape from the prisoner-of-war camps, but not one of them ever succeeded in getting out of the country. Scotland Yard has the reputation of being very efficient, so I don't doubt that Grauber will be behind the bars again within a week or two.'

'Don't you believe it!' said Gregory bitterly. 'Grauber's not like any ordinary German—he speaks English as well as I do, and French, and Dutch, and probably several other languages as well. He's as cunning as a serpent and as slippery as an eel. If he once reaches a big port he'll manage to get out of the country somehow and back to Germany via Spain, or even America and Russia, if need be. He's Himmler's right-hand man and has fifty times the brain of a fellow like Hess, so you can take it from me, Stefan, that his escape is a damn' bad business.'

On the 18th Lacroix was again in Paris, and they had a long secret session with him, during which he was able to give them the good news that the Duke of Aosta was now surrounded with the bulk of the Italian forces at Ambaalgi and had asked for terms of surrender; so the Abyssinian campaign was as good as over.

On the 20th the Germans launched their blitzkrieg against Crete by sending hundreds of dive-bombers to attack the British naval base at Suda Bay and landing two thousand paratroops in its neighbourhood. In the succeeding days Gregory and Kuporovitch were both frantically busy sorting and arranging their masses of documents, but both followed the new campaign with intense interest.

It was the first occasion in history that an attempt had been made to invade and conquer an island by air power alone, and the outcome of the battle might have an extraordinary influence upon the Germans' future operations. Quite apart from that, the holding of Crete by the British was of the first importance, since the loss of it would be a great blow to British sea-power in the Mediterranean. As long as the British could hold Crete they were within easy striking distance of Italy and the coast of Cyrenaica, and could render the passage of the Sicilian Channel extremely hazardous to Axis transports carrying supplies from Italy to North Africa; but if Crete were lost the British Navy would be forced back to its

301

bases at the extreme eastern end of the Mediterranean.

On the second day of the attack the Germans captured the airfield of Maleme and also succeeded in establishing forces in the neighbourhood of Candia and Rethymno; but the Navy had done its part with its usual efficiency and sunk with appalling losses to the Germans all the seaborne troops despatched from the mainland. Candia and Rethymno were recaptured, but by the end of the week the Germans still held Maleme and had established themselves in an area for ten miles round it.

Gregory knew then that the game was up anl cursing long and bitterly. As long as the captured airfield had remained within range of our field batteries the Germans could not land great quantities of troop-carriers and heavy war material on it; but now they had succeeded in pushing back our forces so far they would be able to bring over limitless quantities of reinforcements and arms. As the place was an island far removed from our main bases in Egypt and Palestine the Germans could now throw into it more men and weapons than we could, so it must be only a matter of time before our forces were overcome.

Attention was temporarily diverted from the terrific battles raging in Crete by the appearance of the *Bismarck* in the Atlantic. On the 24th H.M.S. *Hood* was sunk, and for the next three days the world followed with bated breath the chase of the giant German battleship, which ended with its total destruction on the 27th; but this news was heavily offset by the Admiralty announcement that Britain had lost two cruisers and four destroyers in the fighting round Crete.

By the end of the month the position in Crete was desperate, and on June the 1st it was announced that 15,000 British troops, the remnants of a gallant Army, had been safely evacuated.

That night Gregory and Kuporovitch again sat staring at the map of Europe.

'We've got to work fast, Stefan,' Gregory said. 'It'll be a race now—between us and Hitler mounting his next offensive, and you can guess where that will be.'

The Russian nodded. 'Turkey, and a break-out into Asia. Now he's secured himself from a flank attack there's nothing

302

to stop his going right ahead. If only the British had put every man they could spare, with all their tanks, into Crete and the other big Greek islands in the Aegean, in the first place, they might be holding them still, and we'd have had longer to make our preparations. As it is, we'll have to go ahead and chance it.'

'Exactly,' Gregory agreed. 'The tanks that should have smashed up those first German concentrations on the Cretan airfields had already been lost on the Greek mainland. It absolutely passes my comprehension how they can have failed to realize that in the Grand Strategy of the War the mainland was of no real significance, and that they couldn't hold it anyhow; whereas the retention of Crete and the Greek islands was absolutely vital. Now we've lost them the whole of the Aegean will be a nest of German air and submarine bases. We'll never be able to get any convoys through to help Turkey if she's attacked, or send the Navy through the Dardanelles and the Marmara to help her defend her long northern coast in the Black Sea against invasion. Turkey is completely isolated, and now the Germans have got those damned islands they're less than twenty miles from the Turkish coast in several places, and could blitz hell out of Smyrna any night they chose. We can't blame the Turks if they give way to Axis pressure, and if they do, instead of fighting on the Dardanelles and the Bosphoros, where we would have stood a good chance of holding the Hun in the narrow gate, we'll have to take the whole weight of the German Army in Syria and Iraq. It's going to be sheer murder, Stefan, unless we can create some diversion.'

Kuporovitch poured himself another go of cognac. 'You've said it, my friend. The Imperial Forces will have to meet the weight of at least a hundred German divisions in open desert country which is perfect for tank operations. I wouldn't give a brass button for their chances of stopping the Nazis from getting to Suez and the Persian Gulf. Once that happens they'll have all the oil they want and southern Asia for the taking.'

Gregory laughed cynically. 'I reckon your estimate of a hundred divisions is too modest, Stefan. The Nazis know that we're still far too weak to land a new B.E.F. on the Atlantic coast of Europe. They'll fling everything in and use the troops of all the jackal nations—Italy, Hungary, Rumania, Bulgaria and the Vichy men in Syria—into the bargain. At least five million German-led troops will come thundering down into Mesopotamia, and I doubt if we've got even half a million to oppose them. I just shudder when I think what this Greek adventure may yet cost us.'

'Well, ours is a forlorn hope,' Kuporovitch made a grimace; 'but I agree that we should delay no longer.'

'All right then,' Gregory nodded. 'All the arrangements for planting the stuff are made, and Ribaud had better warn two or three of his people to get out tomorrow. After that, we'll do a few more every day, then put the balloon up on the 7th.'

On the following afternoon Kuporovitch got Madeleine on her own and said to her: 'Listen, my loveliness. In a few days now we shall be making our bid to alter the whole course of the war. As you know, I cannot even hint at the form our blow will take, but I can tell you that from now on every member of Lacroix's organization will be in extreme danger. You know how, for weeks past, I have been typing night and day, and that Gregory brought back with him from London hundreds of other forged documents. Since his return we have been sorting and addressing them to various members of the organization.

'Each of these carefully varied sets of paper is to be planted in his own dwelling by the person to whom it is addressed. Then they will leave Paris with their families and be smuggled out into Unoccupied France, or Belgium, or Switzerland. On the last day of the operation our key-members will also plant their special documents, and arrangements are being made to get them away in a body. Then one of us will tip off the Germans that a vast conspiracy exists and turn in the addresses of our friends after they have gone. The Nazis will raid their homes and find all these incriminating papers which vary slightly, but tell the same story.

'While Gregory was in London he made arrangements with the British Secret Service for a similar policy to be pursued upon a smaller scale in Norway, Denmark, Holland and Belgium; so that when it is uncovered the Germans will believe that this conspiracy has its ramifications throughout the whole of their occupied territories. Upon their reactions to what we are leaving for them to discover depends the success or failure of our enterprise; but the next few days will be a period of extreme danger.

'There is no way in which we can prevent individual members of our organization reading the documents that we give them before they put them away in their secret files and leave their homes. If there is a traitor among us we are undone, since he might not only turn over the documents prematurely to the Nazis himself, but consider the time ripe to blow our whole movement sky-high. You know how dearly I love you. Will you, for my sake, agree to leave Paris?'

She smiled up at him. 'No, Stefan, not even for you. It isn't fair to ask me. I don't know what you mean to do, but, whatever it is, you're doing it because of that outburst of mine the night that Gregory first returned to us. This is my party—my vengeance—and nothing in the world will persuade me not to be with you and Gregory when the blow is struck.'

It was so plain that her mind was absolutely made up that he forbore to argue, but he looked very grave as he went upstairs to work, for he knew the extreme risk that they were all now running.

For the next few days there was a great tenseness in the house, and Gregory and Kuporovitch talked very little. They were constantly on the move and held innumerable guarded telephone conversations from a call-box some way along the street with Ribaud and various other members of the organization.

On July the 4th it was reported that German air-borne troops were already landing in Syria, and even Gregory was surprised and disturbed by this indication that within three days of their conquest of Crete the Germans were already so far advanced in the mounting of their next offensive.

On the night of the 5th a last conference was held at the Professor's house, in which Lacroix gave special instructions to his most intimate followers. They were not allowed into the main secret but were told that the night of the 7th had been agreed upon to stage a major blow upon the enemy, and this would necessitate their abandoning their homes with their families. With their relatives and with only such luggage as they could carry in their pockets they were to assemble at the Professor's house during the course of the day—each individual being given a special time so that the seventeen of them who were concerned should not arouse suspicion by arriving in a body.

Lacroix had decided that to endeavour to smuggle seventeen people and their families over the frontier into Unoccupied France, at one time was too great an undertaking, but Ribaud had devised a plan for getting the whole company safely out of the country altogether. He alone was to remain in Paris, as his contacts in the heart of the enemy police system were too valuable to be jeopardized for the sake of one additional person planting some of the faked documents. Lacroix, too, would not be present, as it was important that he should be at his own headquarters in Vichy to get the first reactions of the Germans to the conspiracy when it was unmasked. In consequence, Léon Baras, the bull-necked Communist Deputy, was placed in charge of the arrangements for evacuating the main party.

During the past few days the patients in the Marquise de Villebois' house had been quietly evacuated one by one in Madame Idlefonse's ambulance, and the Marquise herself was to leave Paris with her daughter on the following morning, so on the 6th, for the first time in many weeks, Madeleine found herself without any night duty to perform.

As was his custom, almost immediately after supper Luc Ferrière went up to his room. Pierre, who was in the middle of an interesting book, said that he was going up to bed, and Gregory went out to make some last minute arrangements; so Stefan and Madeleine were left alone.

For a few moments they sat in silence, then he said: 'Time's getting short now, my beautiful. Have you decided what you mean to do when the balloon goes up?'

She looked at him in some surprise. 'Why, stay here with you and Pierre, of course. As there's no question of planting any documents in this house, we shan't have to leave Paris like the others, and we'll be able to see the results of our great coup at first hand.'

He shook his head. 'But no, Madeleine, that is impossible. I thought I made that clear the other day when I urged you to leave for Unoccupied France well before the party started.'

'You asked me to go, and I said I wouldn't. But you didn't say anything about its being impossible for me to stay here after you had sprung your mine.'

'Didn't I—are you sure?' He raised his heavy black eyebrows in well-simulated surprise, since he knew perfectly well that he had intentionally misled her, and went on: 'I thought I'd made it plain that I was only asking you to go a few days earlier than you would have to in any case. That certainly was my intention.'

'But why should we not stay on here?' she asked. 'As I've just said, since Luc Ferrière is not one of us, you won't be planting documents on him, so there's no reason why the house should be raided.'

Kuporovitch looked away a little uncomfortably. He had no wish to discuss with her the matter of Luc Ferrière, as having lived in the Mayor's house for so many months a subtle change had gradually taken place in their relations with him. At first they had regarded him with open hatred, as the man who had betrayed a number of their friends to death and torture; but with the course of time, since they never talked politics with him, they had developed first an indifference and then a semi-friendly tolerance of their host, who from fear and dislike had slowly come to accept them as members of his household. Madeleine was completely merciless as far as the Nazis were concerned, but the Russian feared now that her natural compassion might lead her to make the strongest protest and all sorts of difficulties if he confessed to her that Ferrière was to be made a scapegoat for their enemies.

He had even been a little loth himself to agree to planting documents on the Mayor and leaving him there to be hauled in by the Gestapo, but Gregory had insisted. He had pointed out that the one weakness of their conspiracy was that, as they could not bring themselves to sacrifice any of their own people deliberately, when the raids were made no arrests would follow, which might make the Nazis suspicious.

To counter this they had succeeded in planting documents on a few of their enemies, who would naturally deny all knowledge of the conspiracy when they were arrested; but these were few, and people of no particular importance, whereas Ferrière was a French official of high standing, who ever since the fall of France had been acting in collaboration with the Germans. As Gregory argued, it was the Mayor who had caused the nursing-home to be raided, and the fact that many months had elapsed since then should not be allowed to save him from an appropriate recompense; and just because they had been able to make use of him since was no reason at all why he should be spared when by turning him in they could so materially further the great plan upon which they were engaged.

Looking back at Madeleine, Kuporovitch simply shrugged his shoulders. 'I do not myself know all the details of what has been arranged. I can only tell you that it is by Colonel Lacroix's orders that all of us are to leave this house. I have already spoken to Madame Chautemps, and she will leave in the afternoon to go and stay with her relatives at Rheims. Pierre, of course, knows nothing of the inside of the conspiracy, but will receive his orders to leave by an underground channel for Occupied France in the morning.'

'I see,' she said slowly; 'and where do you and Gregory intend to go?'

'Arrangements have already been made for us to leave the country. Pierre has been given the impression that when the balloon goes up the four of us are leaving together for Unoccupied France, because we did not wish him to know that any arrangements had been made for the principal members of the movement to leave France altogether. As you were unwilling to go when I urged you before, I arranged matters so that you could make your choice at the last moment. You can come with us if you wish, but if you insist on remaining in France, for a time at all events, Lacroix wishes you to move into the unoccupied territory, so I shall fix up for you to leave with Pierre first thing tomorrow.'

He did not add that whatever she decided would also settle his own movements, and that if he could not persuade her to come with Gregory and himself he meant to join her in Unoccupied France as soon as possible. He was taking a big gamble, having intentionally left her in the air until the last moment with the belief she would be able to stay on in Paris with both Pierre and himself. For him everything now hung upon her answer.

It came quickly.

'But, Stefan,' she exclaimed, 'except for those few weeks when you were in England, we've been together now for a whole year. I—I simply don't know what I should do without you.'

He suddenly stood up and took her hand. 'Do you mean that, Madeleine?'

'Of course I do. I couldn't bear to be parted from you, after all this time.'

Looking down into her eyes, he said very gravely: 'A year's a long time, isn't it? Georges has been dead for a year. I know very well that you haven't forgotten him. You never will. But answer me one question: which means more to you now—Georges' memory or myself?'

She came to her feet and faced him. 'Georges was very dear to me, but I never lived under the same roof with him for months on end, and even he could not have given me greater devotion and affection than you have, Stefan. I know you far better than I ever knew him. I don't know where you're going, but wherever it is will you—will you take me with you?'

He knew then that he had won, and his face was radiant. She knew, too, that, although she had refused to admit it to herself, she had loved him almost from the beginning, for his courage, and his chivalry, and the sweetness of his nature.

'You've waited a long time, Stefan,' she whispered. 'I only hope you'll find me worth it.' And as she put her arms round his neck, turning up her face for his kiss, they both knew a glorious moment of great happiness.

One moment later the door opened, and Pierre stood in the doorway, his face a mask of furious anger.

20

The Great Conspiracy

At the sound of the door opening Madeleine and Stefan came out of their embrace and swung round. For a moment there was dead silence. Then Pierre, his eyes blazing fury, snarled at Madeleine:

'So this is why you wouldn't come with me to Limoges! All your fine talk about Georges' memory was just lies. You were in love with Stefan all the time.'

'Yes, Pierre, I was,' she answered frankly; 'but I didn't realize it until I knew that he was going to leave me.'

'I don't believe you,' he stormed. 'When I came down to get my book just now I heard you talking. I've known for days that something was on, but I didn't know that zero hour was tomorrow night. The two of you felt that I might make trouble, so you deliberately planned to fix me. You meant to get out together and leave me to be caught.'

'If you think that, you can only have caught bits of our conversation,' Kuporovitch cut in. 'We don't mean to sacrifice a single one of our members if it can be avoided, and the most careful arrangements have been made for everybody. You will receive your orders tomorrow morning to leave at once by one of the underground routes into Unoccupied France. I offered Madeleine the opportunity of going with you, but she preferred to come with me.'

'That's the truth, Pierre,' Madeleine exclaimed. 'I swear it!'

As he stared into her eyes he could not doubt her, yet he said stubbornly: 'How *can* you think that I should ever have been willing to go off on my own? Wherever you go I'm going too.'

She shook her head. 'I suppose it could be arranged for you

to come with us, but would that be wise? I mean, if we succeed in getting away I intend to marry Stefan, and you'd only be miserable if you remained with us.'

He caught his breath in a sob. 'But, Madeleine, you can't. You'd never be happy. He's much too old for you.'

Kuporovitch's eyes glinted dangerously. 'I'm not too old to throw you out of the window, and half a dozen more like you.'

'Please!' Madeleine interposed. 'My mind's made up, Pierre. I love Stefan, and that's all there is to it. I'm terribly sorry about you—I'd give anything for this not to have happened, but I can't help my own feelings.'

'You may feel like that now,' Pierre persisted, 'but that's only because you've been caught in this pretty little trap he's laid for you. Naturally, you've grown fond of him, through having been with him so much all through this past year. Then he suddenly tells you that he's going away, although I bet he had no intention of letting you go off into Unoccupied France with me really. He just said that to stampede you, and you fell for it. You admit yourself that it was only a few minutes ago that you found out you loved him. That isn't love—it's just a sudden surge of emotion which overcame you when you were taken off your guard. In a day or two you'll feel quite differently again and realize that it's nothing more than strong affection you feel for him. For God's sake, Madeleine, don't let yourself be rushed into anything like this! It isn't fair to any of us, not even to him.'

Again Kuporovitch gambled with tremendous courage, as he said quietly: 'All right, young man. If you honestly believe that, I release Madeleine from the promise to marry me which she made just now. We'll wait until all three of us are out of the wood, then I'll ask her again.'

Madeleine smiled at him. 'You won't have to, Stefan. I know my own mind, and it's already made up.'

But Pierre clutched swiftly at the straw which had been offered him. 'In fairness to me, Madeleine. I beg you to take him at his word. But what about tomorrow? Somehow it must be arranged for all three of us to leave together.'

'All right,' Kuporovitch nodded. 'One extra won't make any difference to such a large party. You'd better ignore the orders which you will receive in the morning to proceed into Unoccupied France. Our party is to rendezvous at the Professor's house; but I shall be busy until the last moment, so you shall take Madeleine there. You should arrive punctually at eight o'clock, and I'll join you as soon after that as I can.'

There was a little silence. There seemed no more to be said, but Pierre was obviously reluctant to leave them, so Madeleine murmured: 'We may be up all tomorrow night, so we'd better get what sleep we can. I think I'll go up to bed.'

With a swift gesture she took Stefan's hand and pressed it. Then the men followed her upstairs.

On the following day none of them left the house. The morning and the afternoon seemed endless, as Madeleine, Kuporovitch and Pierre sat about, waiting for the evening with almost unendurable suspense. Gregory, who had been out most of the previous night, slept through the day.

When he came downstairs Kuporovitch got him alone and told him of the scene that had occurred the night before. Taking both the Russian's arms, Gregory gave him a friendly shake, as he said:

'Well done, Stefan! Madeleine's a grand girl; and I felt certain all along that sooner or later she'd realize her luck in having captivated such a splendid fellow as you. As for young Pierre, it's hard luck on him, but he'll get over it in time. I've got to go out and put the spark to the mine now, so I'll leave the two of them to you. I can manage quite well on my own.'

'No,' said the Russian. 'We'll stick to our original arrangement. As you've got to put your head into the lion's mouth I can at least wait for you; and if you don't come out you'll know anyway that I shall be around somewhere.'

'Good old Stefan!' Gregory smiled. 'If I do slip up, and they detain me, it'll be a big comfort to know that you're still about, ready to seize any chance for a rescue.'

Having said *au revoir* to the others, the two of them set out on what they hoped would be their last walk for a long time to come through the dark depressing streets of Paris. For a little they went forward side by side in silence; then Kuporovitch said: 'I take it you've heard from Ribaud that von Geisenheim had your letter?'

'Yes, I saw Ribaud last night. He told me that the General

was extremely interested and guaranteed me a safe conduct to come and see him at the Crillon at seven-thirty.'

'Do you really think you can trust him?'

'Yes. As you'll remember, it was von Geisenheim who saved my bacon for me in Finland. He's a Prussian aristocrat of the old type and hates the Nazis like hell. That doesn't mean he's anti-German; but he's one of the men who will lead the Army if they ever stage a *coup d'état* against Hitler. Our bull point in this case is that he's a diehard anti-Communist, and he's of the school which always believed that years ago Britain and Germany should have entered into an alliance against Russia. It was extraordinarily good luck his being appointed Inspector-General in Occupied France. Of course, we could have put the balloon up from various other quarters, but von Geisenheim is about the best man for our money that we could possibly get.'

In the Rue Royale they parted. Kuporovitch went into Maxim's, where he intended to have a meal while waiting, and it was agreed that Gregory should join him there after having seen the General. Gregory did not think that his interview would last for more than an hour, but if he had not reappeared by half-past nine Kuporovitch was to telephone Ribaud and find out what had happened.

Walking boldly into the main entrance of the Crillon, Gregory asked for the General, stating that he had an appointment. He gave his name as Lucien Rouxel, and produced the faked passport with which Lacroix had furnished him many months before, to prove his identity. After waiting for about five minutes he was taken up to a big room on the first floor.

Von Geisenheim was seated there smoking a long cigar. He was the thin, hatchet-faced type of Prussian who wore his greying hair long and was dressed with meticulous care. His blue eyes, which were wrinkled at the corners, did not change their expression as Gregory advanced towards him, and it was only when the orderly closed the door that his face broke into a wintry smile.

'Well, well!' he said. 'I had no idea that Monsieur Lucien Rouxel would prove an old acquaintance. Last time we met you were the Colonel Baron von Lutz, and I suppose you have

313

half a dozen other aliases in other countries. I must congratulate you upon having kept alive all this time.'

As he waved towards a chair Gregory sat down and smiled back at him. '*Danke schön, Herr General*. It certainly is a far cry from Voroshilov's Headquarters during the Russo-Finnish War to German-occupied Paris. Quite a lot has happened in the last fifteen months, and, knowing your political opinions, perhaps I should congratulate you, too, upon having kept your head on your shoulders.'

Von Geisenheim pushed forward a big silver box full of the long cigars. 'As I have the walls of this room sounded daily, and everything in it is examined by my military secretary, I don't think the Gestapo has yet succeeded in establishing a dictaphone in it. Nevertheless, one cannot be too careful, so I think we'll keep off the subject of my political opinions.'

'By all means,' Gregory agreed. 'But if my visit is to serve any useful purpose I must ask if they have remained unchanged.'

The General's eyes narrowed, and he lowered his voice a little. 'I have never had any interest but the wellbeing and greatness of Germany. There was a time when certain of us feared that the Nazis might jeopardize that through biting off more than they could chew; but the Fuehrer has proved us wrong, as a glance at the map of Europe as it is today is quite enough to show.'

'At the map of Europe, yes,' Gregory admitted. 'But I have always believed in the Duke of Wellington's dictum that one should always use large maps. Are you quite satisfied when you look at the map of the world, *Herr General*?'

Von Geisenheim nodded. 'The war is very far from being over yet, but our grip on Europe is now unshakable, and with that I don't think we have much to fear.'

'You are prepared to face a war of exhaustion then?'

'That should not be necessary. It is hardly likely that with the immense armaments we now possess the Fuehrer will stand still.'

'An invasion of Britain?' Gregory hazarded.

Von Geisenheim waved his thin hands airily. 'Because I have given you a safe conduct to this interview that does not mean that I am prepared to discuss our future strategy with you.'

'Of course not. I only raised the matter in order to express an opinion that I can hardly expect you to accept, knowing me to be a patriotic Englishman, but which, nevertheless, is absolutely honest. Had you invaded Britain in August 1940 God knows what would have happened. I believe that even then somehow or other we would have managed to drive you out, because you wouldn't have found things the same there as in the other countries which you've overrun. The entire civil population would have risen against you, and we have something in the neighbourhood of forty people for every German soldier you could possibly put over. The slaughter would have been positively appalling, but I don't think you would ever have succeeded in conquering the whole country. As it is, very nearly a year has passed since the collapse of France, and during that time Hitler has missed the boat. If you invaded Britain today you wouldn't stand a dog's chance.'

'That we may perhaps see in due course; but go on, and tell me what bearing this has on what you were going to say.'

'Simply that, whether you attempt to invade Britain, move south into Africa or strike East, any of these things would prove a major operation involving the flower of the German Army, and a very high percentage of its effectives. To be successful you would have to denude the occupied territories of Europe of most of their garrisons. Do you think that in such a case you could continue to hold them down?'

'Why yes. These miserable people are unarmed, so even comparatively light German forces could keep them in order.'

'Not if the whole lot rose at once under proper leadership into a full-scale revolution.'

'Where is such leadership to come from? The natural leaders of these conquered peoples have either come over to us or fled abroad.'

'That's true only of their rulers, politicians and Generals; it is not true of their leaders of tomorrow. They are still here, working underground.'

'You have in mind the Communists?'

'I have, *Herr General*.' Gregory sat forward a little, and spoke more earnestly. 'This is the place where you and I, who are enemies in all other things, meet on common ground. Whatever either of us may say about the prospects of our respective countries to emerge victorious, each of us knows deep down in his heart that both our people are now prepared to fight to the last ditch. There will be no surrender on either side. Frankly, at present I see no prospect at all of the British ever being able to defeat the main German Armies on the Continent of Europe, but, on the other hand, we still hold command of the seas, and we have an ever-growing Air Force, so I see no prospect either of Hitler's being able finally to defeat the British Empire. For both our sakes, sooner or later, we must make a peace of compromise.'

Von Geisenheim shrugged. 'I know that you have connections in varying high places. Am I to take it that you are about to put before me unofficial peace proposals?'

'Oh no!' Gregory smiled. 'I'm hardly in a position to do that. But it's in my interests as much as yours to avert a common danger. If this war goes on until both our countries are in a state of exhaustion, one fine day the Communists will emerge, and the whole structure of organized Government will go down before them, plunging the whole of Europe into a state of anarchy.'

'It will be a long time before that is likely to happen.'

'Perhaps not so long as you think, *Herr General*. Should your main Army undertake any major operation and get itself bogged, as it well might if it attempted the invasion of Britain, or any other move which necessitates its maintaining great forces across water, a Communist rising on a Continent-wide scale will take place behind your backs. Even Germany might be affected, since you know as well as I do that the workers there, although patriotic Germans, are by no means one hundred per cent behind Hitler.'

'There may be something in what you say, but at the moment it seems to me entirely speculation.'

'On the contrary.' Gregory produced some sheets of paper from his pocket. 'You know that I am a British Secret Service agent, and you can guess what I've been doing here—assessing the present state of feelings of the people in Occupied France at first hand. During my enquiries, by pure chance I got on to a certain underground organization. I was

316

absolutely amazed to find how great its ramifications are, and I feel certain they can't be known to you. These last few weeks I've put in some extremely hard work following the thing up, and I have here the names and addresses of over a hundred people, mainly living in Paris, who are connected with this movement. They're not all Communists by a long way, but they've gone over to the Communists as the only hope for forming one coherent body which can throw you out of France when the time is ripe. I have reason to believe, too, that the movement does not concern France alone, but has its ramifications in all the other occupied territories.'

Von Geisenheim's eyes narrowed. 'This is extremely interesting. In view of what you tell me I don't mind admitting that during the past week we've had some most extraordinary reports in from our people in Belgium, Holland, Denmark and Norway. In some raids they made they discovered documents which certainly suggest that such a Continent-wide conspiracy is actually in being.'

Gregory laid a sheaf of papers on the General's desk. 'If you pull these people in and search their homes, I have no doubt at all that you'll find the same sort of thing. To tell the truth, I hesitated a great deal before I came to you, because, temporarily at least, it would be a fine thing for Britain if we read in our papers one morning that every German in Occupied France had had his throat cut; but I've always thought that one should take a long view. If the German Army is tied up in Turkey, or Morocco, and the whole of Europe suddenly goes Bolshevik in its absence, I don't believe we'd ever be able to prevent Communism spreading to Britain. If that happened the whole of the British ruling caste and all that it stands for would go down the drain. It's as certain as that God made little apples that within a year or two at most the British Empire would disintegrate and that's the thing that I am out to stop.'

Von Geisenheim took the papers and nodded. 'You're absolutely right. As national states both Germany and Britain would cease to exist, and it's better even that one of us should emerge from this blood-bath intact than that both should perish utterly. I need hardly say how much I appreciate your having come to me. In any case, I should naturally honour my word, so you will leave this building a free man. In addition, to give you a chance to get clear of any of these people with whom you may be involved, I shall not take any steps against them for some hours. You realize, of course, that should you be caught later I shall not be able to do anything for you, because you are very definitely an enemy agent; but, personally, I have the highest respect for you, and I hope very much that you will succeed in getting home safely.'

'Thank you, *Herr General*,' said Gregory, as he stood up, and they shook hands. 'Doubtless you have your ways of communicating with London, and Boodle's Club will find me when I am in England. If at any time you feel that the stalemate is going a bit too far, let me know, and I'll always take a chance on coming over to see you. We might be able to start the ball rolling for some form of peace by which Germany could save her face before the structure cracks.'

'I don't think Germany is likely to crack,' von Geisenheim laughed; 'but if at any time Britain feels like packing up on reasonable terms, and you care to let me know, I shall always be happy to provide you with a safe conduct to come and see me, wherever I may be.' He pressed a bell on his desk, and the orderly returned to take Gregory downstairs.

As Gregory left the Crillon he was extremely pleased with himself. Whether the huge bomb which he had slung under Hitler's bid for world power would have its desired effect it was still quite impossible to say, but he felt that he had planted it pretty skilfully and that his lies had been convincing. Actually, he was the last person in the world to desire any peace of compromise.

He had an unshakable conviction that this was our last chance to beat the Germans once and for all. Even for Hitler and the Nazis to go was not enough. The whole power of the German race ever to fight again in a big-scale war must be destroyed. Otherwise, within a few years of any patched-up peace the people of Britain would have fallen into their usual lethargy again; our armaments would be reduced once more almost to vanishing point, and when the Germans attacked us under some new warrior leader we would no longer be given that breathing-space to mobilize our man-power and resources

318

which had already saved us from annihilation in two World Wars.

The French were out now—for good and all. Whatever future alliance might be made, they could never again be relied on to hold the Germans for a number of months while we prepared for battle. Next time the Germans would go all out direct for Britain herself in the very first hour of the war, and we should not stand a dog's chance. Only by the utter destruction of the sources of power by which the German people might wage any future war could the people of Britain hope for any permanent security in the future.

Yet his line that the war had reached a deadlock, and that only a peace compromise could save both Britain and Germany from gradual exhaustion and finally disintegration, had been necessary. It was the only logical cover for a British agent betraying to a German General the fact that a conspiracy existed in France and elsewhere for the massacre of the German garrisons when they had been weakened by some great new undertaking.

At quarter past eight Gregory rejoined Kuporovitch at Maxim's, and as he sat down the Russian could see from his face that all had gone well.

Being an optimist by nature, Kuporovitch had ordered two portions of his second course—a saddle of hare—in the hope that Gregory might have time to join him in a quick meal before they left for the Professor's house. He had also ordered a bottle of champagne, and as they toasted each other they thought how fitting it was that they should dine in that famous restaurant, so expressive still of the old spirit of Paris, on this, as they hoped, their last night in the French capital.

They had no time to linger, so by twenty to nine they left the restaurant, and at nine o'clock they reached the secret rendezvous.

The big drawing-room at the back of the house was more crowded than they had ever seen it, as nearly sixty people were now gathered there. Both of them expected to find Madeleine and Pierre in the crush, but with increasing uneasiness while they searched they found after a few moments that the other two were not present. They had been due to arrive at eight o'clock, and it was now just after nine. That

319

they should be a whole hour late for such a vital appointment seemed absolutely inexplicable. Really anxious now, Kuporovitch sought out the Communist Deputy, Léon Baras, who was in charge of the whole party, to ask if he had seen their two missing friends or received any message from them.

Baras expressed great surprise. He said at once that they were not expected as they were not included in his party and had been ordered to make their own way out of Occupied France by one of the underground channels that morning.

'I know,' interrupted Gregory hastily. 'I'm afraid I'm responsible for altering those arrangements; but I had excellent reasons for doing so, and I felt certain that two additional members to such a large party would not make the slightest difference. I told them to ignore their previous orders and report here at eight o'clock.'

'What could have happened to them, then?' said Baras, anxiously. 'You can see for yourself that they are not here, and had any message arrived from them I should certainly have been informed of it.'

'I'd better telephone at once,' muttered Kuporovitch. 'At least we shall know then if they have been detained at Luc Ferrière's house for some unexplained reason.'

The three of them went into the small library and Kuporovitch grabbed up the telephone. When he was put through Luc Ferrière answered him. On Kuporovitch asking him if Madeleine and Pierre were there he replied:

'No. They told me a little after seven o'clock that they were both going out and went upstairs to get their things on. I have not seen them since.'

Kuporovitch thanked him, hung up, and repeated what the Mayor had said.

Gregory heaved a sigh of relief. 'At all events, the place has not been raided. But, dammit, they wouldn't take two hours to get across Paris. What the hell can have happened to them?'

'They may have been involved in a street accident,' the ex-Deputy suggested. 'And if they're not badly injured they'll arrive here later. Nearly everyone else has assembled, but there are still a few members to come in. It's arranged that we should start at ten o'clock, and I do not want to delay our departure, but that gives your friends the best part of an hour's grace.'

They returned to the other room, where Baras mingled with his charges, making a fuss of several children who had been brought with their parents; but Gregory and Kuporovitch stood a little apart, now prey to the blackest forebodings. Even if Madeleine and Pierre had only been involved in a bus smash one or both might have been seriously injured; but there was nothing whatever they could do about it—only wait and hope.

Fifty minutes drifted by, but neither Pierre nor Madeleine appeared, and there was no message from them. At ten o'clock Léon Baras called for silence and addressed the assembly.

'*Messieurs et Mesdames,* you know that tonight we strike a great blow for Freedom. Even I do not know as yet what form that blow will take. That is our Chief's secret; but as part of the plan it was necessary that we should abandon our work here, temporarily at least. Since there are too many of us to have any hope of getting over the border into Unoccupied France in one night, without arousing the suspicions of our enemies, it was decided that for the time being we should go into exile.

'Many of you will wish to ask how, if such a large party could not get safely into the unoccupied territory, it is possible to transport them in reasonable safety right out of France. We owe the idea to the genius of our great Chief. It is simple and, I believe, quite practicable. As you are aware, largely through our own efforts the railway system has become increasingly more difficult and dangerous for our enemies to operate. In consequence, they are now transporting as much as they can of their heavier supplies by water. Each week big convoys of barges are made up in Paris with the munitions that our workers are forced to make under the tommy-guns of the German soldiers. These convoys go down the Seine and are then taken north along the coast, either to the ports of Belgium, Holland or Germany, where they can be more easily transported to their destinations.

'One of the captains of a sea-going tug which tows these chains of barges is a trusted member of our organization. For his next trip he has managed to arrange that all the members of his crew should also be de Gaullists, and we have other friends among the wharf-hands who load the barges. Each tug takes a tow of five, and on this occasion only four of the barges with have been loaded with munitions. One of them has been left empty, except for a good supply of stores to feed you during your journey and a certain amount of rough-and-ready bedding. The trip will take a week, or perhaps longer, so I fear you will have to put up with a period of considerable discomfort, because once you are in the barge you must remain there and only come up for a breath of air at nights, until you are released.

'Where you will be when that happens I cannot at present say, but I have good hopes that it will be among friends. I must ask you not to question me further upon our plans, but to act like the well-disciplined patriots that you are, and place your faith in myself, as your immediate leader, and in our great Chief, who has the safety of us all very near his heart.'

As he finished there was a little subdued applause, followed by an excited murmur of conversation, when the little groups of families and friends began to discuss these first particulars that they had been given of the manner in which they were to be smuggled out of France. It was no news to Gregory and Kuporovitch, as the originators of the coup which necessitated this whole evacuation. They had played a part in planning the escape with Lacroix and Ribaud, and neither of them had been looking forward to a week or ten days cooped up in the dark in the bottom of a barge, but it had seemed the only way in which such a number of people could be conveyed out of Paris on the same night without arousing suspicion.

At the present moment they were much too worried about Madeleine and Pierre to concern themselves with the dreary and uncomfortable days which lay ahead of them. Kuporovitch would not have minded going into this dark voluntary prison for a month if he had Madeleine beside him, but he could not even guess what had happened to her, and his heart was now heavy with an agonizing fear.

Baras came shouldering his way through the crowd towards them and said: 'I'm terribly sorry about our two friends, but as they haven't turned up I'm afraid we really must go now.'

'No, no!' Kuporovitch protested. 'Give them a little longer. Even if there's been an accident it's unlikely that both of them would have been badly hurt, so the other will turn up to let us know what has happened.'

'That's all very well,' the ex-Deputy replied, 'but we must adhere to our time-table.'

'You're quite all right for time,' Gregory said firmly. 'You can afford to give them another half-hour anyway.'

'Well, I'll wait until a quarter past,' Baras conceded reluctantly: 'but if they're not here then we really must start.'

It was already five past ten, and the next ten minutes seemed to go terribly quickly. Then Baras came across to them and said: 'I'm sorry, but time's up.'

Again Gregory remonstrated: 'It's only a quarter past. As I said just now, you could well afford to give them till the half-hour.'

The ex-Deputy shook his head, but Kuporovitch jumped up on a chair and, calling for silence, addressed the crowd.

'My friends! I appeal to you in a great difficulty! Madeleine Lavallière and Pierre Ponsardin, two of our stoutest-hearted comrades, who have been with us from the beginning, have failed to reach this rendezvous. They should have been here at eight o'clock, but we have telephoned their house, and we know that it was not raided. They were quite free when they left to come here. We can only suppose that a street accident must have delayed them. They may be injured or they may have been detained for questioning in connection with one; but in any case it is almost certain that one or both of them will get here as soon as they can. If we start without them they will never be able to find us. The night is still young; so will you not give them a little longer in the hope that they may yet be able to join us before we set out?'

Léon Baras' booming orator's voice rang out as that of the Russian ceased: '*Messieurs et Mesdames,* I am the leader of this party, and it is the order of our Chief that all here should obey me. I am as distressed as any of you can be at the non appearance of these two friends of ours, but I resent having my authority questioned. We were due to leave here at ten o'clock. I have already voluntarily delayed our departure on this account for twenty minutes. As your leader I say that we cannot now delay any longer.'

'One minute,' Gregory raised his voice. 'None of us disputes the leadership of Monsieur Baras, but we are all free people here. We are fighters for Freedom. Again and again we have imperilled our lives in the cause of Freedom. Therefore I maintain that we have the right to decide the limitations of the authority which we are prepared to allow Monsieur Baras to exercise over us. I was partly responsible for making the plans for your escape, and I give you my word that by waiting here another twenty minutes or so you will not jeopardize it in the least. I cannot think that any of you would willingly leave Madeleine and Pierre, now homeless and without any refuge to which they may go in Paris, behind. Let's have a show of hands. Those in favour of leaving our friends in the lurch!'

'That's not a fair way to put it!' shouted Baras, as not a single hand went up.

'Those in favour of hanging on here for another twenty minutes!' shouted Gregory, and practically every person in the room raised a hand.

'Thank you, friends, thank you!' called Kuporovitch, as Gregory turned to Baras and said:

'I'm terribly sorry about this. The last thing that I would do in the ordinary way is to dispute your authority. But I just had to secure this last chance for our friends.'

Baras did not reply. With an angry scowl he turned his back and walked away.

For the next ten minutes the crowd continued to stand and sit about, but it was quieter now. The nervous excitement which had animated the people at the thought of their coming adventure had subsided and given way to an uneasy tension.

Gregory looked at the clock—ten minutes of the extra twenty he had gained had already slipped away, and he whispered to Kuporovitch: 'It doesn't look as though there's much hope now, old chap. What do you intend to do?'

'Why, stay here, of course! Madeleine's bound to turn up some time.'

'I'm afraid you must face it now that she may have been arrested.'

'Then I'll bribe or smash my way into every prison in Paris until I find her.'

Gregory grinned. 'I thought as much. Well, between us we may be able to get her out of trouble yet.'

'No, you must go, Gregory. This is my affair.'

'Nonsense, my dear fellow! I was just hating the thought of those ten days in the bottom of that filthy barge, and I bet it'll be all of that.'

Kuporovitch shook his head. 'No, Gregory, we mustn't joke like this. The inside of that barge means safety, whereas for us the streets of Paris will now be a very different matter. After tonight the Germans and the Quisling police will redouble their guards and precautions everywhere. They're certain to believe that there's much more to this thing than what you gave them. Everybody will be under suspicion, and particularly stray people without jobs or a proper residence. You've blown Luc Ferrière's place up yourself, remember, so we can't go back into hiding there.'

'You're right about the difficulties that we've made for ourselves,' said Gregory soberly. 'But that's all the more reason that you'll need some help. It's no good arguing. I've made up my mind to stick around anyhow.'

They had hardly finished their whispered conversation when the main door of the room was suddenly thrown open, and the Professor's manservant, who did not look like a manservant, stood there, his eyes wide and excited, his face a little white.

'The police!' he gasped. 'They're coming into the courtyard! There's at least twenty of them!'

Suddenly a cry went up from the far corner of the room. 'We are betrayed! We are betrayed!' And the whole crowd broke into a clamour.

'Silence!' thundered Baras. 'Silence! Don't be alarmed. All the windows of this house were fitted with steel shutters months ago, and the doors have special locks. It will take the police at least a quarter of an hour to break one of them in.'

In spite of his reassuring words, the clamour grew. Again and again from various quarters of the room people shouted: 'We have been trapped! We are betrayed! How can we get away now?'

Even through the murmurs and excited shouting they could

now hear the crashing of axes on wood and the ring of steel on steel as the police, who were evidently round the back of the house as well as at its front, strove to break in through one of the steel-curtained windows of the room.

Suddenly a bearded man near Gregory turned, pointed at him and screamed shrilly: 'It is the Englishman and the Russian! It is they who have betrayed us! We should have left here at ten o'clock—over half an hour ago. Léon Baras told us that; but these two succeeded in keeping us here until the police arrived.'

Everyone was now staring at Gregory and Kuporovitch. Fists were raised, and angry faces thrust into theirs, as side by side they backed together towards the nearest wall. Baras forced his way towards them.

'By God! I believe they're right!' he bellowed. 'Ponsardin and the Lavallière girl were never intended to be in my party. That they were coming with us is just a story you put up. I expect they're safely over the frontier by this time and haven't the faintest idea of the dirty double-crossing use you made of their names.'

'Kill the traitors, kill them!' screamed a woman, and a roar went up from the mob which even drowned the battering of the police against the steel shutters.

The two friends knew that their position was desperate. They had not the least idea what had gone wrong, as no mention of the Professor, or his house, had been on the list which Gregory had handed to von Geisenheim. In fact, he had meant to suggest to Kuporovitch that they should pass the night there in case Madeleine and Pierre turned up after all and, if not, use it as their headquaters while they hunted Paris for them. They had not an iota of proof to support their story. It looked as though another minute would see them torn limb from limb. Several of the Frenchmen had already pulled automatics from their pockets. Gregory knew that only instant action could save his friend and himself.

Swinging round, he seized Baras by the lapel of his coat and yelled above the din: 'You're wrong—utterly wrong; but that doesn't matter now. Your job is to get these people out of here, before the police break in. For God's sake, tell them about the cellars, and get them down there while you still have the chance!'

Baras was quick to see the sense of this argument. Jumping on to a chair he bawled for silence. As the shouting died down a little, he said in a lower voice: 'Listen! Whether these two betrayed us I don't know—we'll deal with them later. All that matters for the moment is that we've got to get away from here.'

'How, how?' cried half a dozen panicky voices.

'Silence!' he implored. 'Silence! Keep your heads and listen, unless you all want to see the inside of a Gestapo torture chamber! There's an entrance from the cellars of this house into the catacombs. Surely you're not such fools as to think we'd plan to take over half a hundred people down to those barges in omnibuses at this time of night! The catacombs were the road to safety in our original plan. I've got a map of them, so you needn't be frightened that you'll get lost. We'll take these two fellows with us and sit in judgment on them when we reach the barge. Come on now! Follow me!'

As he jumped off the chair Gregory and Kuporovitch were seized by half a dozen men near to them and hustled after him. To have put up any resistance at that moment would have been quite hopeless, so they allowed themselves to be pushed along, none too gently, into the hall.

The little Professor was already standing there. He led them down the staircase to the basement and into a big cellar where a number of crates were stored. Pulling one of them aside, he uncovered a trapdoor which when opened revealed some old stone steps and an electric switch. The light was flicked on, and some of the men went down the trap. Gregory and Kuporovitch were pushed after them, and the rest of the crowd followed. The Professor came last, having operated a special contraption he had arranged for pulling the packing-case back over the trap when it had been shut.

On reaching the bottom of the steps Gregory and Kuporovitch found themselves in one of the most extraordinary apartments they had ever seen. The catacombs were originally stone-quarries from which in ancient days the masons had hewn the material for constructing the principal buildings of early Paris; and their tunnels ran like a giant rabbit warren in

327

all directions under that part of Paris which lies on the left bank of the Seine. Centuries later, in 1786, when it had been decided to build over many of the city's old burial grounds, the bones and bodies had been collected and thrown at random into the catacombs, converting them into a vast charnel-house. In 1810, after the fury of the Revolution had spent itself, some attempt had been made to arrange the skulls and bones, and they are now stored in various galleries and compartments. It is said that altogether the remains of nearly six million persons are deposited there, but the people who first attempted to put them into some sort of order had the macabre idea of using them for decorative purposes, and a number of underground chapels were constructed out of these hideous materials.

It was to one of these grim chapels that the escaping freedom fighters had descended from the Professor's house, but it was clear that the chapel was no longer used for religious purposes. Against a fantastic background of human skulls, pelvises and whole skeletons, set upright in plaster, were ranged long benches, upon which stood retorts and other scientific instruments and impedimenta.

One glance at them was enough to explain their presence to Gregory. The Professor evidently used this secret retreat under his house to manufacture time-bombs and the infernal machines for the saboteurs. The big chamber made a first-class laboratory, and the altar end of it had been fixed up like an office, with desk, filing cabinet, cupboards, and even a telephone, so that the Professor could be rung up when he was at work without bothering to go upstairs.

As the last member of the party came down into the cellar Baras was studying his map under the central electric light which hung from the ceiling, while several other men crowded about him. Just at that moment the telephone bell rang.

Instantly the murmur of conversation ceased, and everyone turned to stare at the instrument. There was something strange, sinister, frightening about the impatient shrilling of a modern telephone in that ancient crypt, with its weird and horrible wall decorations. No one moved forward to lift the receiver until the Professor, having closed the trap above securely, came down the steps, and walking over to his desk picked up the receiver quite calmly. He listened for a moment, then he looked at Kuporovitch and said: 'It's someone asking for you.'

The Russian started forward, but the men who were holding him pulled him back while Baras, elbowing his way forward, took the instrument.

There was a pause while everyone stared at him expectantly, then he exclaimed: 'It is Mademoiselle Lavallière!'

'There!' cried Gregory triumphantly. 'You see! She didn't leave for Unoccupied France this morning; and the fact she's still in Paris proves that it was not we who betrayed tonight's meeting.'

Baras looked a little abashed as he beckoned Kuporovitch forward; and, releasing their two captives, the nearest men began to mutter apologies.

'Yes, this is Stefan speaking,' Kuporovitch said into the mouthpiece. 'What's happened? Tell me quickly, but be careful what you say.' There was another pause, then he turned to Gregory.

'It was Pierre! The little swine tried to double-cross me. When they went upstairs to get their clothes on at seven o'clock he locked her in her room, and she's only just managed to get out.'

Gregory gave a swift nod. 'Then it's Pierre who gave away to the police the fact that we were all meeting at this house. Evidently he didn't care how many of these people were sacrificed as long as *you* were caught so that he'd get the girl for himself. What the young fool doesn't realize is that Luc Ferrière's place will be raided some time tonight and that both he and Madeleine will fall into the hands of the Gestapo.'

'We must go and get her!' cried Kuporovitch.

Gregory nodded again. 'Ask her if she can be at the Café du Rhône in an hour's time. If she can we'll pick her up there.'

Kuporovitch spoke again into the instrument. Then suddenly he swore; he had been cut off.

In vain he jangled the rest; the line was definitely dead; so he rang the exchange and asked for Luc Ferrière's number.

Baras stepped forward and interposed: 'Look here! I'm sorry we suspected you wrongly, but we dare not wait any longer, really. The police must have broken into the house by this time, and immediately they find it empty they'll search the cellars for some secret way out. If they discover the trap before we're clear there'll be a fight and half our people will get shot or lose themselves in this maze of tunnels as they try to get away in the darkness. We simply must go now.'

'All right!' snarled Kuporovitch. 'Go if you want to but leave this to me.'

'Don't be a fool,' Baras persisted. 'We have only one map of the catacombs, and I must keep that to lead these people out of them. If you don't come with us you'll never find your way out and probably die here.'

'He's right, Stefan,' interposed Gregory quietly.

'But if I can't warn her the police may raid the place while we're on our way there,' Kuporovitch cried, frantic with anxiety.

The Professor spoke with sudden firmness. 'You must go *at once*. Long ago I made arrangements to blow up my house if it were ever raided by the Quisling police. Now, the firing of the mine I have laid will protect us from pursuit. Quick, off you go—all of you; or it will be too late.'

Kuporovitch groaned; but Gregory seized him by the arm and dragged him away with the others as Baras led the way out of the chapel, map in one hand and torch in the other. The rest of the crowd struggled after him. Entering a high-arched tunnel, they hurried forward for about five hundred yards; then they heard an ear-shattering crack, followed by a long-echoing rumble, as the house caved in on its demolished foundations. Little flakes of stone fell from the roof under which they were passing, but soon there was no further sound except of their shuffling feet.

As they stumbled on through what seemed mile after mile of long dark tunnels, occasionally intersected by lofty chambers, or cross-roads at which several tunnels met, the Russian cursed, swore, and almost wept alternately, declaring that if he ever got his hands on Pierre he would cut the little traitor's liver out.

Gregory tried to cheer him up as well as he could by saying that all was not lost yet, and that probably when they reached Luc Ferrière's house they would find Madeleine waiting for them; but he had difficulty in concealing his own anxiety. Von

Geisenheim had said that he would take no action for a few hours, but Gregory had left him soon after eight, and it was now well past eleven. The General might have considered that three hours' start was ample for Gregory to get clear of any conspirators with whom he might personally be involved, and have by now issued instructions for the police to act.

At last the procession slowed up. Murmuring apologies, Gregory and Kuporovitch thrust their way forward to its head to find that Baras had just reached the top of another flight of steps and was pushing up a heavy trapdoor. They followed him out to find themselves in another cellar, and going up more stairs they saw by the light of their torches that they had reached street level again in a disused warehouse.

'Where exactly are we?' Gregory asked.

'On the Quai de la Gare,' replied Baras. 'The barges are moored only two hundred yards from here, on the left bank just this side by the Pont de Bercy. The next job is to get all these people on the empty barge without their being noticed, but we should be able to manage that all right in the course of the next hour of two, if they cross the street two or three at a time at decent intervals.'

'Good!' said Gregory. 'Kuporovitch and I are going off to see if we can collect Madeleine Lavallière. If we can we'll join you on the barge later. If we don't turn up you'll know that she's been caught, and we're staying behind on the chance that we may be able to rescue her.'

'Good luck then!' the ex-Deputy said; 'and don't forget that the empty barge is Number 2 in the string.' As he spoke he led them over to a rickety board doorway and, pulling the staple from its socket, let them out into the night.

As quickly as they could they walked along the quay towards the Gare d'Austerlitz. At the Pont de Bercy they saw the tug—the *Sans Souci*—and the barge which it was hoped would carry out of Paris such an unusual cargo, somewhere about dawn.

The barges were not like that upon which many months before Gregory had made his trip through Northern France into Belgium. They were many times larger, being of the big sea-going barges which cannot pass through canals but are used only on the principal European rivers and for coastal work between the big ports. He noticed, however, that the third in the string was considerably smaller than the other four.

When they reached the station they were greatly relieved to see that it was only just after half-past eleven. It now seemed hours since they had been pulled down into the catacombs as prisoners. They had feared that they would have to walk or hitchhike, on any belated lorries that they might find, half across Paris; but the Metro was open until midnight, so they were still able to get a train after waiting for ten minutes on an almost deserted platform.

Directly they reached the Malesherbes station they hurried along to the Café du Rhône, as Kuporovitch still hoped that Madeleine might have caught his last words before they had been cut off, and have managed to get there. As eleven o'clock was the curfew hour for all cafés, under the German régime, it was shut; but a faint chink of light showed at the side of one of the black-out curtains, so evidently someone was still about inside. They knocked on the door. It was answered by a waiter whom Kuporovitch knew well, and he asked if Madeleine had been there that evening. His heart sank as the waiter shook his head. 'No, she's not been in at all tonight.'

Having thanked the man they proceeded round the corner towards Luc Ferrière's house. The moon was now within two days of full, and the whole street was bathed in its brilliance. Directly they entered the street they saw that a van was standing outside Ferrière's door, and Gregory felt certain now that their worst fears had been realized. He had seen such vans in the Paris streets too often in recent months to be mistaken. It was a police van.

They had not advanced ten yards when the van began to move. Kuporovitch started forward, about to dash down the road in pursuit, but Gregory grabbed his arm with the words: 'Steady, Stefan! You'll never catch it now, and you'll only give yourself away by running after it.'

The pace of the van rapidly increased. In another moment it had disappeared round the corner at the far end of the street. Keeping an iron control over themselves, and trying to assume an air of nonchalance, they walked on more slowly now until they reached Ferrière's house. Two *agents de ville* were still standing outside it talking, but having finished their argument they went back into the house, slamming the door behind them.

Gregory and Kuporovitch knew then that beyond all question they were too late. The house had been raided, and Madeleine was once more in the hands of the Gestapo.

21

Race Against Time

They walked on in silence that could almost be felt. Kuporovitch was in such agony of mind that he could hardly think coherently, and even Gregory was at a complete loss how to console his friend.

He knew that they were now really up against it. When they had had their first fears that Madeleine was in trouble there had at least been the Professor's house which they could have used as a safe refuge, but obviously Pierre had given that away to the police, and it was now a heap of ruins. Had Ferrière's been raided during the previous weeks, or even right up to the previous night, there were a score of places where they could have found safe sanctuary with other members of the movement; but now there was not a single roof in Paris which sheltered friends who could aid them. For a few moments Gregory was utterly stumped, then, on a sudden thought, he snapped his fingers and exclaimed: 'Ribaud!'

Owing to his key position, the French detective alone of all Lacroix's supporters in Paris was remaining there. If they could get on to him he might be able to give them particulars about what was likely to be done with Madeleine. They increased their pace to a run until they reached a call-box, from which they could ring up the *Sûreté*.

Whenever they rang up Ribaud, which was as infrequently as possible, they used the most guarded phrases and, in most cases, terms with a double meaning which had already been agreed on with him. On this occasion he was more abrupt than ever, and when Kuporovitch said that it was essential for them to see him he replied that it was quite impossible for him to come out. The Russian insisted, but Ribaud continued to refuse, and it was only when Kuporovitch threatened to come and see him in his own office that he at last reluctantly consented and said the he would meet them in the porch of Saint-Germain-l'Auxerrois at 12.15.

When they arrived at the rendezvous they found him furiously angry. He had heard that von Geisenheim had done his stuff and turned in the expected list of addresses, but at about the same time he had also heard that a raid was being made on the Professor's house; so he knew that things had gone very badly wrong somewhere. In view of that, he had decided that he must watch his own step more carefully than ever, and that the best way for him to protect himself was to remain in the *Sûreté* all night, so that he would have a perfect alibi and could not be accused of helping any of the conspirators to get away. By forcing him to come out Kuporovitch had wrecked his plan.

For a few moments the Russian and the Frenchman wrangled angrily in the darkened porchway of the old church, which served partially to conceal them from the strong moonlight that lit the street. Then Gregory intervened.

'Listen, you two! We're wasting time; and you, Ribaud, have damn' well got to help us, whether you like it or not. You must for your own protection. Don't you realize that once the Gestapo get their hands on Pierre Ponsardin he'll blow the whole works and you'll be the first for the high jump?'

'*Mon Dieu!* You're right!' exclaimed Ribaud. 'The little swine! It was his crazy jealousy for Kuporovitch which caused him to give the meeting-place away, and he meant to make a bolt for it with the girl: but now the Nazis have got him they'll torture him until he reveals everything he knows. It's not only myself but Lacroix we have to think of.'

'Exactly,' added Kuporovitch; 'so you see how vital it is that, by hook or by crook, we should get him and Madeleine out of their hands.'

'God alone knows how you're going to do that!' moaned the Frenchman despondently. 'If I lift a finger to help either of them I'll immediately become suspect myself.'

'You might be able to lift a finger to help us, though,' Gregory suggested. 'I mean as a signal for the right time to

335

go in and attempt their rescue. As they've only just been pulled in they'll probably be transferred from their cells to the place where they're questioned, or even from prison to prison, in the next twenty-four hours. If you could tip us off when that's likely to happen we might be able to do something.'

'Maybe,' grunted Ribaud, 'but wherever they're taken you can be certain they'll be heavily guarded. Anyhow, I'd better get back now and find out all I can about what's being done. I'll slip out again to meet you here for a few minutes in an hour's time.'

Ribaud moved off along the moonlit street, but the other two remained where they were and sat down in the deep shadow on the steps of the church. There didn't seem any point in their going anywhere else, and for the time being there was nothing at all that they could do.

They were both too anxious to talk of casual things, so for most of the time they sat in silence. The hour seemed a long one, but at a quarter past one they began to show a little more liveliness and keep a lookout for Ribaud.

The moments seemed endless now, but the short, dark figure they were expecting did not appear. Half-past one, a quarter to two o'clock, a quarter past—and still no sign of Ribaud. They had begun to fear now that Pierre, in his terror at being caught, had already denounced the French detective, but their only hope was to hang on where they were on the chance that he would yet turn up. Another half-hour dragged by wearily, then, at last, just after quarter to three, Ribaud came hurrying down the street.

'They've been questioning them for the past three hours,' he said, 'and I knew that nothing would be settled until the preliminary investigation was over. There was no point in my coming out before, and I felt certain that you would wait.'

'Is Madeleine all right?' Kuporovitch demanded anxiously.

'She was looking pretty washed-up after her grilling; but they haven't started in on her physically yet.'

'How about Pierre?' Gregory enquired. 'Do you think he's split?'

Ribaud shrugged. 'I don't think so. It's hardly likely that he would until the Gestapo people began applying their hot-irons to him. If he had I should probably already be under

336

arrest. Anyhow, he's past doing us any further damage now.'

'You mean . . . ?' Kuporovitch muttered.

'I mean that the little traitor's dead. After our people had taken him down to a cell I saw him and gave him a cigarette.'

Gregory nodded. 'That was much the best thing to do, in view of all that's at stake. It was lucky that you had some on you.'

Ribaud's smile was grim. 'I always keep a few in my case; one whiff and the cyanide does its work. I know far too much about the inside of a Gestapo torture chamber now ever to let them get me alive.'

'What do they intend to do with Madeleine next?' Kuporovitch asked.

'At the moment she's in a cell at the *Sûreté*, but they'll transfer her to the *Cherche-Midi*, where they keep most of the women these days. What time that will be I can't tell. It all depends on when there's a police car free to do the job; but I should think they'll take her across within the course of the next two or three hours. Once she's inside you'll stand precious little chance of getting her out. The trick you played before won't work a second time, even if you could find another Luc Ferrière.'

'What happened to him?' Gregory interjected.

'The old chap's protesting his innocence and offering to swear to it on *Mein Kampf*. They're treating him quite decently at the moment, but I doubt if he'll get away with it when they find that stuff you planted in his house. Serve him right, too! The dirty little Quisling was responsible for our nursing-home being raided; and if you knew what those devils have done to poor little Nurse Yolanda and the others who were there you'd be ready to tear that old man's guts out with your naked hands. But, as I was saying, your only chance of rescuing Madeleine is to intercept the car that takes her to the *Cherche-Midi*. Now I must get back, otherwise I shall find myself having to smoke one of my own cigarettes.'

They gave Ribaud two hundred yards' start, then followed him until they reached the *Sûreté*. Walking round it, they took up their positions in a deep doorway on the opposite side of the road to the entrance of the courtyard, from which the police cars always drove in and out.

It was now getting on for half-past three, but another long wait was in store for them. Occasionally it was broken by a sudden tense expectancy as a police car came out of the yard, and they strained their eyes to see if Madeleine was in it. Had it not been for the bright moonlight they would have had no hope at all, but as long as the moon lasted they felt reasonably certain that they would be able to pick out a woman's figure, even if she were seated in the back of a car, some distance away. Four o'clock came, then an intensely worrying period when the moon disappeared behind the roof-tops, and semi-darkness partially obscured their view; but by five the street was lighting with the early summer dawn.

They were both very tired from their long vigil, and incredibly depressed by the thought that, even if they were able to make their attempt, it could only be a forlorn hope. Madeleine's escort was certain to be armed, and the driver of the car would have only to put his foot on the accelerator for it to streak away. Their opportunity would consist of no more than a bare half-minute, as the car turned out of the courtyard before developing its full speed.

Suddenly Kuporovitch gripped Gregory's arm, but at the same second Gregory had seen the same thing. A police car was running quietly out of the yard, and in its back they could plainly see Madeleine seated beside an *agent de ville*. They had long since discussed their method of attack in detail, and now, without an instant's hesitation, they put it into operation.

While Kuporovitch remained concealed in the doorway Gregory stepped out on to the pavement and hailed the driver of the car. Just as the man was about to put on speed he turned with a look of surprise. Letting the car run gently on he called: 'What d'you want?'

Gregory ran swiftly across the road to him, crying as he ran: 'For God's sake come and help me! Some men have broken into my apartment in that house. They've half-murdered my wife, and I only just managed to get away.'

The police chauffeur stopped the car and leant out of it, as he said quickly: 'That's bad luck, but we've got a prisoner and can't leave the car. There are scores of our chaps in the yard of the *Sûreté* there. Give a shout to some of them.'

Gregory was now right close up to the man, and he waited

338

on tenterhooks for the next act in their skilfully staged plot. Suddenly it came—a single shot rang out. Unseen by the driver, Kuporovitch had come up behind the car and fired through its window, shooting through the back the *agent de ville* who was sitting next to Madeleine.

The instant Gregory heard the shot his hand darted forward. Grabbing the police chauffeur by the throat he dragged him from the seat. Then, lifting his fist, he hit the man a hard blow between the eyes, dropping him in the roadway and, scrambling into the car, seized the wheel.

Meanwhile, Kuporovitch had run round the other side of the car. He jumped in beside Gregory, and with his gun still in his hand thrust it in the face of the *agent de ville*; but he had no necessity to shoot again. The man was lying back, either unconscious or dead.

The single report of the Russian's automatic had been enough to raise the alarm in the courtyard of the *Sûreté*. Other policemen were now running from it, shouting at them to halt; but Gregory had the brake off. He let in the clutch and the car shot forward.

A pistol cracked, another and another. The shots echoed through the quiet dawnlit street. A bullet clanged on the metal-work of the car; another hit one of the rear tyres, which went off with a loud plop. The car swerved wildly, but Gregory managed to get it under control. Crouching over the wheel he drove on all out, in spite of the bumping rim.

But he knew that he would never be able to get clear away in the car now. The rim must be cutting the flattened tyre to pieces, and the stout rubber-covered canvas might catch in the axle, causing it to jam. In addition, there had been a number of other cars in the courtyard of the *Sûreté*. In them the police would give chase at once, and he could not hope to outdistance the pursuit with one of his back tyres gone.

He took the first corner to the left at full speed, ran on a little way, then turned right, into the entrance of a mews. 'Come on!' he cried, jumping out. 'We've got to run for it!'

Kuporovitch had been leaning over the back of the seat examining the *agent de ville*. He found that his victim was still breathing, and he hoped the fellow would live. He had little time for the French police who were now co-operating with the Germans, but he knew that they were more or less forced to do so, and it had been particularly distasteful to have to shoot the fellow in the back; but Madeleine's safety being involved, he had not hesitated an instant, as it was so obviously the one certain means of putting the man out of action before he could offer any resistance.

There was no time to examine the policeman further, so Kuporovitch extricated his body from the car and, seizing Madeleine's arm, began to run. Gregory had only waited to see that the other two were out before setting off at a pace which he thought Madeleine could manage.

As it was still early the mews was empty, except for one chauffeur who was cleaning a car, which had a red label *Médecin* pasted on its windscreen. At first the man made as though to intercept them, but Gregory cried: 'Get out of the way! The Germans and the police are after us!'

Immediately the man's expression changed. He pointed to his garage. 'Get in there! I'll tell them you ran past.'

With a hurried word of thanks they ran into the garage and crouched down behind an empty trailer that occupied the back of it, while the chauffeur went on cleaning his car.

A moment later they heard a police car drive up. Excited questions were flung at the man who had hidden them; but apparently the police were satisfied with his replies, as they drove on, and silence again fell in the mews.

After another few minutes the chauffeur came in to them and said: 'The coast's clear now, but they may come back later to make a more careful search. You'd better get out while the going's good.'

As they thanked him for his help he shrugged: 'Oh, that's nothing. It's a treat to be able to put one over on the police, now they've gone in with those filthy Boches.'

Gregory went ahead, telling the other two to follow him a about fifty yards, so that they would have a chance to get away if he ran into trouble on going round a corner. At each corner he paused for a cautious peep into the street ahead before advancing further.

In this manner they gradually worked their way down to the south bank of the river and along it to the Pont de Bercy; but when they reached the bridge they suffered a grievous disappointment. It was now nearly six o'clock, and the *Sans Souci* with her string of barges was no longer there. The many delays with which they had met during the night had made them miss the boat, and now the one lifeline upon which they had pinned their hopes of reaching freedom was cut.

At the corner of the bridge they held a swift consultation. Apart from Ribaud, who dared help them no further, they now had not a single friend left in Paris, and full daylight had come. People were moving in the streets, and Madeleine's description would soon be circulated to every police station in Paris. To attempt to pass the police posts on the outskirts of the city in daytime would be sheer madness, and it was imperative for them to find some cover until nightfall. It was Gregory who suddenly remembered the deserted warehouse into which they had emerged from the catacombs late the previous night.

The moment he suggested they should go there the others agreed to his idea, and they set off. The warehouse lay only a few hundred yards away, on the far side of the quay. Its door had been left ajar, and slipping inside they pushed home the wooden staple.

As their eyes became accustomed to the dim light in the old building they saw some discarded packing-cases in one corner, and going over to them sat down. Then, for the first time, Madeleine was able to bless her rescuers and tell them in detail what had happened.

On the previous night she and Pierre had gone upstairs at seven o'clock to get their things on, preparatory to leaving the house. He had walked into her room, locked the door behind him and told her that he had no intention of taking her to the meeting, as he felt certain that she meant to go off with Kuporovitch.

There had been a frightful scene, in which she had used arguments, entreaties and threats, finally telling him that if he really kept her there all night as he proposed to do Kuporovitch would come back in the morning and beat him to a jelly.

Upon that Pierre had let the cat out of the bag. He was so crazy with jealousy that he had given away the meeting-place

341

to the police solely with the intention of getting his rival out of the way once and for all.

At this horrifying disclosure Madeleine had pleaded with him anew; but he had argued that it was now too late to do anything, even if he wanted to. She had disputed that, but he had pointed out that, although there might still be time to warn the people at the meeting before the police arrived, he would never now be able to conceal the fact that it was he who had given the meeting place away, and the result would be that they'd hunt him down and execute him as a traitor.

When she had asked him about his future plans he had said with all the conceit and stupidity of a weak man who is obsessed by one idea that, since he had put Kuporovitch out of the running, there was no further bar to her coming away with him the following day to his aunt's home in Limoges.

She had been very tempted to claw his face to ribbons with her nails, but she knew that she was not strong enough to overcome him and that the thing which mattered above all else was for her to get a warning to the meeting. Madame Chautemps had gone off that afternoon, as arranged, to her relatives at Rheims, so there was no one else in the house except Luc Ferrière, and Madeleine had felt that she would not get much help from him if she brought him upstairs by shouting. On deciding that her only resort was guile she had then played the part of a weak female and pretended to be entirely overcome.

Pierre had attempted to console her, and after a little she had made a show of accepting her situation philosophically, in the hope that he would go away and leave her; as, even if he locked the door behind him, once she was alone she would have been able to get out of the window by a shed that lay below it, into the backyard. But he had made it clear that he did not trust her and meant to sit up with her all night.

She had then suggested that they might as well have some supper and unpacked the small parcel of things which she had been going to take with her. Among them was a thermos with soup in it, and as she always carried a sleeping draught in her nursing kit in case of emergency, she had managed to put it, while distracting his attention, into Pierre's portion of the soup.

As soon as they had finished their picnic meal she had declared that, even if he was determined to stay there all night, she was not going to allow that to prevent her from getting what sleep she could, and, lying on her bed fully dressed, she had put out the light while he remained seated in an armchair.

Normally the sleeping draught would have done its work in half an hour; but Pierre was in such a state of excited tension that Madeleine began to fear that it was not going to work at all. For what seemed an age she had lain there listening to his breathing, till, at last, the drug and the darkness in which he was sitting made him drop off.

As soon as she heard him snoring gently she had got up, crept out of the room, locked him in and run downstairs to telephone.

To her horror she found that it was already half-past ten, but she had rung up the Professor's as quickly as she could and got on to Kuporovitch, only to be cut off in the middle of their conversation. The line had simply gone dead, so it must have been the exchange, or more probably the police upstairs had switched off the extension to the laboratory by accident, in an attempt to listen-in to the conversation themselves.

She had just heard Kuporovitch say, 'You are to go . . .' before the connection had been broken. She did not know where he wished her to go, and she knew that, owing to Pierre's treachery, the Professor's house might by raided at any moment; so that if she went there she would very likely fall into the hands of the police. In consequence, she had decided that she had better stay where she was in the hope of Stefan getting through to her again. Half an hour later Luc Ferrière's had been raided, and all its inmates had been carted off to the *Sûreté*.

When Madeleine had finished her account, as they were all terribly tired after their exhausting night, they agreed that the first thing to do was to get some sleep. After they wakened, refreshed a little, it would be time enough to discuss possible ways and means out of the wretched situation in which they found themselves. There was nothing that would serve for bedding except some dirty straw in the bottom of the packing-cases, but having collected that they made themselves as comfortable as they could. Since it was a warm June day there was no question of their suffering from the cold, so they soon dropped off and did not wake until the late afternoon.

All three of them found that they were now very hungry, so Gregory said he would go out and see if he could raise some food. That pleasant spicy smell which comes from the Paris grocers, and in normal times is so characteristic of the whole city, had now entirely disappeared, as the shops were empty of everything except small stocks of goods which were unobtainable without ration-cards. But he knew that food of sorts could still be obtained from the station buffets, since they were kept supplied as a convenience for the Germans, who in these days formed more than 90 per cent of the travellers on the French railways.

On reaching the Gare d'Austerlitz he obtained one sandwich, two large coarse biscuits, a bag of cherries and a packet of mixed nuts. He also managed to buy a bottle of cheap French red wine, for which he had to pay the exorbitant price of forty francs. Having purchased a paper, he made his way back to the warehouse. When he reached it his face was grave.

'I'm afraid we're up against it,' he remarked, as he sat down. 'Last night's affair has given the Germans the jitters, and they've instituted that damn' curfew again; so no one will be allowed out in the streets after eight o'clock without a special pass. That puts the lid on our attempting to get out of Paris tonight.'

'I wonder how many days they'll keep it up?' speculated Kuporovitch moodily. 'If only we could have got off tonight we shouldn't have had any great difficulty in catching up with the string of barges; but if we're forced to remain in concealment here for several days we'll miss them altogether, and as far as I can see they're our only hope of getting clean out of the country in safety.'

'The curfew's certain to last for several days,' said Madeleine, 'and while it's on to go out in the streets at night without a pass is simply asking to be picked up by one of the patrols. I think we'd better risk making our first move tomorrow in daylight. If we could get as far as the suburbs we'd be able to hide in a garden there until after dark; then cut across the fields so as to avoid the police posts that they have on all the roads, outside the city.'

Gregory shook his head. 'Unfortunately, we're on the wrong side of Paris, so we've either got to go right through the heart of the city or make a long detour round endless streets to the east and south. We'd never be able to do that without somebody recognizing us.'

'Why?' asked Madeleine. 'Although I've been arrested three times now, I don't suppose that more than twenty Nazis and police have seen me face to face.'

With a rueful grin Gregory held out the paper. 'I'm afraid you underrate the enemy. They've published your photograph here, so every policeman in Paris will be on the lookout for you.'

'Oh dear!' she exclaimed. 'Of course, they took our photographs soon after we reached the *Sûreté* last night.'

'It's not a very good one,' he went on, 'but it's quite good enough to identify you by, and the devil of it is that they're offering fifty thousand francs for your capture, dead or alive, and the same amount for information which will lead to the arrest of the two men who rescued you. They also publish a fairly accurate description of myself, given them, I suppose, by that police chauffeur I knocked out. The Germans don't like admitting their own mistakes when they make them, which God knows, isn't often, and, naturally, in this case they're blaming your getaway on the inefficiency of the French police. Anyhow, the full story is given here, together with an account of Luc Ferrière's arrest, and a statement that your companion Pierre Ponsardin, committed suicide in his cell at the *Sûreté* by smoking a poisoned cigarette.'

'Oh, poor Pierre!' Madeleine sighed.

Gregory ignored her interruption, as he saw no point in telling her that Ribaud had actually been responsible for Pierre's death. 'They blame the French police for that, too, as Pierre should have been searched, and anything he was carrying taken from him, immediately after his arrest. The little party in which you were involved forms the high spot of the night's doings although there's a statement in much more guarded language that many other raids were made, and that a conspiracy against the régime has been uncovered

—hence the fresh imposition of the curfew. One thing stands out as plain as a pikestaff: fifty thousand francs is a lot of money, and there are still far too many Quislings in Paris for us to run the risk of letting you be seen in the streets.'

'But we can't stay here,' Madeleine murmured, casting a glance round their gloomy and uncomfortable retreat.

'I'm afraid we'll have to,' Stefan said despondently. 'But God knows how we'll ever be able to catch up with that string of barges now.'

'Given a little bit of luck we might,' Gregory spoke a little more cheerfully. 'Léon Baras was trying not to depress the others too much when he told them they'd have to remain under the hatches for a week. I had no dealings with the captain of the tug or his crew, but I made a few independent enquiries, and I doubt if they'll reach Le Havre in less than ten days. If the curfew is taken off at the end of the week, and we can find some means of fairly rapid transport once we're out of Paris, we might even be able to pick them up at Rouen.'

Kuporovitch nodded. 'It seems that's the best we can hope for at the moment. In the meantime, we must make ourselves as comfortable as we can in this dismal hole; or perhaps we ought to move down to the cellar. I expect the police are throwing a net over the whole of Paris, and some of them might quite well pay a visit to a deserted warehouse like this during their search.'

'You're right,' Gregory agreed, and getting out his torch he went downstairs to examine the cellar. It was damp and evil-smelling, so pulling up the trap he descended still farther into the catacombs themselves. The air was much fresher there, as it came in from an old disused drain which ran under the street and gave direct onto the Seine. The stone flooring of the tunnel was rough and dry, so he decided that they had better take up their quarters down there and went up to tell the others.

Madeleine was reluctant to sleep down in the catacombs because she was frightened of the rats which she felt certain must swarm there. Gregory told her that the warehouse was just as likely to be overrun and that rats were not dangerous unless they were attacked or starving. In order to keep out of their way as far as possible, it was decided to carry down the

346

packing-cases and make a high flat stack of them on which to sleep, instead of lying on the floor.

When they had carted down the empty cases and arranged the straw on top of them their next worry was light, since Gregory's torch could not be expected to last for more than a few hours. With a view to saving it as much as possible they decided to stay up above as long as daylight lasted, but hold themselves ready to beat a quick retreat to the cellars if they heard anyone approaching the warehouse door.

While they had been talking and making their arrangements they had divided up the meagre fare that Gregory had obtained from the station buffet and made a scratch meal of it; but they were still hungry and greatly depressed by the uncertainty of being able to secure further supplies of food and light. The evening hours of the long summer twilight seemed unending, but at last, when full darkness had fallen, Gregory produced the ancient philosophical tag 'He who sleeps dines,' and suggested that they should go below and turn in.

As they stood up Kuporovitch suddenly announced that he was going out. Without even asking him why he wished to do so the others immediately protested that he would be absolutely crazy to risk himself in the streets now that it was after curfew; but he insisted, simply saying that he had a little job to do which would not take him very far or very long.

Gregory knew the Russian too well to argue with him. To quiet Madeleine's fears Stefan swore that he would do nothing rash, exercise the greatest caution and be back within a couple of hours at most. Then he kissed her gently and slipped out of the door on to the quay.

He more than fulfilled his promise by returning in just over an hour, and with him he brought two heavy sacks slung over his shoulder. He had remembered that the office of the black market racketeer Lavinsky was only a stone's throw from the Gare d'Austerlitz, and he had carried out a second successful raid on it for the benefit of himself and his friends.

As the sacks were emptied by the light of Gregory's torch their contents gave rise to cries of amazement and delight. There were tins of all sorts of luxuries that Madeleine had not seen for many months; not only such things as tinned ham, pineapple, and *foie gras*, but, most precious of all, and only procurable now in Paris at the price of a millionaire's ransom, there were four big bundles of nine-inch candles and two packets of matches.

They carried this almost fabulous treasure down into the catacombs, and the very sight of it had banished their previous despondency from their minds. With candles to light them Madeleine no longer had any dread of the rats, and sorting out the good things again they opened some of them at once to enjoy a first-class picnic supper.

On the following day they decided that, since Gregory's description had been circulated as well as Madeleine's, Kuporovitch was the only one of them who would be reasonably safe out in the streets in daylight, and that even he should only leave the hideout for a short time once a day to get news.

When he brought in the paper there was nothing more in it about the conspiracy which had been revealed the previous day, so they now felt happier in their minds with the thought that Léon Baras and his party in the barge must have succeeded in getting clear of the capital without arousing suspicion. There were, however, banner headlines in the paper. At dawn the previous day, Sunday, June the 8th, British and Free French Forces had invaded Syria, and their armoured units were already reported pressing forward towards Damascus.

Gregory was immensely cheered to know that we had at last taken the bull by the horns and openly thrown overboard all the absurd nonsense about the so-called rights of neutrals in a territory where the administration had definitely shown themselves unfriendly to us and was rendering every possible assistance to our enemies. He felt, too, that a successful campaign in Syria would make an immense difference to the Grand Strategy of the War, since, if Syria could be brought under British control, Turkey would no longer be isolated, and the road would again be open to give her swift assistance if she became the next victim of Axis aggression.

The days that followed proved dreary in the extreme. There was nowhere in either the warehouse or the tunnel below in which they could sit or lie in real comfort. Thanks to Kuporovitch they were quite well off for candles, but, as they found it necessary to keep a couple alight all night, in order to scare away the rats, they did not feel justified in using any during the day; and the warehouse was in a perpetual twilight which made it impossible to read the books and periodicals, which Kuporovitch brought in, for any length of time. He made a trip to the station each morning and evening to get the latest paper, and it cheered them a bit to see that the Syrian campaign was going well; but there was no news as to when the curfew would be lifted, and until that happened they had no option but to continue in their voluntary captivity.

At last, on Saturday, June the 14th, an announcement appeared that, after having been imposed for a week, the curfew would be lifted on the following night, but would be enforced again at the first manifestation of further activities against the régime.

On the Sunday afternoon they made their preparations. Kuporovitch had procured some coarse unrationed material, a big needle and some thick thread with which Madeleine made three haversacks to carry the remainder of their stolen food, divided up between them. For hours, it seemed, they waited while darkness gradually fell, then, one by one, they slipped out of the warehouse and joined up again on the next corner, a hundred yards down the street.

It had already been agreed that they must not take the Metro or a bus across Paris, owing to the danger that Madeleine might be recognized, even in a subdued light; so they were fully prepared to face a long and tiring walk. The moon had been full on the 9th, so it was now six days on the wane. As the night was fine it shone in an almost cloudless sky, giving them ample light to proceed at a good pace without risk of banging into lamp-posts or people in the black-out.

Taking the less frequented thoroughfares, they went up the Montparnasse Hill and down the other side until they reached the Seine again, crossing it by the Pont Mirabeau. A quarter of an hour later they left inner Paris by the Porte d' Auteuil.

They now had the southern edge of the Bois on one side of them and some straggling buildings interspersed with vacant lots on the other, and they felt a little more cheerful, since if they were challenged now there was much more hope of their getting away among the scattered buildings than there would have been in a Paris street.

It was now just on midnight, and they had already walked the best part of six miles, but they knew that the most dangerous part of their night's undertaking was yet to come. The road they were following formed the bowstring to a great southern bend in the Seine, so some two miles farther on they would have to cross the river again at Saint Cloud. From the intelligence supplied by their old sabotage parties they knew that one of the police posts forming the cordon round Paris was situated there.

When they were within a quarter of a mile of the river Gregory turned off the main road, leading his friends down a side road to the left. They followed this for several hundred yards, until they found a path which led towards the river and turning again went on towards it. Having reached the towpath they turned left again, now keeping their eyes skinned for any sign of a boat. It was not long before they came upon a small house, and the light of the moon was sufficient to show them from the weathered board erected outside it that at one time it had been a river-side tea-garden. In front of it, on the other side of the towpath, was a boat-house.

Scrambling down the bank, Gregory tried the door and found it locked, but with the aid of a piece of old iron, which they picked up, they forced it, and felt considerable elation on seeing that there were several boats inside.

The police cordon was more for the purpose of trapping the unwary who endeavoured to get in and out of Paris by road without a permit than with the idea that it would serve to keep Paris's two million citizens inside their city. It would have needed thousands of police and troops on duty all night to do that, and the Germans were not the sort of people to deny themselves the pleasure of the river during the summer months to the extent of confiscating all boats. Thus, although Gregory had feared that it might take them much longer to secure a boat than it actually had, he had felt pretty certain that they would be able to find one sooner or later and get through the cordon by crossing the river in it.

There was still the danger that they might be seen while crossing and challenged by a patrolling sentry upon the other bank, and on this account they now had reason to dread the moon, but it was a risk which had to be taken.

Selecting a two-foot-six punt they lay down at full length in it, in order to make themselves less conspicuous. Then using two pieces of board as paddles, since there had been none in the boat-house, the two men began to propel the boat across, taking great care to dip their pieces of board into the water as noiselessly as possible.

To their great relief they reached the other side without being challenged. Having made the punt fast to a ring in some wooden steps they scrambled up the far bank and set off across a field, gradually edging north-eastward until they struck the main road again beyond Saint Cloud.

Wishing to get as far away from Paris as they could that night, they pressed on until nearly three o'clock in the morning. By that time, having covered over twelve miles, it was clear that Madeleine could go no farther: so they left the road and made themselves as comfortable as possible in a grassy hollow that was screened from view by some trees. Fortunately, as it was high summer, the ground was dry, and the night warm, so they soon dropped off to sleep.

In the morning they ate some of their iron rations, then set off again. On entering a pleasant village Madeleine recognized it as Marly, so was able to confirm that they were on the right road. Later they hoped to get a lift on a lorry, but Gregory did not wish to invite awkward questions until they were farther from Paris. With a few minutes' halt every hour and a long rest at noon they walked for the best part of the day, except for a stretch of about three miles over which a countryman with a pony and trap had spontaneously given them a lift. By evening they had accomplished a further nineteen miles and were approaching the outskirts of Mantes.

After selecting a small coppice as their headquarters Gregory left the other two to rest, and went on into the town; his object was to find a carter who might be leaving the following day in the direction of Rouen. He spent the best part of two hours visiting several cheap bars and eating-houses, where he got into casual conversation with a number of workmen.

Madeleine and Stefan had long since eaten their supper and were getting a little anxious about him when at length he rejoined them about ten o'clock. He reported that he had had the luck to find a lorry-driver who was actually leaving for Rouen the following morning, and for a price that had been agreed he had been willing to take them with him.

After sleeping in the open again they were up very early next morning and walked through the town while it was still shrouded in the misty light of the summer dawn. Half a mile beyond it they waited on the crest of a hill with some anxiety to see if their man would, after all, arrive to pick them up. A quarter of an hour later he appeared. The lorry pulled up, and Gregory went forward to greet him.

The man was a dark, sinewy-looking little Basque whose name was Sabarros. Later they learned that he had been a soldier in the Maginot Line at the time of the collapse, but had managed to borrow a suit of civilian clothes and so escape capture and internment. Gregory paid over half the money that had been agreed on; then he and his friends settled themselves on the hard boards of the lorry among some great wicker-covered carboys containing acid, which screened them from view. It was hard going for them, and before the day was out they were wretchedly sore from the bumping they received. When the lorry made one of its periodical halts late in the afternoon Sabarros came round to tell them that they must get out as they were only a mile from Rouen, and he did not mean to risk taking them right into the city.

Having paid him the rest of his money they took a fork road. Some way along it they found a disused chalk quarry at the bottom of which some bushes were growing. Leaving the other two to scramble down into it, Gregory cut across the fields towards Rouen. During their long walk on the previous day they had passed quite a number of German troops, but nothing like so many as there were here. The old town absolutely swarmed with them, but none of them took any notice of Gregory as he wound his way in and out of narrow turnings down to the docks.

It was June 17th, exactly a year to the day since the collapse of France, and on every hand there was ample evidence of the damage which the British bombers had done throughout the year to this important invasion base. There were so many wrecked buildings on the waterfront that the Germans no longer troubled to try to conceal them; but in spite of the havoc, the port itself was still functioning, and there was a considerable amount of shipping there.

After looking in vain for the *Sans Souci* and her tow of barges Gregory got into conversation with several watermen until he learned that she had arrived on the 15th and left on the 16th.

He was not unduly disappointed as he had hardly expected to be lucky enough to catch her there. By a quick reckoning he worked out that as she had taken seven days to cover the hundred and sixty odd miles of water between Paris and Rouen she would be at least three days in covering the remaining eighty miles of water from Rouen to Havre. As against that his own party had succeeded in making the eighty-mile journey overland from Paris to Rouen in two days and a night; so, given equal luck, they should be able to get overland to Le Havre in thirty-six hours. As the *Sans Souci* had left on the 16th she was not due at Le Havre until the 19th, so they had, on his reckoning, at least a day to spare.

When he had worked this out to his satisfaction he began a discreet enquiry in the hope of finding another lorry-driver who would take them on to Le Havre the following morning; but there he met with much more difficulty than he had expected. All French territory between Rouen and the coast was now in the special zone occupied by the German armies which sooner or later might yet receive orders to invade England. With their usual thoroughness the Germans were leaving nothing undone to keep their preparations secret.

In consequence, there were special road patrols and innumerable barriers at cross-roads, at which all civilian transport was halted and examined. All the lorry-men he could contact told him that it was more than lives were worth to attempt to smuggle three people through, none of whom had passes. Late that night he returned to the chalk quarry, and as gently as he could broke the disquieting news to the others that they would have to make the rest of the journey on foot, and that it was now going to be a race against time as to whether they could reach Le Havre before the *Sans Souci* left it.

Early next morning they were on their way, and night found

them at the little town of Caudebec after a most exhausting day. They had accomplished twenty miles of their journey, but in the late afternoon they had come into the area that was forbidden to all civilians without passes; so for the last two hours of daylight they constantly had to get off the road and take lonely by-paths, or hide in the woods when they saw German patrols approaching in the distance. To add to their distress, as twilight fell it had begun to rain, and they passed a most uncomfortable night in a small coppice.

Next morning they made another few miles, but they had to hide so frequently that they decided that it would be better to rest during the day and go on at night.

Night travel also proved to have its disadvantages. The moon was now ten days past full and only a waning sickle in a sky of scudding clouds. Bright moonlight would have added to their dangers, as sentries would have been able to take pot-shots at them from some considerable distance with a good chance of bringing one of them down; but in the darkness they had to face the peril of running into troops without warning, and three times during the night they had to take to their heels at a sudden challenge.

It was the night of the 19th, and the day that the *Sans Souci* could be expected to reach Havre; yet they had covered only another ten miles when from sheer fatigue they were compelled to camp again near Lillebonne. They still had the best part of twenty miles to go, and if the *Sans Souci* had arrived at Havre on the previous day she might sail with the tide in the morning.

Gregory tried to cheer the others by saying that the *Sans Souci* might easily take four days between Rouen and Le Havre. Three and a half was the absolute minimum, so the probability was that she would not arrive till the 20th and sail again on the 21st, but he knew that their chances of catching her were now decreasing with every hour, and in this troop-infested country they dared not go on in daylight.

As darkness fell on the night of the 20th they started off once more, determined to make the most desperate effort to reach Le Havre before the morning. The hours of darkness proved a veritable nightmare. Again and again they had to turn back or get off the road at the sound of movement in

354

front. On five occasions they were challenged, and on three they were fired at. The two men helped Madeleine as much as they could, but when dawn came all three were desperately weary. By their unshakable determination they had succeeded in covering fifteen miles during the night, but they had only reached Harfleur, which lay the best part of five miles outside Le Havre.

On the flat uplands there was little cover, but they managed to find another chalk-pit which had a small cave in it. Kuporo-vitch's haul of iron rations had served them splendidly, but they were now nearly exhausted, and to recruit their strength the little party ate the last of them before stretching themselves out to sleep.

Being old campaigners, Gregory and Stefan had both developed the capacity for waking at a given time. Before they settled down they agreed that they would only sleep till midday, as it seemed now that their last chance of catching the *Sans Souci*, even if she were still at Le Havre, would be a cross-country dash in full daylight, so that they could reach the harbour before the evening tide.

Shortly after midday they climbed out of the chalk-pit and set off across the fields. They could now see the city spread out below them, and the English channel, beyond which lay safety and freedom, calm and peaceful in the summer sunshine. To their great relief they found the last part of their journey much less hazardous than they had expected. There were not so many German troops about as there had been farther inland, and apparently the local inhabitants were allowed to roam about freely within a few miles of the city, so that the little party was not particularly conspicuous, owing to the numerous men and women working in the fields. At a little after two o'clock they entered the town and made their way down to the port.

It had been blitzed by the R.A.F. to an even greater extent than had Rouen, and here again the damage was so extensive that the Germans were making no attempt to conceal it. For a quarter of an hour they walked along the quays, their eyes frantically searching the shipping for the *Sans Souci* and her tow.

Suddenly Gregory raised his arm and pointed. He could

have cried aloud with joy. The *Sans Souci* had not yet sailed, and was lying at the end of a long jetty. She was too far off for him to read her name, but he knew her at once from the fact that the third in her string of barges was considerably smaller than the other four.

The next thing was to be aboard her, but, as they had feared, they found the entrance to the jetty guarded. Two stolid-faced Germans, one with a rifle and fixed bayonet, the other with a tommy-gun, stood there.

Gregory took his party into a waterside café, and at once began to make discreet enquiries as to when the *Sans Souci* was due to sail. There were no German soldiers in the place, only French wharf-hands, so they answered his questions without any hesitation and seemed willing enough to help him in any way they could. None of them could give him the information he required, but one of them went out to make enquiries, and came back to report that she would sail about half an hour after midnight. Gregory then asked how he could best get aboard her. The men shook their heads glumly, and all agreed that there was no chance of that unless he could get a special pass.

He enquired if there were any way of contacting the tug's captain or one of the members of her crew, but again the men shook their heads. No one was allowed on to such tugs, and no one was allowed off them. That was one of the German regulations, and they were extremely strict about enforcing it. The *Sans Souci* had put into Le Havre in order to pick up her escort, as she would be proceeding in convoy up the coast with a number of other vessels. She had arrived two days before and was there still only because the convoy had not yet been made up, but none of her crew had been allowed ashore, even to buy a drink.

A square-shouldered man, who seemed somewhat better educated that the rest, had proved most helpful, so Gregory took him outside and asked him if he could suggest any method by which three people could be smuggled on board the *Sans Souci* that night. The man said that, if they were prepared to risk being shot at, it might be accomplished after dark with the aid of a small boat. He even went so far as to say that he had a boat and would have taken on the job himself but for the fact that his niece was getting married from his house that evening, so he could not possibly let down his family and the friends who had been invited by disappearing for an hour or two in the middle of the party.

Gregory suggested that if he could be shown where the boat lay he and his friends would take it out on their own, and, as they would have to abandon it if they were successful in reaching the *Sans Souci*, he was perfectly willing to buy the boat outright. He further pressed his argument by stressing the fact that if they could do as he suggested his new friend would run no personal risk at all.

After a little discussion the waterman, whose name was Boucheron, agreed and led Gregory about a quarter of a mile along the quay to the place where his rowing boat was tied up. They did not approach it, but Gregory took careful note of its situation and that of the German sentries nearest to it. Then Boucheron asked: 'What do you intend to do with yourself in the meantime?'

Gregory looked at his watch. It was only just on half-past three, so he and his friends had the best part of nine hours to fill in, and he replied with a shrug: 'Goodness knows! Just hang about until it's close on time for her to sail, I suppose.'

'Then why don't you and your friends come along to my place?' suggested Boucheron. 'It'll be rough-and-ready, mind, but we've managed to collect a bit of food and a few bottles of wine for the occasion. This damn' war's grim enough, and one must try to forget it sometimes. Anyhow, I didn't see why my little niece should be robbed of her fun on the day of her marriage.'

'That's awfully kind of you,' Gregory replied. 'There's nothing we should like better. But before accepting it's only fair to warn you that we're on the run.'

'That didn't take much guessing,' Boucheron smiled. 'I tumbled to that the moment that you spoke of trying to get aboard the *Sans Souci* without a pass. I don't want to know your business—it's enough for me that you're up against these German brigands; but we won't tell the wife anything about it, in case she gets a bit nervous. I'll just say that I used to know you when I was working in the shipyards at Brest and that I asked you and your friends to come along.'

They walked back to the café and collected the other two, whom Gregory introduced as Pauline Vaquière and Alexis Tambov, since he considered it wisest to guard against possible future complications that might arise if Madame Boucheron, or any of her friends, happened to remember Madeleine's name in connection with the police notices which had been published a fortnight earlier.

Boucheron had a small house in the Rue Amiral Courbet, and on the way there they agreed on a story that the strangers had just arrived by train from Paris to take up work with the harbour authorities.

Madame Boucheron received them very kindly, putting down the state of their clothes and their untidy appearance to the fact that they were only poor working-people who had travelled third-class in one of the trains which now took a day and a night to get through from Paris to Le Havre.

Her brother was with her, as he had come to stay with them for the wedding. He was a tall man named Picquette, with sunken eyes and a ragged moustache. They were both hard at work preparing for the wedding-party, so Boucheron took his guests upstairs in order that they could tidy themselves and rest, turning over to them a room that had been his son's until the boy had fallen fighting on the Somme during the previous summer.

When they had cleaned themselves up as well as they could Madeleine lay down on the bed, while the men stretched themselves out on the floor, and they all got in three hours' badly needed sleep before Boucheron came up to tell them that it was now seven o'clock and the wedding guests were assembling.

The little parlour downstairs was soon crowded with people; the men were all dressed in their Sunday black, and the women had brought out their best bits of finery for the occasion. Their roughened hands and garlic-smelling breath betrayed the fact that they were all working-people, but they were a kindly, good-natured lot, only too happy to have this chance of forgetting the war for a few hours. There was much hearty laughter and a certain amount of crude fun poked at the bridegroom, a stalwart young fellow who looked most uncomfortable in his very high white collar, and at the bride, a pretty buxom girl of twenty named Colette.

The marriage was a civil one, and the functionary who performed it was treated with great deference. When it had been duly solemnized the whole party adjourned to a small hall nearby which had been taken for the reception and a dance.

Everyone exclaimed at the good things, so rare in these hard times, that Madame Boucheron had managed to provide for her buffet, although nearly all the guests had made some contribution to the feast themselves. Healths were drunk, there was much hand-shaking, and as the wine began to circulate they all gave free reign to their high spirits. Now that they had rested Gregory and his friends were able to join in the fun. He had a dance with the bride, and during it he asked her if she could keep a secret.

'Of course I can!' she smiled up at him. 'What is it?'

'Simply that my friends and I would like to give you a wedding present, but we've had no time to buy one, so we want you to buy it yourself; but you must promise me that you won't say anything at all about it to your mother, or even to your husband, until tomorrow morning.'

As he spoke he pressed a *mille* note into her hand. It was his way of rewarding the Boucheron family for their kindness, but he knew that the gift of so large a sum coming from a poor workman would excite comment from the girl's mother and friends if they learned about it before his party were safe out of Le Havre.

'A thousand francs!' the girl whispered. 'But how can you possibly afford it?'

'That's all right,' Gregory smiled. 'Your uncle has done me a great service, and I have more money than you might suppose from looking at me. I hope your marriage will be very happy.'

All the time they were dancing or talking among the crowd round the buffet the three friends were keeping a watchful eye on the clock, and at half-past eleven Gregory caught the eyes of the other two. After a few minutes they disengaged themselves from their partners and joined him.

'Time to go home,' he said with a quiet smile. 'We won't make our adieux to anybody. Boucheron will understand and explain to his wife tomorrow. There's a small ante-room at the far end of the hall, and it has a side-door leading on to the street. If we slip out that way nobody's likely to notice our disappearance.'

Madeleine and Stefan danced the length of the floor while Gregory strolled slowly behind them; then all three walked casually into the ante-room. The cloak-rooms were just beyond it, and having collected their hats and coats they came back to the little room with the side-entrance. To their annoyance they found Madame Boucheron's brother, Monsieur Picquette, standing in it. He had evidently just entered and closed the door to the dance-hall behind him.

'Hallo!' said Gregory cheerfully.

Picquette did not smile, but asked in a gruff voice: 'Where are you three off to?'

'It's pretty hot in there, so we thought we'd go out for a breath of air,' George replied lightly. 'We didn't want to catch a chill after dancing, though, so we thought it best to get our coats.' Then he pulled a pretty bluff by adding: 'Care to come along?'

'No, thank you,' said Picquette. 'I'm not going out, and neither are you.' Suddenly he produced a revolver from behind his back and pointed it at them.

'What the devil are you doing with that thing?' Gregory asked with a laugh, although he knew now that Fate was evening up the scales. The fickle goddess had sent them Boucheron in their hour of need, but now she had dealt them out this sunken-eyed fellow; and it was quite clear that he meant to make trouble of some kind.

'You don't remember me, do you?' Picquette went on. 'But I remember you all right—all three of you. Perhaps you recall a certain nursing-home in Paris that was raided by the police last November? I was one of the *agents de ville* that you tried to shoot in that affair. I'm only here on leave from Paris to see my niece married, but it will be a real pleasure to hand you over to the Nazis.'

22

Sitting on Dynamite

'So that's it,' nodded Gregory. 'All right, I'm not denying anything, and I take my hat off to you as a first-class policeman for having recognized us after all this time. But as you're a Frenchman it's only reasonable to assume that you've no real love for the Nazis. Let's make this a business deal. What's it worth to you to let us go?'

'Nothing that you could pay,' came the prompt reply. 'That girl with you is Madeleine Lavallière, and the Germans are offering fifty thousand francs for her apprehension. They're offering another fifty thousand francs for you two men. That's big money to a man like myself, so you can save your breath and stay where you are until the Nazis come for you.'

'How about your brother-in-law?' Madeleine said swiftly.

'Are you prepared to get him into trouble for having taken us into his house?'

Picquette shrugged. 'You needn't bother your head about Boucheron. No one can prove he knew who you were, so I'll fix things for him all right.'

'As you say we're to remain here until the Nazis come for us I take it you've already tipped them off?' remarked Gregory.

'That's right; I put a call through to Paris within five minutes of setting eyes on you this afternoon. I didn't want any local big-wigs interfering with my kill, so I spoke to Major Schaub, the man you knocked out—remember?—in that nursing-home affair. He was as pleased as a dog with two tails when he heard that I'd got you taped. I told him about this place and that we'd be here tonight and that I'd keep an eye on you; so he said that he'd come from Paris himself to pull you in. As a matter of fact, I expected him here about eleven o'clock, so he and his "black boys" may turn up any time now.'

The Quisling policeman had not even told Gregory and Stefan to put their hands up; but he knew his stuff. His revolver was pointing straight at Madeleine. He was banking on the fact that neither of the others would dare to attack him knowing that whatever happened she would be shot.

Gregory and Stefan were horribly conscious of his strategy. In such a desperate situation either of them would have taken the risk of rushing him. but as it was they dared not move; yet their whole escape was now in jeopardy, and their only chance lay in doing something before the Nazi police cars arrived upon the scene.

Madeleine too had sized up the situation. She knew that it was up to her. With splendid courage she suddenly began to walk the few steps forward which separated her from the barrel of the gun.

'Stand back!' cried Picquette. 'Stand back, or I shoot!'

But his momentary hesitation to kill a woman cost him exactly one hundred thousand francs. As his finger squeezed the trigger Madeleine flung herself headlong on the floor; Gregory and Stefan sprang at the same instant. Picquette's revolver was wrenched out of his hand. Kuporovitch dealt him a terrific punch which landed on the side of his jaw, sending him backwards, so that his head crashed against the wall. He fell, limp and bleeding. in the corner.

The crash of the single shot had hardly ceased to echo before Madeleine had picked herself up and all three of them were outside the building running down the street.

All was quiet outside, as in the occupied cities few people remained out after ten o'clock. For the first fifty paces all Gregory's thoughts were riveted on the sounds which were coming from the blacked-out windows of the hall. Everything now hung on whether Picquette's shot had been heard by anyone in the dance-hall. If it had, his unconscious form would be discovered within a few seconds and a score of men would come running out into the street to see if his attackers were still in sight. If they were, a hue and cry would start, the nearest police would join in, and once the human pack was after them it would be difficult, if not impossible, to shake it off.

But Dame Fortune had turned the smiling side of her face to them again. Evidently the music of the accordions, and the stamping feet of the dancers, had drowned the noise of the shot. The merry-making continued unabated, and with a quick word to his companions Gregory brought their pace down to a walk.

'It's all right,' he said. 'We've got a few minutes' grace anyway, and if we run we may attract the attention of some patrolling *gendarme*. We'll have to hurry, though, as that fellow caused us to lose quite a bit of time.'

'I told you before that I thought you were leaving it a bit late,' said Kuporovitch.

'We'd have had ample time if we hadn't been held up,' Gregory replied, 'and I fixed the time of our departure as late as possible for two reasons: firstly, I didn't want to leave the party sooner than we had to in case some Quisling there wondered where we had got to and started to make enquiries about us; secondly, we've still got to get into Boucheron's boat and out to the *Sans Souci* unseen. We shouldn't have stood a dog's chance of doing that earlier in the evening while there were still lots of people moving about among the cafés on the waterfront. They don't close till eleven anyhow, and we had to give them a bit of time to settle down for the night, so the longer we could leave it the better.'

Boucheron's boat was in the Arrière Port, so from the Rue Amiral Courbet they had to make their way right round the inland basins and across the railway. That meant a good two miles' walk, and it was now twenty to twelve. But the *Sans Souci* was not due to sail until well after midnight, and Boucheron had been confident that she would not get under way until half-past twelve at the earliest.

There was no traffic in the streets, and very few pedestrians, so they were able to put their best foot forward. Gregory had made a careful study of the route they would follow when walking back from the Arrière Port with Boucheron that afternoon, so he had little fear of losing his way. Nevertheless, in the tricky turnings between the railway station and the Quai Georges they did lose it, and a precious ten minutes sped past before they managed to find it again. In consequence, it was twenty minutes after midnight before they reached the Arrière Port, and they were all now in a state of suppressed anxiety, as they felt that their margin had become terribly narrow.

There was no time left to make a cautious investigation of the wharf side, to satisfy themselves that no fresh sentries had been posted to keep watch on the small craft during the night. They could only take a chance on the sentries being at the same posts as they had occupied that afternoon and go boldly forward to the steps beneath which the boat lay.

Luck favoured them again. The challenge that they dreaded to hear each second did not ring out. Treading as gently as they could, they covered the last few yards of *pavé*, slipped down the stairs and into the boat. Gregory took the tiller, while Kuporovitch undid the painter and got out the oars. Next moment they were off.

If the Russian had used the full strength of his arms he could have sent the rowing-boat ahead at a fine pace, but dared not do so from fear that the splashing of the oars would attract attention. He could only paddle gently, keeping well into the shadow of the wharf side. The minutes seemed to fly by as they slowly progressed and rounded the corner into the Avant Port, where the *Sans Souci* had lain that afternoon. Gregory and Madeleine strained their eyes ahead into the darkness, endeavouring to pick out the jetty where the tug and her string of barges had been tied up. At last they saw it, but to their dismay the *Sans Souci* was no longer there.

With a sudden pull on the tiller-ropes Gregory turned the boat's nose out to sea, as he said grimly: 'We'll have to risk someone hearing the splash of the oars now. Come on, Stefan! Put your back into it! Row for all you're worth.'

Instantly the Russian dipped his oars deep and exerted all his strength. The boat shot forward with a quick hissing sound, while Madeleine looked anxiously behind them, and Gregory again strained his eyes, peering into the gloom to seaward.

For the next ten minutes they did not exchange a word, as with heave after heave Kuporovitch sent the dinghy bouncing forward. Then Gregory exclaimed: 'Stick to it, Stefan, stick to it! I can see something ahead.'

The moon was now in its dark quarter, but faint starlight enabled them to see a little distance, and as they advanced Gregory could now make out a black mass that he had sighted across the water with growing distinctness. His heart leapt with joy. He was certain now that it was the *Sans Souci* with her string of barges. Another five minutes' hard pulling and they were under the stern of the rearmost barge.

But the *Sans Souci* was just passing the harbour mouth. The size of the waves was increasing, and having cleared the entrance she was now putting on speed. It was all that Kuporovitch could do, even by the mightiest efforts, to keep up with the rearmost barge. At Madeleine's urging he put on a final spurt, then standing up in the dinghy, Gregory cast its small anchor up on to the barge. It caught on the low rim which ran round the deck, and by hauling on the anchor rope he was able to pull the dinghy up under the barge's counter.

For a few minutes Kuporovitch rested from his exertions, while Gregory lashed the anchor rope to the boat's thwart and got a second grip on the barge with a boat-hook. The Russian then prepared for the difficult job of getting on board.

The side of the barge was eight feet or more out of the water but by standing on the little triangular foredeck of the boat he reduced the distance by two feet. The anchor rope was too thin for him to climb, and the only way that he could reach the barge was to jump.

With the boat now tossing in the waves it was a most hazardous attempt to make. For a few seconds he balanced himself precariously until a wave-crest carried the boat up; then, knowing that if he failed to secure a hold he would be dashed overboard and swept away in the darkness beyond hope of rescue, he sprang.

His fingers caught the wooden rim above the barge's deck. For a moment he hung there kicking wildly, while Gregory and Madeleine watched him fearfully. Then, with a frantic wriggle, he managed to lever himself up and tumbled head foremost into safety.

A moment later, now lying on the deck, he put his hands and arms over the side. Madeleine was all ready for him. As she jumped he caught her in his arms and hauled her in. As soon as he had released her he turned again, and gripping Gregory's hand pulled him up too.

For a full minute all three of them sat panting there on the deck, then Madeleine cried: 'We've done it, we've done it! We're safe at last!'

'Yes, we've done it, thank God!' Gregory echoed. 'But I'm afraid we're only safe for the moment. The devil of it is that through that wretched fellow Picquette holding us up we were unable to join our friends, and I don't see how we can do so. We caught the boat all right, but we're in the wrong barge.'

'What does that matter?' Madeleine shrugged.

'It matters a hell of a lot,' Gregory said with unusual seriousness. 'Now we're out of France I can tell you the plan we hatched for conveying all our Paris friends to safety. These barges are bound for a Dutch or German port, so they've got to pass through the Straits of Dover. Reconnaissance aircraft of the R.A.F. are keeping a daily watch for them. The recognition sign is that the third barge in the string is much smaller than the other four. When we're sighted the Royal Navy will get busy. The Nazi escort ships will be sunk, and the people in Baras' barge will be rescued and taken to England.'

'But how marvellous!' exclaimed Madeleine. 'And in that case why ever should you worry? When the Navy comes on the scene we have only to show ourselves and shout, and they'll take us off too.'

Gregory grunted. 'That sounds all right, if the Nazis don't spot us first and shoot us; and if the British come near enough to hear our voices. The trouble is that four out of five of these barges are filled with high explosives. The Navy has orders to cut out the barge which has our friends on board and blow the others sky-high. As I've just pointed out, we're on the wrong barge, and, as far as I can see, have no means of reaching the right one.'

The more they thought about their situation the less they liked it. The five barges were strung together with twenty-fathom lengths of steel cable, and there was no way at all in which they could cross those yawning gulfs to reach Léon Baras' party, which occupied the second barge in the string.

'We'll have to wait till daylight,' Kuporovitch said. 'The captain and the crew of the *Sans Souci* are in the secret. If we signal them they'll slow down so that we can get back into Boucheron's boat and row along to join our friends.'

'I'm afraid there's not much hope of that,' Gregory sighed. 'You seem to have forgotten, Stefan, that this string of barges now forms part of a convoy with a German escort. What the escort consists of we shan't discover until daylight, but I expect there'll be at least one Ack-Ack ship and probably several E-boats. Directly we stand up to start signalling the Germans will wonder who we are and come on board to investigate. There's another thing. We'll have to cast off the boat before morning. Otherwise the Nazis will spot it and guess that some unauthorized persons came out to this barge in it under cover of darkness.'

'Wait a moment, though,' said Madeleine. 'If the British Navy is going to capture Baras' barge and tow it to England why shouldn't they capture the whole string? This great cargo of explosives would be as useful to the British as to the Germans, and surely the Navy will have thought of that. You must be wrong in thinking they mean to sink all the other barges.'

Gregory laughed. 'I'm afraid you don't understand the difficulties of such an operation. The Germans aren't going to take this little party lying down. We shall be hugging the French coast the whole time, and once the balloon goes up scores of German aircraft will take off to bomb the British ships. They'll probably despatch to the spot any other fast E-boats they may have within thirty miles and a submarine or so into the bargain.

'To capture a whole string of barges and tow them back to an English port with the British ships being attacked both by sea and air while they're on the job would be one hell of an undertaking. Speed is their best defence against such an attack, so there wouldn't even be time for them to send boarding-parties on to the barges to undo the hawsers and attach each one to a separate ship. They'll simply come alongside Baras' barge and throw him a rope. Directly it's made fast, and he's cast off from the barges ahead and astern, they'll pull him out of the string as quickly as they possibly

367

can. When they've got his barge to a safe distance they'll blow up the other four barges by gunfire in order to create confusion among the Germans and destroy this big cargo of enemy war material.'

'I see,' said Madeleine softly. 'Of course, one always thinks of the British Navy as all-powerful, and that there's simply nothing that it cannot do.'

'I'm afraid that even the Royal Navy has its limits,' Gregory smiled, 'but it's nice that people should think of it in the way that you say, and actually far too little appreciation is given to the amazing things it has accomplished. The fact of the matter is that the English are not given to talking very much. They're not very good at bringing home to other people the real basic fact that without them Hitler would have won his war and had the whole of Europe in the bag long ago.'

'That's entirely on account of your incredibly ill-managed propaganda in the first two years of the war,' Kuporovitch remarked. 'Nine-tenths of the people outside Britain still believe that the English are decadent and that their fighting is being done for them by the troops of the Dominions and a few gallant Scottish regiments. But where would all the others be without them? No portion of the Empire could continue to exist without the homeland, unless they allowed themselves to be taken over by the United States. And where would the United States be if Britain fell? If Hitler had every shipyard in the whole of Europe, including Britain, to build the greatest Navy that the world has ever seen for his assault on the Americas, they couldn't possibly compete in such a building race. Within five years the Stars and Stripes would be swept from the seas.'

Gregory nodded. 'You're right, Stefan. And it's a rotten shame that this idea that everyone else is doing the fighting should still persist. When I was last in London a great husky Australian stuck a finger in my chest and said: "If you don't soon get down to business in this war I'll be meeting you in New York one day with *Free English* written on your shoulder. How would you like that?" '

'Of course, it's quite true that we're terribly slow in the uptake, and we're not fighting all out yet. We need, and we're thundering glad to have, all the help that we can get in this titanic struggle, both from the peoples of our own Empire and the Free Forces of all the peoples who are fighting with us, but that does not affect the fact that the people of the homeland are the rock upon which Hitler will break.'

He paused a moment, then went on: 'In no other country in the world is there quite the same solidity and strength of purpose as in the little island where the three ancient races are now merged into one; and that brings us back to the Royal Navy. Every other people on earth that is fighting for, or even prepared to fight for, its freedom, is now dependent on Britain keeping free the seas; and, although not many people realize it, over eighty-five per cent of the officers and men who man our fighting ships are drawn from the Southern Counties of England.'

There was another short silence, then he gave a cynical little laugh and added: 'Of course, the men of Devon and Hampshire and Kent don't get much credit for the fact that Hitler isn't occupying Buckingham Palace, or that Britain is still far and away the best fed and most comfortable country among the warring Powers in which to live. Neither do the people of all the other towns and counties between John o' Groats and Land's End, who provide much the biggest proportion of the Imperial Armies and Air Forces; yet it is *their* blood, and *their* tradition, which permeates all the other Anglo-Saxon peoples of the world. That indomitable spirit, which has made the Empire, lives in it still today, and without it all else which sustains our Commonwealth of Nations must perish.'

'You're right, Gregory, absolutely right,' Kuporovitch agreed, 'and we'll see the Navy doing its stuff tomorrow—if all goes well. Perhaps, though, if we slept for a bit we'd be able to think up some way of getting rid of our ringside seats. It's quite clear now that they're going to be far too near the performance to be comfortable.'

Getting up from the deck, Gregory set Boucheron's boat adrift, then they went down into the small cabin in the stern of the barge, which was occupied by a watchman when it was in port. There were two bunks in it, and on one a couple of coarse blankets had been left neatly folded. Madeleine lay down on one bunk, while Gregory and Stefan tossed up for the other. Gregory won, so the Russian found some old sacking and made himself as comfortable as his makeshift bedding permitted, on the floor. Although they had slept for three hours that afternoon they were still terribly fatigued from their long journey and desperate exertions, so within a few moments they were all asleep.

When Kuporovitch awoke it was daylight. He roused Gregory, and the two of them went cautiously up the short companionway to take a look round and find out the composition of the convoy. They soon saw that none of the ships was within several hundred yards of them, so they were in little danger of being spotted, provided that they did not let more than the top of their heads appear above the hatch.

To their right they could see the coast of France very clearly. They were not more than a mile from shore and were heading up-channel. They were just passing a town that Gregory could not definitely identify but thought was probably Fécamp, and they found that their string of barges formed the second in the convoy, which consisted of six strings altogether. On their seaward side there was a small grey-painted motor yacht, which had doubtless been commandeered from some French port and converted into a Flak-ship. There were also three E-boats, spaced out at intervals along the line. In addition, they also saw that each of the six tugs towing the strings of barges was now flying a balloon as a precaution against aerial attack.

'The balloon puts paid to any chance of our making our presence known to the people in our tug,' said Gregory. 'There must be German Air Arm men on board to fly it, and I expect they rigged up their winches while we were at Boucheron's yesterday afternoon.'

'No, we can't expect any help from that quarter,' Kuporovitch agreed. 'Even if there weren't Germans on board her their friends in the escort ships would see our signals. You were quite right last night in your prediction of the fix in which we'd find ourselves. As far as I can see, the only thing for us to do, when the party starts, is to jump overboard and trust to luck that the British will pick us up.'

'But you can't swim,' Gregory objected.

'I know; but I can make some sort of raft, or, anyhow, lash

together all the spare bits of wood that I can find as something to which to cling.'

When they went below again they found that Madeleine was awake and rummaging in the lockers of the little cabin in the hope of finding some odds and ends of food; but she was disappointed. They had to go breakfastless, and instead employed themselves on making three good-sized floats from cupboard doors which they wrenched off, broom-handles and other wooden gear. There was plenty of twine in one of the lockers, and by the time they had finished, although each of the floats looked like a large bundle of junk, they felt certain that they were large enough and sufficiently strongly tied together, to support the weight of a body in the water for several hours.

From time to time one or other of them went up the companionway so as to be informed at once if any unusual activity was going on. They saw several German planes, and about nine o'clock one that Gregory believed to be British, flying very high. He wondered if its pilot was even then examining the convoy through his observation glasses with special interest.

They thanked God that the weather was fine, as if the plane that Gregory had seen had not identified the *Sans Souci* and her tow it was a virtual certainty that some other British plane would report the big barge convoy during the course of the morning.

But in any case several hours must elapse before the attack could be expected, as the Admiralty would certainly not be holding a force in perpetual readiness for this minor operation, and even in wartime instructions could not be issued and ships sent to sea at a bare few minutes' warning. There was also the question of air co-operation and the fact that the British flotilla would have to cross the Channel before it could attack the enemy's escort.

Aircraft continued to come and go in the sky above, and on two occasions they saw a brief air battle in which Nazi planes came spiralling down into the sea, leaving a long black smoky trail behind them.

Soon after eleven o'clock, as they were beating up towards a large town which Gregory felt certain was Dieppe, Kuporovitch noticed a motor launch leave the pier and come racing out towards the convoy. The launch feathered through the water until it reached the leading tug. Soon afterwards a signal was hoisted, and the convoy came down to half speed, while the various escort vessels closed in upon it.

The Russian had already called the others up, and with some perturbation they began to wonder what was happening. All too soon they knew. Each of the escort vessels picked a barge, and German sailors from the E-boats began to scramble on board them.

'Hell!' exclaimed Gregory. 'What cursed luck! The Nazis have tumbled to something at the eleventh hour. They must have got wind of it somehow that one of the barges contains Baras and the rest of our friends, so the men in the E-boats have been ordered to search them.'

'Oh, poor wretches!' Madeleine sighed. 'It's too terrible to think of their being caught and hauled back to suffer God knows what horrors when they've been cooped up in that barge for a fortnight and are so very near being rescued.'

'If they search every barge they'll find us too,' remarked Kuporovitch grimly.

'I think that depends on if they stumble on us first,' Gregory replied. 'If they find the others they probably won't bother to search any further. Thank goodness none of the E-boats picked Baras' barge to start off with, as it'll probably work the other way too, and if they find us first they'll be satisfied.'

Madeleine nodded. 'It's really a question as to what information they have. If they're looking for sixty or seventy people they won't be content with us three, but, if they've just been tipped off that there are some stowaways on one of the barges, finding us would put them off the track of the others altogether.'

Gregory and Kuporovitch remained silent, but looked quickly at each other. They both knew what was in Madeleine's mind; if they showed themselves at once, and gave themselves up, that might be the means of saving some sixty other people from death and torture.

It was a terrible decision to have to make. The Gestapo would show them no mercy, and once they had given themselves up, with all three of them as prisoners, and no one outside to give them aid, they knew that there was very little chance of their being able to escape again. Yet, in the past weeks they had suffered so much already, and were now so very near freedom. Even though they were standing above a great mass of high explosive the odds would have been about even on their being picked up by the British after they had taken to the water, if only they could swim far enough from the barge before it was blown sky-high. It was Madeleine who decided their terrible problem for them by saying:

'I think we ought to, don't you?'

The others both knew what she meant, and they nodded slowly. Then she walked up the few remaining steps of the companionway on to the open deck, and that tough man Stefan Kuporovitch felt that it could have been no braver sight to have witnessed Marie Antoinette walking up the steps of the guillotine.

The men followed her out from their hiding-place and waved to the Germans in the nearest E-boat. The boat cast off from the barge ahead of them, which it had just been examining. An officer in it spoke to one of the sailors, who stood up in its prow and began to semaphore the other boats. Immediately the men in them gave up their search, and together with the launch which had put out from Dieppe they all headed for the barge on which Madeleine and her friends were standing.

The nearest E-boat pulled up alongside, but none of its crew attempted to come aboard. Two of them covered the stowaways with automatic rifles and waited until the launch arrived. A black-uniformed figure was standing in its stern, and with grim forebodings the little party on the barge recognized him as their old enemy, Major Wolfram Schaub.

Two sailors scrambled on to the barge, then two S.S. men, then the Major. As he came forward his strong nobbly face was wreathed in smiles.

'*So!*' he said. 'I've got you after all. It was a near thing, after that idiot policeman messed things up last night.'

'Congratulations,' said Gregory cynically, 'on your marvellous staff work. We've been up against every Gestapo man in France for the past fortnight and made our way through

373

the German lines of the forbidden coastal area; yet you owe it to pure chance, and a dumb-headed French Quisling having recognized us, that you got on our track before we could get clean away.'

'Enough!' snapped Schaub. 'I will teach you manners and to cringe at the name of the Gestapo before you're very much older. Get down in the boat, all of you.'

There was nothing to do but to obey, so they lowered themselves over the side into the stern of the launch. All took as long as possible, as it seemed to them now that every second counted, and they were still hoping against hope that the British Navy might come on the scene before Schaub actually get them into Dieppe.

With eager, desperate gaze they searched the sea and sky; but there was not a sign of any shipping except that in the convoy, and above them only two patrolling Messerschmitts circled lazily.

When they were in the boat Schaub ordered the young naval officer in it to return to Dieppe. Their speed increased and the launch shot forward. They had not more than two miles at the outside to cover, and as they sped away they now kept their eyes fixed sadly on the string of barges that for so many days they had struggled so desperately to catch, and which, as it proceeded slowly up-channel, carried away their last hopes of life and freedom.

They were half-way to the shore when Gregory suddenly spoke: 'You haven't got Léon Baras yet, have you?'

Schaub looked at him quickly. 'No, why do you ask?'

'Because I don't like Baras. He once did me a dirty trick, and sooner or later I always get even with my enemies. Would you make it any easier for us if I told you where you could lay your hands on Baras?'

'Yes, I'd do a deal,' the Major replied. 'The Communist Deputies have been giving us a lot of trouble, and I'd like to make an example of one of them. Naturally, you'll understand that all three of you will face a firing-squad, but I can arrange matters so that you face it standing up, instead of lying on the ground already beaten to a pulp.'

'All right, then,' Gregory nodded. 'I've only got your word, and I wouldn't do it if I didn't want to get even with Baras, but I'm going to trust you about seeing to it that we're not tortured before we're shot. Baras was in our party, but we disliked each other so much that he decided to travel in a different barge. If you like to turn back you'll find him in the second barge of the second string.'

Madeleine and Stefan had been listening to Gregory and wondering what on earth he was trying to do. Now they both stared at him in open amazement. Either of them would have given a great deal to escape torture and flogging before they died, but having decided to give themselves up in order to save all those other people, it seemed a poor cowardly business not to go through with it right to the end, as if Baras was discovered all the others must be too.

Suddenly they caught a faint rat-tat-tat high above their heads and, looking up, they saw something they had not noticed while listening to Gregory. Two squadrons of British fighter planes had suddenly come on the scene, diving from a great height at terrific speed right out of the sun on to the two German Messerschmitts. Gregory's strong eyes had seen those squadrons first, and the sight of them had convinced him that the party was on.

Air battles were nothing new to Major Schaub, and with hardly a glance above his head he ordered the launch back to the string of barges. Before they were half-way there the two Messerschmitts, caught napping, disintegrated under an absolute hail of cannon-shells from the swarm of British fighters, and the pieces came fluttering down into the sea. The two squadrons then divided; one turning south, and the other north, they curved away in opposite directions across the coast of France.

The Germans in the launch cursed a little and shook their fists in impotent anger as they saw the wreckage of the Messerschmitts tumbling down from the sky. The Ack-Ack escort ship had come into action, as also had the anti-aircraft guns in the E-boats, but after a few moments they all ceased fire, as the British squadrons had passed out of range. As far as the Germans were concerned it was just an episode of the war, which was now over.

The guns had hardly ceased firing when the launch reached the barge where Léon Baras and his friends were confined.

Once more two sailors went aboard, then two S.S. men, then Major Schaub. The three prisoners remained seated in the stern of the launch, listening with all their ears and wondering what the devil was going to happen.

Suddenly there was the sound of shots and shouting from the barge. The shots increased to a din as more and more rifles and automatics came into action. As Gregory had guessed, Baras and his companions, all of whom were armed, were not going to allow themselves to be taken without a struggle, and there were at least twenty Frenchmen to the five Germans. Gregory had led the Major into a pretty trap.

One by one the Germans had disappeared down the companionway in the after-part of the barge. Now one of the S.S. men reappeared and dashed to its side. 'Help! Help!' he shouted. 'The barge is full of these damned Frenchmen, and they've all got guns! Quick! Up you come, all of you, and lend a hand!'

There were two more S.S. men in the launch, guarding the prisoners, one sailor up in the bows, and the young naval officer who was standing by the tiller. One of the S.S. men turned to the officer and with a wave towards the prisoners cried: 'Here, you, look after these people!' Then both of them hauled themselves up over the barge's side; the sailor in the bow jumped after them.

As Gregory and Kuporovitch had only just given themselves up they had not yet been searched or disarmed. No sooner were the S.S. men out of the way than they pulled their guns from their pockets. The young officer made a quick grab at his holster, but too late. As he turned to face Gregory, Kuporovitch hit him a mighty backhander, and he toppled overboard. Next minute the two friends had come into action with their guns, taking the S.S. men on the barge in the rear. They shot both of them in the back.

Madeleine grabbed up a boat-hook and fixed it into the barge's deck-rim so that the launch should not drift away from it, as she cried to the other two: 'Up you go! I can manage to hang on. I'll be all right here.'

Stefan shook his head. 'No, Baras and the rest are more than enough to tackle those Nazis. But there'll be more of

376

them arriving in the other boats in a minute. I'm staying here with you.'

The sounds of firing had already attracted attention. The convoy had come down to slow, and the three E-boats were all racing towards them.

Gregory was now desperately anxious. If he had been wrong about those two squadrons of fighter planes, and they had no special interest in the convoy, but had merely appeared above it by chance on one of their daily patrols, the fat was in the fire with a vengeance. The Germans in the E-boats and the Flak-ship were more numerous and better armed than Baras and his friends. It would be a frightful business if all of them were now killed or captured as a result of his clutching at a straw, and if, in the hope of saving his own party after all, he had wrecked everything by his premature disclosure that Baras was in the barge. The launch was on the landward side of the barge. With a quick glance at the oncoming E-boats he sprang on to her deck to stare wildly at the sea horizon.

For a moment he believed the game was up. Then he thought he saw some faint smudges of smoke on the skyline. Shading his eyes with his hand he stared again. Yes, he was right—there were six of them. The Germans had seen them too; a hooter on the Ack-Ack ship began to wail.

After that everything seemed to happen incredibly quickly. The planes were back again, circling overhead; the smudges of smoke increased and grew nearer with fantastic speed, turning into six long low destroyers. They were still several miles away when they opened fire with their biggest guns. Shells began to scream overhead and plunge into the water among the other strings of barges, sending up great fountains of foam. The German E-boats were within a few hundred yards of the launch, but all of them now changed their courses and swerved out to seaward of the line of barges. Below the barge's deck fighting was still in progress. Revolvers cracked, and every moment there came the scream or curse of a wounded man.

Fascinated by the sight of the action as he was, Gregory forced his eyes away from it and, turning, yelled to Madeleine: 'Come on up! You'll be all right here now.' Stooping, he grasped her hands to drag her on board. Kuporovitch

377

hauled himself up after her, and when he got to his feet Gregory saw that he was laughing.

'Well done!' exclaimed the Russian. 'Well done, my friend! It was a stroke of genius on your part to get Schaub himself to take us off that cargo of dynamite and deliver us safely to this barge and our friends.'

'It was more by luck than judgment.' Gregory grinned. 'If those planes of ours hadn't turned up just at that moment I would never have dared to risk it, and as it was I gambled on their being in on this show. Come on! Let's clear one of the hawsers. Even the Navy will want all the help we can give them in a party like this, where time is everything.'

The two of them ran forward and with frantic fingers began to release the great wire cable which attached the barge to the one ahead.

The R.A.F. fighters were now dealing with the balloons, sending streams of tracer and explosive bullets into them. One after the other the great blimps burst into flames and came gently sailing down, their cables coiling in loose curves as they dipped into the sea. The *Sans Souci* had already unhitched herself. The sailors were fighting the German balloon men on her deck, and her captain had turned her nose north-westwards to get behind the protective screen of the British destroyers.

The Ack-Ack ship was in flames and sinking. One of the E-boats blew up with a terrific bang, as a shell exploded among its torpedoes. The other two had turned once more, and with every ounce of speed they had were racing for the shelter of Dieppe.

Several coast batteries had now come into action. German shells were falling among the destroyers. One was hit and had the top part of its mast carried away. Amidst the crash of the explosions and the banging of the pom-poms, the rat-tat-tat of machine-guns and the individual crack of rifle-shots, the droning of the many planes made constant thunder in the sky. Several flights of the Luftwaffe came screaming out of the blue sky over the coast; some attempted to dive-bomb the warships, while others attacked the British squadrons.

There were fifty dog-fights going on at once. The planes swooped and circled in an indescribable *mêlée* with such speed

378

that it was impossible to follow their individual movements. The sky above the convoy was now a haze of curving vapour trails. Five aircraft burst into flames and fell within a few seconds of one another; from four the pilots had managed to bale out, and swaying from side to side under their graceful parachutes they gently floated down.

When Gregory and Stefan had run forward to cast off the forward hawser they left Madeleine standing alone amidships. She had her back turned to the companionway, and it was the sound of running feet which caused her suddenly to swing round. A single figure had emerged from the interior of the barge. Hatless, bleeding from a wound in the face, and his left arm hanging limp from his side, he ran towards her. It was Wolfram Schaub.

With demoniacal fury in his face he raised his pistol to fire at her. She sprang back with a quick cry, but the pistol only clicked. Its magazine was empty.

For an instant they stood glaring at each other, then with the courage of intense hatred she flung herself straight at him.

It had never entered his head that a woman would go for him with her bare hands. Taken off his guard, he made one step back, but he was not quick enough. The violence of her onslaught carried him off his balance; clutching frantically at the air, he fell backwards into the sea with a wailing cry that was only cut short as the water closed over his head.

For a moment Madeleine swayed wildly, very nearly taking a header after him. With a terrific effort she recovered her balance. Pale and shaking, she turned to see that one of the destroyers had left the others and in a graceful curve was now coming alongside.

As the destroyer approached, Baras and his men came tumbling up on deck from the companionway. The sailors threw some ropes. Gregory caught one at the forward end of the barge and at the after end some of the Frenchmen near Baras caught another. The destroyer had reversed her engines, and, oblivious of the battle that was raging all round, a naval lieutenant sprang down on the the barge's deck. Raising a megaphone which he held in one hand he shouted through it: 'Is Mr. Sallust aboard?' And with an answering shout Gregory ran along the deck to him.

379

'I was asked to find you,' said the N.O. quickly. 'I gather you're in charge here. Will you get all the people up from below as quickly as you can so that we can take them off?'

'Aren't you going to take the barge in tow?' Gregory asked.'

'Good God, no! Towing a thing like this would reduce our speed to about fifteen knots, and we've got to get out of here just as quickly as we can.'

'Right-oh!' said Gregory, and he began to shout orders in French.

In a very few minutes the whole party, except those who had been killed in the recent fighting with Schaub and his men, were up on deck, and with willing hands the British sailors helped them on to the destroyer.

Gregory left last with the Lieutenant, who said that the Captain commanding the flotilla wished to see him as soon as they were clear of the scrap. The destroyer's lines had already been hauled in, and her engines were turning over once more at full speed, thrusting her out to sea.

In a bare two minutes she had covered the best part of a mile. Then there was a colossal explosion. One after another, the barges of ammunition disintegrated in huge sheets of flame as they blew up. Turning into line ahead, the flotilla, with its anti-aircraft guns still belching fire and smoke at individual Nazi aircraft, raced away, its work accomplished.

When the guns had ceased to thunder Gregory sought out the Captain on the bridge and thanked him on behalf of all concerned for the brilliant feat of rescue work that the Navy, with R.A.F. help, had carried out.

'Oh, that's quite all right,' smiled the Captain. 'It's all in the day's work, you know. We're very happy to have been of service to you and got so many of these poor people out of the clutches of the Nazis. By the by, I don't suppose you've heard the latest news: the war's taken quite a new turn since this morning. Hitler's decided to try to cut his old friend Stalin's throat. The German Army attacked at dawn along the whole front of the Russian-held territories.'

'Is it really war, do you think?' asked Gregory anxiously. 'Are the Russians fighting back?'

'Oh Lord, yes!' the Captain laughed. 'They've announced

that since Hitler's double-crossed them they mean to fight to the death.' And he went on to give the full story of that Sunday morning's world-shaking news.

With a little sigh of satisfaction Gregory went below to find Madeleine and Stefan, to tell them all about it. In a single hour the whole orientation of the Second World War had been fundamentally changed. He had never believed that in any possible circumstances Hitler could achieve complete and final victory. Now he knew that the Germans could not even hope for a stalemate and that this now aggression must shorten the war by years.

When Madeleine heard the news she exclaimed: 'But why should Hitler have attacked Russia? He really *must* be crazy.'

Stefan smiled as he took her hands. 'You didn't tumble, then, to what we've been up to all these weeks?'

'Surely,' Gregory laughed, 'the report of Hitler's speech at the time he launched the attack, which I've just given you, must have provided you with the clue.'

She shook her head. 'I'm afraid I still don't get it. He said that Russia had been trying to stab Germany in the back while pretending to be her friend, didn't he? And that therefore he must settle with her and render her impotent before he smashed Britain for good and all.'

'That's it,' Gregory agreed. 'But don't you remember the bit about the great conspiracy, having its ramifications all over Europe, that he said the Gestapo had uncovered; how, although supposed to be his Allies, Stalin and Co. had been plotting all the time with the Freedom groups in the occupied territories, so that when he was up to the neck in a death-grapple with Britain they would be sufficiently well organized to rise up and rend him? Well, that was our party.'

He paused a moment, then corrected himself. 'No, I'm wrong—it was your party, Madeleine. You were the one who started it all, by laying down the law to Stefan and myself that the people in the occupied territories would just die of starvation in a year or two, unless somehow the whole war could be given an entirely new twist. We talked it over and we made a plan. I went back to London and got things moving there, while Stefan sat in Paris typing documents night and day.'

'Of course,' Madeleine interrupted. 'All those hundreds of letters on the typewriter with a Russian set of characters, that he had such a job to obtain.'

'That's it,' Gregory smiled. 'They were supposed to be instructions from the Soviet Government to their secret agents in Occupied France. Meanwhile in London we forged countless letters in French, Dutch, Norwegian, Danish, Czech, Polish and German, with which we were able to build up huge correspondence files. The documents in those files were supposed to have been received by the Freedom fighters in all those different countries, and every one of them told the same story: they were being financed and instructed by Moscow in their work of sabotage and fermenting revolution. London made arrangements for the people in other countries: Stefan and I, with Lacroix's consent, handled Occupied France. We planted the files with the most trusted members of our organization, then at the beginning of this month we started to smuggle our friends out, and immediately they'd left split on them one by one. Their homes were raided, the files were discovered hidden in all sorts of cunning places. The Nazis put two and two together, then four and four, and finally added hundred to hundred when we blew up the whole works a fortnight ago.'

Kuporovitch chuckled. 'We must have given Himmler and all the Gestapo people the greatest headache that they've ever had.'

'I'll bet we did,' Gregory grinned back. 'And they couldn't laugh off such a great accumulation of evidence from so many different quarters. We provided them with chapter and verse, which made them dead certain that a vast conspiracy existed in the whole of the German conquered lands, inspired by Moscow, to rise against them when the time was ripe. Mind you, we were taking a colossal gamble. I don't wonder that Lacroix hesitated before he came in with us. We were simply betting on the fact that, although Russia would never attack Germany, she would fight if she were attacked; and it was our work to force the Nazis' hand, so that they should be absolutely convinced that they'd lose the war unless they settled with Russia before attempting to tackle Britain.'

'Oh, it was marvellous!' Madeleine whispered. 'Absolutely

marvellous! Perhaps now in a year or so France may be free again, and these filthy German brutes will get their just deserts.'

Gregory nodded. 'I hope so. You wanted vengeance, Madeleine, and now you've got it; not a little vengeance, like the killing of Schaub because he shot your Georges, or the sabotaging of a few trains containing German soldiers—but a real vengeance. At dawn today Hitler took on 200,000,000 new enemies, and before this job is through every living German will curse his name. Next winter they'll be dying by the million in the biting winds and freezing snows of the Russian plains. You weren't content to take an eye for an eye and a tooth for a tooth. But you needn't worry—your will to break Hitler is going to destroy the flower of the whole German race.'

They were silent for a little, then Gregory said: 'You've never been to England, have you, Madeleine? I do hope you'll like it.'

'I'm sure I shall,' she laughed, 'as Stefan and I are going to get married there. Wherever we may go afterwards, we shall always think of England as our second home.'

'Bless you both,' Gregory smiled back. 'I insist on being best man, and old Pellinore will dig out some champagne for the wedding. I hate weddings as a rule, but I'm going to love this one, because I'm so damn' certain that both of you are going to be marvellously happy.'

He left the two lovers then and went up on deck to get some air. At last he could allow himself the luxury of savouring the joy of a good job well done, and feel that he had earned the right to take a little time off to be once more with his beautiful Erika. That night, if he were lucky, or, at least, tomorrow, he would hold her in his arms.

An hour or so later he was still leaning on the rail thinking of her and watching the white cliffs of Dover as they rose out of the sea, when the Lieutenant who had jumped down on to the barge came up to him, and said: 'Pretty good business this—old Hitler going for the Ruskies, isn't it? Might even keep him busy for a few weeks!'

'Yes,' said Gregory quietly. 'I rather think it might.' And a few minutes later, as the Lieutenant was called away by some message from the bridge, Gregory smiled to himself.

Those few words had been so typical of the English spirit. Evidently the nice efficient young officer had not yet visualized the vast potentialities of the Soviet Union—the greatest land Power in the world. He regarded the new war as another episode in the war between Britain and Germany which might prove helpful to the British cause. Without thinking very much about it, he was just calmly and superbly confident that, whoever might come in with or against Britain, she was bound to be victorious in the end.

As the afternoon sunlight played on Dover's cliffs Gregory was very proud to be an Englishman.